HITKIDS

SHANE BRIANT

PROLOGUE

Los Angeles. October. '97

Despite the gag, the fat kid was making one hell of a racket. Not that it mattered, no one could hear his screams out in the hills.

He was nine years old, four feet four inches tall, and weighed 110 pounds – twenty too much. Congential obesity.

He lay face down across the gleaming silver line, his cheek pressed against the blue metal chips on the far side of the track.

The ropes on his wrists and ankles were tied so tight he hadn't been able to feel his fingers or toes for more than five minutes. He was terrified that any second he might throw up and choke to death on his own puke.

Despite the heat of the day, the rail felt cold against his bare stomach where the t-shirt had bunched up, exposing several rolls of blubbery flesh.

The rest of his body was on fire. His khaki shorts, underpants and short-sleeved shirt were drenched with the cold sweat of abject fear.

He'd never met the two kids before that afternoon.

They'd seemed so nice and friendly outside the school. They'd promised to show him a cougar. They'd seen it in the hills. They knew where it hung out. It'd be fun.

They'd lied.

At his head crouched the younger of the two boys; around his own age, chubby faced, pink-cheeked, fair-skinned, blonde hair neatly cut and brushed. He'd looked like a regular kid – 'cept for the eyes, they were scary, they burnt a hole clean through you.

The other kid was older by maybe five or six years, taller by six inches, swarthier in appearance, with dark wavy hair. Man, was he strong.

The fat boy's heart hammered in his chest as an image of the weird blonde kid sprang into his consciousness. He was the bossman. The kid with the scary eyes called the shots.

A fit of coughing suddenly wracked his sweating body and he felt short fingers tugging at his gag, which immediately fell free.

"You scream all you like, blubberboy. Be my guest," the voice at his head cooed lazily into his ear.

The fat boy quickly twisted his head upwards as he gasped for air.

"Please don't hurt me!" he pleaded, tears streaming from under the blindfold down his fleshy cheeks. "Please don't do this! Please. I beg you!"

"Pardon me boys is that the Chattanooga choo-choo," he heard the blonde boy sing softly, up close to his face. His breath smelled of lemon candy.

The fat boy lowered his head to the blue metal chips and began to sob quietly as he mouthed the Lord's prayer.

Our father, who art in heaven...

The blonde kid's lips brushed his ear. "Track twenty-nine. Boy you can give me a shine, " he continued.

The boy at his feet began laughing.

"How long now?" the blonde boy cut a sidelong glance at his buddy, a smile as broad as Death Valley making twin apples of his chubby cheeks.

"Three minutes – maybe less," his companion replied, sniggering.

"How do you feel now, porky?" The voice was teasing. Soft, smooth and silky. Like liquid velvet. It made the fat boy's blood run cold.

The blonde boy immediately recommenced singing. "When you hear the whistle blowin' eight to the bar. Then you know that Tennesee is not very far..."

"Oh jeez, man, fatso's peed his pants!" his dark-haired buddy shouted, pointing at a stain spreading on the fat boys shorts. "Gross-out!"

The blonde kid leant over and took the lobe of the fat kid's ear between his thumb and forefinger and began to apply steady pressure with his nails. "You're a dirty, dirty bird! No one ever taught you manners? Now you've pissed me off."

The older boy pointed to his wrist watch. "Two minutes, man. Let's get out of here. We can watch from up there," he said, pointing to the embankment behind them that separated the north from the southbound tracks.

"Sure thing. Wouldn't want to be too close when the train comes on through," the blonde kid replied, letting go the fat boy's ear. "There's gonna be bits sprayed all over."

The fat boy immediately jerked and twisted like crazy, his heart running faster than the approaching locomotive. He was going to die for sure, he knew that. Any second he'd hear the horn sound and a hundred and thirty tons of steel would cut right through him like a chainsaw through a tub of peanut butter.

Then he felt a faint vibration in the rail. It buzzed through the flesh of his stomach, as if someone had driven a white hot needle into his spine.

Oh sweet Jesus help me, it's coming. Oh momma, momma, don't let me die.!

Up on the embankment the blonde boy pulled a small digital camera from his shorts' pocket and focussed on the body strapped to the southbound track below him – the fat boy was shaking like an aspen leaf in a hurricane.

Click, click, click.

The screaming continued. No words – just one continuous shriek.

Snap, snap, snap. Memories were made of this.

The locomotive was only fifty feet down the line when the driver sounded the horn. The sound was ear-splitting.

The blonde boy immediately sprang to his feet, cupping his hands to his mouth, screaming down at the fat kid on the track as the train hurtled the final thirty-five feet towards them. "FIVE... FOUR... THREE... TWO... ONE... "

The train thundered through on the northbound line behind them with an explosive shockwave that blew the grass flat for twenty feet either side of both tracks.

The fat kid's body arched so violently it was as if he'd been strapped to the electric chair and the executioner had pulled the switch.

The blonde boy purred with satisfaction.

Man, this was wild!

It took fully three minutes for all the wagons to barrel past, the sound eventually fading to nothing.

Then there was silence, broken only by the wind blowing through the long grass.

The fat boy lay very still.

"Would you ever friggin' believe it?" the dark-haired boy murmured incredulously. "the dumbo actually fell for it."

Down at the southbound track the blonde boy nudged the side of the fat boy's head with the toe of his sneaker.

"Hey, blubberman, wake up," the blonde boy said, pulling the blindfold away.

The fat boy's eyes were open wide, staring down at the ground unfocussed.

As consciousness returned, he raised his eyes and was suddenly looking deep into the blue eyes of madness.

"I'm going to cut your hands free, butterball. You cut your legs free yourself."

The game was over.

The blonde boy stood. He pulled a roll of hard candy from his shorts pocket and popped a lemon sherbet into his mouth, smiling briefly at his buddy.

"Some good things, eh?" he said.

It was time to get home. Supper'd be on the table.

PART ONE

Los Angeles.
Thursday. lst August. '99

1.

The pain was indescribable. I was trapped in that utterly powerless no man's land between sleep and consciousness. I knew I was dreaming, yet my terror was no less intense. My nightmare world was inhabited by unspeakable demons. I felt a crushing sensation in my head as though my brain had been surgically removed and placed between the jaws of an industrial vice. Voices of the damned screamed at me with a ferocity and anger I'd never experienced before. I was transfixed like a rabbit in a beam of light, unable to break through into reality. It was the terrible premonition of things to come.

Then with a terrible rush I was suddenly thrust through the storm clouds and my eyes blinked open for an instant. A phone was ringing. I was alive. I could feel my chest heaving as the first tidal waves of anxiety hit me.

What day was it? Quick calculation. Thursday. Maybe.

I reached for the phone and balanced it on the pillow, at the same time noticing my white shirt cuff and suit sleeve. Shit. I'd slept in my clothes again.

"Jay? It's Nathaniel. Faith's tossed our package out the window. She's hired Helen Lowenstein. The woman's tough as Teflon. No way Faith'll accept our offer now, that bitch won't let her. Now she'll want everything, and she'll probably get it. Same fuckin' justice as ever for the good guys. Same old story. What can I tell you."

I lay on my back, breathing as steadily as I could as I fought for equilibrium. Nate's words were a blur. The clock on the nightstand told me it was 5.10 p.m. Rays of the late afternoon sun angled obliquely through the window above the bed.

The room was a pigsty.

"Hell, the line's dropped out," I heard Nate mutter in my ear.

"No, I'm still here," I managed, my stomach heaving. "Why did you call anyway? This is a good-news-only time of my life."

Silence.

"Come on, Nate. Do you expect me to clap or something?"

"Have to keep you up to speed, Jay. That's my job," Nate replied. I'd hurt his feelings. We'd been close buddies for over six years.

"I'll try working a few angles," he continued. "But if you've got any spare moolah salted away for a rainy day, I'd spend it pronto while the sun's out."

Nate had never been one to imbue a client with overconfidence. Good friend; not a lawyer people fought to retain.

"I'll be in touch, Jay. Get lucky."

I didn't have the strength to lean across to the nightstand, so I dropped the phone by the bed and continued the laboured breathing.

What an ass I was. When had liquor ever helped? She was gone. That was it, pure and simple. I'd spent the past month trying to hate her when I knew damned well I'd love her forever. Stupid. I had to let her go.

At her tender age the decisions came easy. They were cut and dried. There was no room for sentimentality in the logic of a twenty-six year old.

The question was, how much did she have it it mind to take with her? The company was practically bankrupt and the house was mortgaged. My soul was hers already. What the hell else did she think I had?

The room stank of booze and some bastard had painted the roof of my mouth with plaster while I slept.

You will self-destruct in ten seconds Mr Phelps.

The imperative was to get out of the house immediately, find a corner of some halfway friendly bar and recover as best I could.

It was a short walk down Sunshine to the Santa Fe Grill.

I'd eyed the place a thousand times, but it would've been too vulgar for Faith. No pools of cold pressed olive oil on the tables, no manufactured La La smiles.

Now that I was my own man I decided to make the most of it. I'd mingle with the hoi polloi.

I ordered a bowl of green chili stew and a jug of Margies. The stew was hot as hell – just the way I liked it.

Now I had my corner of the world. I knew nobody. I felt invisible.

Everyone in the place was sweating. For a while I thought it might have been the air-conditioning on the blink, then I remembered how hot it had been outside; Ventura had been a furnace when I walked down from the house.

Could have been all that spicy food.

With the second jug around halfway through, I began to feel the tequila course its way through my veins. The relief was immense. I knew that without it's medicinal qualities I'd have been on a metal tray and toe-tagged long ago.

He must have been sitting in the diner when I arrived; I just hadn't noticed him.

If I hadn't heard his voice, I probably would have just ordered a third jug, then struggled back up the hill in a drunken stupor.

He was standing at the cash register with his back to me. "The doloroso, m'old china," he said.

The gravelled voice was his signature, the accent pure Elephant and Castle. It had to be Jack.

The doloroso – the sad one. The Spanish expression had always appealed to Jack. Not that a bill had ever saddened him in his life. He'd always had enough change.

Twelve years ago in London we'd unwittingly shared the sexual favours of a girl called Kitty Maynard.

Neither of us knew our personal share of her mind and body was never more than fifty per cent till she screwed up her dates, and we both showed up for a 'special brekkie' on the same day.

Jack and I ended up good friends, sharing a big old house near Battersea Bridge for just over four years.

Those were good bachelor days.

Then on a whim I moved lock stock and barrel to the States. To this day I don't know why. Maybe to get away from my crazy brother, Raymond.

I wrote to Jack every now and then. I missed him. But I knew letter-writing just wasn't his thing.

In the end I let go. That's a part of life; friends just drift apart.

I knew if our paths crossed again it'd be as if he'd snuck out to buy a pack of cigarettes. He was that kind of an easy-going guy. Tough as nails, but true to his friends. A definite straight-shooter.

That was years ago. Christ, how many? Nine? Ten? Possibly more. Could this really be Jack? Here in LA?

I called out.

"Jack Corr! Is that you, you old bastard? Have you forgotten your old friends entirely?"

He turned to face me.

The look of shocked surprise was suddenly replaced by his trademark grin – wide as the Thames at Westminster. The ladies had always loved it.

"Bugger me if it isn't Jay Benedict!" he thundered, oblivious to the looks of disapproval around him.

He looked much older than his forty-four years.

He was carrying a good deal of extra weight. Maybe as much as twenty pounds. His hair was no longer black as pitch. His face looked bloated. The cheeks were jowls, and the skin had an unhealthy pinkish tinge.

I was shocked. What had happened to the Lothario of Camberwell Road?

He grinned, his eyes sparkling, then flung his arms wide and wrapped them round me.

"Well, what do you know. Been years, no?"

He stood back and looked me up and down.

"Must be at least nine," I replied, suddenly aware that without his firm grip I was now swaying. The booze was beginning to take its toll.

"Eleven, matey. Close to twelve I'd say. Harold's eleven."

"Harold?"

"My boy. I'm married." He beamed at me in anticipation of some wisecrack.

"So someone ground you down after all," I said, not wishing to disappoint.

I gripped the edge of the table to steady myself.

He winked. "Stella. My lovely Stella. Love her to death. As Yankee-doodle as I'm a London lad. Heart as big as Clapham Common."

He glanced at his watch. "Jesus H! Got to get moving, china. I'm late. Shouldn't have stopped anyway. Just felt like it. A snackie – know what I mean?"

I nodded, very aware of movement in my small intestine.

"Hey, what you say! Why don't you come meet Stella?"
His eyes pleaded with me to say yes.
"Can you? It's been twelve years, for Christ's sake."
What could I say? It seemed like a good idea.
Providing I could keep the green chili stew down.

2.

Back then, when I first knew him, Jack did a bit of everything to earn a crust. Not all legal. But who cared? Certainly didn't bother me. I was younger then and didn't take a lot seriously.

Besides, he never involved me in his nefarious schemes.

Every now and then, at odd times of the night, there'd be a knock at the door and a couple of thickset strangers would be standing on the step, come to remind Jack of some debt or other.

But he always had a stash, so this never presented much of a problem. He'd usually just forgotten he owed someone or other money.

Jack told me he had a place on Old Topanga Canyon Road. As we fed into Highway 101 heading West, he pencil-sketched the missing twelve years.

A few months after I emigrated to the States, he decided to jump a plane.

"Took off to avoid a bit of unpleasantness", he told me. "For once in my life I didn't have enough 'readies' on hand. Couple of nasties from the Mile End Road caught me on the hop. Applied for a U.S. visa in Paris, then headed over here.

"Set myself up in Canoga Park and jumped straight into the classic car trade; bought fifties classics and shipped 'em back to a mate of mine in the Elephant and Castle. Made a fortune."

When he clapped eyes on Stella for the first time, she was sitting outside Johnny Rocket's on Melrose. He'd just taken delivery of a '69 red two door Thunderbird with chromed fins a mile long. She was eating a sundae, and she was on her own.

"Looked like a cheerleader; thought like Bertrand Russell," he said laughing as we approached the Calabasas off-ramp.

"She was finishing a doctorate at UCLA. Psychology. Pretty racy thesis. 'A role for women amongst Nietsche's Ubermensch!'"

He chuckled. "She loved the car; I loved her. We got hitched two months later. Simple as that. Before I knew it she was up the duff with young Harold."

He swung the Trans Am into Topanga Canyon Boulevard. "By the way, how's your love life, old china?"

I gave Jack the whistle-stop resumé. The nuts and bolts of the last twelve years of *my* life. The successes, the failures, the highs, the lows.

He listened intently, filing it all away.

I told him of my computer games company – the small fortune I'd made out of 'The Five Guardian's' video game, and the way I'd managed to lose it on a succession of dud ideas.

I told him of Faith, our love, our fruitless efforts to secure succession to the Benedict dynasty, the fact she'd pissed off with a smart aleck media exec young enough to be my son – someone who no doubt had a significantly higher sperm count.

I did my best to mask my despair.

The more I spoke, the more I realized how badly I'd fucked up my life; that it was no one's fault but my own. It was suddenly clear as day. There was no blaming Faith, it was me.

"The cruelty of youth, Jay old son," Jack said. "Just don't tell me you want her back or I'll cuff you round the ear."

He grinned. Jack had always been pretty black and white.

We turned into Old Topanga Canyon Road.

It was surprisingly rural out here. Reasonably wild. Reminded me of Spain.

"So what happens if she makes good her threat to bleed you dry?"

"Any hope of keeping the company afloat goes out the window. The idea was to raise another mortgage on the house. That's out of the question now. Everything'll be frozen. Every brass razoo. She's got one smart lawyer."

"The bottom line is what?"

"I go under. She gets rich. I get lonely."

I smiled wryly, attempting to make light of it.

Then I cast a glance at Jack. His face was all storm clouds.

"Fuck it. It doesn't matter, eh? Forget the bitch. Believe me, she'll get hers, one way or another. That's karma, matey."

He pointed. "Our place is just up ahead."

The drive was lined with lemon trees. Though the fruit was still green, I could have sworn I could smell them. Maybe it was just wish fulfilment – it was just so good to be with an old friend, someplace other than the desolation of what had once been a home.

As the car drew up outside the house my eyes drifted upwards. A silhouetted figure was staring down at us from a gabled window. The effect was eerie, reminiscent of Wuthering Heights. I couldn't take my eyes off the spectre.

Just then a woman called out from the back of the house, diverting my attention. It was a mother's voice. I don't know how I knew. It just was. Comfortable, easy-going and full of love. The voice of a mum I'd never had. It had to be Stella.

"We've got company, love," Jack called out as we stepped onto the verandah. "Old pal of mine. Come and meet him."

Jack made for the bar in the far corner of the cathedral lounge room.

The house was a curious mixture of a California ranch and South London; post and rail leather sofas, Victorian sideboard, Wurlitzer juke box, three quarter size English billiard table against the window.

He asked some pretty searching questions about Faith. I think he felt sorry for me – maybe guilty that here he was, happy as a clam, while I was in the deepest possible conubial shit.

I could see that what really struck a nerve with him was that, not content to fry me emotionally, Faith had it in mind to bankrupt me into the bargain.

"How about I pay her a visit? Have a chat with her and her fancy man?" he said, narrowing his eyes theatrically. "What's his name?"

"Larry Loman. Works for Lorimar. Slick second-rater."

"I'm serious," he continued, like a dog with a bone. "Do you want me to have a word in his shell-like?" he asked.

This time Jack wasn't smiling.

A word in Larry's ear? Strong arm tactics from Jack on my behalf? That was all I needed. Helen Lowenstein would just lap it up, spit it out in court and I'd be well and truly screwed. As would Jack, for his trouble.

"Thanks, but no thanks. I've enough problems."

Jack shrugged, then looked over his shoulder into the living room, willing Stella to hurry up and join us on the veranda.

"He's got Stella's brain, thank God, and my nose for mischief." The words came out of left field.

My brain jerked back into gear. "Harold?"

"Harold. He's in the 'Command Module' – that's what he calls his room. It's a grown-ups-free area. Strictly off-limits. He's good enough to let Conchita clean it every Tuesday."

He chuckled. "Mind you, it's a supervised cleansing. As if she's going to steal something."

He laughed again.

Just then we were joined by Stella.

She lived up to my every expectation. I'd never seen Jack with any girl less than stunning.

Unlike Jack, who's build was stocky, Stella was tall, long-limbed, with a gentle happy face. Perfect skin, shortish primrose-yellow hair that neatly framed her perfectly defined features, and electric blue eyes that held you like a magnet.

She held out a hand; her smile lit up the room.

Maybe Jack was doing me a favour, but each time the conversation veered towards my ongoing marital situation, Jack steered it away to calmer waters. Nearly always he'd bring the subject back to some anecdote about Harold. The boy was clearly the focal point of their lives.

The kid was forming intelligible words at nine months, walking at twelve months, reading children's books at three years, and capable of quite abstruce conceptual thought by the time he was five.

I wasn't really listening. Staying awake was hard enough.

"Harry's seriously-gifted, that's been obvious since ever," Stella informed me in soft tones, "but we're determined to keep his life as normal as possible. There's plenty of time to let genius blossom, I think. We don't want him to miss his childhood."

"Not that we've held him back," Jack cut in eagerly. "He's had every opportunity to grow intellectually.

"We enrolled him at the Centre for Early Education when he was three. Outstanding place. Trifle snooty, but right on the money.

"Schools cost a fortune the world over. America's no different. Do you realise at the Centre there's even a special lane in the driveway just for limosines! Doesn't that just blow you away?"

I sipped on my bullshot, doing my best to look interested, but my brain had slipped into that stultifying shadow world of inebriation, and I was concerned I might embarrass myself by dozing off at any second.

"Harold's been in the 'gifted program' since he was seven. He'll be at UCLA in a couple of years max. You bet your life on it! Imagine that, at thirteen!"

Stella let Jack dominate the conversation. She sat in a basket chair that hung from a beam on the porch, her legs tucked up under her while her husband bragged on about their issue.

It was close to ten when Jack offered to drive me home.

My relief was so intense I was embarrassed that it might have shown on my face. At that moment bed seemed the next best thing to the peace of the grave.

"Wish you could have met Harold," I vaguely heard Jack mutter as we drove away from the house, the imagined sweet fragrance of lemons invading my semi-conscious senses.

I had no recollection of saying goodbye to Stella. I suppose I must have done so.

Next thing I knew we were parked nose to the wrought iron gates of my home and Jack was shaking my shoulder.

"You got the clicker?" he asked.

I stumbled from the Trans Am. "Mind if I don't invite you in right now? Feel pretty bad."

I shuffled surprisingly competently to the side gate, pulling my keys from my pocket, then waved feebly from inside the driveway.

"Call me tomorrow," Jack shouted from the car, his expression heavy with concern.

I smiled back, trying to make a brave fist of it all. "Will do. Thanks for being there for me. You always were."

"Always will be. Go to bed, china. And no more booze tonight."

3.

It was good seeing Jack again.

When we'd shared the house in London, life had presented few problems. Sure, I was short of cash every now and then, but that's par for the course when you're young and single. Besides Jack was always happy to tide me over till my next cheque arrived.

Strangely enough, when I broke through into consciousness the next morning my head was relatively clear.

There was no time to clean up my pigsty of a bedroom, just enough to shower, grab some clean clothes and check the messages.

There was just one. It was Faith. I felt the usual low voltage shockwave of depression.

She wanted to arrange a time to collect a few things she'd left behind. I couldn't imagine what she had in mind – the wardrobes were bare.

A time when I'd be out, she added.

Her tone was uncaring and businesslike. She knew damned well I was suffering, but it wasn't her problem.

I drove over to the Cyberkitchen, the name we'd given to our computer games company in Van Nuys. It was a two story cement building on Oxnard, standing practically beneath the Hollywood Freeway. It was pig ugly.

I felt truly bad about Charlie, my partner with the patience of Job. There were no two ways about it, I'd let the business roll downhill while I wallowed in self-pity.

We'd gone into partnership after the financial success of 'The Five Guardians', but despite Charlie's obvious talent we'd managed to miss the target for the next five long years.

Nancy, our receptionist, handed me another wad of messages.

Nate had been trying to reach me. Presumably with some last vestige of bad news he'd omitted to dump on me the day before.

I wasn't disappointed. Nate warned me to expect a process server. There'd be little to be gained in avoiding process. They'd get me one way or another.

I walked Charlie round the corner to the Brazillia Lounge, a surprisingly upbeat coffee shop for that neck of the woods.

I had to tell him what was happening. If I was forced to split my assets with Faith, then the company was through. We wouldn't be able to service the loans.

There were only six of us at the 'Kitchen; Charlie and me, plus four employees. Lissie, Mort and Scuzz, our indefatigable propellorheads, and Nancy our general person Friday. So our wages bill wasn't huge.

Nevertheless, until the cash deal with Lanyard Bell went through we were about as liquid as quartz.

I felt like an undertaker making arrangments for the burial of poor Charlie's career. There was no question that for the time being it was dead. There was, however, a choice of caskets.

He took it well. He just listened patiently as he drank his strawberry flavoured soya milkshake while I explained just how broke we were, and how the divorce would affect matters.

But Charlie was a survivor born of optimism. Didn't let things get him down.

Mind you, he was only twenty-eight. I was that way once.

Only time I'd ever seen Charlie without a smile was when he was staring at a computer screen. Then he'd be really buzzing. Completely wired.

I was so sorry for Charlie. He'd have been so much better off had he never met me.

We discussed how best to divide up the company assets. There was no way I was about to let Faith grab what was rightfully Charlie's.

It was all such a shame. Such terribly bad timing. We were close as a wafer's width to the finish line with a new game with the working title of 'Sleuthhound'. Lanyard Bell had promised a decision a week ago.

I had it in my mind to suggest he take the title with him, but I knew the intangible assets of a company like ours would be the first thing Lowenstein would sniff out – there wasn't much else worth a damn.

Besides, Faith knew I thought Sleuthhound was our ticket to financial nirvana.

I poured a hit of Stoli into my double short black. Charlie knitted his brows and tut-tutted as he spooned some fragments of strawberry debris at the bottom of the glass into his mouth.

I think he was worried for me. That was his nature. Just when he should have been more concerned with his own future, he was thinking about mine.

If only I could have interchanged his and Faith's philanthropy quotient.

We walked back to the CyberKitchen. The sidewalk smelled of burning rubber, and the air of wood barely one degree below its combustion point.

A beat-up silver seventies Lincoln was parked opposite, the engine running, the windows rolled down.

Someone was sitting behind the wheel.

Considering the heat, whoever it was must have had a death wish. Maybe he had Valvoline engine oil in his veins.

It had to be the process server.

As Charlie opened the door of the building, the door of the Lincoln was pushed open and a young man in an open-necked banana shirt skipped across the road, thrusting an envelope into my hand.

The lad was scarcely old enough to be in possession of a driver's licence. No way would anyone have served him liquor without an ID.

Maybe this was his first day on what he'd soon discover was a shit of a job.

I rolled up the envelope and stuffed it in my pants pocket. I needed a drink, things were beginning to move too fast for my liking. Who knew, there was a more than fair chance I'd be divorced and bankrupt into the bargain before I had time to shake my DT's.

But first I had to force myself to deal with business affairs that couldn't wait. I owed it to Charlie and our five employees. I'd selfishly let myself go for several days now and the company was beginning to wallow without someone at the helm.

The company needed me just now.

Charlie's area was cybertechnics, his speciality the 'tools'; the programs that allowed one to make the movies. His hard-on was the product of cool technology. Charlie's technical ideas were often mind-blowing, yet if implemented would have bankrupted the company, no question, because he had no nose for cost control.

My forte was ideas, the writing, and business management. I was the hard head, the numbers cruncher. That was what was supposed to bring *me* off.

In the old days it did. I knew the numbers of product shipped by every company in our specialised industry. I knew their cash flow and projections.

Together, Charlie and I worked well. If Faith could have given us another six months, the Lanyard Bell deal would have come good. I would have bet the house on it.

Which was exactly what I'd intended to do. A second mortgage. Because six months from now we'd have our title on five million machines.

Somehow or other I had to figure a way out of our financial problems.

By 2.20 pm I'd been running on empty for well over an hour. I'd achieved as much as was humanly possible, now it was a question of taking care of number one. I had to send some reinforcements after the shots of Stoli – they'd been holding the fort since breakfast.

Charlie hadn't moved from his office since we'd returned from the Brazillia. I didn't say goodbye.

Nancy looked up from her desk, smiling encouragingly at me as I walked to the door. She knew we were all in trouble. Everyone did.

I instinctively made for the Santa Fe Grill. Subconsciously maybe I half-expected Jack to be there again. Consciously I reminded myself the place served damned good Margaritas – a cut above the watered variety so prevalent in the cheap Valley joints.

At the Santa Fe they kicked like Bruce Lee. Not too sweet either.

The first jug was heaven. The second was sheer indulgence. I thought about a third.

Put it down to paranoia, but I could have sworn the young kid behind the bar was sneaking furtive looks at me. Like I could end up being a problem.

That did it. I paid and stepped outside.

The heat hit me like a hammer.

For a moment I thought I might pass out. The world was revolving as fast as a CD, and my skin was flushing white hot. No way was I fit to drive.

When my father died it was of a massive heart attack. It was in the family genes. He was forty two. So was I last week.

As I steadied myself on the hood of the Pontiac, I remember thinking that then was as good a time as any to meet my maker.

That didn't mean I wasn't frightened. I was scared to death.

I hung on to the door and dragged it open, pulling on a lever by the side of the passenger seat and lying practically horizontal in the car. I closed my eyes while I prayed. If there was a God, he'd help me I knew that for a fact. In my panic I suddenly believed he was right there in the car with me, holding my hand.

It was a miracle. My heart stopped racing. My thoughts became a jumbled mess of nonsense, and I slipped into a divine dreamworld.

Many times I felt myself rising to the surface and each time I dived back into the delicious oblivion of sleep.

This time I knew I wouldn't be able to make it down again till I'd come up for air. Someone was tapp-tapping on the window.

I struggled to open my eyes.

An apparition was pressed to the window. The face of a woman around fifty. Totally moonstruck; eyes wide as French breakfast saucers.

She looked as though she'd been drinking a lot; she was mouthing something incomprehensible, her bloated lips awash with saliva.

As I sat up, she wagged a finger at me then staggered away between the cars in the parking lot.

There was something about her that reminded me of my mother. It wasn't the booze, though that had been a pretty major part of mum's life, and consequently mine. It was the manic look of expectancy in the eyes.

I closed my eyes again, my first instinct to sink back yet again into the reassuring darkness. This time I made it down again.

When I woke the second time the clock on the dash told me it was just on half past six in the evening. I'd been out for two to three hours all told.

Strangely enough, I didn't feel too bad, despite the fact that the interior of the Pontiac was a hundred per cent humidity, and my clothes were drenched.

It was time to get home.

4.

His fingers kept drifting back down to the butt of the gun. Just to caress the blue metal with his short fingers sent a thrill through his body.

He glanced up at the window on the fifth floor. He could clearly see a woman. It had to be her. She was in the guy's apartment after all.

Of course he'd have to check her out, make sure, that went without saying. No point in putting a bullet in the wrong customer.

The woman ran a hand through her hair, then moved away from the window.

He glanced at his watch in annoyance. 3.50 pm. How long was the bitch going to make him wait? He'd been here for over an hour now doing his best to blend in with the shoppers in the Promenade. Soon as he pulled the trigger and blew her away the cops would be sniffing around asking questions. *See anything out of the ordinary, mister? Anyone hanging around outside?*

Yes, a low profile was everything.

His forefinger inched down over the butt of the Ruger and closed over the edge of the trigger.

Come on! Whoever you are, come down here, for Christ's sake. Let's check you out and get this done!

He flicked off the safety and took up the first pressure. He liked to flirt with danger. It gave him a rush.

The woman was back at the window, looking down into the Promenade, doing something to her hair; pushing it up behind her head and sticking a comb or something in it.

He ground his teeth together, willing her to leave the building. *Come on down, bitch. I've got one killer surprise for you.*

Then the woman stepped back and a curtain was pulled across the window. *Shit, shit, shit!*

He stamped his foot down hard on the sidewalk. He wanted to do it now! Now, for Christ's sake. He was ready, his mind screamed!

What the hell was going on? Had he miscalculated? Was the guy in there with her after all? Were they going to screw each other or something?

Annoyance was turning to serious anger. So the bitch was keeping him waiting? He had a good mind to 'off' her whether or not she was the one. Screw her!

His eyes drifted from the window down to the entrance to the building.

As though in answer to his prayers the door miraculously opened.

It was the woman from the fifth floor apartment for sure, he could tell by the hair pinned up behind her head.

He watched her stride out across the Promenade. She was making straight for him.

Quickly he turned his back to her and followed her reflection in the glass of the pharmacy window facing him. Which way was she heading? Through to 4th Street? The parking station maybe?

His heart leapt at the thought. *Please, please, please,* he pleaded, squeezing his eyes tight shut for a fraction of a second.

He watched her make a right, heading directly for the cut through to parking station 5.

He almost laughed aloud. Sweet Jesus, this was too good to be true.

Here we go, lady. Party time.

Only maybe fifteen feet separated them now. She was moving fast. Occasionally she'd look to one side or other and he'd see her face. She looked real mad.

As she skipped down the six steps to level two he glanced quickly left, right, ahead, and behind. The only movement on the entire level was a red Mustang turning into the exit ramp at the far end. Otherwise they were alone.

Excellente!

The woman stopped at the rear of a blue Ford Discovery and began rummaging inside her purse.

He slowed up six feet from her. One last quick look around.

No one.

This is as lucky as you get, man. Go for it!

He walked forward, his heart racing like crazy. It was the most extreme buzz he'd ever felt. It was huge.

His hand closed on the butt of the gun, easing it up a couple of inches.

Then he locked eyes with the woman for the first time and he smiled.

Bang, bang, you're dead, he half-whispered to himself, as she stared curiously into his deep blue eyes.

5.

As I drove up Sunshine I reached for the clicker.

Only then did I notice the burgundy Chevy two door parked to the left of the driveway gates.

Two men were leaning against the beat-up car. One was dressed casually – open-necked plaid shirt and slacks. The other wore a third-rate suit.

As I nosed towards the gate the formal one held up a hand and motioned to me to roll down the window.

He then leaned in the window, pulled out his police badge, and flipped it casually open at his and my face level.

"Detective Yant. Santa Monica Police Department. Over there's my partner, Detective Wahl."

He indicated the man in the shirt behind him.

"Are you Jay Benedict, sir?" he asked. He was simultaneously polite, yet off-hand. Not much heart was lurking beneath his ten dollar business shirt.

I nodded my head. My heart was suddenly pounding again with some precognition of calamity. This didn't happen in real life – only in the movies.

Tragedy was seconds away, had to be. Cops didn't wait to deliver news of a windfall. What terrible sledgehammer of evil tidings was this uncaring policeman about to hit me with?

"May we come in, Mr Benedict? I think this is something best not discussed in the street."

"What's this about?" I stammered. It was scarcely more than a whisper. I wasn't breathing. Though I knew something terrible had happened, I had no inkling of what he was about to say. I was thinking accidents; the death of my brother in London maybe.

"The matter concerns your wife, Mr Benedict. There's been a shooting. I'm sorry, sir. She's dead."

To this day I have no recollection of the following few moments.

Shock plays strange games with the nervous system. My brain must have shut down in much the same way as a computer does to conserve power.

Then suddenly I was aware of the detective shaking my shoulders hard and shouting back at his partner to call an ambulance.

I tried to shout something, but found my lungs were empty – I hadn't been breathing since I heard the word 'dead'.

I remember trying to tell the detective not to call the ambulance. "Inside," I mouthed. "Let's go inside."

Neither Yant nor Wahl wished to sit.

Wahl, the short fat detective was good enough to fetch me some water.

I sat in my TV chair. It had always been our favourite spot. Oversize. Not really big enough for two, but plenty big enough for lovers. Faith would sit in my lap and we'd sometimes fall asleep watching the late movies.

Right then I felt like a six-year-old lost in grandpa's wingchair.

The detectives stood, flanking me like statues.

Yant pulled out a notebook, constantly referring to it as he spoke.

Wahl's eyes never left mine for a second. I found this disturbing. Every time my eyes drifted back and locked with his he was boring a hole through me; as though he were trying to look into my soul for the truth.

He never blinked.

Yant read a prepared speech in a tone he obviously reserved for breaking news of death. Quiet, efficient, with just a hint of pathos.

Faith's body had been discovered slumped beside her Ford Discovery on the second level of parking station number 5 on 4th Street, Santa Monica.

Dispatch logged a 911 call at 4.38. The legal time of death was determined by patrol division to be 4.45. This was the time the cops actually saw the body for the first time.

An investigator from the corner's office had, prior to the findings of an autopsy, loosely determined the time of death to be closer to 4 o'clock.

Faith had taken one shot to the center-left chest area, and one to the side of the head. Either would have caused death.

She had died instantly – at least that was what had been initially determined at the crime scene.

Robbery didn't appear at first sight to be a motive. A few hundred dollars and several major credit cards were still present in her purse. Her rings were still on her fingers.

No one had been apprehended in connection with the shooting.

"I have to ask this question, Mr Benedict," Yant continued. "Can you think of anyone who might have harboured a grudge against your wife?"

A grudge? Such an archaic choice of words. Someone who'd want to put a bullet through her? No, the idea was unimaginable. She'd had no enemies. Faith was the most straightforward person I'd ever met. Like her, hate her, or love her. When she knew I couldn't give her babies, that was it. I had to go. Life had to continue. Faith had to be cruel to others so she could be kind to Faith.

The irony was she'd always seen herself as a survivor.

She'd been wrong.

Wahl studied me with his unblinking steady gaze. I think he thought I should have been weeping, or maybe biting the carpet with grief. To hell with him, I thought. I had a deal of weeping to come. But not with Wahl and Yant as my witnesses.

Detective Yant asked me if I knew why she'd been in Santa Monica that afternoon.

Perhaps she'd been shopping, I replied instinctively. For some unfathomable reason I still couldn't bring myself to tell him about Loman. I just didn't want to bring him into the equation. Not then. At that precise moment Faith was my wife. This had nothing whatsoever to do with Loman.

However, I was sane enough to register that I'd have to tell them about him pretty damn soon. They'd find it decidedly odd if I didn't and they just happened on the information at some later stage – as they most assuredly would.

Besides, Wahl was already definitely giving me the prime suspect stare. Why wouldn't he? Start at the center and move outwards.

"My wife and I are separated. At least, she chose to separate herself from me," I said in language I thought Wahl might comprehend, cutting him a quick glance.

Wahl stared back, the suspicion of a smile playing on his lips. Yant looked up from his notebook briefly. My reply had been unexpected.

"When exactly did she move out, Mr Benedict?" he asked with an expression which gave nothing away.

"A week ago. Last Wednesday, 8.45 pm."

"You're a precise man, Mr Benedict," Wahl observed dryly.

"It was the worst day of my life. How could I forget it?"

"Did your wife have a lover, Mr Benedict?"

Yant didn't apologize for his bluntness. Maybe there just wasn't time for basic human compassion in his line of work. Too many bodies littering the sidewalk.

"Yes," I whispered, barely audibly. "Larry Loman. Works for Lorimar."

"Movies?"

"Televison. Same thing. He's an executive."

Yant made more notes.

"And he lives in Santa Monica?"

"That was my line of thinking," I replied.

I looked at my hands. They were shaking.

"Suite 5. 1230 3rd Street Promenade. It's a walk through to the parking on 4th."

"How well do you know this Loman?" It was Wahl who spoke.

"I don't. All I know about the man is what my wife told me. His name, and that he's young and rich."

"That covers most bases these days," Wahl mumbled.

Yant threw a disapproving glance at his partner.

"Was your wife living with Loman, Mr Benedict?" Yant enquired.

I replied that I presumed she had been, and that since she'd left she no longer gave me a blow by blow account of her day to day life.

Yant gave me a lengthy thoughtful stare, as if debating whether to continue. Then he snapped his notebook shut.

"All right, Mr Benedict. That's about it for now. I'm sorry to have had to ask so many painful questions right now. Goes with my job, I'm afraid. Doesn't mean I like it one bit."

He paused as he stuck a finger in his ear and thrashed his arm about to relieve an irritation.

"Now the hard part, Mr Benedict. I have to ask you to come with us to the county morgue to identify your wife's body."

I knew this was coming.

Wait till someone looks you in the eyes and says the same thing.

6.

I once passed an auto accident. I was ten and in the passenger seat. I happened to look left as we passed a van.

There was a cadaver still sitting slumped back in the driver's seat, held fast by his seatbelt. The door and the side of the driver's head were missing.

I recall thinking later how strange it was there was no blood. No red anywhere. Rather, the open side of his head was just black as pitch. The collision must just have occured. As I flashed by, I felt as though I'd been touched with a white hot branding iron.

Faith had already been assigned a number and toe-tagged when I arrived at the morgue. The top of her head had been draped with a cloth. Possibly the wound to her head was considered too shocking.

The room was ice cold after the humidity outside. The salt sweat instantly dried and caked under my eyes and on my temples.

Someone pulled back the sheet.

I felt a Buddha-like composure as I looked at her young once graceful face – why, I shall never know. I was removed, as though I were having an out of body experience. For the first time in my life I was having some kind of a religious episode and I was shocked by its intensity. There was a sudden overwhelming understanding and acceptance of my own mortality. It had nothing to do with insensitivity or heartlessness, and it had nothing to do with Faith. Everything around me was slowing down as if I were observing life frame by frame.

I noticed she was still clothed. There was a glimpse of a blouse.

Yant was at my side.

I stared down at Faith in my personal dreamscape, scrutinizing each detail of the face for future reference, as would a computer scanner. Then I gradually became aware of the real world around me. Detective Yant was repeating a phrase, over and over, ever louder. "Mr Benedict. Is this your wife? Please answer yes or no."

I nodded my head.

The Medical Examiner's assistant pulled the sheet back over Faith's head and pushed her slowly into the wall, the metal rollers resonating round the airless sanitized basement.

I was escorted outside.

There Yant and I met up again with detective Wahl. He'd managed to scare up a chili dog somewhere. With all the fixings.

Sensitive man, Wahl.

"How do you feel about helping us out at the station house, Mr Benedict?" Yant asked. "I mean right now. Tonight. I'll understand if you tell me you'd rather wait till morning, but we find a lot of people want to get in there right away – find the bastard who did it. Know what I mean?"

I looked Yant dead in the eye. He just wanted to grill me. I knew that. He knew that. Hell, even Wahl was smirking openly – he had the guilty husband on the run, seriously rattled, about to make a mistake.

Instead of anger I only felt sadness. What the hell could make a man so mean-spirited?

"Tomorrow," I said to Yant. "I need some space. I can't breathe in here. Can you understand that?"

Yant nodded. Wahl looked pissed; he'd have liked to shine a bright light in my face till morning. He could almost taste a confession.

7.

Charlie lived in a converted garage halfway down Abbott Kinney. Actually it was more like a small falling down bungalow with a garage at the side. When he set up his computer hardware in the lean-to, it went without saying he set up his bed there too.

First thing he did when he moved in was black out the one small window. I swear he's the closest a human can get to a mole.

I couldn't think of anyone else to turn to. To call Jack right now was out of the question. I didn't feel right about it.

I suppose I realized instinctively that the years had distanced us somewhat. Anyway, things had changed. Then we'd been best buddies. Now he was a family man, that was his focus.

He'd grown up.

Yant offered to drive me home, but I knew that without some semblance of human warmth I might start thinking of walking out to sea at Santa Monica. Besides I had to steel myself to make the call to Faith's mum and dad. I knew I couldn't hack that alone.

So it had to be Charlie; a fundamentally decent man, few words, big heart. I knew he'd spare me some time. He'd care.

Yant had let me call him from the station house. I didn't tell him about Faith – just that I'd received some bad news and needed a friend.

He was standing in the street when we drew up outside the dilapidated wreck of a building young Charlie called home. Black T-shirt, mole-brown pants and bare feet. Sartorially he was a disaster. He had no conception of how he looked. I'd never seen a mirror in his shack and it showed.

As Yant's Chevy took off up Abbott Kinney towards Lincoln, Charlie put an arm round my shoulder.

"Tell me about it when you're ready, Jay. Meantime, let's eat."

His kind face was suffused with compassion. How did I deserve a friend like this? A few hours ago I'd been the catalyst that had threatened to send him broke.

I stood behind him in the small galley kitchen as he splashed a dash of this and a shake of that into a steaming wok.

I asked if I could use the telephone. I had to call Faith's parents. If they hadn't lived in Tempe I wouldn't have dreamt of breaking the news on the phone. But there was no other option. They had to know, and that meant right now.

Hal answered. I thanked God it hadn't been Alice. Though I knew from the word go that they both disapproved of our marriage, Hal had always done his best to keep it to himself.

Alice, by contrast, made no secret of her antipathy towards me.

For starters I was an Englishman. She'd have been happier if Faith had married a Somalian bandit or an East Timorese fisherman.

Then there was the added insult that I was only two years younger than her husband.

Hal was a doctor. A staid, reasonably humorless honest man. His father had been a doctor, as had his grandfather before him. All had lived and died in Tempe, Arizona. For Faith to choose a career path in fashion was a low enough blow to them both. But her sudden determination to marry a man whose lifelong contribution to humanity was to be the creation of ineffectual computer games for small children was the kiss of death.

Alice had shown up at the wedding, but it had been under suffrance. Hal had made her.

I broke the terrible news to Hal.

He listened in silence. No interruptions.

I don't think I was particularly clever in the way I put things. I could hear the rhythm of his breathing changing, and I knew he was fighting for control.

How the hell can you dress up words that spell the end of someone's world?

He told me that Alice was at a bridge club meeting. His voice was thin as a reed. He'd tell her when she got in. He expected her any minute. Had I made any of the 'arrangements'?

I replied that it was too premature to even think of such things. There was to be an autopsy. I supposed that would be a matter of course in these cases.

Hal told me they'd catch a plane first thing in the morning. He just wanted to be close to Faith, he said. And so would Alice.

He suddenly broke off. He had to hang up. Alice was home.

I felt immeasurably sorry for Hal. Now it was *his* turn.

I stood in the shadowy hallway, trembling. I could feel a tidal wave of emotion welling up inside me. So far I'd managed to keep a pretty even keel. I knew I had about two minutes left before the cyclone hit.

With his usual sixth sense Charlie came out from the kitchen and hugged me.

I've never been a man to shy away from physical intimacy between friends, be they male or female. Of course this runs against the norm as far as Englishmen are concerned; a race renowned for its stiff upper lip and legendary *sang-froid*.

So Charlie's gesture was a touch of magic.

"I overheard," he said simply. "I figured no one needed to tell anyone something like that twice over, so I kept on listening. Any way I can help, you let me know."

"Can I sit in the lounge for a bit?" I asked.

"Sure," he replied. "Take as long as you want. When you need to talk I'll be around."

As I began to walk into the darkness of the lounge he caught my elbow. "Let it out, Jay. Let go."

I cried like a baby for over an hour. I hadn't felt so desolate since the day at school the headmaster told me my mother had died of a stroke.

I'd never known my father, he'd taken off the second mum told him she was in the pudding club for the second time. He'd never much cared for children. One was tolerable; two was out of the question.

I was twelve when mum died. The emptiness was numbing. I'd looked after her since I was seven.

On one occasion I'd returned from school at tea time to find the house empty, the oven door open, and a cushion inside. That was the first of mum's many aborted suicide attempts.

My brother Raymond had never been much help. He was seldom at home.

Eight years older than me, he was always 'out there doing things'. Quite what they were, mum and I never really knew. They certainly didn't bring home any bacon.

I came to the conclusion that whatever 'things' he was doing, they were mostly for his own benefit. He just didn't have much time for mum or me; we had to muddle through, and she just wasn't up to it most of the time.

They told me she'd died of a stroke, but that was just a white lie. In actual fact she'd taken barbiturates.

They hoped to save me undue pain. But I knew. Don't ask me how, I just knew. Kids do. They have an understanding of life, an intuition that's usually blunted as the years roll by.

Right then, I didn't know much of anything.

I managed to pull myself together marginally, and joined Charlie in the garage. His advice had been sound. The cathartic outporing of tears had helped enormously.

We sat on a low sofa facing his bank of computer hardware, our faces bathed in the eerie light of twin computer screens. Charlie looked quite ghostly.

"I'm really sorry about the business," I said. Amongst all the present horrors, concerns for Charlie's well-being kept nagging me.

He hadn't complained for a second, even though he didn't have a cent to his name, and lived in that dreary garage. Now his business was about to crash round his ears.

"You realise Faith's death might change a heap of variables," he said softly, after a few moments silence.

This hadn't struck me. But of course it was true. Now that Faith was dead, I was a widower. No divorce, no lawyers, no frozen assets, no process servers. It was all mine; the house, my few miserable savings, the car.

"I didn't mean –" he began.

"I know you didn't, Charlie. I know. But I hear you talking."

"Did the detectives tell you how they saw it?" he asked. "If you don't want to talk about it, I'll understand."

"They didn't say much. Asked the usual questions. Did she have enemies? That kind of thing."

"Did she?"

"No way," I replied. Then another thought shook me. I closed my eyes in shame. "Shit! Loman. No one's told that poor bastard."

"Did you tell the cops she was living with him?"

A surge of relief. Yes I had. I'd told them about Lorimar. They'd have spoken to him for sure. Thank Christ. Saved me the torture of calling him. I sank back into the threadbare sofa, the springs moving accommodatingly.

"There's no way –?" Charlie began tentatively, shooting me a look loaded with innuendo.

"No," I replied simply. The idea was laughable. Larry shoot Faith dead in a parking lot? The man was as innocuous as a short drink of Perrier water. The seminal rich Hollywood yuppie.

"You're going to need a lawyer," Charlie said a few seconds later, interrupting a nightmare image of Faith's death mask lying on a steel tray. "Nate's just not up to it, Jay."

I looked up, startled by Charlie's train of thought.

"A lawyer?"

"Someone who knows what he's doing. Just in case. Know what I mean?"

"In case of what?" I asked. I didn't follow at all.

"Faith was having an affair with another man," Charlie began uncertainly. "Your marriage was on the rocks. She was about to stick it to you financially in the divorce courts. Then she ends up dead. Gunned down for no apparent reason in a parking lot, and robbery wasn't a motive. Isn't that what you told Hal?"

"That's right."

"Well, I have to say it the way I see it. Who are they going to be paying close attention to? Which is the more attractive scenario? A pointless thrill-killing, or a crime of passion?"

I suddenly saw quite clearly what Charlie was getting at, yet I didn't much care. Right that moment, if the cops had arrived in a black and white, hand-cuffed me and taken me away, it wouldn't have bothered me.

"You have to think about it from their point of view, Jay. Especially if you ever think of raising any money on your house to keep the 'Kitchen afloat. Remember, that wasn't possible while Faith was alive."

He had a point. Like it or not, I'd have to seriously consider my position pretty damn soon.

An image of the smirking Wahl flashed before me. There wasn't much doubt in that detective's tiny mind who was responsible for Faith's murder, and it wasn't some young punk from the wrong side of Pico.

For a while I tried to get into the mind of someone like Yant. Difficult but not impossible.

Statistics, and all those years on the street, would have me checking out the husband pretty thoroughly. Motive? Sure, the husband had motive; wife off screwing some young buck, and a fancy divorce lawyer was about to squeeze the husband dry. Anyone else with a reason to gun down the DOA? No one immediately apparent.

Okay, so where was the husband at the time of the killing?

I fought to clear my fuddled brain and think back clearly. What had Yant told me? The legal time of death had been determined at 4.45. Presumably that meant the time the first police officer arrived on the scene and determined she was clinically dead.

But the *actual* time of death – the time of the shooting, since she'd died instantly – had been estimated at closer to 4 pm.

Where the hell had I been then? In the Santa Fe Grill.

I struggled to remember clearly, but hard as I tried I couldn't remember exactly.

Hell, I'd been drunk as a skunk; I hadn't been checking the time. I remembered leaving the Cyberkitchen around two-twenty. It was the last time I recalled looking at my watch.

That put me at the Santa Fe around a quarter to three. Two jugs, the way I was lapping them up, saw me sauced and dead to the world in the front of the Pontiac by three-thirty.

Some alibi.

Yes, if I was detective Yant, I'd be checking out the English asshole pretty thoroughly.

Right then the only person with a grip on reality was Charlie. He was spelling things out to me pretty clearly, and making a lot of sense. It never actually crossed my mind anyone would think I had a hand in the shooting till Charlie had delicately brought it to my attention in the garage.

"I've got a few beers in the fridge, Jay. Nothing hard though. Can I get you one?"

Charlie was all through with his advice. Now it was up to me whether I took it and dumped Nate.

I shook my head. No more alcohol. It was time to think of other people for a change. Charlie, Hal and Alice.

It would soon be time to bury the dead.

8.

My grandmother was the master of the hackneyed aphorism. Drove my mother nuts. There wasn't an original idea in her wrinkled head. One of her favorites was 'it can only get better.'

As far as my mother was concerned it never did; it got progressively worse till the day she decided to end it all. Didn't stop my granny though. She actually whispered the same words to me as she tucked into the funeral baked meats less than an hour after burying her daughter.

Within two weeks she herself was dead. So she'd been wrong, it didn't always get better. Unless one believed in a God.

In my experience one of the great truths of life is that when you stumble, there's invariably someone right up your butt ready to offer a swift kick.

It wasn't too long before I got mine.

Charlie was kind enough to offer me the sofa bed in the lounge room, so I bunked down for the night. And, miracle of miracles, I slept the sleep of the dead from just after eleven that night to eight the following morning. No dreams, no hob goblins.

Thanks to the absence of the usual quantities of alcohol in my bloodstream, I was mercifully free of the 'mean reds' the following morning.

Charlie had left for the 'Kitchen when I dragged myself from the sofa. Weekends meant nothing to him. They were just two more days. The freeways weren't so jammed, that was the one difference. Day in, day out Charlie was always first in at the office. Around 6 am.

He'd left me a note in the kitchen. *Sorry, no caffeine, buddy. Take care. See you when I see you. C.*

It took the cab the best part of half an hour to arrive, so I didn't make it home across the hill to Studio City till around nine thirty.

On the way I made some mental notes of priorities for the day. If Hal didn't call me, I'd have to call him back to find out when he and Alice were arriving from Phoenix. Then I'd need to call Yant to find out when they planned to release Faith's body to me.

As the cab turned into Sunshine I looked over the driver's shoulder in astonishment.

Ahead, parked by the gates, was Yant's familiar dirty brown two-door Chevy.

The tall detective was leaning against the door, smoking. Beside him was an even taller man. Yant must have been six-two – this man would have made any basketball team he'd wished.

I paid off the cab while the two men watched. Yant wore his usual shabby suit, the man at his elbow a much snazzier variety. Neat and crisp and even.

As I walked across to them I noticed Wahl was still sitting in the Chevy. He was busy flossing his teeth. He showed little interest in me.

Yant extended a hand without a smile. "We've been trying to reach you, Mr Benedict," Yant said, almost accusingly, as though I should have been wearing a pager just for his personal benefit.

"Well, you can relax. I'm here now." The remark came out smart-arsed flippant. It was quite unintentional.

A look of annoyance momentarily darkened Yant's features. "This is Investigator Kifley," he said, indicating the giant beside him. "He's with the Federal Bureau of Investigation."

I shook Kifley's hand. It was a vice. "May we talk to you inside?" the FBI man said, the muscles in his hollow cheeks twitching.

I stared up into the dead fish eyes of the Federal agent. The FBI? This was a major shift of jurisdiction. How was the bureau involved? Perhaps they had a handle on the man or woman responsible for Faith's death, and he was from out of state. Christ, they must have moved fast.

Yant and I sat opposite each other in the living room, he on the sofa, me in the TV chair. Kifley preferred to stand, towering over us both. Wahl had seen fit to stay in the car.

"Just how is the FBI involved, Mr Kifley?" I asked, craning my head up to the stars.

The unsmiling giant said nothing, but rather opened a leather attaché case, extracting a sheaf of glossy eight by ten black and white photographs.

Fully expecting him to pass them over, I held out a hand. Instead he held them close to his chest, shooting a glance at Yant.

"You know a man by the name of Jack Corr, Mr Benedict?" Yant said in a reasonably friendly manner as he studied my reaction to the mention of Jack's name.

I stared at him in confusion. What the hell did Jack have to do with anything? The question was the last thing I expected him to come up with.

For close to twelve years Jack had been a man from the past. Forty-eight hours ago our paths had crossed, purely fortuitously. Suddenly a detective from the LAPD, together with an FBI agent, were in my living room asking me whether I knew Jack. Strange coincidence, to say the least.

"Do you know Jack Corr, Mr Benedict?" Yant reiterated, this time rather more forcibly.

"Yes I do. Can you tell me why?"

"How long have you known Mr Corr?" This time it was Kifley who asked the question.

"I can't think exactly. Around sixteen years, maybe slightly more. Why?" I was annoyed that they were ignoring my question.

"When did you last see Mr Corr?" Yant enquired.

"The night before last. Thursday. We met quite by chance in a restaurant on Ventura. I hadn't seen him in years."

"Really," said Yant. The word was so laced with sarcastic disbelief it immediately got my back up.

"Yes. Really," I snapped back. My nerves were still very close to the surface.

I was staring across at Yant, so I didn't notice Kifley stoop to place the eight by tens on the coffee table in front of me. Suddenly, plop, they were there.

I broke eye contact with Yant and looked down at the photos. My surprise must have been clearly evident to them both.

The topmost was a pretty grainy shot of the exterior of the Santa Fe Grill, sidewalk and all. It looked as though it had been taken with quite a powerful telephoto lens. Jack was standing at the entrance, one hand on the door. He was looking back over his shoulder down the street.

"There are others. Take a look, Mr Benedict," said Kifley.

I was curious, so I picked them up.

The second shot was of Jack and myself. I was shocked by my appearance; I'd no idea I looked so gaunt and haunted. My shirt was hanging out at the side, and my hair was standing out at the side of my head like a sail.

The third shot was another shot of Jack and myself outside the diner. This time however it was a medium close-up, and consequently the texture of the photograph was more grainy.

Under this photo were several snaps of us walking down Ventura. It was evident that we were talking to each other. Yet I couldn't help noticing that in all the photos Jack was looking either to his left across the street, or behind him down the sidewalk. In none of the shots was he looking at me.

The last shot was of Jack's Trans Am. I was already sitting slumped inside. Jack was in the process of climbing in behind the wheel. Again he was looking back down the street, as if watching his back.

I was annoyed. What the hell was going down here?

I tossed the photos on to the coffee table. They fell with a loud slap.

The gesture wasn't lost on Kifley who nodded to himself as if some projected reaction on my part had been confirmed.

"Perhaps you'll tell me why you've been taking photographs of me, Mr Kifley."

"We were taking shots of your pal Corr, not you, Mr Benedict." He said. Again he looked for a reaction. "Does that surprise you?"

I was silent. The FBI taking snaps of either of us surprised me a whole lot.

"You say you met Jack Corr quite by accident at the Santa Fe Grill? Would that be right?" Kifley asked.

"Correct," I replied.

"And before that meeting, you hadn't seen him for years. How many years exactly?"

"Eleven. Possibly twelve."

"How long have you lived in Los Angeles, Mr Benedict?"

"About as many years."

Kifley nodded his head slowly, more as a theatrical gesture for my benefit than confirming the fact in his mind. None of this was news to him. He was leading me by the nose, like an old trial lawyer about to stun the jury with some startling revelation.

"How well would you say you knew Jack Corr?"

"As well as I know anyone, I guess," I replied. "We were pretty close in London. As I said, we hadn't seen each other in a long time, but he didn't seem to have changed much. Looked a lot older, that's about all."

Another annoying nod from the FBI man. We were slowly getting there.

"Well, I'd say we at the Bureau knew Jack a good deal better than you did." He smiled. "That'd be my guess anyway."

I couldn't stand the smug look of self-satisfaction a second longer. "Mr Kifley, if you have something to ask me, could you cut to the chase? I don't know whether detective Yant has filled you in yet, but my wife was shot to death yesterday. I can do without all this."

"Yes. I'm familiar with the circumstances of your wife's death, Mr Benedict," Kifley replied without apology.

Then he paused, as though marshalling his thoughts.

"Would it surprise you to know that the Bureau has a file several inches thick on your pal Jack Corr?"

"Yes, it would," I replied evenly. "What's he supposed to have done?"

"Done? You want to know what he's done? Well, I'll tell you, Mr Benedict." He crouched down in front of me. His face was right in mine. "We believe for the past ten years Jack Corr worked as a contract killer for the Russian Mafia in New York."

Kifley delivered this bombshell without a hint of theatrics. It was a simple statement of fact. His eyes were twinkling nevertheless.

My mind blanked out temporarily. My brain spat out the information in the same way as an Apple Mac computer spits out an IBM disc. Kifley's statement just wasn't compatible with the man I knew as Jack Corr.

"That has to be nonsense," I replied almost at once.

"We don't build files this thick on fanciful notions," he said, indicating a width with his thumb and forefinger, "No sir. However, I'm not interested in what you think, Mr Benedict. I'd be happy if you'd just tell me why you arranged to meet with Mr Corr on Thursday."

It was a pretty damned obvious trick question. "We met by chance. I told you earlier," I replied.

Kifley feigned recollection. "Right," he drawled, drawing out the word to signify his disbelief. "Of course. You just happened to bump into a professional contract killer the day before your wife gets blown away in a parking structure in Santa Monica."

His tone was so cold it seemed the temperature in the room had fallen a good five degrees in one second.

I was dumbfounded by the inference. Was he really suggesting I'd hired Jack to murder Faith? It just wasn't possible.

I opened my mouth to tell the man to get out of my house when he held up a hand and ploughed straight on.

"We know for a fact that Jack Corr shot Jacob Vacek to death outside his house in the Hamptons October '89. We just can't prove it in a court of law. Tainted evidence. That's the only time we got real close. But it's common knowledge he was used by Sergei Krolov in his rise to prominence in Brighton Beach. Kerchenko, Osolov, Gretchkin, Harrison – they all died or disappeared between '90 and '96. I tell a lie, Harrison was pulled out of the Hudson over in Hobokin with a bullet to the head less than three months ago. You remember?"

I'd no idea who or what he was referring to. I just stared back at him.

He shrugged. "Don't you read the papers? Harrison was a major player. Everyone knew it was Corr. He was good."

Kifley smiled, as though in admiration of a true professional. "We knew damn well it was Corr. Too many trademarks. Killing's not a trade you can keep a secret. People have got to know you're out there or how do you get the jobs?" He chuckled. He clearly thought it was a laughing matter. "Best you can hope for is never to make a mistake.

"But forensics has come a very long way in the past few years. It's now a very exact science. We would have had him sooner or later. No question. I think he knew that. Word on the street was he was getting out."

He paused for a couple of seconds. He could see I'd shut my mouth. I was no longer arguing; I was listening hard.

"Now, when I say we *think* he was Krolov's hired help, that's what he damned well was. Take my word for it, Mr Benedict. The question is, is this news to you?"

He waved an arm indicating Yant. "See, that's what's been bothering my friend, detective Yant. Our professional paths crossed the moment Corr walked into that diner and spoke to you."

"It's plain stupid for anyone to even consider I approached Jack to harm my wife. I didn't even know he was still alive, for Christ's sake. We hadn't been in touch for years!"

"Maybe. We checked with Corr's phone company records. Doesn't mean you didn't keep in touch some other way. Corr was a careful man, Mr Benedict. That's the reason he lasted so long. Last thing he'd do would be to leave fingerprints, so to speak. He'd hardly call you from home. Neither would you, if you had anything to hide."

Something about what Kifley'd been saying was bugging me. Apart from the obvious damning inference that I had procured Faith's death. Bells were ringing.

Then it came to me.

"You're speaking of Jack in the past tense," I said.

"That's right. He's dead." His eyes drilled a hole in mine. This was the kicker. How would I react?

My mind just bubbled. I hadn't yet come to terms with Kifley's imputation that Jack was a contract killer, let alone the inference that I was an accessory to Faith's killing. Now Jack was dead?

How? When? Had he been killed in an internecine gang war? Without thinking I was already subconsciously accepting Kifley's first premise, that Jack was a criminal.

During the few seconds silence that followed Kifley's bombshell, the FBI agent shot a meaningful glance at Yant, who was looking disappointed at the way things were panning out. Possibly he'd hoped I'd give more away. Maybe I looked too convincing in my astonishment.

Kifley turned away and began to pace slowly round the room. Yant leant forward. "Jack Corr was killed in an auto accident on the Santa Monica Freeway past Cloverfield heading east. Suffered a cerebral embolism at the wheel."

I was quite speechless. Every new second of my life was bringing fresh catastrophe. I was close to overload.

"Question that's bugging me is this. What was Jack Corr *doing* on Interstate Highway 10 at 4.20 yesterday? So close to 4th Street." He raised his eyebrows theatrically. "Now that's what I call a *real* coincidence. Wouldn't you agree, Mr Benedict?"

9.

I've always been of the opinion that we have little or no choice in our destiny. In a way my mum and I were agreed on this point. Karma was very much a focal point of her life.

My mother professed to being a Buddhist. This didn't have much to do with a close examination of the basic tenets of the religion, but rather with her belief that its founder, Gautama, had identified more closely with animals than Jesus, who had chosen to leave that side of things to St Francis.

Her continuing nightmare was that Cleo, her beloved Boxer dog, wouldn't find a place in the next world. Gautama assured this.

My brother had no time for what he considered her ridiculous quirks. She paid him no attention. Her religion was a comfort to her. She even bought a small carved wooden Buddha and placed it in the ageing dog's basket.

Right now it was *my* karma, my destiny, to be badgered by detective Yant.

The day he'd come to break the news of Faith's death, he'd asked me politely if I'd spare some time at the station house; now it wasn't so much of a request as a demand.

Of course I could have refused, but I didn't. If I'd been thinking at all clearly, I would have taken Charlie's advice and retained a top-class criminal lawyer, but I didn't.

I didn't even call Nate. Very stupid. I should have seen the storm clouds gathering.

Kifley and Yant waited not too patiently in my lounge room as I checked my messages and made some essential calls that couldn't wait.

Hal and Alice were flying down that afternoon. They'd chosen a Howard Johnson motel down the road in Universal City.

They'd already left for the airport by the time I called, so I couldn't do the right thing and insist they stay with me. Maybe it was just as well – Alice's blatant antipathy would have been mind-blowing.

I then called the number on the business card Jack had given me at his house.

'Corr's Classic Cars' it read across the centre. Underneath was his home address and phone number.

I had no idea what I was going to say to Stella as I waited for her to pick up. I hoped the right words would come to me. After all, I judged I had a fair idea how she'd be feeling. We were both drifting in the same boat, sans paddles, trying to get through the day for the sake of others. In her case for her boy.

An answering service picked up my call after an interminable time.

Some sullen drawling woman with her roots somewhere in the Deep South took my message. It must have been obvious from the words that there'd been a death in the family, but it didn't soften her attitude any.

I showered and changed as quickly as possible, then the detectives and I drove in convoy to the precinct house in Santa Monica.

10.

In real life, police stations are pretty much the way they are on TV.

I was shown into an interview room. Yant directed me to sit as he hung his crumpled jacket over the back of a chair.

Kifley stood by the door.

Wahl, thank God, had decided he had better things to do. I could see him through the glass door stabbing at his Olivetti with two fingers like an idiot. The quintissential caricature of a cop. TV shows have certainly researched the Wahls of this world pretty thoroughly.

A tape was set running. Yant identified Kifley and himself, the time, the fact that I had volunteered the interview, finally noting that I had declined an offer of legal representation.

I was in that air-conditioned room for the best part of an hour.

Yant asked me questions about my personal life, and Kifley questions that impacted on my relationship with, and knowledge of, Jack Corr.

The deeper Yant delved into my financial affairs, the more it became apparent to me that had *I* been the detective, I would have been looking at myself with a decidedly jaded eye; Thursday I was on the verge of bankruptcy, four o'clock Friday I was a man of means. The fact that most married couples take out mutual insurance policies as a matter of course didn't come in to the equation. When it came right down to it, my 'windfall', as he so tactfully referred to it, amounted to a quarter of a million dollars.

He asked me if I'd sign an authorisation allowing the police department to study both my bank accounts, and the company finances in detail. I agreed at once. After all, I had nothing to hide.

Eventually it came down to the crunch question. I'd wondered for some time whether Yant would be bare-faced enough to ask it. Actually I'd banked on it.

"Can you itemize your exact movements from midday Friday till you returned home at six-forty?"

I told him as concisely as possible. I was pretty sure the kid in the Santa Fe would remember I was in there from around a quarter to three for the best part of an hour.

"You were asleep in the parking lot from approximately a quarter to four till six-thirty. Is that correct?"

I nodded.

"Could you please vocalize your response for the recording, Mr Benedict."

"That is correct," I said stonily.

"There'd be no way of corroborating that I suppose."

"Since I was by definition unconscious, I would suppose not," I replied. I'd forgotten about the bag lady.

Yant stared for a few moments up at the ceiling, then closed his eyes. His mind was an open book. It was incredible; one minute he was intimating I'd hired Jack to kill Faith, the next he was considering whether I'd pulled the trigger myself.

I spoke very slowly and deliberately. "I very much doubt I could have made it to 4th Street in time to shoot my wife."

"I'm not suggesting you did, Mr Benedict," he replied, as if shocked by the inference. "But since you raise the possibility –"

I cut him short. "I could scarcely walk when I left the diner. Ask the staff. There's no way I could have controlled an automobile."

"Possibly that's where your pal Corr enters the picture."

Kifley's remark was barely a whisper. But it was a very deliberate attempt to anger me, to throw me for a loop.

It was the most offensive remark I'd ever had directed at me in my life.

"If you are suggesting Jack Corr shot my wife with my collusion, why don't you have the balls to say so?" I asked.

Kifley said nothing. He just tried to outstare me.

He failed. Ultimately he looked away.

"There are aspects of your wife's murder that are very curious – aspects that came to light during the autopsy."

Yant reached for a manila folder and shuffled through some papers.

"The cause of your wife's death was clearly apparent. She was shot. The mechanism of death was a practically simultaneous lasceration of the heart muscle caused by a bullet to the chest, together with bleeding into the brain caused by a bullet to the right temple. The estimated time of death is as close to 4 pm as makes no difference. We know this for a number of reasons. The patrol officers were at the scene at 4.45. Lividity, the purplish discolorisation and waxiness of the skin, together with the pooling of blood, suggests she had been lying undiscovered for at least half an hour, possibly a few minutes more. Her body temperature had fallen by just under one degree. There was also evidence of green flies in the mouth, ears and nose."

Yant looked up from the autopsy sheet. He'd been reading out aloud without thinking. He clearly wished he hadn't run on. There was, after all, a human being sitting opposite him.

My thoughts were suddenly consumed by nightmare images.

Kifley cleared his throat. Yant continued.

"The medical examiner, together with the firearms examiner have concluded that your wife was shot twice with a .22 caliber Ruger Mark II automatic loaded with subsonic ammunition. Almost certainly a suppressor was fitted, muffling the detonation. The shot to the heart was at a range of less than an inch, so the clothes would have taken care of the muzzle blast. The slug causing this wound was recovered and found to be only lightly damaged – hence an accurate identification of the make of murder weapon was possible.

"The second wound – that to the right temple – was fired at skin touch range causing star-burst splitting of the skin at the temple. The gun had been pressed to the skin with direct contact. This usually causes the bullet to rattle around the brain causing maximum damage for a slug its size. Only fragments of this projectile were recovered."

Yant was about to continue when I cut in angrily. "I *need* to know this kind of detail?" I was breathing hard. "Do you have children, detective Yant? If one of them were knocked down and killed by a truck would you wish to have the visceral injuries itemised to you in graphic detail? Would you care to know the kid's guts were hanging over the fender?"

I think I made my point. Yant nodded his head by way of an apology – it was the best I was going to get.

"The reason I felt it necessary to detail the wounds was –" He broke off abruptly then fixed me with a steady look. "We are in little doubt that whoever shot and killed your wife was a professional killer. The weapon used is a preferred one. I mention in passing that it was Jack Corr's tool of choice. It's practically certain that the shot to the head was the second wound. The first shot to the heart was quite sufficient to cause death. So why the shot to the temple?"

He shrugged his shoulders, then studied me.

How was I to answer? Was I supposed to understand the vagaries of professional hit-men?

"This was no thrill-killing, Mr Benedict. I guarantee you that," he continued, searching among the papers in front of him.

"Here on the evidence sheet is a list of effects taken from your wife's body. By 'effects' I mean jewellery. I'm excluding the contents of the purse.

"You'll note there was also a pair of sunglasses. Would you mind taking a look? Then you can tell me if there's anything you know for a fact that's missing. Maybe a ring she always wore, a pendant? You know, that sort of thing."

He swivelled the sheet of paper round for me to look at it, keeping a finger on the edge so I couldn't pick it up.

I glanced down.

Diamond engagement ring. Wedding ring. Cabochon emerald ring. They were all itemized.

"Nothing's missing," I replied.

He took the evidence sheet back.

"That figures. There was no evidence of robbery. Her wallet was still in her purse, full of cash. No, this wasn't the result of some impulsive act. There were no signs of a struggle."

I could see he was leading me. Right then, I didn't know where.

"You'd imagine that if approached by a strange man or woman carrying a hand gun there'd be some indication that your wife attempted to turn away from her assailant. To shield herself. She did not. She was clearly unafraid. She either knew her assailant, or it's possible he or she announced themselves in such a way as to lead your wife to believe they meant her no harm. You see, there is absolutely no evidence of a struggle. She just went down like a sack of potatoes. I have to ask myself, why?"

"What the hell makes you think you've got the right to ask me these kinds of questions?" I shouted. "You're clearly suggesting I'm responsible. Well, I'm here to tell you I loved my wife very dearly, despite the fact she had ceased to love *me*. I could not even dream of harming her in any way, so back off right now!"

The silence in the room was only interrupted by my heavy breathing.

I noticed Wahl through the glass. He'd turned to look at me; my yelling had been audible thoughout the station house.

"I'm not pointing a finger now, nor have I done so," Yant continued in a soothing tone. "Yet I reiterate, it's clear this was the work of a professional killer. It seems clear there was premeditation. So I have to ask myself the question – who was the employer?"

I was still fighting for control. Fortunately I was winning, the last outburst had helped release a little tension.

Yant pressed on relentlessly. "You keep telling me she had no enemies; that you can't think of anyone who could possibly wish her dead. But, hey, I have to tell you, the facts speak for themselves. They scream you're plain wrong."

It was a cue for Mr Nice Guy to replace Mr Nasty. "Why don't we break for some coffee," Kifley interjected affably.

I stood. "I'm out of here."

No one else moved.

"You know something?" said Yant. "I can't believe you haven't asked me what your ex-pal Corr was doing in Santa Monica right around the time your wife was shot. Now *that's* been bugging me since we came in here. I know if I were you I'*d* be asking the question." He let the remark hang in the air, as he glanced up at Kifley. "Unless of course I *knew*. Then it wouldn't occur to me to ask."

I walked to the door. Still neither Yant nor Kifley moved.

As I turned the handle, I stopped dead. Yant was pushing my buttons, and he'd hit the spot. I had to know.

"Okay. You got me. Are you going to tell me? Do you know?"

"We don't *know*, no," he replied. "I can tell you what his wife told us, that's about all."

"What did Stella tell you?"

"He took his son over to see a young pal of his. Dropped him off on Montana and 5th around 3.30. We checked it out. Left ten minutes later."

"Sounds pretty innocent to me, detective Yant."

"Doesn't take forty minutes to get to the Cloverfield turn-off."

He raised his eyebrows at me.

11.

My brother Raymond took care of the funeral when mum died. To me, aged twelve, he was a grown up. Actually the poor bugger was just a big kid of twenty.

It turned out to be the last thing he ever did to help me. From that day on he left me to shift for myself, while he carried on 'doing things.'

I had an inkling even then that most of these 'things' were contrary to the law, but I was too busy avoiding the bureaucrats whose thinking was that an orphanage was more preferable to life with my very eccentric Aunt Eileen.

When I got back home from the precinct house the silence in the house was palpable.

All around me, life carried on as usual. The neighbours were taking the kids to the beach and walking their dogs in the park. I had to call a funeral home to 'make arrangements'. Yant had called to tell me they'd be releasing Faith's body that evening. She'd be ready for collection any time after six.

I made a call.

Apparently there are degrees of luxury involved in the process of passing over to the other side; hand-carved caskets of exotic Caribbean hardwood, silken interior finishes, gold-plated accessories.

In the subtlest of ways it was brought to my attention that a man of my position in society should be spending big. People would be watching. Look at India, the funeral director noted. Impressive stuff in that neck of the woods. No costs spared by the well-to-do. It was a yardstick of respect. I should choose the best; the man clearly equated my English accent with wealth.

I found the entire conversation disgusting. It wasn't a question of the money. It was the commercialization of death, sorrow, helplessness and despair.

Nevertheless, I settled for the five star treatment. I was thinking of Hal and Alice. They'd want the best for their girl.

The cremation was scheduled for Tuesday.

Next call was to Loman.

I didn't feel like speaking to the man one bit, but I just had this nagging feeling that it was the decent thing to do. God knows why.

He sounded pole-axed when I told him who I was. Major embarrassment. The husband calling.

He mumbled and 'er-ummed' for a bit. Didn't sound too upset about Faith's death, which made me really resentful that Faith had chosen this emotionless yuppie over me.

The tragedy was that he'd ultimately cared so little for her. The thing that clearly shocked him most was that she'd been shot in broad daylight so close to where he lived.

I picked up Hal and Alice at around midday at the airport. To my great surprise Alice flung her arms round me at the arrival gate and burst into tears.

I held her close as the sobs wracked her body, staring at Hal over her shoulder. He'd aged about thirty years.

We spent the afternoon at the house. Hal had been right. Alice wanted to be among Faith's things. It comforted her.

She retrieved Chub-Chub, the faithful old Teddy that she'd given Faith on her third birthday. He'd belonged to her once, and her mother before that. Quite the old soldier was Chub-Chub. The scrawny bear had certainly seen many a campaign: one glass eye, one button eye, left arm sewn back on more than once.

Alice sat on the end of our bed cradling the bear, rocking back and forth.

I called Stella several times during the afternoon and again left messages. I thought perhaps she and her son had gone to stay with her parents or friends.

At six that night I drove Alice and Hal to their motel. I suggested they change their minds and stay with me, but they declined. The bitter irony of Faith's death was that it had served to bring Alice and me much closer.

On my return home the message light was blinking at me.

It was Stella.

She timed her call at 7.35, thanking me for the fractured condolences I'd left on her machine.

Her voice was calm; her tone solicitous. She said she'd been told of my wife's death and couldn't find adequate words to express her sympathy.

There was a short gap of silence on the tape.

By now you will most probably have heard –, she began again, then her voice stopped abruptly.

After a second or two she continued. *I'm sure it must be the worst possible time for you, but I'd really appreciate it if you could come out and see us. I'm really confused, you know. Stupid. Do you think – ?* Again she halted, as though regretting she'd said anything.

Oh, look. Don't worry. I'll be fine. Take care. I'm so very sorry about your wife.

She rang off.

I called her back at once. The phone rang twice then was picked up. A young boy's voice. It had to be Harold.

I introduced myself and asked if I could speak to his mother.

His manner was surprisingly sophisticated for an eleven-year-old.

"Of course, you're my father's friend from England," the boy replied. "Cybernetics. That's what you do, isn't it? Multipath movies?"

I was taken aback. Erudite polite conversation was the last thing I expected from a lad his age. Everything came straight out of left field; his manner, his assurance, his knowledge of what I did for a living. Though Jack knew my field was computer games – it always had been – I couldn't remember having told him I'd branched into a new genre of interactive computer generated movies.

Maybe the kid was into my kind of stuff. If he was a keen games geek he'd probably have heard of me and my 'Five Guardian's' game somewhere on the Web. That was the most obvious answer.

But right now wasn't the time to chat about video games.

"That's right. I'm a friend of your father's," I replied. "May I speak to your mother? Is she at home?"

"*Were.* You *were*," he replied, matter-of-factly.

"Were what?" My mind was on what I was going to say to Stella.

"*Were* a friend of my father. He's dead, you know."

He suddenly had me right on the back foot. Here was an eleven-year-old talking to an adult; he'd lost a father, I'd lost my wife. They'd probably died within minutes of each other. And who was in control?

He was one cool customer.

"Yes, I know. I'm very sorry indeed." I was trying to mask my awkwardness. "Look, I'm returning your mother's call. Is she there?"

"We've both suffered a tragedy, I gather," the boy continued. It was only then it struck me how odd it was that the boy didn't have a trace of an American accent. It was BBC Queen's English. Where did he get it from? Was it pure affectation? Even Jack was typical 'likely lad' South London working class. What had Jack thought about it? Added to which was a pomposity that was the province of an Oxford don, not a school kid. Gifted programme or not, this boy took himself very seriously.

"Look, I have to speak to your mother right now. It's urgent. Do you understand?"

"Of course I understand, Mr Benedict," he replied in clipped tones. "What do you take me for. I'm not a fool. Quite the contrary, as a matter of fact." There was an edge to his voice. "I'll get my mother for you right away. I didn't realize you were in such a hurry."

"Thank you."

"We'll talk later," he added after a five second hiatus. The aggrieved tone had suddenly vanished. I could have sworn there was now the hint of a smile in the voice.

Before I had time to interpret the boy's strange attitude Stella was on the line.

"Jay. Thanks so much for calling back. Look, it's really great of you to call, but don't worry about coming over. I acted really stupidly. Just got it into my head I needed to talk to someone who was really close to Jack. I mean we have plenty of friends, but –" Her voice trailed off.

"Look, Stella. I have to get out of this house. It's suffocating me. So how about I come see you?" It was true. I could smell Faith's perfume in every room. The walls were closing in and crushing me. Maybe Stella and I could help each other.

Her voice brightened immediately. "Well... Yes then. Oh please. That'd be great."

On my way over I did my best to organize my thoughts. They were coming thick and fast from all directions. What I needed badly was a system organizer brain implant.

Was it conceivable that the unthinkable was true? That the best friend I'd ever had had been a murderer by trade? True, we hadn't seen each other in close to twelve years. Nevertheless, surely no one changed that radically? Or did they? Maybe it wasn't such a fantastic notion. Killers would hardly advertise their profession to the world at large.

I cast my mind back to the Jack I'd known in London.

Jack was at heart a kind man. Always had been. Gave up great chunks of his spare time to charities. Mostly for children. Dr Barnados. The Variety Club. He was easy-going and loved life with a vengeance. He wasn't particularly avaricious – liked nice things, expensive women and a better class of booze, but that didn't require a fortune.

Could the Bureau have got it all wrong?

The file Kifley had waved at me was certainly pretty damned thick. There must have been a hell of a lot of evidence in those pages. And Kifley seemed convinced beyond a doubt. He said it was common knowledge in the criminal underworld that Jack was a hired gun. What had he said? Jack had shot Jacob Vacek to death outside his house in the Hamptons? *We just can't prove it in a court of law. Tainted evidence.* I couldn't imagine the Bureau would choose their task force subjects with anything less than solid evidence.

And Stella? If the Bureau were right, had she known? That would make her an accessory, even if she'd played no active part in Jack's activities.

Of course it went without saying that she knew now. Kifley would have grilled her with the same sensitivity he'd shown me.

His suggestion that Jack had had a hand in Faith's death I dismissed out of hand. Even if the FBI man was correct about Jack being a professional killer, why on earth would he have done such a thing? He was my friend. He cared for me. He knew how much I loved Faith. He'd even asked me whether I wanted him to put a little pressure on Loman, and I'd rejected the idea without a second's thought.

I turned off the 101 onto Topanga Canyon Boulevard.

The countryside surrounding Old Topanga Road was quiet as an English country lane at sunset.

Because the house was set so far from its closest neighbour, all I could hear as I opened the car door was the rustle of the lemon leaves as they danced in the slight breeze.

There was no one on the porch to greet me, though it stood to reason Stella must have heard my car approach. I conjectured she may have been cooking, or in the bathroom.

As I stepped up onto the verandah I happened to glance upwards. I could see a figure standing at the gabled bedroom window looking down at me just as before, the night Jack brought me here. This time I wasn't drunk and could make out that it was a child. Not too tall.

It had to be Harold.

I waved and mouthed a greeting.

He must have seen me, yet he didn't move an inch. It was the strangest thing, he remained stock-still, staring down at me like a phantom. It was almost unnerving.

I wasn't about to hang around any further so I walked through the house towards the verandah where Jack, Stella and I had sat two days before.

She was curled up in her basket like the Doormouse in Alice in Wonderland, her hands like small paws either side of her slim face, her nose framed on either side by the primrose hair.

I stood there for quite a while debating what course of action to take.

As I turned to leave she started to whimper, as a puppy does in a dream of fear.

She woke with a start.

As she caught sight of me, she let out a stifled cry, lifting the back of one hand to her mouth. She took a deep breath and smiled embarrassedly.

"Jay! I'm so sorry. How long have you been standing there?" she said, immediately disentangling herself and stepping from the basket.

"A couple of seconds," I lied.

She offered me food, which I declined, then fixed us two very stiff vodka martinis and we returned to the verandah.

The conversation flowed like molasses as we tip-toed around each other's emotions. As usual, it was the female that eventually came to the point.

"They're saying some dreadful things about Jack."

It was time to take the bull by the horns. "Detective Yant told me."

She didn't look in the least surprised. She merely nodded, staring out into the darkness.

"Can you believe them?" she asked.

There was absolutely no point in evasion, nor pussyfooting around. It was imperative we talk this out.

"It's not the Jack I used to know. The concept is quite overwhelming. I can't come to terms with it," I replied.

It was the strangest thing, but even in the shadows I thought I saw the faintest suspicion of a smile touch her face.

"I lived with Jack for just under twelve years. I have a doctorate in psychology. I've practiced for ten years, giving sound advice to countless lost souls. Now some dumb policeman tells me I was married all these years to a cold-blooded killer. Says a lot for my judgment if he's right, doesn't it?"

What the hell could I say? The point was, much as I was fighting the reality of my thoughts, I was no longer sure the idea was so far-fetched. Could the Bureau be so far off base?

As far as Stella was concerned, she convinced me without question – if it was true about Jack, she'd never known.

We tried to talk it through for the best part of an hour. She asked a thousand questions about Jack's past; the years we'd spent in London. I pumped her for knowledge of Jack's life in the States.

Sixty minutes later we'd both exchanged a score of stories that painted Jack as the perfect husband, father, and friend. Hardly a candidate for 'Button Man of the Year'.

"Harold's my strength," she said, handing me a refill. "I know I can fall apart for a while if I want to, and he'll see me through. He's pretty incredible."

"For an eleven-year-old," I added, to make a point. It hardly seemed fair to me that she should be leaning so heavily on the shoulders of one so young.

"He loved Jack like crazy. Worshipped him."

"Dad the hero?"

She half-smiled, half-laughed. "You'd better believe it."

"I spoke to Harold briefly on the phone earlier this evening. He seems to be taking it very well."

"He's always been that way. Keeps his emotions bottled up. I wish he'd let it all out. It worries me. He's always been a bit of a loner – the product of having nothing much in common with other kids his own age. He identifies with sixteen-year-olds, but to them he's just a kid. That's the reason he's bonded so closely with Jack and me."

I had to ask, and this was as good a time as any. "Harold's never been to England, has he?"

"No." She smiled. "I know, you're going to ask me why he doesn't speak like normal American kids. That's it, isn't it?'

She hadn't taken offence. I was relieved. I nodded.

"His accent was mine till he was six, Jack's till he was nine, then he took it into his head to change it."

"Why?"

"He thinks it's cool – simple as that. When he went through his 'do everything like Dad' phase, he thought the cockney accent was *just excellent!*" She mimicked a typical young kid. "Now he wants to talk like an English gentleman."

She laughed and her face shone with beauty. "Look, I don't worry about little things like that. That's what makes him a kid and I love it. Hell, I thought it was just terrific to be a cheerleader!"

I left just before midnight. We hadn't overdone the Martinis. I think we both knew we had too much on our plates to even contemplate a hangover.

Jack's funeral was to take place Tuesday, the same day as Faith. I promised Stella I'd be there – fortunately the scheduling didn't conflict. Faith's service was at 10 am, Jack's burial at 3 pm.

It was going to be a bone-crushing day.

12.

I took Alice and Hal up Pacific Coast Highway on Sunday. It was imperative I get them out of the house; they were fast sinking into a bottomless pit of nostalgia. Somehow I had to separate Alice from Chub-Chub. I couldn't bear to see her wandering around the house, clutching the bear like a security blanket to her chest, while Hal stared vacantly at the framed photos of Faith on my desk.

For me the drive was an escape from the reality I'd have to face on Tuesday. I deliberately left my cellphone behind.

We sat in silence as we drove along the coast, the sun roasting the weekenders on the beach to our left. There wasn't a cloud in the sky nor a breath of wind. The kids were having a ball, and the air was thick with the smell of fat from the short order cafés either side of the highway.

Despite the air-conditioning, the greasy smell somehow found its way into the car.

As we passed the turn-off to Topanga, I remember wondering how Stella and Harold were coping with their personal loss.

The rest of the day was a blur of sadness and emptiness. Hal and Alice said little or nothing. Neither could face food. I craved a hit of liquor but curbed my desires.

At six I dropped them off at their motel and returned to the silence of my home.

Thankfully there were no messages. Maybe Yant actually took one day off a week to be with his wife and kids. I wondered if he had any – I don't think he'd have been a very laugh-a-minute dad.

At nine that night I took a valium and went to bed. As I drifted off to sleep, a line of Samuel Daniel's sprang to mind; *Care-charmer Sleep, son of the sable Night, Brother to Death, in silent darkness born, relieve my languish and restore the light.*

It only felt as if a couple of seconds had passed before I was clawing my way towards consciousness.

The phone was ringing.

"Mr Benedict? Is that you?"

Unbelievably, it was young Harold Corr.

I glanced at the illuminated display on the nightstand. It was 10.30 pm. I found it incredible that the boy was actually calling me at this hour.

"Is that you, Harold?" I asked drowsily.

"Yes. That's right. It's me. Harold Corr. My mother asked me to confirm you will be attending my father's funeral on Tuesday."

I felt a momentary tinge of annoyance. This call had nothing to do with his mother. I was certain of that. This was all about Harold Corr. For some reason best known to himself, the young boy was playing games. Calling people at this late hour to check on funeral arrangements was almost certainly calculated to annoy. I wasn't going to rise to it.

Yet quite possibly Stella hadn't told the boy I was coming. Maybe he was just trying to do his best. Maybe he was suffering from some kind of delayed shock.

Maybe.

"Of course I'll be there," I replied equably, giving the boy the benefit of the doubt.

"You're aware of the venue?"

"I am." Stella had told me.

"My mother will be attending the funeral of your wife at ten. Sadly, I shall not be able to accompany her. Prior commitments, you understand. Please accept my apology."

I shook my head in an attempt to clear my thoughts. What the hell was this kid talking about? *Prior commitments, you understand.* Who the hell did he think he was? If he was merely trying to get my back up, he was succeeding.

"Apologies accepted. I'll see you on Tuesday. Look after your mum."

"I've done so all my life," he replied, quick as a whip. "I shall look forward to meeting you. We have lots to discuss."

I replaced the receiver before he could continue, then took it off the hook.

13.

Monday came and went.

I called Alice at her motel in the morning. She told me Hal was in the grip of one of his migraines. She'd more or less taken over the details of the cremation. The family Baptist Minister was flying in from Tempe.

Such a dear man.

Hal and Alice felt it appropriate that he should say a few words. Did I mind? Of course not.

I spent a good hour on the phone to Nate. We discussed the details of a second mortgage on the house to raise money for the Cyberkitchen.

I'd initially thought this was a lay down misère, but apparently until probate was granted on Faith's will, there were problems in this area. Nate was going to fix them.

I though it prudent to discuss the aggressive position the SMPD had taken towards me. Nate took the matter extremely seriously. He was anxious the local media shouldn't get the smallest whiff that there was any doubt whatsoever about my innocence. A man accused, he told me, even if cleared absolutely some place down the line, is never viewed the same way.

You heard 'bout that Jay Benedict guy? Put a contract out on his wife. That's what the cops thought, anyways. Couldn't prove it most likely.

He made me promise to include him in any further discussions with Yant.

No one from the Santa Monica Police Department called that day. Small mercies.

I took Alice to dinner at the Lincoln. Hal was in a darkened bedroom back at the motel with a wet facecloth over his eyes.

We ate in silence; Alice a breath away from tears throughout. During coffee she reached out and held my hand without even looking up from the table. She'd found a courage she never knew she had, and I respected her for it.

I couldn't sleep Monday night, despite a double dose of barbiturates. I knew Tuesday would be my Armageddon.

14.

I was surprised by the numbers inside the chapel. Must have been fifty or more.

I sat on the left of Alice and Hal in the front row. I gripped her small hand and held on. Who was supporting whom?

I remember seeing Charlie, Nate, and several distant relations of Faith's I vaguely recollected meeting at our wedding but hadn't seen since.

And Stella.

She was there, sitting alone in a dark grey suit, her face ashen. Quite how she'd summoned up the strength to show up is a mystery I will take with me to the grave.

The Baptist Minister from Tempe, Lance Scone, had his say. As did I. Alice sobbed, Hal looked as though he'd retreated into a transcendental state of grace.

The coffin disappeared on invisible rollers and Faith was gone.

If anyone was expecting a wake they were disappointed.

I spoke to the Minister and a few family members who'd made the trip from Tempe. I hoped the others would understand. I knew Charlie and Nate would.

Stella had vanished by the time I looked for her.

I then drove Alice and Hal to the airport. They took Faith's ashes with them. I felt a surprisingly fierce pang of loss when the four of them boarded the plane.

Faith and Chub-Chub were going home.

For some inexplicable reason, as I funnelled onto the Golden State Freeway on my way to Jack's funeral in Chatsworth, I couldn't help thinking of young Harold Corr. The kid was plain odd. A child prodigy quite possibly, yet so unlike his devil-may-care father.

What had made him the way he was? Stella was loose and easy. Was it just a generational thing, or was he simply rebelling against the laid-back attitude of his parents?

Twenty minutes later I parked my car at the cemetery. A dark-suited usher directed me to 'the Corr burial'.

On the way over I passed Kifley and another man I hadn't met before. They were standing at the crossroads of pathways fifty feet from the mourners.

They didn't look in the least sheepish. I presumed they'd come to check out the guests. Who did they expect? Bugsy Malone?

There were approximately twenty gathered round the grave site. I stood to one side, at the edge of the semi circle.

Stella hadn't changed out of her gray suit. Harold was standing so straight he looked much older than his eleven years.

I guessed the boy stood about four feet eight. He clearly hadn't inherited Stella's genes when it came to height, but rather Jack's. He reminded me of an older John-John that day at Arlington when they buried JFK. He stood ramrod straight, schoolboy blonde hair neatly brushed and parted, hands by his side.

A minister stood across from us.

As he opened a prayer book and began to speak, I studied the gathering. I couldn't see anyone who even vaguely resembled the popular notion of a crime boss. Everyone present looked genuinely sad-faced. I doubted that a single person had turned up simply as a polite gesture of respect.

As my eyes returned to Stella, I felt the boy's eyes on me. It was as if I'd walked beneath a high voltage cable.

I won't go as far as saying I actually found it disturbing at the time, but it was that 'hairs rising on the back of your neck' feeling you get when you know you're being watched. Women get it more than men. And the funny thing was that, for some reason I couldn't explain, I couldn't bring myself to meet his gaze.

I immediately cut my glance from Stella to the minister, then down at the coffin at the graveside. I felt really dumb. An adult embarrassed by a quirky kid.

I stuck it out a good two minutes. Then I just couldn't help myself. I still felt the weight of his eyes on me.

He was the mongoose, I the rabbit.

I had to look.

Even at a distance of twelve feet, the eyes were mesmeric. Electric blue, like his mother. Acid blue perhaps, if there's such a colour. Acid came to mind because it was the only word that described the penetration of those eyes. *I am Harold Corr*, they told me emphatically. *I am someone to be reckoned with. Ignore me at your peril.*

As our eyes locked, his expression changed barely perceptibly. Could I have read the suspicion of a smile?

Abruptly he looked up at his mother and took her hand in his. As he did so, Stella's shoulders shook and she began to weep softly.

The music was really loud, unnecessarily so. Jimi Hendrix, Voodoo Chile.

Stella had begged me to come back to the house. She needed to be among friends to celebrate Jack's life, rather than dwell on his death. She wanted to talk about him; feel as though he was still there with her somewhere, still alive in her soul.

How could I refuse?

Now that I was in the house, a captive audience, Harold chose to ignore me. I knew it was deliberate because in my peripheral vision I'd noticed him occasionally searching the room to check that I hadn't left.

I was still sipping my first beer an hour later, determined never to slip back into an abyss of alcoholism, when I felt the boy's presence.

"Mr Benedict. Hello. I'm Harold Corr."

He held out a short-fingered childish hand.

"Pleased to meet you," I replied, equally formally. I can't think why.

"Thanks for coming today. I know it helped my mother. It's nice that at least one of dad's friends from the past was there. He would have liked that."

There was a beat. His eyes never left mine. Nor did he blink.

I smiled. The boy handled himself well. He'd made a nice speech, Jack would have been proud of his maturity.

"Your father was a good friend to me," I replied. "I know you'll miss him greatly, and it'll be hard. When we were in London -"

"Would you like to see my room?" he cut in. He obviously was in no mood for syrupy sympathy. He was a grown-up.

"Your room?" I asked uncertainly; he always came up with the unexpected.

"Yes, my room. You know, the Command Module. My father told you about it."

I tried to recall. I'd been so drunk when I'd last talked to Jack. But yes, I seemed to remember. But how did he know, he'd been in bed at the time?

"I thought no one was allowed access to the Module without a visa?" I joked.

"Please leave your drink down here. I don't care for alcohol in my room. It smells," he replied, without any acknowledgment of my feeble attempt at humour.

There's neat and there's anal. That's what I've always thought anyway. My mother was neither. Pots and pans were stacked higgledy-piggledy in the kitchen, clothes tossed in a heap in the bedrooms. Nothing was actually dirty; it was just ready for use. Right at your feet, so to speak.

Harold's room could easily have been designed and assembled by NASA.

There wasn't an overabundance of computer hardware. That wasn't really the point. It was the feel of the place. Stark flat white walls, floor and ceiling; three screens standing on a bleached wood trestle table – two computer monitors, one television screen. Cables bound together by tape in three bunches of seven or more, feeding from behind the table somewhere up into the guts of his processors.

What the pupose of all the color coded cables were, even I couldn't imagine. It certainly wasn't power.

"You've got a pretty elaborate system here," I said, hoping I wasn't sounding too patronizing.

"It's how you configure it that counts. But then, I don't need to tell you that, I'm sure," young Harold replied. "It wasn't dad's thing. Computers never appealed to Jack. I mean he had one; couldn't have operated his business without one, but it was never his bag."

He drew up a chair, placing it next to his at the trestle table.

"Take a seat, Jay."

I sat, mesmerized by the boy's cool manner. There wasn't any aspect of the boy that was predictable, either in his speech or actions. One moment I was 'Mr Benedict' and he was treating me with the respect a child might give an adult, the next I was the familiar 'Jay', as though there were no generation gap. One second he was referring to his father as 'dad', the next it was 'my father'. Now it was 'Jack'. Perhaps it characterized the degrees of empathy he felt at any moment towards his father.

He sat down beside me, switching on the computer.

"My father had nothing to do with your wife's murder. You know that, don't you?"

For a second or two I was quite speechless. "Of course I do, Harold," I replied at length, stunned by the remark. "Why on earth would you say that?"

"Because of what he did for a living. You might be excused for believing he had a hand in the matter. It's important you understand this is not the case."

"What he did for a living? What has dealing in cars got to do with the murder of my wife."

"Car dealing?" A slow burn spread across the young boy's pink cheeks. "My father was a mercenary, Jay. Surely you knew that."

The conversation was getting bleaker by the second. Who'd told him this? What was he coming up with next? Try as I might, I couldn't think of a word to say. I was open-mouthed with shock.

"I prefer the appellation, mercenary," he continued. "Desperado isn't bad."

He stared at me. "You look surprised. I felt sure by now the authorities would have brought all this to your attention. A man by the name of Kifley was at the funeral. He's Bureau. He came to see my father over a year ago when Harrison disappeared. He was pretty angry, I can tell you. He knew dad was responsible, just couldn't nail him. Same old story."

The child sitting beside me actually chuckled at the memory.

I stood to leave. There was no way I was about to listen to any more of this. If he was trying to shock me, he'd succeeded. The most immediate question was how the hell should I handle this? It was hardly the time to confront Stella downstairs.

The shocking irony was that what young Harold was telling me was most probably true.

Quite possibly the boy was psychologically disturbed and needed specialist help. My response demanded very careful thought. Right then I knew it was best to get out of there.

"Please don't leave yet,' Harold said, as I reached for the door handle. "You look angry. Why? I'm hardly to blame for the sins of my father, am I?"

"Of course not," I replied.

"In actual fact you have a great deal to thank me for. But more of that later."

At the time this struck me as an odd non sequitor, and I was about to take him up on it when he started tapping at the keyboard.

"Look Harold," I began, on a different tack, "What you're suggesting is nonsense. I have no idea where you're getting your wild ideas. Anyway, I have to go."

"Are you familiar with PGP, Jay?" he said, as a photograph of a semi-naked girl slowly unfolded down the screen.

"The computer program?" I asked. I still had my hand on the door handle, yet something held me inside the room.

"Yes. Pretty Good Privacy."

As all things software orientated were my field, I knew quite a good deal about PGP. It was one of the most popular examples of the new wave of information security technology. The multi nationals swore by it – industrial espionage was a very real day to day threat.

With the PGP software program on a simple floppy disc, anyone could encrypt messages and post them on the Internet.

The problem in the past had been that it was always theoretically possible to break the codes. Plus there was the added problem that third parties might intercept the key to the cypher, and be able to unscramble the encrypted message.

The joy of PGP was that the system was composed of a public key, available to all and sundry, and a private one that only the receiver was privy to. The message could be encoded with the public key, but could only be decoded by the owner of the private key.

"Jack swore by PGP," Harold continued matter-of-factly. "For a man in his business it was a godsend. Easy to use, and absolutely no record of contractual matters. Mind you, Jack's key was woefully short. I'd have used a hundred and twenty eight bit key myself. I'll have to change that soon."

I was spellbound. This boy was only eleven years old, for Christ's sake!

"Dad used a Finnish web site. Very cunning. Called Penet remailer. It's an anonymous server, provides a front for sending mail messages and posting untraceable news items. All you need are the passwords. The addressee's and your own.

"Jack's and mine is kind of interesting. 666jACK666. It's a killer system – no pun intended." He smiled. "No one knows who sends it, or who receives it. Just them and us. Don't you just love it?"

I couldn't think of a thing to say. I was stunned by the child's depth of understanding of the most complex aspects of computing technology.

He pointed to the larger of the computer monitors. "Look there. Watch the photograph."

I did so. I kind of knew what was about to happen. Jack must have installed the Stay-Go system of encryption. Stay-Go took each digit of an encoded message, encrypted with the help of PGP, and hid it inside one of the thousand pixels that made up a digital photo. The obvious advantage of the system was that no one knew you were sending an encoded message, so you never aroused suspicion.

As I watched, the photograph dissolved, revealing a fast-moving jumble of numbers that flashed across the screen at high speed. The code itself, the algorithm, had scrambled the ones and zeros that made up the digital data.

Harold snuck a conspiratorial look at me as he tapped in his private key. Almost immediately the screen revealed a single line of words.

Hello Mr Benedict. Welcome to my thoughts.

Harold swung his chair round and stared at me. His expression was now serious. The fun bit was over, it was time to get to the point.

"This is how my father did business, Mr Benedict. How he took his orders, so to speak. As soon as he read his instructions he destroyed them. It was always quite simple. A name, an address; sometimes a sense of urgency, sometimes not. You see, only a very few knew the keys, and as far as Jack was concerned it didn't much matter which one of them was sending the message. They always paid – the money was always credited. Wouldn't have been in their interests to do otherwise – Jack would have hunted them down. And the joy was that there was never a record of the details. His reply was action or lack thereof. Payment was arranged through a numbered account in the Turks and Caicos Islands."

Harold's fingers danced on the keys and the message vanished, replaced by a blinking cursor.

Much as my reason commanded me to leave, an overwhelming curiosity bade me stay. How did the kid know these details? It was beyond belief to suggest that Jack had shared this information with a young boy. So how did he know? And why was the PGP software on Harold's PC?

Come to think of it, how had he known that Jack had told me about the Command Module? Had he mentioned it to his son the following day? It was such an insignificant remark, I doubted he would have.

"Tell me one thing, Harold," I began. I had to know.

"Fire away. I have all the answers," he cut in sharply without any humour.

"How is it you know all these things? How come you have Stay-Go and PGP on your system?"

"You're thinking – did dad know I knew. Correct?"

I held his eyes for once. "That's right."

"The answer is no. I took possession of the programmes the night my father died. He had no further use for them. Besides, I was concerned the Bureau would come with a warrant to search his den."

"Then how do you profess to know of his business? You're just guessing, are you? You have a very vivid imagination, Harold, I'll grant you that."

"No, Jay. Quite wrong. No guesswork. You see, I've had my father under surveillance for over a year."

I could feel the blood pounding in my temples. This was all quite incredible.

"It happened quite by chance," he began. He was talking quickly, enjoying his explanation. "I was working on a science program at school. 'Video camera miniturization and its uses in sports.' Lenses can be very discreet nowadays, you know.

"I conjectured whether it would be possible to set cameras throughout the house without my father or mother's knowledge."

"The equipment – ?" I began.

"I stole the money and bought it all piecemeal – mail order. It was so very simple. You see, mum and dad agreed that this room, the Command Module, was my very personal territory, and they respected my space."

He pressed a few keys and a four-way split screen image of rooms in the house appeared on the television monitor to the right of the computer screens. "I set up four optical and audio surveillance probes – they were, and are, my eyes and ears in this house. They operate with miniature pin-hole lenses. You only need eight millimetre insertion holes. Cover's a ninety degree field of vision. The omni directional microphone feeds sound into a voice activated amplifier."

I watched the screen in amazement as he played with the controls. The top-left picture was of the living room.

Harold followed my gaze. His fingers played with the keyboard, and immediately that picture took over the entire screen.

Stella was sitting talking to a young attractive couple. The camera zoomed in on her face.

"Pretty neat, eh?" he said as the camera began to rove round the room. "Of course the batteries need changing every now and then. Otherwise it's completely wireless."

"Doesn't it bother you to know you're spying on your mother?"

"No. It started as fun. Then, as you can imagine, it became more serious."

I knew what he meant, but said nothing.

He switched screens to the camera in Jack's den. The room was empty.

"Dad always kept the den locked. I had to think smart to get the camera in there." He smiled, pleased with himself.

"Naturally, I soon became aware of what he was up to. Then it was only a matter of time."

His eyes twinkled with excitement. "It was like a real life drama. I knew who had been targetted, and whether dad had filled the order. Then I watched the news. You see, I knew what the future held for that particular guy. I knew." He was so excited he was practically breathless.

"Watch carefully," he continued.

I was watching extremely carefully.

The camera zoomed in with surprising speed towards the computer monitor on Jack's desk until Jack's screen became Harold's screen.

"I could see everything. His private key became mine."

He switched back to a shot of the verandah. A couple of teenagers I'd seen with their parents at the funeral were standing pressed up against each other. The boy looked around furtively then kissed the girl on the lips, at the same time placing a hand on her left breast. Harold giggled.

"Occasionally I keep copies of the tapes. But very rarely. You see, if there's any confidential information, like identities of employers – and needless to say, items such as the private key cypher – I commit it to memory. But sometimes I keep tapes just for fun. I'll give you a for instance."

He punched the play button on a VCR to the right of the keyboard. He'd clearly inserted the relevant tape well in advance.

Immediately the screen filled with a close-up of myself.

I looked drunk as all hell. My eyes were half closed and my voice was slurred and heavy. I watched myself slug down the remains of my drink then look up.

How about I pay her a visit I heard Jack say from off camera. Then the framing adjusted to include Jack. *Have a chat with her and her fancy man. What's his name?*

Loman! I heard myself shout triumphantly. A dribble of fluid was leaking from the corner of my mouth. I looked disgustingly dissolute.

Want me to have a word in his shell-like?

Harold hit the pause button and turned to me. My heart was pounding. The frozen image was nightmarish.

"And to think that less than twenty-four hours later, your wife was dead." He paused. I was still glued to the screen. "Wouldn't look too good to an investigator, now would it?"

My eyes snapped round to the boy. Investigator? What was he up to now? Was this the precursor to some veiled threat? I felt a surge of real anger. My eyes were blazing. "What the hell do you mean?"

"Take it easy, Jay. I'm just kidding around," he said. It was suddenly a kid's voice, and of course I instinctively backed off. Jesus, the boy was manipulative.

"Hey, I just thought it'd be fun to show it to you. Besides, you said no to dad, didn't you?" He smiled at me, then looked thoughtfully away as though debating the idea. "I suppose *some* would say you weren't that forceful about it, maybe. Might have changed your mind overnight, I suppose."

My anger had abated slightly, but not a lot.

So young Harold was just getting off his jollies teasing me, was he? It certainly wasn't my idea of fun. The sooner I got out of there, the better.

"Oh Jay?" he said abruptly, turning away from me. "Could you get that for me? It's my lucky coin."

I stared at him. He could change his mood like a chamelian.

"What are you talking about? Get what?"

"It must have fallen off the table. It's on the floor by your feet somewhere."

I looked down, but couldn't see a thing. "Pick it up yourself," I replied.

As Harold made the smallest move to rise from his chair, I realized I was being childish myself, so I crouched down and searched unsuccessfully between the cabinet and the trestle table for the coin.

"Look, thanks Jay. But forget it," he said after a couple of seconds. "I'll look for it later."

The incident with the coin had broken the spell. I knew it was time to get out, go home and think about my best course of action. Should I tell Stella of the conversation, or did she have enough on her plate right now?

Again I placed my hand on the door handle.

"We're not finished," I heard him say in clipped tones as I turned to leave. The timber of his voice was cold as ice. It was a command – no two ways about it.

I turned. How did this boy dare to talk to me like this?

The eyes were again those I'd witnessed at the funeral. I felt another of those hairs rising on the back of the neck sensations. But this time there was something *very* disturbing about the boy's demeanour. His expression was now full of menace.

"You owe me money, Mr Benedict."

Again anger welled up inside me. I was hard pressed to remember Harold was just a young kid. Every instinct screamed at me to clip him round the ear.

"Money? Owe you money? I don't owe you a red cent, kid." Then it occured to me that perhaps he'd meant I owed Jack money, so I added, "nor did I owe your father money."

"This has nothing to do with Jack. *You* owe *me*. Jack would have charged considerably more. My fees are much more reasonable. Got to start small and build up a business if I'm to fill Jack's shoes. If you'd only let go the handle of that door and sit down, I'll explain."

Much as I wanted to slap the boy's smug face, my better judgement prevailed. "Okay, junior. Why don't you tell me." The 'junior' bit was deliberate. I know it was a cheap shot; I couldn't help myself. I knew it'd hit the mark – Harold's expression darkened.

"Your wife was insured? It's common practice, no?"

He sounded like a lazy insurance salesman pitching to a client. But this time, I didn't let his manner get to me. I'd just made a decision. I'd hear the brat out, let him get to the point without interrupting him. So I just nodded my head.

"You told my father your wife was living with someone else and it broke you up. Right?"

Again I nodded. It must have all been on the tape. The little bastard had been listening to all the personal details.

"And the video games business was going down the tubes?"

This time he didn't wait for a response. "So, the death of your wife solved a whole heap of problems. Today you're cashed up, the business is back on track, and divorce doesn't figure. Of course it's sad that your wife had to be sacrificed, but them's the breaks, as they say in the movies. I'd say $10,000 is very reasonable. That's what you owe me."

If he'd been an adult I'd have creamed him. I'd had enough of the kid's aspersions. Now he seemed to be attempting to blackmail me.

I held up a hand, I wasn't going to listen to another word. "I didn't kill my wife."

"I know," he replied simply, without emotion. "I did."

15.

There are moments of everyone's life that with the benefit of hindsight we wish we'd handled differently. I expect Chamberlain died wishing he could go back to Munich and start again.

For me, I'd give ten years of my life to be able to rewind to the moment that little monster spoke those shattering two words – *I did.*

I was overcome with a terrible all-consuming rage. At that particular moment it made no difference that he was a young kid – Harold was merely the focal point of a terrible fury. It's actually a tribute to my basic good nature that I didn't rip the boy limb from limb that very second.

As it was, I grasped hold of his shirt lapels and lifted him clean off his stool, bringing him to my eye level.

"Look, you little brat! Don't you ever say something like that again in my hearing, or you'll be sorrier than you can ever imagine!"

I was breathing hard, the blood pounding in my veins. My shoulders were heaving with emotion as I stared at the boy. I hadn't had time to let go of my emotional feelings at Faith's death. I'd had to keep them bottled up inside me while I took care of Alice and Hal. I was a soda bottle that had been shaken for days in the hot sun. Every shred of me was bursting for release.

I held him less than an inch from my face. His face began to turn blotchy as the shirt tightened round his throat. To my surprise, the kid seemed quite unafraid.

"You hurt me, Mr Benedict, and you'll be very sorry. Repeat any part of this conversation to a living soul and you'll wish you'd never been born. I'll get you, you'd better believe it," The words were a hiss through clenched teeth. His feet dangled in space.

I don't know what went through my mind just then, I can't remember. My thoughts had no cohesion whatsoever. But a part of me knew that if I didn't let the boy go, I'd kill him right then and there. So I dropped him to the floor and closed my eyes tight shut.

Harold's voice ground on inexorably as he stood. "Is it because you *believe* me that you're angry, or because you *don't*? Because if it's the latter, you'd better think again.

"I did you a terrific favour, you know. I knew dad was thinking along the same lines. That's why he asked you if you wanted him to help you out. Remember?

"I figured later that you were in two minds. Couldn't make the cruel decision. You didn't want your wife's blood on your own sweet hands, so you needed someone else to make the move for you. Sure, you were going to miss her. Sure, you'd feel guilty.

"The more I thought about it, the more I knew I'd have to make it. You were too piss weak. I mean, she didn't love you any more. She'd dumped you, for Christ's sake. She was never going to make you happy. And there was Charlie to think of. His future. Your future. It all stacked up."

He stopped speaking for a moment.

I could hear the computer screen buzzing. My fists were balled so tight no blood was reaching my fingertips. My head felt as though it was about to explode.

Then somewhere in the deepest recesses of my brain I heard him continue.

"Are you still listening, Mr Benedict. I hope so."

I couldn't move a fibre of my body. I was reacting like a mainframe consumed by a strong virus. I was melting down.

"I knew what I had to do," he continued. "So I borrowed one of dad's Rugers. I knew where he kept them. He wouldn't notice it was gone – he wasn't on a contract, see? The rest was easy. I found Loman in the directory. Asked dad to take me over to Phil's place in Santa Monica. Phil's a good buddy.

"Then I watched Loman's place. I got lucky right away, I saw her almost immediately. Followed her from his place to the parking station. Had the gun inside my shirt. 'Course I had to be sure who she was, so I walked right up to her and asked her. She had the car door open. *What's it to you, kid,* she said. Not too friendly. So I said. *You're Faith Benedict aren't you?*

"She just stared at me, as if I was a piece of shit. So I said, *Well, I got a real big surprise for you.* Then I pushed the gun to her chest and pulled the trigger. After that I gave her Jack's signature to the head. It was simple. So simple."

Two seconds later I was pounding his body against the bedroom wall. I'd lost it completely and had no idea what was happening.

I have a vague recollection that the kid was screaming blue murder. Then I felt a crushing blow on my back and neck and I guess I passed out.

16.

The pain was back with a vengeance. It was of Olympian proportions.

As my brain booted up and consciousness returned, I thought for a moment I was surfacing after another bender. Then I realized that this time booze wasn't the culprit – I'd been slugged.

I knew I was downstairs in Jack's study, lying on a sofa. A woman I didn't know was sitting at my side watching me, holding a wet facecloth, occasionally dabbing at my temples. Her expression was something less than solicitous.

At the far end of the sofa, facing me, was a burly looking man who scowled at me with all the latent violence of a doberman on a short leash. He'd taken off his jacket, and had his hands on his hips. He was breathing hard.

Was he the tough guy who'd whacked me from behind and torn me off young Harold? It seemed logical. He was most likely out of breath because he'd carried me unconscious downstairs from Harold's bedroom.

I could just make out Stella in the shadows, sitting in an armchair to my left, her right hand cupped over her mouth. She'd been crying. Her face was set in horror.

I tried to move my head to face her. I wanted to say something; God only knew what.

Immediately, waves of nausea welled up from my stomach so precipitously I called a halt to movement of any kind, save very shallow breathing.

"Why?" I heard her say in the shadows to my left. "Why would you *do* such a thing? He's just a boy for heaven's sake."

I closed my eyes. Immediately the dabbing at my temples resumed.

"He ain't nothin' but a gutless bastard." The words came from the end of the sofa. Must have been the redneck.

I couldn't reply. Breathing was the imperative just then. Besides, I knew no one was in a mood for any justifications, despite Stella's rhetorical question. I was a monster, a gutless bastard who'd quite gratuitously ripped into a poor defenceless child.

Poor Harold. I was a hundred and seventy-five pounds, and six feet one – he was just under a hundred, and four feet eight,

The forty minutes I was lying in Jack's study were a torture of an unusual kind. They were waiting for their pound of flesh. They felt they deserved an answer – the reason why.

However, there was no way in the world I could have undergone an interrogation and lived through the pain. I knew I had to feign unconsciousness, then get the hell out of the house and make for some killer pain relief. Explanations would have to wait. Right now I was in self-preservation mode.

I must have been convincing, because one by one they left the room. Stella first. Then her burly minder. Then the dabbing halted, and I heard the shuffling of feet towards the door.

The house seemed deserted as I slunk from the study to the front door and out to the car.

Somewhere behind me I could just make out the soft melody of a Carpenters' song. Another of Stella and Jack's memories no doubt.

As I drove past the lemon trees, I tried to balance my head on my shoulders so as not to put the damaged muscles of my neck to any use. It helped a bit, but not a lot. Enough to see me home and into the medicine drawer.

Twenty minutes later I was on my back again, and dead to the world thanks to the wonderfully potent mixture of prescription Codeine Forte and Librium, washed down with Rose's lime juice. All icy cold.

My mum would have been proud of the cocktail.

17.

My brother Raymond had the worst temper. When we were kids he was forever flying off the handle and laying into me. Considering I was eight years his junior, I usually didn't do too badly for myself.

Mostly he used his fists on me, though there were occasions when he found bats or sticks handily placed.

There was one occasion when he came at me with a knife. Fortunately for me, Dick Conway our neighbour saw the glint of steel and pulled Raymond off me. I had both my hands on his knife arm and was scared to death. I don't think he meant to stab me, but he was like that; he got so angry he didn't know what he was doing. When he was angry he was like an insane man on crack.

Now me. I'm different. Maybe Raymond took both doses of violent anger when the genetic architecture of the Benedicts was being handed out. Perhaps our creator thought, *Better give young Raymond all the violent goodies, Jay can have something else. A sweet tooth? A love of animals?*

Either way, though you could never have called me placid, I'd never gone over the edge the way I did that evening with Harold.

I suppose it was time for the soda bottle to burst. Harold was unlucky enough to fiddle with the screw-top.

My rage was still very much in evidence the following day as I talked it out with Charlie at the Cyberkitchen. I had a swelling the size of a mango on the side of my neck to which Nancy had very solicitously applied a dishcloth packed with ice.

As usual Charlie was 'ol' reliable'; the person I called when I needed help.

He has an inestimable calmness. He sees the world with a dazzling objective clarity, withdrawn as he is from the real world, living in the virtual reality of his garage.

"So what are you telling me, man? That you reckon the kid actually took a gun and shot her? Come on..." he said, giving me a doubtful look.

"Of course I don't think the kid shot Faith!" I replied, trying to keep the lid on my temper. The last thing I wanted to do was to snap at Charlie. He was my one friend, I needed to feel his stability.

"Then what *are* you saying?"

"Shit, Charlie. I don't know! But how the hell would the kid know so much detail, for Christ's sake? The type of gun, the two wounds, one close to the chest, one to the head?"

"He read it in the L.A Times. Don't ask me. It must have been reported some place."

"But why would the kid want to tear me apart like that? What on earth have I ever done to him?"

"He's just a vindictive little bastard. Added to which he's obviously major smart, so why wouldn't he be major sick into the bargain? I mean, he wires the house. Cameras everywhere. Plays peekaboo with mom and dad. And if what he says is true about his pop, and the kid's been watching it all on his tapes, then he's been living in the sickest of possible dreamworlds for over a year. Isn't that about how long he's been spying on them?"

I couldn't remember exactly. "Yeah, a year; maybe more. But remember, he never *showed* me any of that stuff. Just the tape of Jack and me the night I went round there. How do I know any of that other stuff is true? Any more than I know any of Kifley's Bureau information is true?"

"Hold it, Jay. Let's get this straight. You believe Kifley, don't you?"

He had a point. Reluctantly, I did believe Kifley. It was hard not to – that file was so damned thick.

"So are you angry because you think the kid's lying, and you don't know why he's behaving like such a little shit? Or is what's driving you crazy the fact that you think somewhere in the Corr household there's a link with Faith's death, and you don't know what it is? We'd better get that straight before we go any further."

It was a good line of thinking. I had to begin to understand my anger, or at least direct it properly.

"Whatever you do, Jay, go see Yant. Whether or not you think it's all a heap of bull or not. Even if you think the kid's giving you the most evil ride of your life, you've just got to have your side on record. I mean, the cops are going to think it's major strange if you don't tell them. You never know where things like this are going to lead, do you?"

It was true. Yant had to know. Which brought up the question of Stella. What was I going to say to her? I could hardly let her hear the news of Harold's confession to me from detective Yant of the SFPD?

Yet how would she take it if I told her myself? First thing Harold would do would be to deny the conversation ever took place. So who was she going to believe?

Charlie read my mind, as ever. "You going to tell the mother?"

"That her eleven-year-old told me he'd borrowed his father's gun and murdered my wife?"

Charlie mulled this over. "Jeez, it's a hard one."

We sat in silence for a while.

"So go with the alternative, Jay. Go see Yant. Hand it all over; let him run with it, for God's sake. That's what he's there for; to investigate where the hell the little bastard was when Faith was shot, whether Jack had any guns in the house, and if the kid could have got access to them. I mean, there's a whole barrel full of forensic tests he can do on the kid's clothes for instance. Just let him get on with it."

"What really terrifies me is that everything he said was so convincing. It all made sense. The PGP programme's tailor made for someone in Jack's line of business."

"If we accept that it *was* his business," Charlie cut in.

"I think I'm beginning to," I conceded. "And the Stay-Go program? Could Harold have just invented the whole thing? See, until I see some solid evidence, I can't be sure it isn't his imagination running wild."

Possibly the worst part of the entire episode was having assaulted an eleven-year-old boy. *Whatever* the reason. The redneck was right about one thing last night. It was the action of a gutless bastard to launch into a young boy and bang him up against a wall.

Just as the ice-pack began to slide down my back, the telephone rang.

"It's detective Yant on line two, Jay," Nancy warned me. I put the call on speakerphone for Charlie's benefit.

"Detective, I was on the point of calling you." It sounded like a dumb lie, but it was of course true.

Yant replied predictably. A deliberate doubtful tone. "Is that right, Mr Benedict? Well, I'm sure glad. See, it came to my attention this morning that there was a 911 made around 6.20 yesterday evening. Domestic violence call. Outside of the city limits. Down Tapanga Canyon way."

He paused to see if I'd take the opportunity to chip in. I decided not to.

I was annoyed that Yant was playing around like this. Why didn't he just come out with it?

"When the officers arrived, they were assured everything was under control. It was all a big mistake – that's what they were told."

I could hear a huge intake of breath, then he released the air through his teeth. "Know anything about it?"

"You haven't said exactly where this occured, detective."

"I didn't? Why, it was up at Jack Corr's place. I got the message this morning from Mr Kifley. He doesn't miss much, and he's kind enough to share things with us down here.

"So I thought to myself, *hey, Jack's only just been laid in the ground a couple of hours, and the shit's hitting the fan already.*"

"I need to speak to you in person, detective."

"Well, why don't you come right on down, as they say on the TV." Yant chuckled down the line.

"Sounds like he knows more than he's saying," Charlie said as Yant rang off.

What could he know, I pondered? Someone must have made the call when they heard the screaming upstairs. Then when Stella had discovered it was me, she must have told someone to tell the patrolmen it had been a mistake. After all, it was no big deal. I was pretty damned sure I hadn't inflicted anything worse than a few bruises on the boy's back. What was Stella going to do? Have me arrested and taken downtown?

The major question was, had Stella reported the matter subsequently to the authorities? If so, what had she said? And what on earth had been Harold's version of events?

"Go see the man, Jay. Tell him everything. Just like it happened. I know you, Jay. I can just see you saying,*Hell, this is all pretty damned silly. No way was Harold Corr involved in any of this. Let's just forget it – save Stella the angst.*"

This time Charlie had got me all wrong. No way was I going to leave out one syllable. Like it or not, Yant was going to hear the lot.

18.

I'd gone to see Detective Yant of my own free will; it had been my suggestion. Yet you'd never have guessed it.

I was back in that damned suffocating interview room with the fan on the blink, the tape was running and I was being given a grilling just short of the third degree.

Worst of all, that smug pig of a detective Wahl was there in place of Kifley. The FBI agent was 'unavailable'.

Wahl lounged against the door, chewing on a toothpick.

My memory's always been one of my greatest assets. Seen me top of the class at school, and second top at University. I'd reckon my memory is pretty close to total recall over less than a week. Over that and it falls from ninety per cent to around eighty. So when I say I gave Yant an exact account of the conversation between young Harold and me, I think I did exactly that. I don't think I missed a detail; maybe how tight I grabbed him by the lapels, but not much else.

Yant just let me ramble on. To give the man his due he listened intently, occasionally cutting a glance to Wahl.

"Then I was hit from behind. I don't know who did it – doesn't really matter, there's no way I'm about to press charges. I should never have lost my temper anyway."

Yant leant across the table. "This interview is terminated at –" he checked his watch, "10.43 am."

He leant the chair on two legs, threaded his fingers together behind his head and whistled softly. "Mr Benedict. That was quite some story."

Wahl snorted briefly with laughter. Yant shot him a look of reproach.

"That was no *story*," I shot back.

"Whatever. I have to say that in all my sixteen years on the force, I've never heard the likes of it. Closest I ever got to it was a few years back in South Central. But that was a drive-by shooting. The kids were teenagers. The youngest was fourteen."

He swayed gently back and forth on the chair. Detective Wahl continued to pick his teeth.

"But this ain't South Central, Mr Benedict. And it's not Rampart. We're talking yuppie-land here. We're talking privileged kids. Kids like Harold Corr.

"Now, I'm not saying rich kids don't go apeshit and start killing people. I mean, hey, look at the Menendez brothers." He smiled, then abruptly leant forward, placing his elbows on the interview table. "But you're talking about an eleven-year-old, for God's sake. A kid who probably gets sent to bed by his mom at 9.30 pm."

I had a fair idea of his mindset, and it didn't have much room for gun-toting children.

I stood up. Better to leave before I got really angry. Not so much with Yant; I had to see it from his point of view, it was a pretty bizarre story to say the least. But the impulse to plant one in the centre of Wahl's self-satified face as he grinned at me from the door was overwhelming.

"I dunno, Bob," Wahl chipped in from the door. "They say Mose'art was composing symphonies at around the age of five." The composer came out sounding like a Jewish gallery. "That kind of puts the Corr kid in the retard category."

Yant stood and walked over to my side of the interview table. "Tell you what I'm going to do. I'll take a ride over to Calabasas today. Have a word with Mrs Corr and the boy.

"I'll get to the bottom of all this, Mr Benedict – you can count on it. I know you're as anxious as I am that we make a quick arrest and put this whole thing behind us. But right now there's not so much to go on. No witnesses, no murder weapon." He shrugged. "Fact is, the only one with a motive is yourself. Sorry to be so blunt, you know. But that's a fact."

I didn't much care for Yant's arm which he'd draped around my shoulder. It didn't feel at all friendly, but rather the precursor to handcuffs.

I couldn't make out from the detective's rheumy eyes whether or not he still had a sneaky suspicion that I'd somehow been involved in Faith's shooting. He'd surely have checked with the Santa Fe Grill by now, so he'd know that though technically possible, it would have been the equivalent of a paraplegic climbing K2 for a man as drunk as I was that night to have driven across town to Santa Monica and shot Faith in the time available to me.

"Let me ask you a question, detective Yant," I said in my most friendly tone. If he and his arm were going to 'buddy' me, why not return the serve.

"Fire ahead. Anything I can do."

"What on earth would I have to gain by coming down here and telling you all this if it weren't true? I mean, why would I do such a thing?"

Yant rubbed his chin. "My, that's a hard one," he began with a pensive expression. "I have to tell you a whole heap of people tell me strange and wonderful things 'cos they're just plain crazy. Nothin' to gain, just looney-tunes.

"In all the years I've been in the force I'd say over ninety per cent of what folks told me to my face were lies. Now I'm not saying you're a liar, Mr Benedict, but I have to consider the possibility. Right?"

"Right," I replied. I'd had enough of Yant. I pulled away from him. He was now using my shoulder as a lamp post.

"Tell me, detective," I said, addressing Yant while pointing a finger at Wahl. "What does that asshole over there do exactly? I mean apart from training as a dental hygienist."

Suddenly Wahl wasn't laughing. The fat cop made a move in my direction. Yant held up a hand.

"Mr Benedict. Let's get this straight. It's one hell of a strange story you just told me. Now I said just now I'd check it out. So let's just keep a button on our language, shall we? Wouldn't want my partner here to get cranky."

There was little doubt of the implied threat of violence.

"I'd take a search warrant with me, detective, if I were you. And while you're looking for the Ruger, don't forget to check out the computers – the kid's got one in his room. Jack's is downstairs."

"I do know what I'm doing, Mr Benedict." Yant replied stonily.

Wahl reluctantly stood to one side as I fronted him at the door. There was nothing to be gained by staying. They had my version of the conversation on tape. It was now a matter of record. They could do what they liked with it.

19.

Nathanial Berg's office is just past La Brea on Wilshire.

Nate's a lovely guy with a good nature. He's honest and altruistic – characteristics that are as prevalent in lawyers as truth is in politicians.

Once a senior associate at Levi, Butt, & Levenstein, he was eaten up and spat out by a new wave of brave young turks in the mid eighties.

So he ended up in a three room situation on the fifth floor of a charmless building downtown, mothered by the most heavenly paralegal in the whole world – a two-hundred and twenty pound Senegalise woman from Dakar who went by the name of Mama Poule.

She was fifty-two years old, eight more than Nate. She organized his work and play, and loved him with a vengeance.

He reciprocated with an equal intensity, referring to her as 'his better two-thirds'.

Her soubriquet, Poule, translated in her mother tongue to 'hen'. It was Nate's affectionate nickname because she looked after him so well.

Nate never made much money. He was too charitable. Pro bono work took up an inordinate amount of his time.

Mama Poule encouraged this side of his practice. She'd never had much material wealth back home in Senegal, and had seen too many people suffer to worry whether she and Nate drove a fancy car or ate in the most fashionable restaurants.

Yet the sad fact was that, nice as he was, the man just wasn't one of life's winners. At least as far as appearances went.

And Charlie had made a very good point; perhaps right now wasn't the very best of times to have such a man on my team. Not when it seemed more than likely I was heading inexorably towards a conflict with men the likes of Yant, Kifley and the disgusting Wahl.

Earlier, back at the Cyberkitchen, Charlie had made me promise to dump poor Nate. He'd literally shaken me by the shoulders until I'd reluctantly agreed. But as far as I was concerned, a coerced agreement was no agreement whatsoever.

As I waited the usual interminable time for the slowest elevator in the western world to grind its way down to the lobby, a very vivid image of Faith leapt into my mind. She was on tip-toe reaching up to place the white fairy on the top of the Christmas tree. She looked about sixteen and quite adorable.

My chest immediately started hammering.

The image was immediately replaced by one of Harold Corr. *I did,* he said, his eyes cutting through me.

My mouth went dry.

I eventually arrived at Nate's fifth floor offices.

Mama Poule drew me to her superbly ample bosom and I was temporarily lost to view in massive folds of flesh and calico shift.

"I so wished to be with you when they laid your sweet girl down," she wept into my ear. "You understood I couldn't, didn't you? One of us had to stay back?"

I tried to reply, but she was holding me so fast my lips were wedged in folds of warm flesh.

"I think of you all the time, Jay," she continued. "How've you been taking care of yourself? I hope you're eating right? Food's a mighty fine healer. Take me, I've never had a day's sickness in my life."

She held me at arms length then wiped her tears on her sleeve and abruptly shook with laughter as she realized what she'd said. Her ego was the size of a pea.

She showed me through into the 'inner coop', as Nate referred to his office. Nate looked up from some papers on his desk, through bifocals as thick as one of Zabar's New York shaved pastrami sandwiches. He took my right hand in both of his and clasped it firmly.

Twenty minutes later I'd unloaded every detail of Harold's extraordinary confession, together with details of both my meetings with Yant in Santa Monica.

It was hard to tell what horrified him more – Harold's claim that he'd killed Faith, or the fact I'd now been interviewed on tape twice by the SMPD, and on both occasions had waived my right to have an attorney present.

"I know I'm no Perry Mason, Jay. But even you can see that was downright foolish, eh?"

"What can I tell you, Nate? It seemed right at the time. You had to be there. Hell, the first time it was within minutes of the shock of hearing the news. I wanted to help."

"I know, Jay," he said in a soothing voice.

"Second time, I just got it in my head to go on down there and tell them what the little bastard said. Charlie kept pushing and pushing. Eventually I gave in."

"Well, it's not as if you've said anything that's incriminating. For once in my life I've a client in my office that hasn't got blood on his hands. I mean that figuratively, of course." The greater part of Nate's pro bono clients consisted of disadvantaged ethnics who'd gotten themselves in trouble, were guilty as all hell, and merely needed a little help with plea bargaining. That or some of Nate's fancy eloquence at sentencing time.

"Do you think I should call Stella? Explain?" I felt bad about her, I'd let her down.

"Can't do any harm. If it were me, I think I'd have to. I couldn't let her think I didn't care about her feelings. She had nothing to do with what happened in Harold's room. Question is, what did the boy tell her went down? You have to think about that."

I *had* thought about it. I'd thought about it a lot. The way he'd threatened me when I'd grabbed him left me in little doubt he was no shrinking violet. He didn't seem to know the meaning of fear.

Repeat any part of this conversation to a living soul and you'll wish you'd never been born. I'll get you, you'd better believe it.

So what story would he spin his mother? What reason could he possibly give for me laying in to him? It'd be interesting to learn that one.

"The police are going over to the Corr place this afternoon, soon as they get their search warrant. That's what Yant told me."

"The boy'd be damned stupid to keep any of that stuff hanging around on his hard drive," Nate reasoned softly. "I'd say he'd make copies and hide them. Same with the tapes. Shouldn't be too hard to find."

Mama Poule brought us some coffee, together with two dishes of homemade chocolate date nut cake; one of her specialities.

"Why don't you give her a call from here," Nate suggested as he spooned a wedge of the cholesterol explosion into his mouth. "I can listen in on the other line."

It seemed like a good idea.

The phone rang four times, then was picked up.

Silence.

"May I speak to Stella Corr, please," I asked.

Still no one spoke, but this time I thought I detected breathing on the line.

Finally a voice. "This is Harold Corr, speaking. Who is that, please?" It was the voice of feigned naïveté.

Who was speaking? He knew damned well who it was, I was convinced of that. He was speaking that way for the benefit of others in the room with him.

"This is Jay Benedict. Please may I speak to your mother."

The boy didn't respond. I merely heard a sound as though the receiver had been dropped, then I heard Harold cry out in alarm. "Mom! It's him! He's on the phone!"

Little bastard. He was doing a great job. Very convincing. Next thing, I could just make out a man and a woman speaking in the background. Then the receiver was picked up.

"Jay? It's Stella. It's not at all convenient your calling right now. I have the police here." She sounded rattled, but not overly antagonistic.

"Look, I'm sorry if it's a bad time. I'll let you go in a couple of minutes. Just wanted to explain about last night–"

"I can't imagine how you could possibly explain away what happened," she cut in. "Harry was terrified. I had to give him a sedative. The only reason I didn't agree to file charges was because I knew what you'd been going through."

"What did he tell you?"

"Harry? He told me everything."

"What did he tell you, Stella?" I wanted her to tell me exactly.

"Look, Jay. I don't have the time or the inclination to go into all that. I have the police turning the house upside down. I have Harry in tears in his room. And now I've got you on the phone. Not content to apologize for hitting my boy, you're asking me a whole heap of damn fool questions. Are you for a second suggesting he gave you *cause* to hit him? Go on, answer me that!" She was working herself up into a real state.

"Is he saying I just upped and hit him? Out of the blue, so to speak? Just laid into him for no reason?"

Silence.

"Come on, Stella. You must know I wouldn't do that. I know Jack would believe me."

"Just keep Jack out of it, will you!" It was a shout. She was really upset now.

"I'm sorry, Stella. Shouldn't have mentioned Jack. I'm sorry. I just can't believe your son would say I hit him for no reason."

"Of course he didn't say that! I keep telling you, he told me everything, for God's sake. He's deeply ashamed of what he did. I was really angry when he told me."

I could see Nate out of the corner of my eye frantically signalling me to keep pressing her.

"Told you what?"

"About all the cameras! Spying on us all! What else, for heaven's sake? He told me he played you the tape of you and Jack chatting the night before he died, and you just flew at him."

So that was it. Pretty clever.

"Oh Stella. What can I tell you? If that's what he said, and you believe him –"

Now she was screaming at me – out of control. There was no future in arguing with her, so I didn't interrupt. "Jay! I saw that tape! Harry showed it to me. I can understand how you'd feel, talking that way about Faith the night before she died. I'm a psychologist, for heaven's sake! But you had no right to take it out on my child. No right at all. And right now I haven't got time for you, Jay. I just want you to leave us alone. Call yourself a friend of Jack's? Jesus H Christ!"

She slammed the receiver down. Nate and I sat in silence mulling it all over.

"From what you've told me about the boy, I'd say he's going to put on quite a show for the cops, Jay," Nate said after a second or two.

I had to admit he was right. The little bugger was probably blubbing his way out of a jam as we spoke. I just hoped against hope that he'd slipped up hiding the discs and tapes. I'd have loved to see him blub his way out of that one.

"I'd say detective Yant is sitting down to the première of the 'Jack and Jay Show' right now," I said, thinking a bit of levity might lighten the solemnity that had descended on us all. "Not a pretty sight, the drunken Benedict."

Nate looked concerned. "Can you remember exactly what was said?"

"No. Not exactly. I was drunk as a lord. The part I remember most is the bit that little tyke showed me last night – when Jack offered to have a word with Loman, sort him out."

"But you demurred? There's no question of that, is there?"

"None. I told him I had enough problems without his laying into Loman for me."

Nate winced.

"Did I say something wrong?" I asked, all innocent.

"Well, I'd have preferred it if you'd demonstrated some kind of outrage at the suggestion he go round to Loman's place and sort it out. Instead, you tell him it would only add to your problems, thereby intimating it might have been a good idea had the circumstances been different."

"Oh come on, Nate. It's just a turn of phrase! Give me a break."

But Nate had a point. I could just hear the prosecuting attorney labouring this very same point in court.

"Better wait and see what the police turn up at the Corr household," Nate said. "I'll call our friend detective Yant later this afternoon. Explain I'm your lawyer. In the meantime, my advice is to give Stella and the boy a very wide berth. Let the cops do their thing."

I couldn't have thought of anything I wanted more. I needed some private time. Time to grieve. Time to regroup.

20.

Thursday came and went. So did Friday.

As I drove back to work from Nate's office that Wednesday, a doggie bag of chocolate date nut cake in the glove department, I fondly imagined I could put the memory of that terrible afternoon in Harold Corr's bedroom behind me.

I was wrong. Very wrong.

My every waking minute was consumed with the need to know what had transpired at Old Topanga Canyon Road the afternoon detective Yant had executed his search warrant. My curiosity was burning me up like a butterfly in a brush fire. I couldn't think of anything else.

I tried burying myself in my work at the Cyberkitchen until I was so fatigued I could scarcely keep my eyes open. I walked for miles at lunchtime, but nothing could erase Harold's image, it was ever ready to jump into my mind.

I called Nate Thursday lunchtime. He told me he'd left several messages for Yant, but the detective hadn't returned fire.

I called the SMPD myself at 6 pm to be told that detective Yant was unavailable. *Gone home I guess.* I was assured he'd be sure to get back to me.

He didn't. Not Thursday night. Not Friday morning. Not Friday afternoon.

6.45 pm Friday I was really busting for some news. What the hell had the police found? What had the kid told them?

I again called Nate. He told me he'd left messages all day. Yant was still unavailable. I suggested we meet for dinner.

Mama Poule chose a place on Abbott Kinney close to Charlie's place. A Creole bar with plenty of atmosphere, an eclectic mix of diners, and spicy food. Mama Poule knew what I needed; somewhere loud and busy, a place that didn't allow too much room for depressive thought.

"You're going to have to let go, Jay," Nate told me over a dish of curried goat, "It's going to drive you insane. It doesn't matter what the kid told the cops. Can't you see what he's doing to you? Don't give the little ankle-biter the satisfaction. Get on with your life. He's just a kid with one major personality problem, pretending he's a Wiseguy like his father. *He* needs help, not you."

Saturday 9 am I couldn't stand it a second longer so I drove over to Santa Monica and asked the duty sergeant at the station house if detective Yant was around.

The officer asked my name and quizzed me as to what the matter concerned. So I told him. My name appeared to ring a bell.

He picked up an internal phone and spoke in low tones with his back to me so that I couldn't overhear the conversation.

Half a minute later, detective Wahl walked through the door from the squad room. He was positively beaming with delight.

"Well, what do you know. It's Mr Benedict. In the wrong place at the wrong time." He chuckled at his own private joke.

"What do you mean, exactly?" I asked politely, containing my revulsion.

"Why, there's a team on its way over to your place right now. We called you fifteen minutes ago. 'Course you were on your way over here."

He glanced at his watch.

"Tell you what," he said lazily, thrusting his bullet head aggressively close to mine, deliberately invading my personal space, "Why don't you get your dumb ass home. Wouldn't waste too much time, computer man; the boys don't like to wait too long. They might end up taking the cutters to that fancy gate o' yours."

"You have a search warrant for my house?" I was too stunned to even think of a smartass reply.

"Sure have, computer man. Personally I can't *wait* to see what we dig up." He winked at me. "If you know what I mean."

This time I called Nate immediately. He and Mama Poule were halfway to Santa Barbara with a picnic lunch. He told me to get home pronto, make a note of everything the police did, and say nothing till he got there.

The gates were wide open when I arrived.

I drove up the driveway and stopped outside the front of my home. Three patrol cars and a white truck were parked outside the house. The front door was wide open. A patrolman was standing to one side. In the garden facing me were two men in blue overalls, LAPD printed in large letters on their backs. One had a shovel, the other a mid-sized plastic bag.

There was a call from inside the house.

"Mr Benedict! We tried calling you," Yant shouted, striding out into the sunshine, waving about a piece of official looking paper. "Detective Wahl just called to say you were on your way over. Don't worry, we didn't break a thing, these boys are damned ingenious when it comes to locks."

He handed me the paper. "By the way, you'd better take a look at this." I didn't study it too hard – I presumed it was the search warrant.

"I've been trying to reach you since Thursday morning, detective Yant. You didn't return my calls."

"Nah, I'm afraid I was up to here in it," he said gesturing to his scrawny throat. "Got a few calls from a guy called Berg. Says he's your lawyer. That right?"

"That's right."

"Well, let's hope you don't need one, Mr Benedict." The smile had all the genuine tight lipped warmth of Bozo the Clown.

"Are you going to tell me what you found, if anything, at Jack Corr's house on Wednesday?"

"Sure, I'll tell you," he replied, fixing me with a hard stare. The mask of 'Comedy' transformed to 'Tragedy' in less than a second. "We found an eleven-year-old kid who's having a nervous breakdown 'cos some asshole decided to beat the shit out of him. That's what we found." He began prodding my chest aggressively with the index finger of his right hand. "And do you know why this fuckwit decided to give the kid the once-over? Because he didn't like the movies the kid took of him. Made him look the jerk that he was. And all just a couple of hours after the poor tyke had just finished burying his dad"

I suddenly remembered my promise to Nate. *Say nothing.* But I just had to. The man was so damned arrogant. And it seemed clear that he'd made up his mind I'd invented the whole thing.

"So, no murder weapon, I take it?" I said as casually as I could. "No list of Mafia bosses?"

"Let's see what we turn up here before we make too many wisecracks, eh?" Yant snapped back.

I walked past him into the house. Two detectives and four uniformed officers were going through the place in pairs, all wearing rubber gloves. My home looked as though the windows had been left open during a windstorm.

I'd always thought TV cop shows overplayed the lack of respect police show Joe Citizen when they search for evidence.

Not so.

The kitchen was devastated. Every shelf emptied – nothing put back. The living room had been turned upside down, cushions everywhere on the floor, furniture stacked in the centre of the room well away from the walls.

In the master bedroom they'd emptied drawers of clothes onto the bed and left them there. The walk-in wardrobe was bare, all the clothes in a heap on the floor as they checked for secret compartments.

In my den, papers, files and folders had been lifted from my desk and scattered on the floor. Again furniture had been pulled away from the walls to see if they would reveal caches of goodies or concealed safes.

No one paid any attention to me, they just carried on destroying my home and my peace of mind, invading my privacy, driving me into what I was convinced was a totally justifiable rage.

As they went about their business, they helped themselves to whatever they fancied. They liked the look of it? Into the plastic bag it went. Evidence.

"What do you think you're doing with that?" I asked a heavy-gauge Latino woman, as she tossed a plastic box containing at least fifty floppies together with a dozen or so zip disks into a large plastic bag, and began writing on the evidence tag.

She looked lazily over her shoulder and studied me as though I'd just padded soft dog shit into the den with me.

"Evidence. If you've got a problem with that, see the primary. That's detective Yant. He's around here somewhere."

She continued to riffle through the filing cabinets in my office.

As I walked back to the front door, a car braked heavily on the gravel outside the front door, gouging grooves in the driveway.

It was the pig-man, detective Wahl. I distinctly saw his eyes drift towards me, but he pretended he hadn't seen me and made straight for Yant who was standing over by the pool.

I decided to join them.

"I suppose the law says it's okay to help yourself to whatever you feel like. Is that about it?"

Yant was making a note of something. He didn't even bother to acknowledge my presence. Wahl mimicked my English accent. "That's about it, Mr Benedict."

I was seriously angry by now but realized I'd have to tread carefully. "Look I know you're a bit busy destroying my home right now, but I'd really like to know what you found on Jack Corr's computer. And his son's. I don't think that's pushing the envelope too far."

Yant flipped his pad shut and stuck it in his jacket. He still wouldn't meet my eye.

"Me and agent Kifley found diddly squat. That make you happy?"

Before I could interject some stunning piece of repartee, Yant plowed on. "And let me tell you something else. If we'd found the kid with a smokin' gun, I wouldn't be about to share the fact with you." He abruptly swivelled his head to face me. "Am I being plain enough?"

"Clear as day, detective." I wasn't about to back down. We were now toe to toe, and I was getting stuck in. "Tell me one thing, though. What the hell makes you so fucking aggressive? It didn't start after the incident with the kid. For some reason you decided you didn't like me the first time you saw me. Why is that?"

He gave me the full-on slow burn. "If you're looking to aggravate me, Mr Benedict, you're doing a damn fine job."

That was it. Not a trace of logic. Not a jot of sense.

I opened my mouth to speak, about to dig a very deep hole for myself, when my train of thought was interrupted by a shout from one of the overalled policemen poking around the far side of the pool.

"Detective Yant, sir!"

I followed Yant and Wahl over.

The policeman was pointing down into the soft earth beside the pool pump.

Yant and Wahl crouched. I tried to peer over their shoulders.

Though it was by no means clear what I was looking at – the package was smudged with a good deal of dirt – I had a sinking feeling that they were looking at a gun wrapped in plastic. It was secured by black plastic tape.

Yant held out a hand, and the overalled cop handed him a plastic bag.

He took a small brush from his inside pocket and very carefully cleaned as much dirt as was possible from the package. He then began to ease it into the plastic bag. Meanwhile, Wahl took the opportunity to turn his head in my direction and wink. He'd won first prize in the lottery.

They both stood and faced me.

"Know what this is, Mr Benedict?" Yant said, holding the plastic bag up next to his face.

I screwed up my eyes and feigned really intensive scrutiny. "A weapon of some kind?" I was so angry, I was in two minds whether it was worth decking the man. It didn't look to me as though I had the least thing to lose. In their book I was both a wife-killer and a child beater. If they were going to arrest me, then they could just go ahead. What the hell else could they do to me?

"You figure it could be a weapon, eh? Well, let's see." Yant's self-control was palpable. "Detective Wahl, if you had to be more specific, what would *you* say?"

Wahl took the plastic bag with extreme care from Yant with his thumb and forefinger, and studied it closely. The gesture reminded me of the way my granny used to drink her Earl Gray at teatime.

"Ruger Mark II automatic. .22 caliber." Wahl cut a glance at me and raised his eyebrows.

"No silencer?" I managed to reply, despite my white-hot anger.

It was then, thank God, that Nate arrived. It was only then that I realised what an ass I was making of myself.

What had Nate told me? Only one thing. Watch and keep silent. Yet here I was a hair's breadth away from a fist fight with the detective charged with investigating my wife's murder.

Nate stepped from his stationwagon and strode purposefully across the lawn towards the three of us. Mama Poule followed at a pace more suited to her bulk.

"Sorry I took so long, Jay," he said, taking the warrant from me and giving it the cursory once-over.

He looked Yant in the eye. "Nathaniel Berg. I'm Mr Benedict's lawyer."

"Couldn't have shown up at a better time, Mr Berg. Looks like we found a weapon answering the description of the murder weapon exactly. A Ruger Mark II .22 caliber automatic."

"Nothing too special about a Ruger. Seen a lot of them in my time, detective," Mama Poule observed dryly.

"And you are?" Yant asked not too politely.

"Mr Berg's paralegal. I'm familiar with most handguns in common usage – have to be in our business, don't we?" She was all sweetness. "The Ruger's nothing out of the ordinary. Must be thousands of them in the county."

"Found any buried in your garden recently?" Wahl quipped.

Nobody cracked a smile.

"I was about to ask your client if he knows anything about the weapon." Yant folded his arms.

"I wouldn't imagine he does," Nate replied before I could draw breath.

"Perhaps I could hear it from the horse's mouth, Mr Berg."

"Mr Benedict has no intention of answering any further questions at this time," Nate replied, then put an arm round my shoulder, walking me away from the gathering and back towards his stationwagon.

Mama Poule stayed by the pool to observe the police.

As Nate opened the driver's door, Yant called from the poolside. "Please don't think of driving Mr Benedict out of here. Let's see how we go for an hour or so."

We sat in the car. "Don't even think of explaining. I know damn well you knew nothing of the gun. Question is, who's up to the funny business?"

"Nate, I'm afraid you're going to hate me, but I talked to those bastards before you arrived."

My long-suffering lawyer merely drew a deep breath.

"I didn't say much," I said, like a child scolded by a dark look on mother's face.

"Jay, for shit's sake why can't you keep your big yap shut? God knows I'm doing my best, but you make it so damn hard." The rebuke wasn't too harsh. It was almost sympathetic.

"Won't happen again, Nate. That's a promise."

"Not too sure if you can actually do much more damage. Even from that small exchange, it's plain as day they think you're *it*. How did you manage to get them that antagonistic in such a short time?"

"Can they really help themselves to whatever they like?" I asked.

Nate studied the warrant. "Says here they can search the house, garden and all outbuildings. Unusually broad parameters. Yant would have had to have stated what he was looking for in the affidavit, and where he thought he'd find it. The hard part would have been providing probable cause – why he thought he was going to find something buried by the pool or hidden in the house."

"What possible cause could they have?" I was genuinely puzzled.

"There's no point in second-guessing Yant's reasons right now."

I watched the police digging by the pool for a short while, trying to figure out what was happening to me. Nate re-read the search warrant.

"They went to see the boy and he spun them a sob story," I said eventually. "Naturally they didn't find anything incriminating because the little bastard must have guessed they'd be coming, and managed to hide all the software. So right now they think I'm either a cold-blooded killer, or I need immediate psychiatric help."

In the silence that followed, I watched the pantomime in the garden continue. Wherever Yant and Wahl went, so did Mama Poule – like Mary's Little Lamb. Yant would turn around every minute or so and stare at her aggressively. She'd just smile back, her hands clasped behind her back.

"You have to take this very seriously, Jay. I mean that."

"I am, Nate. You'd better believe it. I know I sound a bit flip occasionally. That's my way, I suppose. A defense mechanism. Right now, I have to admit I'm a bit scared. What do you figure their next move will be? Is it cuffs and down to the lock-up?"

Actually, I was more than a bit scared. At that precise moment I was damned scared. Everything was running out of control. The policemen in my garden had it their power to arrest me for the murder of my wife. After that it was a lottery. A good lawyer, and the guilty walked free. A bad one and the innocent eventually took the lethal injection.

"There's no way they'll charge you right now. Yant'll have to run it all past the DA first. Remember you're an educated white man living in a nice LA neighbourhood. The police wouldn't be too quick to make an arrest unless they found you standing over Faith's dead body with the gun in your hand. And then probably only if you confessed on tape."

"You fill me with confidence," I replied. For once I wasn't being flip. He did. It felt good to have an ally with vultures like Yant and Wahl flapping around me.

"The downside – and there's always a downside – is that they've probably got enough to make the DA at least sit up and think. There's motive. Faith was divorcing you and taking you to the cleaners. Instead, she ends up dead and you breeze past Go and collect a quarter of a million dollars insurance.

"Secondly, there was a window of opportunity to commit the crime – albeit on a tight schedule.

"Thirdly, the murder weapon is dug up in your garden. That's motive, means and opportunity in anyone's language."

"No one's that blinkered, for Heaven's sake. Surely they've been around long enough to smell whether or not the gun's a plant or not?"

"I asked around about detective Yant. He's not such a bad guy, would you believe. The way he's reacting to you right now, you'd think we were in Italy and you'd told him to his face that his mother was a whore. But the word is, he's basically a smart man. And smart is good news for us. I don't see them issuing a warrant on the basis of discovery of the murder weapon.

"The DA will want to make sure he's got a tight case. My guess is they'll do a complete forensic number on the Ruger. When they find the gun's clean as a whistle – and it will be, take my word for it – they'll think very seriously about the possibility that it was planted to frame you. That is, if it *is* the murder weapon. Quite possibly it's not."

Things didn't look quite as bleak as they had five minutes earlier. He was a walking valium, was Nate.

Then a very odd thought brought on by Nate's last observation struck a nerve.

"You don't think the boy found one of his father's guns and thought he'd bury it in my garden as a payback for duffing him up in his room?"

I watched Nate to gauge his reaction. Would he take the notion seriously or dismiss it out of hand.

"It's certainly a very real possibility. If that's the way it happened, there's a fair chance he got his buddy Phil Tampico to telephone in an anonymous tip from a pay phone. He couldn't have done it himself because his voice hasn't broken. If that proves to be the case, they'll have a spot of trouble explaining the phone call as sufficient probable cause if this thing ever goes any further."

"Why's that?"

"Well, you can apply for a warrant on the basis of an informant's evidence, but the judge won't grant it to you unless you can show the informant's got a good track record."

"You mean an informant who's proved accurate in the past?"

"You got it. One single anonymous tip counts for next to nothing. No track record, you see. I'll argue forcibly that the search warrant should never have been granted."

"And?"

"There's an outside chance someone will rule the evidence was tainted."

Outside chance? I didn't much care for that. Sounded to me as though Nate was clutching at straws.

"One thing's certain, no way will they arrest you. They've got nowhere near enough to convince a grand jury to indict. No judge is going to send you to trial based on their present evidence."

"It's the strangest thing, Nate, but I hadn't even considered the possibility of actually standing trial for Faith's murder. It's so shocking it takes my breath away."

"I know. And it won't happen, Jay. Believe it. You're as clean as driven snow, for heaven's sake."

"Actually, I *was* arrested in London once. A demonstration in Grosvenor Square. But apart from a few driving citations that's been it up till now."

The skin tightened barely perceptibly at Nate's temples. "Oh yeah? Well, that's nothing much, is it. That was political, no?"

"Yes," I replied.

He nodded his head. But I could see he was already thinking along other lines. "You remember you told me an old bag lady woke you in the parking lot outside the Santa Fe Grill?"

"Of course."

"I'll put someone on scaring her up. It may not give you a cast iron alibi because it might still have been feasible for you to drive over there and be back in time to pretend you were asleep. But it would sure put a mite of doubt in the minds of a jury."

Just when Nate was doing so well, making me feel so secure, he had to go and talk in terms of a judge and jury as though he fully expected me to face the music sooner or later.

The police were there for another two and a quarter hours.

Mama Poule dogged their every step in the garden, while Nate made an inventory of everything I told him was missing so he could tally it with Yant's list.

At 12.30 pm they called it a day. Nate had noted that Yant made two calls from his car. "Calling in to the ADA again, I'd imagine," he observed as Yant made the second trip at 12.20 pm. "He'd love to wrap it all up right now, and take the weekend off. Problem is, he knows the gun on its own's just not enough."

Yant was the last to leave. He handed me the inventory of the items they'd seized.

"You'd better advise your client to stick around for a while. We'll be in touch shortly," he said, avoiding any eye-contact with me.

For once I was in control and said nothing to antagonize him.

"What was your probable cause, detective?"

"That's police business. You'll know soon enough."

"Informant?" Nate ventured, but Yant was already walking towards his car.

"He'll get the Ruger down to forensics right away. For all I know it may very well be the murder weapon, but if he's pinning his hopes on the hundred to one shot that they'll come up with your prints he's going to be major disappointed, isn't he. And that should be end of story as far as you're concerned."

I remember at the time feeling relieved. After all, it made sense. First of all, I was innocent of any wrong doing, and secondly, the gun had to have been planted – that must have been clear to anyone. I'd hardly wipe the gun free of prints then bury the damn thing in my garden!

So I felt a good deal more relaxed as I waved Nate and Mama Poule goodbye.

That was another big mistake. I should have been watching my back.

Things can only get better?

The storm clouds were gathering. Today had been a shower, the twister was snaking down the road.

21.

When Faith packed a small bag and walked out the door, I was angry. Yet at the same time I felt a surge of panic. Was this actually happening? Was she going to another man's bed? It was completely unbearable. So I drank to forget. Not too original. It certainly didn't show too much of the right stuff. I let myself down badly.

Now I knew life had gone one step further. Faith was dead. There was no longer the fond hope she'd come home to me.

When I was about the same age as Harold, I'd fallen in puppy love for the first time. Her name was Ina.

I was staying with a school friend at Wraysbury on Thames. She was a Swedish girl on holiday in the house next door. The three of us would fish for gudgeon with plastic rods.

After five days I plucked up the courage to hold her hand. She didn't mind too much. To us it was the real thing, very grown up.

The day before the holiday ended I kissed her on corner of the mouth. It was a pretty major move. Quite courageous.

I watched her leave the following morning, and I knew I'd never see her again. I also knew I'd never love again. A kid of nine knows these things.

That was then. I was ten. Now I was forty-two, and I knew I'd never love again. I'd be a kid till I died. But it didn't stop the hurt. Without Faith I was in a row boat without oars. And the worst thing was I didn't care.

The weekend passed slowly. Mama Poule had asked me to join them on Saturday for the picnic, but I needed some time out. I felt as though I'd been trudging across soft sand; I was emotionally and physically exhausted.

I checked on Hal and Alice. He sounded like a zombie, but she seemed to be coming to terms with a life without Faith. The strength of the relationship was, as usual, with the woman.

Alice kept talking about the casket. She couldn't decide which of around twenty ash-scattering destinations Faith would have preferred.

I've never been strong on ash dispersal. It's a romanitc load of guff as far as I'm concerned, and has little to do with the sentiments of the departed. But if it gave Alice a grip on sanity, what harm was there in it?

Funnily enough I didn't give Yant a second's thought. Nate had given me a feeling of impregnability.

Monday melded into Tuesday, which led inexorably to Wednesday.

Before I knew where I was it was Thursday. I'd worked four sixteen hour days single-mindedly at the Cyberkitchen. Otherwise life ground on. I was in the eye of the hurricane, lulled into a false sense of security by the lack of bad news.

Mama Poule called Thursday evening. She'd hired a PI with the ominously portentous name of Stir, to execute an extensive door to door with a perimeter of three blocks around my home. Unfortunately no one had seen a young boy acting in a suspicious manner. I'd rather doubted anyone would, it wasn't the sort of of neighbourhood where little old ladies spied on the world from behind lace curtains.

She told me that Nate had tried, unsuccessfully, to reach anyone associated with the investigation. They'd clearly decided to clam up, and weren't about to share anything with us.

Friday afternoon around five I stopped by the Galleria in Sherman Oaks on the corner of Sepulveda. I needed a few general things for the home. Faith had always looked after the running of the house; now I found I was running out of basic items such as lightbulbs, toilet paper, soap – the usual. In my ignorance, I thought I could buy them at the Mall.

As I often do, I forgot entirely where I'd parked the car, so I was mighty relieved when I caught sight of it after a mere thirty minutes search on three levels.

I had the key in the lock when I heard someone call my name behind me. I looked round but didn't see a familiar face, so I pulled open the door of the car and climbed in.

As I did so a bright red Mustang cruised up and stopped, blocking my exit. I could vaguely make out the shape of a male driver in my rear view mirror. He was wearing dark glasses and had his hand draped out the window, beckoning me.

"Mr Benedict? Is that you?" he called.

I opened my door and stepped out, annoyed that the driver hadn't had the courtesy to do so himself. After all, it wasn't *me* that was calling *his* name.

If I'd been a cop I'd have checked his ID for sure – if he was sixteen he was a very late developer.

Either way, he had five years or so on each of the four other kids who were crammed into the Mustang.

The girl in the passenger seat reminded me of Jodie Foster in 'Taxi Driver' – a child dressed as an adult.

In the rear seat was another elfin girl with more paint on her face than Marlene Dietrich. She was wedged between two acned boys.

Everyone was well-dressed in the predictable GAP type clothes. They clearly had one thing in common – designer parents.

"Yes, I'm Mr Benedict. Do I know you?" I said, eyeballing the driver.

The kid had a self-important smirk on his face. Not a good look on someone young enough to deliver the Sunday papers. "Harold wants to speak to you," he said, lazily unwrapping a stick of gum , then flicking it into his mouth. It struck me at the time as the sort of thing the kid practiced in front of a mirror at night.

Then I felt all the eyes in the car on me.

"Harold *Corr*?" I asked. Not that I knew any other Harolds.

"He's over in Toy Universe. Down Ventura. He's waiting. It's important. He says you won't want to miss out."

"Miss out on what?"

"Why not find out, man."

More giggling.

I could feel my temper flaring yet again. I'd really have to put a lid on it soon, no two ways about it.

"What's all this about? Is this some kind of a kid's game?" I was angry. It must have shown in my tone of voice.

"Hey, don't get uptight with me, man," the kid replied easily, chewing his gum. "Don't shoot the messenger, eh?"

'Jodie' in the front seat snickered, elaborately crossing and re-crossing her legs for my benefit. I wept for her parents.

The kids in the back seat laughed out loud at 'Jodie's' sideshow.

"Well, right now I'm busy," I said. "So tell your good buddy I'll take a rain check. Okay?"

The kid driver shrugged. "That's your call."

He then took off his sun glasses and winked at me. Again his acolytes roared their approval. What a funny guy was their hero.

"If I were you, I'd take these kids back home right now – it's well past their bedtime. And while you're about it, why don't you take daddy back his wheels before he gets real mad."

I didn't wait for a reaction. I turned back to my car and heard the Mustang scream off, burning a lot of rubber. Maybe I'd been that assinine when I'd been a kid. The more I thought about it, the more I doubted it.

There was no way I was about to meet with Harold Corr. It was out of the question for many reasons.

Firstly, it wouldn't have been fair on Nate. I'd ignored his advice in the past, and had stepped right in it as a consequence. He'd specifically warned me to give the kid a wide berth. I was duty bound to heed his advice.

Secondly, it wasn't fair to Stella. I knew her opinion of me wasn't up to much, and there wasn't a lot I could do to correct this impression. But my heart went out to her. To have suffered the way she had over the past week, the last thing she needed was more problems with her disfunctional son.

But as I nosed out of the parking structure into Ventura curiosity was gaining ground.

What was young Harold up to now? He wanted to talk to me? What about? Surely we'd done our talking the night of Jack's funeral. What more was there to say?

Was he about to apologize? It didn't seem likely, the kid had an overweening ego.

If the attitude of his buddies was anything to go by, this looked like being more of a childish prank.

I pulled in to the curb and left the engine running. It was getting worse; I was being devoured by curiosity now. It was a virus. Why would he have sent his friends to find me? And how did they find me? It couldn't possibly have been coincidence that they'd come upon me in all those floors of car spaces.

They must have been following me. Probably from the Cyberkitchen to the Galleria.

If that was the case, the whole thing had been carefully planned. And the fact that I'd lost myself in the parking structure meant that Harold Corr would have already been waiting at least three quarters of an hour in Toy Universe.

I tapped my fingers on the wheel. I was an alcoholic with a full bottle of Bourbon opened up and waiting for me on the bar. I hated myself for it, and I knew Nate'd have my guts for it, but I had to know. Was the baby-faced driver I'd just encountered the buddy Jack had taken his son to see; the friend who lived on Montana and 5th?

And the jackpot question? What did Harold have in mind for me this time?

Toy Universe was as busy as ever. On this particular day it was packed with adults rather than children.

I made one whistle-stop tour of the entire ground floor, cutting my eyes quickly from left to right for signs of Harold.

By the time I'd returned to the entrance, I figured I must have missed him. All told, bearing in mind the half hour I'd wasted looking for my car, he'd probably waited the best part of an hour. The boy must have reckoned I wasn't coming.

I felt deflated, like a kid on Christmas morning who gets all the wrong presents. The adrenalin was really pumping. Now I'd have to go home and let the contagion of curiosity eat away at me there.

A woman turned her head and gave me a disapproving look as I swore out loud without thinking.

It was only as I pushed the door open with my right hand to leave that I saw him reflected in the glass behind me.

If it hadn't been for those demon eyes, I wouldn't have recognized him. He'd clearly dressed carefully for the appointment. Goody two-shoes was window shopping for toys.

He was wearing a pair of olive shorts, a white short-sleeved open-knecked shirt, long socks pulled up neatly to just under his knees, and leather school shoes. He looked even younger than his eleven years, if that were possible.

His blonde hair was, as usual, sensibly and neatly brushed, a razor sharp parting on the left hand side. His feet were together and his hands were behind his back.

He was standing by a spectacular Leggo display that stood eight feet high. The giant plastic Swiss Mountain had most probably obscured him as I'd initially tried to find him.

He was neither smiling nor scowling. It was a kind of nothing expression, as though he were in a trance.

As I walked over to him, the blue lasers tilted up and fixed me with a powerful gaze.

"I knew you'd come. You're predictable, Mr Benedict, and that's a fact."

"Curiosity," I replied calmly.

He couldn't resist the smallest semblance of a smile. "Curiosity. Yes. Kitty-kitty." He snickered. "That's exactly what I meant. I knew you'd have to know."

"Know what?"

His eyes left mine and drifted round the store as he tilted his head from side to side. "Oh, you know, whether or not I was putting you on about your wife. Whether I was serious about the money. That kind of thing."

"Is this the best you can do for an apology?"

"Quite an exhibit," he said airily, as though I hadn't spoken, studying the Leggo mountain.

As usual, the little brat was beginning to get to me, despite my best efforts. He knew exactly which buttons to press, and when to press them. But then, kids always do. Same as animals.

"The Ruger in my garden. That was you?"

He picked a piece of Leggo from the display and studied it. "No. That was Phil. I couldn't make it. It would have been a bit obvious if *I'd* been seen digging up the rose beds, wouldn't it?"

Steady, Jay. Steady.

Thoughts buzzed through my head. He's trying it on again. Don't fall for it. You smack the little bastard while he's looking the innocent moppet, and in a toyshop to boot, and you're in the worst conceivable trouble. Keep him talking. He'll make a mistake, and talk his way into a corner. He won't be able to help himself. Trap him, for God's sake. Don't let him get the upper hand!

"Who's Phil?" I asked.

"You met him just now. He's a good friend of mine. Helps me out when he can. We make quite a team, Phil and I. You see, I can't drive, so he's real useful there."

"*Really* useful," I corrected. "If you want to act like Little Lord Fauntleroy, you'll have to learn to speak properly, kid."

He flicked the Leggo piece away and stared at me with venom.

"Keep the gun as a souvenir, Jay. It's the one I used to kill your wife," he hissed. The pupils of his eyes were as wide as egg cups. "Plenty where that one came from."

Just to confuse the little monster I smiled at him. It was an unbelievable achievement, I can tell you. Every instinct told me to tear him limb from limb.

Our eyes locked for perhaps twenty seconds. The blood was boiling through my arteries.

"Why did you ask me here, Harold? What's with you?"

"Oh, I didn't tell you the good news." The excitement of a new thought was evident.

I waited for him to tell me. I knew he would.

"We're in business at last," he continued. "I've gone into partnership with Phil.

"As I said, he's useful – he can drive. Got to have wheels in our line of work."

"What line of work would that be, Harold?"

"Oh, come on, Jay. You know. I don't need to spell it out do I?"

"Maybe you do," I replied. I was milking him, but then he must have known that.

"Be sure to catch the six o'clock news tomorrow." He winked as he said it. It chilled me to the bone.

"You still haven't told me why you asked me here, Harold? Was it just to show off? To act grown-up? More games of let's pretend?"

His eyes narrowed. "I called you here, Jay, to give you one last chance to pay me the money you owe me. Remember? I did you a favour, and you owe me. 'Cept the price has gone up. Because of what you did in my room you owe me an extra five thousand."

I was speechless with fury.

His eyes locked onto mine. "You lay a finger on me again and I promise you, I'll see you go down."

I stood rock still, fists clenched at my sides. Let the little bastard talk, my mind screamed!

"Go down?"

"For the murder of 'pretty girl' Faith, Jay. Clear enough?"

Against all the odds I managed not to strike the child. I was chafing at the bit, the muscles in my jaw rock hard.

"Now I've got a surprise for *you*, Harold," I said, my voice trembling with the effort to remain still. "I've been wearing a wire. What do you think of that?"

To my surprise and anguish, the young boy just laughed out loud.

"You *wish* you had, don't you! You wish! But you're just not that smart are you, asshole? And now it's too late." He laughed again, his fat cheeks pink balloons of happiness.

Nah, nah, ne nah, nah, his eyes screamed at me. It tore me to shreds inside.

"So. You going to pay me, asshole?" he said coldly after a moment's silence.

"In your dreams, sonny," I replied slowly and evenly, enunciating each syllable very carefully. "But I tell you what I *am* going to do. I'll see you in juvenile hall, and that's a promise."

"Oh yeah? Well, you're a dead man, Mr Benedict."

Then he pulled a move that shook me rigid.

His left hand moved so quickly it was a blur.

In a microsecond I felt a stab of pressure on my breastbone. Instantly I looked down. The black muzzle of a gun was pressed to my chest.

"Bang, bang, you're dead!" Harold cried suddenly, his eyes dancing with excitement.

Without thinking I swept the barrel aside with a sharp blow of my hand; just as you'd flick a tarantula off your skin.

Harold cried out in pain as he fell heavily backwards against the Leggo mountain.

There was a loud explosion of plastic pieces as the entire exhibit disinegrated.

Suddenly everyone in the immediate vicinity had stopped still and was staring at us, open-mouthed.

I swore inwardly as I met the accusing looks of the parents around me. Small children clung to moms and pops for security.

He'd done me again. This time the little shit had me on toast. It looked to everyone as though I'd slapped him to the ground.

As I swung round in an attempt to vocalise some kind of justification to the adults around me, I heard a high-pitched unbroken voice at my back. For some weird reason I thought it was someone other than Harold – the voice was pure La La land American. "Sorry, dad! I'm okay! My fault. I slipped. Have I broken any of the Leggo?"

I turned.

To my immense surprise, Harold was standing at my side, brushing himself down, a broad grin on his face. He was massaging his left hand where I'd connected with it. It clearly hurt, yet he didn't want his audience to know.

"You dropped your water pistol, kid," an elderly man said, handing Harold back his black plastic automatic. 'Gramps' couldn't help shooting me a reproving glance; it was obvious he thought the boy was covering for my bad temper.

"Thanks, mister," Harold replied with a sugary smile. Werther's candy wouldn't have melted in his mouth.

A few moments later, the rubber-neckers dispersed and Harold and I were left alone again. He slowly raised the pistol, as though to taunt me, and squirted a jet of water onto my shirtfront.

"Just a toy, Jay. No need to get all excited," he said smoothly. Little Lord Fauntleroy was back, the English accent crisp as a spring lettuce.

He dropped the water pistol at my feet and brushed past me. A couple of seconds later he'd mingled with the crowd.

22.

It was as unbearable as the worst pain I'd ever suffered. It was unadulterated torture.

Imagine how you'd feel; constantly flicked in the face with a wet towel by an eleven-year-old, in the full knowledge that there's no question of revenge because you're an adult and he's just a kid. And we're talking about a kid who's telling you he murdered the person that meant more to you than anything in the world.

However, Harold Corr was the exception. He wasn't just a kid. A murderer with the mind of an eighteen year old, in the body of a child a little over half that age. That was young Harold.

As far as I could judge, there was not a hint of insanity or even psychological imbalance in him. I know the liberal do-gooders would have said there was, but I knew better. He just had a hundred times the normal adolescent allotment of the cruelty of youth.

The airconditioning was on full fan, yet I was burning up.

I looked at the digital read-out on the dash as I drove down Ventura. It told me the unit was straining to lower the temperature to sixty-five degrees. I wasn't at all sure it was succeeding. Maybe it had nothing to do with the heat in the streets – maybe my blood was just boiling with frustration.

So what to do now? Same old question. Each time I crossed paths with Harold Corr, he painted me into a corner. He was a devious little devil, that was for sure.

If I were to inform the police, what could I possibly tell them? I knew damn well Yant would think I was raving. I'd been summoned by an eleven-year-old to a meeting in Toy Universe to discuss payment for the contract killing of my wife? He'd have me in cuffs and down to the psych ward within minutes. He hadn't believed me before, why should he now? I mean, who had the better reason to be in a toy store. A young kid or a grown man?

And if he cared to check with the store, what would he find? That I'd been shouting at the boy, and had then knocked the little shaver clear off his feet backwards into a display of Leggo! Another cue for the cuffs. I didn't think Yant had much time for child abusers.

Naturally, Phil and the other kids would deny ever having set eyes on me. They didn't know me did they? Jay who?

And how was it possible for them to have chanced upon me in a parking structure the size of the Galleria? It was just too improbable.

No, my best course of action was to pretend the meeting had never taken place. Say nothing, that was it. I'd tell Nate for sure, but certainly never breathe a word to Yant. As far as the police were concerned, I never saw the boy.

As I shot past Carney's hot dog stand, a little voice in my head warned me I was driving too fast. It came seconds too late. I heard the siren behind me and saw the flash of headlights in my rear view mirror. I'd reacted just a mite too slowly to save myself.

Five minutes and an expensive citation later, I was turning into Sunshine. I was no longer mentally screaming. I'd been forced to act calm and cool. The presence of the patrolman had helped to keep the lid on my temper.

But as I approached my home, the demons were back gnawing at me. What had Harold said about tomorrow?

We're in business. Be sure to catch the six o'clock news.

I stood on the brakes as the terrible realization hit me with the force of a cruise missile.

Jesus H Christ! I'd missed the point entirely. What he'd been telling me was that he'd scored his first contract. He and Phil were going to kill someone within the next twenty-four hours.

We're in business. The killing business. Like father, like son. He'd accepted his first contract. Someone had visited his web site with a name.

Tomorrow someone was going to die.

I wasn't going to let him kill again. No way.

PART TWO

23.

The gun felt cool and delicious. Harold loved the feel of it. One day he'd be able to handle it with one hand the way they did in the movies. That would be really something. Cool as ice. Held sideways at forty-five degrees. Man that'd be a real buzz!

"Slow down, asshole. You nuts or something?" he snapped from the rear seat of the Camaro.

They'd picked up the car on Palisades Beach.

When it came to locks, security systems and hot-wiring, Phil was the main man. He could be inside with the engine running from a standing start in under a minute.

"We get pulled over, end of story, numbnuts!"

Phil didn't reply. He merely eased off the gas. He knew who called the shots. It didn't matter that Harold was five years his junior. The kid was a genius. There was this *thing* about him. Always had been, ever since he'd first met him. He was plain scary. It was in the eyes. One day the boss kid would let *him* do someone. That'd be real neat.

Harold slipped off the rear seat of the black Camaro. He hunkered down on the floor behind Phil and held his breath for over a minute, watching the street signs flash by at the intersections.

Veteran, Kelton, Midvale, Westwood.

Not far now.

It was an adrenalin buzz of the purest kind. One he'd experienced only the one time – the day he'd put two bullets in the Benedict woman.

What's it to you, kid? she'd said.

Stupid bitch. Not too smart a move was it, as things panned out? But, hey! That look of surprise in her eyes, shit that was something else!

Co-ol!

Harold carefully wiped his chubby hands on the sides of his Super Mario Brothers T-shirt. His hands were sticky from doughnuts.

He pulled out the Ruger's magazine and examined it, then snapped it back in place, humming Voodoo Chile softly to himself as he pulled the suppressor from the pocket of his shorts and screwed it in place. He then held the gun at arms length, taking up the first pressure on the trigger, and aiming it up at the rear window.

Only the top joints of his forefingers closed round the trigger. They overlapped by just a quarter of an inch.

He grinned.

Bang-bang, you're dead!

"Avenue of the Stars, man," Phil called out from the front.

Half a mile to Wilshire.

Harold checked his watch. Right on schedule. Four minutes should do it. Two to get there, one to park, one to get to the rear of the building.

He placed the gun on the floor next to him and relaxed the muscles of his fingers.

It was really wild, no? The guy was walking around his apartment right now, happy as a clam. A few minutes from now he'd be dead. Weird.

He'd received the mail Thursday. The usual encryption.

The boss man had used Stay-Go. Same as before.

Of course the major problem now that dad was dead, was collection. Harold was the only one who knew of the numbered accounts in the Turks and Caicos, and no banker was about to hand out that kind of money to a kid.

He brushed the thought from his mind. He'd worry about all that later. Money was so easily moved electronically. Besides, he didn't give a short shit about the cash. It was the buzz that drove him.

He ran his hand over the cold metal of the Ruger. First things first. He had to show he could do the job. That he was reliable. The second anyone knew his identity, all bets would be off. There was no question about that. Who the hell would hire a kid to do a man's work? The boss man was testing the waters. Had someone taken over Jack Corr's business?

"Turning into Wilshire, man," Phil called from in front.

Thirty seconds later the car swung into Comstock. Harold watched the apartments scud by.

They'd scouted the block earlier that day and made their choices; where to park, where best to gain entry. Slowest time of day, eight-thirty Saturday morning.

Phil turned down a side street and pulled over. He stepped out and fed the metre. A glance up and down the street, then he whistled to Harold.

They walked in through the service entrance.

Harold opened the swing door an inch and peered through the crack into the main foyer.

The elderly uniformed commissionaire he'd seen earlier from the car was standing by his desk as usual, reading a newspaper.

"Let's do it," Harold whispered.

Phil pushed open the door and walked across the marble floor towards the old man. He held Harold's hand – like he was with his kid brother.

The commissionaire looked up from the sports page.

"What can I do for you boys?"

"We're meeting mom upstairs. She's with Mr Gardenas. That's up on the seventh, right?"

The commissionaire checked the duty book in front of him for a second, puzzled, then looked the kids up and down. The taller of them reminded him of his nephew, Jake. Good kid, Jake. Training to be a paramedic. He'd go far, he felt sure. Took a pride in his appearance. Like these two kids did. Pity there weren't more kids like this around. America'd be a better place. A safer place.

"You sure your mom's up there?"

Harold glanced at the apartment list on the wall behind him. 701: Hasker. 702: Balcombe. 703: Gardenas. He cut a quick look sideways through the wide plate glass entrance doors. A good twenty feet down the canopied walkway, the sidewalk was deserted.

Now was as good a time as any. Time was everything.

He pulled down the zip on his Mets jacket and reached inside.

"She said to meet us here, sir," Phil said. "She stayed the night. Maybe we're too early. Is Mr Gardenas in right now?"

"Far as I know. Hasn't stepped out since I came on duty. If he was in last night, he's still upstairs."

Phil smiled as he ran a hand through his perfectly groomed hair. "Think you could call up Mr Gardenas for us. Tell him we're here?"

"Sure can, son," the old man replied at once, reaching for the phone. Why the hell weren't there more like this boy? he thought. Good manners were sadly a thing of the past. *Sir*. Who'd called him *sir* in the last ten years? No one, that's who. Los Angeles had gone to the dogs and no mistake.

As the commissionaire brought the receiver to his ear, Harold pressed the barrel of the suppressor up against the spot where the old man's spine met his cranium, and pulled the trigger.

The Ruger spasmed lightly in his hands.

A thrill ran through Harold's body. This was the best of all possible feelings. He'd told Phil all about it after his first kill and his buddy had told him it was most probably like sex. Like when you came. But who needed girls when you could get a kick like this?

The old man jack-knifed forward on to his desk.

"Move!" Harold hissed, then padded softly across the marble to the elevators.

As the doors closed, he could see Phil pushing the commissionaire's body into the open frame of the desk.

Apartment 703. Forty-five seconds since entry and counting.

Harold rang the bell and stood back from the door so that Gardenas could see him clearly through the spy hole. The Ruger was back in the waistband of his shorts, under his Mets jacket.

This was the best moment. The very best, except the actual pulling of the trigger. The adrenalin was charging through his bloodstream like white water in the Rockies. His hands were wet, his mouth was dry, his breathing short.

He was Doctor Death.

He was God.

The seconds ticked by.

Shit! He'd counted ten. No fucking answer. Where was he? He couldn't wait here in the corridor much longer.

Anyone sees us, we're out of there.

Abruptly the silence in the empty corridor was broken. "What do you want, kid." The voice from behind the heavy door was sharp and unfriendly.

Harold stepped forward, pressing his lips to the crack of the door. He had to keep noise to a minimum. "Sorry to bother you, Mr Gardenas, but I'm locked out. Mr Hasker gave me the wrong key. Can I use your bathroom please? It's kind of pretty urgent, sir."

Harold heard a muffled expletive. His heart was beating faster than a diesel locomotive.

He heard the locks being freed, and the tingling feeling he'd experienced in the 4th street parking structure swept through him again.

Rush, rush, rush.

The final bolt was pulled down and the door opened. Michael Gardenas stood there, wearing a burgundy silk dressing gown, a grim look of annoyance on his wrinkled face as he waved the boy forward into the apartment.

"Come on then, kid. Snap it up, will you. Haven't got all day. Take your leak and get outta here."

Harold stepped forward, his right hand already reaching inside his jacket for the butt of the gun.

Almost instantaneously the gun was out, clutched in both hands and pushed up and into the killing zone. Harold had heard it described on one of those hospital dramas on TV – *in the fourth intercostal space, ten centimeters from the mid line of the sternum.* He'd practised on Phil with his index finger till he could feel the spot with his eyes shut.

"What the fuck –?" Gardenas groaned as the bullet tore through the soft tissue of his chest and smacked against a rib. He was staring open-mouthed at the gun, with a mixed expression of bemusement and horror. "Jesus H Christ, boy, you fuckin' shot me."

Harold's eyes were glued to Gardenas'. He knew he'd fucked up immediately. He'd fired too low. Missed the heart entirely.

He pushed the gun up higher and fired again; twice, in quick succession but the suppressor snagged in the folds of the dressing gown. Suddenly the big man's hands were round his thoat, choking him.

Harold's eyes began to bulge, he couldn't breath.

Shit, shit, shit. I'm going to die!

Then Phil was bursting through the doorway, clubbing Gardenas on the back of the head with the fists of both hands. Crunching blow followed crunching blow.

After several seconds the big man's legs gave way and he began to fall like a giant Sequoia, loosing his grip on Harold.

"We gotta get outta here, man! We've been too long!" Phil was straddling Gardenas' back, breathing heavily from the exertion, pulling the dying man's arms up behind his back.

"Shut the fuck up!" Harold snapped back, pushing Gardenas' head down to the floor with his brown newbuck Boks.

Blood was pooling on the pale carpet round Gardenas' chest. Harold had the Ruger clasped in both hands as he danced round Gardenas and Phil, jockeying for a good angle, but the man's head kept twitching – he couldn't get a good shot!

It was the best fun nevertheless. Quite amazing. Three shots point blank to the chest and the man was still thrashing. Next time he'd use hollow point shells.

Gardenas was groaning, his body twitching and jerking as he struggled against Phil's hold on him.

Phil looked down at him, mesmerised. "Shit, what's happening, man. He's still alive!"

"Shut the fuck up, Phil! I haven't finished, have I? Hold him *still*, for Christ's sake!" Harold replied sharply as he crouched down beside Gardenas, pushing the suppressor against the big man's temple, forcing his face into the carpet.

At last, the *coup de grace*.

Phil watched Harold's fingers begin to squeeze the trigger. "Oh shit, man. Let me do it! Can I off him? *Please*, man. You gotta give me a turn sometime!" Phil was really pumped.

Harold ignored him. He pulled the trigger and Gardenas body instantly quit jerking around. The old man's mouth began to froth pink purple. Then there was a rush of air and liquid through his nose and mouth onto the carpet.

"We're out of here," Harold said checking his watch as he thrust the gun back in his waistband. Two minutes ten and counting. Far too long.

"Give me the strap man! I want to whack him too!"

Harold suddenly angled the gun across at Phil, taking up first pressure. His eyes were ablaze. "It's a *gun*, Phil!" he snapped. "You're not a freaking homeboy, for Christ's sake!" Harold despised street jargon. "Shut the door, we're out of here," he snapped, as he reached down and picked the shell casings from the floor next to Gardenas' body.

It was then he saw the spots of blood on his jacket where Gardenas had held him, and he swore silently. It was one of his favorites.

Less than thirty seconds later they were back in the Camaro, heading home. Two minutes forty all up.

Though Phil was pumped to flashpoint, he drove at a steady forty-five.

Harold was again hunkered down on the floor behind him, disassembling the Ruger.

They dumped the Camaro within fifty feet of where they'd taken it fifty-two minutes earlier. Then they split up, approaching the fire stairs of Phil's apartment block on Montana independently.

Harold had reversed his Mets jacket; the bloodspots were now to the inside. The component parts of the Ruger had been equally distributed between them in the car, the butt pushed down into Phil's undershorts, the barrel and magazine into Harold's jockey's.

Phil was first through his bedroom window.

The Hip Hop music was still playing loudly.

As Harold followed through the window, Phil opened the bedroom door and called down the corridor. Mrs Tampico, Phil's mother, was cooking her famous red sauce. Tonight was pasta night.

"Mom! Can I have the car later?"

"Sure, honey," Mrs Tampico replied. She glanced at her watch. "I'll need it midday till around five. When do you want it?"

"Five's fine, Mom," Phil replied.

It was 9.10 am. Betty Tampico never knew they'd been gone.

24.

My grandmother's life was such an obstacle course of hardship and grief, but she always knew who her true friends were. She told me proudly once that she could number them on the fingers of one hand. To her, having so few friends was an achievement.

Personally, I've always maintained that it's only when friendships are tested that their true mettle becomes apparent.

Nate Berg's friendship was one I valued. He was a true eccentric, and we shared the same taste in booze, food and ethics. We differed in our tastes for women – that was all.

Charlie judged him a loser simply because he didn't make a heap of money, nor drive a fancy car. Not that these things were important to Charlie; he merely viewed them as a sine qua non of successful LA attorneys.

I knew Nate's meagre income was the product of his refusal to play the corporate legal game. A principled attorney in Los Angeles was always bound to end up in the poor house.

I reached Nate's law offices roughly forty minutes after I'd been stopped for speeding. I was totally focussed. Harold Corr had murdered Faith in cold blood. Just for kicks; of that I was now totally convinced. I'd make it my life's business to see the boy brought to book. I remember thinking right then that it was not retribution, but justice I was after.

And it was no longer simply to do with Faith. If there was the slightest chance that Harold planned to carry out another killing, he'd have to be stopped. That meant I'd have to make sure I was believed; that my story was credible.

I didn't give a damn what anyone thought of me, provided some action was taken before it was too late – before another innocent died. If that meant breaking down the District Attorney's office door, so be it.

I'd read recently in the International Herald Tribune that an eight-year-old boy in Winnepeg had shot his babysitter to death with a sawn-off shotgun just because the child was angry. In view of such incidents – bizarre though they might be - it was kind of odd that Yant refused to countenance the notion that Harold Corr could conceivably have pulled the trigger. Maybe in all the sixteen years he kept telling me about, walking the semi-privileged streets of Santa Monica, he'd been somehow sheltered from gang violence, living in the eye of a hurricane of violence that was consuming Los Angeles.

But he must have been living in a dream world if he thought kids in the '90's didn't know one end of a zip gun from the other. If he thought that street gangs recognized some kind of imaginary perimeter fence at Pico he'd have to be mad.

There was a handwritten notice taped to the elevator in Nate's building. *Oldest and most loyal. Will not be sadly missed. Expired 13th August 1997. RIP.*

I took the fire stairs and sweated my way up to Nate's office.

Nate was in a closed doors meeting with a Peurto Rican juvenile and his mother.

Mama Poule brought me a cup of tea to calm me down while I waited. I must have come across a bit crazy.

Ten minutes later I was in the 'inner coop'.

Nate put an arm round my shoulder. He told me to relax and recount every word, every action. I was not to miss the smallest detail.

He then set a tape running, sat back and began sipping a herbal tea.

I was thirty seconds into unloading my version of events when he held up a hand, called in Mama Poule, and asked me to start again at the beginnning – for her benefit. He was shocked, and that was saying something – he'd seen a good deal of the seamier side of life in LA.

An hour later I watched Nate get to work. I'd never seen him so angry.

"It's a bad time to get anyone to move their asses," he said in between calls. "No one wants to know anything this late on a Friday evening. They want to hold fire till the next shift kicks in, then turn it over to them. Besides, I've spoken to Gail Goodrich at the DA's office, and she wants to talk it through with the SMPD before she agrees to meet."

"They wouldn't take the risk of doing nothing, would they? That'd be political suicide. They've got to do something just to cover their asses, eh?"

"Oh sure. I guarantee Goodrich will call me back before half six."

Gail Goodrich was an Assistant District Attorney. Nate had a lot of time for her. She worked hard, didn't have a rascist bone in her body, and was usually approachable in emergencies. Their paths had crossed quite a lot during the past two years, mainly because of the amount of pro bono work Nate had put in. He regarded her as a friend, and thought the feeling was reciprocated.

She'd listened to Nate's initial pitch, and suggested a meeting first thing in her office the following morning.

She didn't give any indication as to whether or not she considered my 'story' broke the barriers of credibility. I presumed it didn't, since she'd hardly have wasted her time, or that of her colleagues, on the ravings of an insane man. It had to be treated in the same way as a terrorist threat – checked out, just in case. As soon as Nate had called her officially, it was her ass on the line. She was going to play it by the book. She'd have to confirm the meeting. She'd call back.

"Maybe they'll say the kid read all about Faith's murder in the newspapers," I said. "But tell me this, how the hell did he know the police had found the Ruger in my garden if he didn't put it there."

"Hold on a second," Nate said as he re-wound the tape.

We listened to my version of the conversation.

"See, it was *you* who brought up the subject of the Ruger. *The Ruger in my garden? That was you?* That's what you told me you said, or something very similar. Yant'll merely say he's a bright kid, he put two and two together, guessed the cops had found a gun in your garden and was just running with the ball."

I swore. It was true. That's exactly what Yant would say.

At 6.28 pm Goodrich called back. The meeting was on. 8.30 am. Her office. Present would be Senior Detective Bob Yant, Detective Stacy Wahl, Joyce Bufor of the California Youth Authority, Goodrich, Nate, and myself.

I couldn't believe Goodrich thought a breakfast meeting was a sufficiently urgent response. Neither could Nate, though it didn't show in his voice on the phone. I could sense he was mad as a cut snake. What if Corr and his pals planned a breakfast killing? There wasn't much point in sitting round a table with coffee and doughnuts then, was there?

25.

I'm no stranger to the waiting game. I learned how to cope at an early age.

When I was nine, a couple of years younger than Harold, I was picked up one day at school by my granny. Though she initially pretended everything was hunky-dory, I knew something was very wrong when we took the Hammersmith turn-off. It was only then she told me that mum had been taken ill, and that we were going to visit her in the West London Hospital.

Mum was lying unconscious in a big ward. She was in a bed next to the door.

Someone at school whose grandfather had died during the holidays had once told me that beds close to the door were always kept free for people the doctors thought mightn't make it through the night. That way they didn't have to truck the dead bodies past all the patients and scare them to death.

If you ever find yourself in a general hospital, dumped in a bed by the door, watch out.

Granny and I sat by mum's bedside for about ten minutes. I held her limp hand while granny talked quietly into her ear. Then a doctor came in and screens were trolleyed round the bed. We were then asked to wait in the hall.

Though nothing was said, I knew Mum had taken more of the red and white pills.

I waited in the corridor with granny for four hours. She looked very stoic.

Though I didn't know it at the time, the doctors had told her they didn't think mum would make it; her heart was so weak. I was being kept on hand in the corridor just in case she came round in time to say goodbye.

They were the worst four hours of my life until the news of Faith's murder was broken to me thirty three years later.

Now I was in another corridor, waiting to be called in to witness the main event. It was just after nine o'clock in the morning, and I was on the third floor of the building that was home to Assistant District Attorney, Gail Goodrich.

Nate and I had met outside at 8.15 am. Goodrich was already in her office. We were the first to arrive.

She reminded me of Shirley Temple.

It wasn't just the curly hair and freckles; she had the most ingenuous smile. It was quite captivating. Nate had said she looked young for her twenty-six years, but this was ridiculous. Maybe this was my year to be surprised by youth. Maybe I was just getting old.

Just before 8.30 a.m. Joyce Bufor arrived. By contrast to 'Sweetness and Light' Goodrich, Bufor was 'Cruella de Ville'. Her face was out of Madame Tussauds Chamber of Horrors. Her demeanour left no room for a smile. It screamed, *life's a hard business, let's get through it as quickly and painlessly as possible.*

I shook Bufor's hand, then waited for the blood to return from my shoulder to the fingers.

On the dot of 8.30 a.m., there was a rap at the door and detectives Yant and Wahl strode in.

Yant avoided my glance till he'd exchanged pleasantries with Goodrich, whom he knew; and Bufor, whom he didn't.

He threw me a cursory glance and nodded.

Wahl didn't bother to even acknowledge my presence.

It was at this point that I was asked to leave the room and wait in the corridor.

The request took me quite by surprise. I'd fully expected everyone to sit around while I recounted my version of the events of the previous afternoon. Instead, they asked me to wait outside.

Twenty minutes later Goodrich opened the door, and politely asked me inside.

It was then she explained that Nate had played them the tape he'd recorded in his office.

No one spoke for several seconds. They all expected Goodrich to start us off. Instead she riffled through some papers on her desk.

In the silent hiatus I looked at the faces that surrounded me. Bufor studied me with all the suspicion a young gazelle might have had of a lion near a waterhole. The distrust was manifest.

Wahl looked bored and churlish; Yant as though he'd just love a five minute knucklefest with me in a dark alley. He was clearly seriously pissed to have been summoned by Goodrich.

Nate had a forced cheery look on his face, attempting to imbue me with confidence.

Goodrich looked like Dorothy in the Land of Oz.

The ADA then proceeded to make a very diplomatic speech. It was obviously for my benefit.

While the others twiddled their thumbs, she told me that she and detective Yant had discussed the ongoing investigation of 'the Benedict slaying' the previous evening.

She explained that although she wasn't disposed to indicate any details of the progress of the investigation, she was able to tell me that Harold Corr was not, and had never been, considered a suspect. Though she wouldn't at this time go into the reasons for this decision, there were many.

Nate pressed her hard to explain hers and Yant's rationale, and she reluctantly did so.

The Santa Monica Police Department, she said, were of the opinion that a boy as small as Harold Corr would have had great difficulty even holding a weapon as heavy as the Ruger Mark II, let alone carry it round town and shoot it as accurately as the autopsy had demonstrated.

Secondly, upon receiving my statement concerning the boys alleged confession, the SMPD had made extensive enquiries. Harold Corr had spent the afternoon with a friend named Phil Tampico in Santa Monica. Tampico's mother had supported both boys' contention that they were at home all afternoon. Other young persons were present that afternoon at the Tampico's apartment. They had also been interviewed, all corroborating the boys version of events.

Thirdly, there was absolutely no motive.

I could see that Nate was set to interrupt when Goodrich passed the baton to the Wicked Witch of the West.

She proceeded to inform us that she'd tracked down and spoken to the principal of Harold Corr's school – the William C Buckman Academy – the previous evening. Not an easy task in the middle of the school holidays, she informed us with a self-congratulatory air.

Not only was Corr a gifted boy to say the very least, years ahead of his age group, he was also a model pupil. There wasn't the smallest blemish on his record. He didn't fight with other boys, nor answer back to the teachers. One couldn't ask for more.

She then fixed me with a confrontational stare. "Yet here is Mr Benedict, maintaining this self-same child is some kind of cold blooded killer."

She closed her mouth, reminding me of how French farmer's closed stable doors for the night; there was a sense of finality about it.

Goodrich gestured to Nate.

"Could Detective Yant tell us whether a statement has been released to the press concerning the automatic pistol found buried in Mr Benedict's garden?" Nate asked Yant.

"No such statement has been released," Yant replied. "But let me make your client's day, Mr Berg. The weapon found *was* the murder weapon – there's no doubt about that. Ballistics have matched the slug taken from the muscle tissue surrounding the decedant's heart."

"Were any prints found on the weapon that might link my client to the firearm?" Nate shot back.

"Look, Berg," Yant spat back rather rudely, "I don't know why you bother to waste all of our time here asking a damn fool question like that. We're all professionals here, barring your client. You're not talking to the press now, so come on. When did you last hear of anyone lifting a set of prints from a murder weapon?"

Nate remained silent. Prints lifted from recently fired guns was the stuff of movies.

Yant snorted, then continued. "Given a choice between a kid who's only just reached double figures and a grown man well on the way to fifty as murder suspects, I have to say I'd always lean towards the big guy. Call me quirky if you like. Guess I'm just made that way."

"Ms Goodrich," Nate cut in, angry; he didn't appreciate Yant's patronising attitude. "I'm sure we're all here for the best possible motives. Detective Yant's attitude is no help to anyone."

Yant looked expectantly at the ADA. Who's side was she on anyway?

"Let's try to keep humour to a minimum, detective. What do you say?" she ventured diplomatically.

"That's just fine with me, Ms Goodrich. Fact is, I don't find any of this the least bit funny," Yant replied. "Point is, the last time Mr Benedict came out with a similar dumb story, I went visiting. I spoke to the kid's mother, and talked one on one with the boy. Took a real close look at his things. All I came away with was the feeling that I should be so lucky as to have a son the likes of Harold Corr.

"Now your client's back with more of the same. First time he tells us the kid admitted to murdering his wife. Now he's telling us that the kid told him in a toy store that he's going to whack someone sometime today. Mr Benedict doesn't know who, doesn't know when, 'cos the kid didn't tell him. And what's the kid going to use? He ain't got the gun no more, 'cos Mr Benedict over there says the kid buried it in his garden. So what's he going to use? His bare little hands?"

"His father's weapons, for God's sake! You tell me it's a matter of record that Jack Corr was a contract killer – why is it so fantastic to believe he had more than one gun, for Christ's sake?"

"Please allow detective Yant to finish, Mr Benedict," Goodrich cut in.

"He threw me a question surely I'm entitled to respond?" I replied.

"It was purely rhetorical, Mr Benedict. Please control yourself."

"Thank you, Ms Goodrich," Yant continued, as I bit my tongue and buttoned my lip obligingly. "Okay, Jack Corr had a stash of weapons. You know this for a fact, Mr Benedict? If so, tell us right here and now where we can pick 'em up, and I'll be on my way."

I was busting up inside with fury, but what could I say? I had no idea where they were hidden. Why was I so sure Harold had access to other weapons? Because Harold had told me.

"I guess you don't know the answer to that one, eh?" The words were a sneer. "Now, I've thought long and hard about this, and a couple of things don't sit right. Firstly, Mr Benedict keeps asking us why he should be telling us these fanciful stories if they weren't the truth. And here he has a point. Why should he?

"Of course the flip side of that coin is this. Why the hell should a highly intelligent kid with a bright future, suddenly decide to take a gun and kill a perfect stranger? More interestingly, why kill the wife of one of his dad's oldest and closest friends?"

"For the kicks! Who knows? Maybe for the money!" I exploded.

"Mr Benedict, if you interrupt again I'm going to have to ask you to leave this room, and we'll continue the meeting in the presence of your attorney." Dorothy looked stern.

Yant thanked Goodrich, then continued. "Well, that's mighty interesting, Mr Benedict. For the money, eh? You see, you're trying to tell us that young Harold Corr has decided to keep the business in the family. He wants to become the youngest torpedo in the history of modern crime? Well, tell me this one. Who the hell would pay an eleven-year-old kid to kill anyone? It's the dumbest idea I ever heard. Secondly, how the hell's the kid going to collect? And even if he did, what's he going to do with the money? Spend it on candy?"

He stared at me, willing me to speak and thereby be banished from the room. Wahl's eyes were twinkling with anticipation.

I kept my trap shut. Nate looked relieved.

"The only reason my client is here today is an altruistic one. He is fearful that the child will make good the threats he made yesterday in the toy store."

I winced. The mere mention of the words *toy store* colored everything Nate was saying. It all sounded quite ridiculous.

"Whether or not the boy is prepared or able to carry out his threat is debatable," Nate continued. "Either way, Mr Benedict has absolutely nothing to gain by wasting anyone's time with fabrications. If you could give us some kind of assurance that a close watch will be kept on the boy during the next few weeks, that is all we seek at present. Naturally, we're of the opinion that, as investigations progress into the death of Faith Benedict, the involvement of Harold Corr will become evident, and charges will be laid against him. In the meantime, we beg you to keep a close eye on the youth. My client believes that this very day he plans to use one of his father's guns to kill someone – guns we presume his father kept hidden somewhere other than in his home. If Mr Benedict could be more specific, he would. Obviously."

"Hey, you just tell me something. Why the bejesus would a happy kid want to do a thing like that? Come on Berg, let's get real for Christ's sake." It was the first time Wahl had parted his thick lips.

"Because he's obviously a deeply disturbed boy," I shot back. "My God, he came home one day, switched on his closed circuit TV and discovered his dad had been a murderer all his life! And as for the ridiculous contention that the poor little fellow couldn't possibly clasp a handgun as heavy as a Ruger in his fat little fingers, I'd like to point out that the greater percentage of all West Central African rebel army recruits are children. Hell, the average age of a Hutu or Tutsi terrorist in Rwanda is under twelve, and he's carrying an AK-47 for Christ's sake!"

Goodrich' rebuke was swift and sharp. "This is a discussion, Mr Benedict. This is absolutely a last warning. Keep your voice down or leave the room."

I apologized at once.

Nate jumped in quickly. "Could the youth be persuaded to undergo a psychological profile, Ms Goodrich? We know absolutely nothing first hand about him. All we have is the hearsay opinions of his school principal."

This remark didn't please Cruella much. She wasn't used to having her opinions questioned. She glared at Nate.

"I have absolutely no cause to order such a step," Goodrich replied. "The child's mother would have every reason to object. Any normal mother would inquire why such a request had been made in the first place. To reply that we were treating her son as a possible murder suspect, solely on the hearsay evidence of the same man who assaulted the child a week or so previously, would make a laughing stock of this office. She'd have attorneys on our backs in a matter of hours. And with good reason. So, no, I will not ask a judge to order such a psychiatric profile. Nor will I ask Mrs Corr to provide one voluntarily. I never make requests I know will be refused. Mrs Corr would be justifiably outraged."

Yant spoke deliberately and his tone was hard. "There's one thing I'd like to add before I get back to the remaining twelve hours of my eighteen hour shift. Two matters, come to think of it. First off, I want it on the record I take great exception to the presence of Mr Benedict at this meeting. He has not been cleared of involvement in the Benedict slaying either by the District Attorney's Office, or the SMPD. He has absolutely no business here today. Nevertheless, I'm obliged to him for coming forward with his 'information'." His expression screamed otherwise. "However, I'm unwilling to discuss the smallest detail of our investigation in his earshot.

"And now for the other matter. And this is for the benefit of my good colleagues; Ms Goodrich here, and Ms Bufor."

Quite why Goodrich allowed him to continue in such a insulting tone was a mystery to me. But she did.

"I've been a cop for sixteen years, and a detective for twelve of 'em. During that time, many many people have confessed to my face to terrible crimes. And a whole heap of those misguided people were never guilty of a damned thing. It just entered their heads at the time to say they'd done something real bad. Some craved a little attention. Some wanted to be famous. Some wanted to take the blame for someone they loved. Some wanted to shock the shit out of me. Some were just plain crazy. Doesn't really matter what the reasons were. Bottom line was, they plain didn't do nothing."

"Cut to the chase please, detective," Goodrich cut in as she glanced at her watch. She'd had enough of being talked down to.

"My point is this. You can either believe Mr Benedict's story – that the kid confessed to him that he killed Mrs Benedict. Or you can disbelieve it. Hell, let's just for the sake of argument say the kid *did* confess. Okay? Well, the next logical question must be, was he telling the truth? And who the hell knows that? Sure as hell, Mr Benedict doesn't, 'cos he ain't got a single shred of evidence to support his argument." He held up his arms in a gesture of supplication. All eyes turned to me. "Or have you?"

It was true. I didn't. I remained silent.

"Right! So I humbly suggest Mr Benedict goes home and lets the police department get on with its job."

"Will the child be kept under surveillance?" Nate asked as the air cooled. "Because if by any chance Mr Benedict's concerns bear fruit today, and the Corr boy is ultimately held responsible for a homicide in this city, a lot of people are quite justifiably going to ask why such steps were not taken."

It was a very thinly veiled threat indeed, yet I could see that unless Nate had made it, Yant had no intention of doing anything of the kind.

"Thank you Mr Berg and Mr Benedict for coming in today." Goodrich's voice was soothing. "If you'd like to leave us now I'd be obliged, we need to continue our meeting in private."

Nate walked me to my car. He assured me I'd done my best. I could do no more. It was up to Goodrich now. He was sure she'd bring appropriate pressure to bear on Yant to keep an eye on the kid for a while. If the boy had any ideas about making good his promises, he'd feel a hand on his collar. The SMPD weren't stupid, they'd do as they were told by the DA's office.

I checked the time as I turned on the ignition. It was 9.10 a.m.

26.

I put it down to delayed shock. I thought I'd been coping so well. After all, I'd staggered through both funerals, taken care of Hal and Alice, and re-financed the business. So why in God's name was I so completely lost and confused now, two weeks down the line? Why was it only now that I felt I was falling apart?

I sat in Faith's and my TV chair that Saturday morning surfing the local television stations for news reports. I was in a complete daze, desperately attempting to reconsider Harold's position both objectively and rationally.

I did. I'll never forget those words, nor the way he spoke them.

That day in his bedroom when he'd claimed it was he who'd shot Faith, my instinctive reaction was one of incredulity that a boy as young as Harold would have taken it into his head to say such a cruel thing to the bereaved. It never entered my head that what he was telling me might be the truth. I'd dismissed the thought out of hand. As would any normal person.

So why was I so certain that the child had pulled the trigger? Was it solely because he'd *said* so once too often? Because he'd been so damned convincing about going into his father's business? Or was it because I was losing the balance of my mind, destroyed by the vicious games of a cruel child?

I'd been so absolutely certain of his guilt as I'd driven home from the toy store down Ventura. I'd known Harold Corr was Faith's killer with the same degree of certainty as the Pope knew the Virgin Mary was the Mother of God. But what made me so sure?

I knew somehow I'd have to clear my present prejudices and think things through clearly. Yant, all his antagonism and aggression aside, had given me cause to re-examine my present convictions.

The geography of the crime scene, the wounds, the position of the body – all these the boy could have learned from the newspapers.

What's it to you, kid? That's what he claimed Faith had said just before he shot her. This was different. To me this *was* evidence. I could almost hear Faith speaking when he told me.

To most people it was a pretty run of the mill phrase. To Faith and me it was different. *What's it to you, kid?* It had always been a catchphrase. So, a coincidence? It was a long shot.

Keep the gun as a souvenir. Surely anyone on God's earth who could come up with a remark like that needed urgent psychiatric help.

But logically Harold's boast of having been responsible for planting the Ruger in my garden wasn't proof of anything. As Nate pointed out, it had been I, not the kid, that had raised the subject of a gun being found on my property; Harold's lawyers would maintain he'd merely run with the ball to bate me.

The heart of the matter was this. Either Harold Corr was bent on torturing me with the lie that he'd shot and killed Faith, or he had actually done so. If the former were the case, he was doing a brilliant job – he deserved an Oscar.

But if he was just playing a terrible game, it begged the question *why me*?

The alternative was that it was all true. He'd decided to kill someone for kicks, thought killing Faith was doing me a favour, and that I'd be grateful she was out of the way. Because of my ingratitude he'd decided to drive me insane.

No matter which way you cut it, in my book Harold Corr was guilty as all hell. He'd shown me the PGP and Stay-go programs on his computer, he knew his father had been a professional killer and was proud of it. He idolized his father, and was determined to follow in his footsteps. He knew where Jack kept his weapons, and so burying the murder weapon in my garden in order to frame me had been a breeze – there were plenty of others to choose from. He probably thought killing people was cool.

My heart bled for Stella. As if it wasn't terrible enough to come to terms with the reality that her husband had been a contract killer, it was only a matter of time before her son broke her heart for a second time.

I was about to make myself coffee, when the quiz show I was watching was abruptly interrupted by a fast-breaking news story. My entire body tensed for a couple of seconds, then relaxed equally as quickly as the story unfolded with a video close-up of bodies lying on a sidewalk.

Two teenagers, believed to be gang members, had been shot dead by police officers following an attempted car-jacking in Marina Del Rey. Another teenager was in a critical condition.

The victim of the car-jacking had been discovered with his throat cut in the trunk of the Infiniti. The camera panned to include the car. We were mercifully spared a look inside.

It was only as I waited for the coffee machine to function that it struck me how inured I'd become to such everyday violence. I'd been waiting for a very specific item of news. Who really cared any more about three or four dead in Marina Del Rey? It happened every day, didn't it?

I remember when I was a kid, growing up in the late fifties in South London, a murder was really big news. Front page stuff. Happened maybe once a month. If that. Now, it was part of the shabby fabric of life.

We'd all got so used to seeing graphic film footage of dead bodies, first in Vietnam in the sixties, and thereafter on the poorer streets of major cities, that Joe Citizen now passed the dead by with just the barest moment of detached discomforted curiosity.

This realisation shocked me so much that I switched off the percolator and returned to the living room. I could neither eat nor drink with such thoughts racing through my mind.

The quiz show was back on the tube as I sat, yet my thoughts returned to Harold Corr's words in the toy store. *Be sure to catch the six o'clock news tomorrow.*

Whatever he planned to do, he clearly thought I'd recognise his handiwork. The only reason I'd been watching the television so early was just in case a story broke prematurely. Besides, what was I going to do till six? Go watch a movie?

At eleven I started to pace the room like a caged animal. Each second was lasting minutes. I found myself counting them, willing the time to pass.

At 11.20 am I swallowed a barbiturate, but my heart kept pounding. The pill hadn't broken the skin of the custard.

At 11.55 am I was in the car on my way to Calabasas. I had to know if the police were watching Harold. Because if they weren't, sure as hell *I* was going to. To hell with Judge Earnshaw! Possibly I was already too late, due to my piss-weak indecision.

It was only as I pulled over to the side of the road a mile or so from the lemon-lined driveway to Jack's place that I realized I had no idea what I was going to do or say when I got there. Was I going to stake the place out? If so, I'd better make sure the kid was at home before I spent the rest of the afternoon sitting in my car watching the house from a respectable distance.

I decided on a drive past. At least that would give me some idea of what was going on there; plain clothes police presence, whether or not Stella's car was in the driveway – that kind of thing.

Even at thirty miles an hour I clearly saw a green Honda in the drive as I passed. I seemed to remember stumbling past it as I fled Jack's wake.

It was most probably Stella's. But as I drew up further down Old Topanga Canyon Road, prior to making a U-turn half a mile on, I realised I hadn't passed another car of any description.

So much for police surveillance.

Without mentally debating the issue, I pulled out my cellphone and dialled Stella's number. I've always been pretty good at retaining telephone numbers, and hers was a breeze because the first two digits were my birthday, the second two my age. An odd coincidence.

I had no idea what I was going to say, I just hoped the right words would come to me. I prayed hard.

The telephone was picked up after the fourth ring.

"Yes?" she said simply.

"Hello, Stella. It's Jay Benedict. Please don't ring off. I'm calling to say how very sorry I am about what happened with Harold after Jack's funeral. I didn't call before because I thought you'd still be angry and wouldn't listen."

I paused briefly so I could judge her reaction. There was merely silence. At least she was listening.

"What I did was inexcusable. I've never done anything like it in my whole life. I guess I'd been a little out of control all the day. It must have been the pills I took to calm me down; I don't really know."

Again I paused.

"So I was hoping you and Harold might find it in you to forgive me. There's not much else I can do but say I'm sorry."

"Thanks for calling, Jay," Stella said at last. A surge of relief flooded through me.

"I'll never understand why you did what you did, or said those terrible things about Harry. But if you're truly sorry, then – sure – okay, I forgive you. Whatever. I just think that it's better if we don't see each other again. Best for you. Best for me. Best for Harry."

Somehow I had to ascertain whether the boy was at home or out at Santa Monica with his neanderthal buddy, Phil.

"Look, I understand absolutely, Stella, and it's very generous of you to see things in such a forgiving way. Tell me though, how is Harold? Not still upset, I hope?"

"He's still really broken up about his father's death. I had to tell him the things they're saying about Jack. Better coming from me than reading about it in the papers. He refuses to believe any of the stories."

"And you?"

She took a deep breath. "I just don't know, Jay. I just don't know."

"Would it help heal any wounds if I apologized to Harold right now on the phone. Face to face might scare him still maybe, but on the phone...? I feel so bad about it all. If there's any way –"

She cut me short. "I don't think so, Jay. He's still really scared about you. He had bruises all down his back, you know. And I had to tell him what the police told me you claimed he'd said. You see, he didn't understand why they were asking him such peculiar questions about guns and software programs; as if he'd done something wrong. I don't think he'll ever forgive you for that. He can't understand why his dad's best friend would lie about him like that – try to make out he's some kind of monster. Neither can I frankly, but we'd best put these things behind us."

"Don't you think if I spoke –"

"No. I don't think that's a good idea at all, Jay. Not at all. Besides, he's not here. He's with friends." Her tone sounded a trifle alarmist, as though she'd got it into her head that I was thinking of coming round to see her. "So let's just leave it, huh? Leave us alone. It's hard enough to even get through another day without having to worry about your conscience. Sorry to put it that way, but I've got to think about us now."

"I understand, Stella," I replied as I heard the click of the receiver.

So, Harold was with his friends.

Of course he could have been visiting any one of a dozen buddies, but I had to put my money on Phil. Perhaps the cops had followed Harold there. It explained their absence from his home.

I made a quick call to directory assistance. There was only one Tampico listed with a Santa Monica number. The operator was helpful enough to give me the address on Montana.

I started up the engine.

27.

Two detectives sat in a car across from the apartment building where Phil Tampico lived. One was eating a hot dog, while his partner sipped coffee from a paper cup. Their eyes were trained on the entrance.

I parked on the next block and switched off the engine. From this vantage point I could observe the cops as well as the door to Tampico's building.

I relaxed slightly for the first time in hours. It was reassuring that Goodrich, Yant, or both, had ultimately decided it was a smart move to keep a close watch on Harold Corr – at least for the duration of the day. Just to cover themselves against the unforeseen.

Three and a quarter hours later, I'd counted only three people entering the building; an elderly man, and two elderly women.

At 4.30 pm the door was pushed open and the Jodie Foster look-alike exited.

Unlike the last time I'd seen her, she was dressed like any normal pubescent teenager. A pair of baggy jeans and a loose fitting sweat shirt. Her hair was held back by a floral alice band.

The innocent lamb, no less.

I reached into the glovebox and pulled out a small digital camera. If no one believed what I said, perhaps they might believe the evidence of their eyes. I'd take a few shots, see what I ended up with.

Sweet Miss Purity stood on the sidewalk for a while, her hands on her slim hips, looking lazily up and down the street. I noticed her briefly glance across Montana at the cops in their Chevy.

I took a few quick shots through the window of my car.

She strolled back into the building.

You didn't have to be a genius to figure Phil and Harold were inside. The girl had been sent out to see if the cops were still there; presumably because the Tampico apartment didn't offer a view of Montana.

At 5.10 a yellow Volkswagan Beetle pulled up outside the apartment building and an olive-skinned woman of around forty walked inside. I debated whether this could have been Phil's mother. Even at a distance, I thought I'd seen a resemblance to the Tampico boy.

Twenty minutes later the door to the building opened and Harold walked out. He was closely followed by Phil and the girl. Harold was clutching a baseball mitt, while Phil carried a bat.

I took some more shots with the camera.

So the kids were going to play in the park. Well, what would you expect? After all, to the world at large they were just a bunch of normal kids.

I knew better. They might fool the police, they didn't me. There had to be a reason for this charade.

The three climbed into the yellow Beetle. It was facing away from me, towards the ocean.

I fired up my engine as I watched the Beetle approach in my rear view mirror. The Chevy had pulled out behind them, two cars back. My, they were subtle when it came to a tail.

The traffic was flowing pretty slowly as the Beetle crawled towards me. I was sitting right down in the driver's seat hoping Harold wouldn't notice me.

Again I'd underestimated the boy.

As the yellow car came alongside, Harold wound down the passenger window, looked straight at me, and grinned.

Behind him, in the rear seat, Jodie had her tongue pressed to the window.

He'd known I was up ahead. The girl must have seen me earlier.

I pulled out into the traffic after the Chevy had passed.

The three kids played softball in the park for an hour. I watched them from a vantage point fifty yards or so down the street.

The detectives sat in the Chevy just across the road from the entrance to the park.

At 6.45 pm, the kids decided to pack it in.

As he climbed back into the VW, Harold shot a glance in my direction. It was an arrogant look of victory. This bothered me. What was his game?

Resentment burned like hot coals within me. As usual, Harold Corr had taken the upper ground. I was furious that again I was impotent to do anything to wipe the self-satified smile off the little bastard's face.

We drove back towards Montana in a ridiculous convoy; the VW, the Chevy, then me. I didn't much care whether the cops noticed me. I had every right to be there.

At Ninth Street they stopped briefly to let 'Jodie' out. Then Phil headed back towards the ocean, taking the slip road across Palisades Park onto Pacific Coast Highway.

The charade continued at Old Topanga Canyon Road. The cops parked at the end of the Corr drive; I parked twenty feet down the road. I looked at my watch. It was 7.50 pm.

Five minutes later Phil left. Harold stood at the gate for a moment, staring down the road at me. I picked up the camera and took some pictures with the telephoto lens.

Finally he went inside.

Ten minutes later, one of the detectives climbed out of the Chevy and walked down the road towards me. He reminded me of a young Popeye Doyle.

The detective gave me a *wind down the window* gesture with his index finger as he pulled out his badge.

I hit a button and the window slid down.

"Something wrong, detective?" I asked.

"Driver's licence please, sir," he replied pleasantly.

I handed it over. He studied it, then handed it back. The name clearly meant nothing to him. He must have been pretty poorly briefed at the station house.

"You've been on our tail since Douglas Park. What's the idea?"

"Just coincidence, I guess."

"Well, my partner and I are on important police business, and you're in the way. So could you please move someplace else?"

"In the way? Here, in the middle of nowhere?" I asked.

"I'm not going to argue with you, sir," he replied. "You're hindering a police investigation. Please move on."

I started up the engine and backed up the roadway a good two hundred feet.

The detective stood in the roadway where I'd left him, staring at me. Then he ambled back to the Chevy.

At midnight I called it off and drove home. Harold had told me he'd kill someone today, and today was over. That was good enough for me. For now, anyway.

Back home I rewound the extended play video tape and watched every news programme that had been aired on Channel 5 since 4 pm.

Apart from the three dead car-jacking teenagers, the streets of LA had been relatively quiet during the afternoon.

I put my feet over the arm of the TV chair and closed my eyes.

Maybe I'd saved someone's life.

28.

Harold sat in the Command Module, watching the television screen. He listened through earphones so as not to disturb his mother asleep down the hallway.

He was angry.

He'd screwed up his first professional kill, and he felt like smashing everything in the house to tiny pieces. He wanted to hurt someone.

Killing the Benedict woman had been such fun. That had been a breeze. So why the boner this time? Perhaps there really was more to this kind of killing than met the eye.

Dad had always made it look so easy. He was the ultimate pro. The contract came though on Penet, then bang-bang some schmuck was dead. Neat photos in the LA Times the following day. Sheer poetry.

It was always the same with the best around. Take Tiger Woods. Looked as though he was swatting a fly, not smacking the shit out of the golf ball.

His thumb danced on the clicker. The channels flashed by at half second intervals. His expression darkened with frustration.

He'd been waiting for 'breaking news' all day; first at Phil's, next on the 'all news, all the time' radio stations on the way to play ball. Finally all the way home. Nothing. Nada.

What the hell was going on? Why had no one found the dumb asshole? Didn't the dude have any friends, for Christ's sake? The guy was a big shot, wasn't he? A major man. Everyone in the city knew councilman Gardenas didn't they? So how come there was nothing on the tube?

He hooked his sneakers on the metal rung under his swivel seat and spun it around a couple of times.

Jesus H Christ, boy, you fuckin' shot me.!

Harold clamped a hand over his mouth to stiffle the belly laugh as he remembered the look on the old man's face as the first bullet ripped into his chest. Major surprise, dude!

Dad would have been really proud.

Then his concentration returned to the television screen, and his face again clouded with annoyance.

If someone didn't find Gardenas soon, he'd look real stupid. This was his first job. The family reputation was on the line. They'd want to *know* the guy was dead.

He reached for the bag of hard candy on the edge of the trestle table, popping one into his mouth and rolling it around his fat cheeks. Lemon drops filled with sherbet. He loved the sour ones, they made you shiver.

What if he called the cops anonymously from a phone booth?

Nah. Not such a good idea. Not with the cops watching him twenty-four hours a day, thanks to that birdturd Benedict.

Benedict was the cause of it all. If it hadn't been for him there'd be no cops nosing around, getting in his way.

He smacked his hand down hard in anger on the trestle table, sending a lance of pain up his arm.

The lemon candy burst open in his mouth, flooding his pink tongue with acid sherbet. Immediately he felt better.

Maybe now was the time for the 'insurance'.

The bracelet.

It was risky. He'd have to play it real smart. But what the hell; why not? He'd planned for just such an eventuality. Now was the time. It was worth the risk to see 'birdturd' up to his waist in bird shit.

The idea was irresistable. He'd do it. Tomorrow Benedict would wish he'd never been born.

29.

The Five Guardians earned Charlie and me a whole heap of money. Though I'd written the game, Charlie shared the profits as part of our subsequent partnership agreement.

In its day the Five Guardians was the hottest game around. Now it was a dinosaur.

My first primitive attempts at writing computer games sadly left little room for any imaginative input by the player. There was usually some ostensible goal to be achieved, but once you won the pot of gold, freed the damsel, passed the checkered flag, that was it. Nothing changed except your level of expertise.

And once you'd bought the game, you played it for free, there were no writer's residuals.

I knew even then I couldn't continue with this stultifying work for ever. I wanted to try something new. Technology was roaring ahead so fast anything and everything was possible.

I wasn't alone. Others in the same industry saw the market for a new genre of entertainment. Charlie was one of them. So we teamed up and formed the Cyberkitchen.

Charlie and I began to think less in terms of a video game per se, and more in terms of interactive movies where the player actually had hands-on control of the story as he watched it. The outcome was his to choose.

With the increasing Internet culture, Charlie and I figured that an ever-increasing amount of people were going to want to 'browse', rather than merely win or lose some dumb game. So we set out to try to combine browsing with a traditional story.

As programmers, we attacked it from a programming angle. Our aim was to allow the player, or 'browser', to branch every twenty seconds, by way of the user interface that linked him or her to the video. He chose from a selection of possible alternative storylines, exploring where the plot would lead, given the mood swings of the main characters. We also allowed the browser to move backwards in time and explore other parts of the story.

Essentially the browser was making his personal plot choices, given the multi paths available to him or her. More romantic? Hit the button. A touch more agression? Hit another. Kiss the girl? Make her cry? The choice was his or hers.

The idea was for people to view our multi-path movies on the Internet. The CD Rom containing the characters and background were free. We'd make money by charging a fee to hit our Internet site to watch multiple episodes.

The ultimate goal, my personal goal, was some day to create an artificial intelligence in the progamming somewhere so that every eventuality didn't have to be scripted by the writer. The AI chip would have thought of them all, and patch in every conceivable answer.

That would have been my nerd heaven.

The deal we'd been a hair's breadth from closing when Faith's lawyer had frozen my assets was a bundle deal with Lanyard Bell.

It worked out this way. Six million LB machines would be sold with our product on each one. The bundle contained only the first ten minutes of the movie. It was a teaser. To watch the rest of the movie you had to hit our Internet site. The cost? A mere two to three bucks per movie.

We named our product Sleuthhound.

The little red light was blinking when I got in at 12.45 Sunday morning.

I let it blink, and went to bed. I desperately needed sleep.

Charlie called at 7 am Sunday. He was so excited his speech was scarcely intelligible.

He castigated me for switching off my cellphone. How could I do it to him – just vanish into thin air at such a critical moment?

I kept shouting into the receiver that I was sorry, but he didn't seem to hear me. He just babbled on. He had the most fantastic news.

Lanyard Bell had given us the green light. Nate had closed the deal at 2.30 pm. Because I'd been unreachable, Charlie had signed on behalf of us both.

The teaser was to be one of several CD freebies to be given away with the new Lanyard Bell machine – the LB Taskmaster 5000. The general US release date was scheduled for two weeks from Monday. The CD's were in production.

It was time to post Sleuthhound on the Internet.

For the first time since Faith had walked out, I felt elated. The smallest ray of hope was shining into my life and I could feel its warmth. Two long years of hard work and dedication had come to fruition. Now we'd see if the title was any good and whether we'd judged the market accurately.

Just possibly there was a life without Faith.

30.

Sunday started out as the most wonderful day.

It was time to celebrate the Lanyard Bell deal, so Charlie and I rounded up Nate, Mama Poule and Nancy. I wasn't able to reach Lissie, Scuzz and Mort.

Charlie had somehow muscled an old threadbare armchair out of the garage and onto the tray of his aged Chevy truck. Charlie, Nancy and Nate rode up front in the cab, while Mama Poule and I rode out back.

Mama Poule looked as regal as Queen Seloti of Tonga. I hung on to the leg of her armchair as we sped up the coast towards Malibu.

Lunch at the Charthouse lasted three hours. We sat on the deck overlooking the ocean, the sun roasting our backs. We ate ourselves to a standstill, and toasted our success in at least four magnums of French champagne. Everyone made speeches – speeches which became less and less coherent as the afternoon wore on.

Then at three-thirty Nancy went quite mad. Whooping and hollering, she stripped down to her bra and pants, and ran down the stairs onto the sand and into the ocean.

This proved such a hit with the other Charthouse patrons that Mama Poule immediately took it into her head to follow Nancy's example.

The cheering must have been audible in Santa Barbara.

Since it was undoubtedly a case of *all for one and one for all*, we three men were next. We stripped down to our jocks and ran into the surf like a bunch of kids.

To watch Mama Poule bellyflop into the Pacific was something the like of which I will never see again. I swear the tide rose an inch in Long Beach.

It was all quite blissful, and there was no corner of my mind available for dark thoughts.

Eventually, Charlie drew the short straw. To him fell the task of chauffeuring us drunks home. He sat on his lonesome in the cab while the rest of us rode the tray of the truck. Mama Poule sang some colourful Senegalese tribal songs her mother had taught her. Her voice was rich and unbelievably strong, drawing many a look of approval along PCH.

It was only as we passed Old Malibu Road I realized how close we were to Tapanga Canyon, and I mentally froze.

Harold Corr lived close by. Harold had murdered my Faith and was laughing at the world.

From that moment on, though I did my best to mask my fundamental mood change from my friends, my joy was over.

Charlie dropped off Nate and Mama Poule, then Nancy. Finally, he took me back to Studio City.

I knew he could sense my emotional metamorphosis, yet he made no reference to it. He merely put an arm round my shoulder.

"A new life's beginning, Jay. You've got to put the past aside. Not forget – I don't mean that – I just mean move forward. You've planted the trees and watched them grow. Now go pick the fruit."

As I watched him back out of the driveway, the gates swinging shut behind him, I knew that there was no way I could move forward till I'd addressed the past.

I had no idea how this was possible, given Yant's antipathy and the less than sympathetic attitude I'd sensed from Goodrich in the DA's offices.

I knew I was on my own.

That evening I again surfed the TV news reports.

Despite the fact my brain was only taking in every third word thanks to all the booze at lunch, I gathered that again it had been an unremarkable day in La La Land as far as homicides were concerned.

To make up for the low murder count, the death toll was topped up by an appalling accident on the San Bernadino Freeway – an eighteen wheeler carrying engine parts had jack-knifed, careering into a coachload of tourists.

Twelve had died.

I heard the entry buzzer sound just as I'd taken my coffee from the microwave. I weaved unsteadily to the front door and pressed the intercom.

"Yes?" I shouted into the console.

"Detective Yant, Mr Benedict. Santa Monica Police Department. Open the gates."

"What can I do for you, detective?" I answered. I had no wish to discuss anything with him right now. I just wanted to drink my coffee and sleep off the booze.

"I'm not asking you, Mr Benedict. I'm telling you. Open the gates or we'll be forced to cut them open."

"What's this about?" I asked.

There was no reply, so I did the sensible thing and pressed the release button. No point in antagonizing a cop clearly equipped with bolt cutters.

As the Chevy swung past the living room window, I could see Wahl was at the wheel of the surprisingly spotless Chevy two-door.

Wahl deliberately stood hard on the brakes, once more gouging a couple of feet of gravel from the driveway.

They were standing side by side facing me as I opened the door. Yant drilled me with a stony stare. Wahl's expression was the usual fixed self-satisfied grin.

I was about to ask them both inside when Wahl reached behind his back and pulled out his cuffs. I gazed blankly in surprise at Yant as the detective began to say the words I'd only heard spoken in the movies.

"Jay Benedict, I arrest you for the murder of Faith Benedict. You have the right to remain silent. Anything you *do* say may be held against you in a court of law. You have the right to an attorney..."

It felt as though a trap door had opened beneath my feet and I was falling into an abyss. There aren't words to describe the depth of my shock and horror as Yant finished the Miranda caution.

I was vaguely aware of Wahl walking round behind me and frisking me.

He then cuffed me. It was the strangest feeling. I felt totally vulnerable, as though I'd been stripped naked in a medieval village square, prior to being pilloried.

I asked if I could call Nate before we left, and Yant told me I could do it at the precinct house. This clearly pleased pig-face Wahl, who would have preferred to have me lie face down on the gravel while I'd been read my rights.

Thirty minutes later I was in the interview room down at the precinct house. I'd made my one call.

Nate was shocked to hell and back by the turn of events.

Judging by the way he was slurring his words, I guessed like me he was still pretty intoxicated and wouldn't be much good to anyone right then. Nevertheless he commanded me in the strongest possible terms to say absolutely nothing to anyone until he arrived at the station house. Innocence, he told me, had nothing to do with anything. Every word could be twisted by smart lawyers, such as he.

I took his advice to heart and sealed my lips.

While we waited for Nate, Wahl took great personal pleasure in fingerprinting me, then taking the police mugshots.

God only knows what I looked like; probably worse than that terrible shot of Hugh Grant released to the press after his little indiscretion up on Sunset.

Rather than put me in a holding cell, Yant chose to have me wait in the interview room. He told me he was doing me a favor; there were some pretty unsavory people packing the cells right then. That's what he said, anyway. My guess was that he hoped I'd start yapping, angrily asserting my innocence.

He'd certainly read me right – I was burning to have it out with him.

Wahl and Yant seated themselves facing me. A tape recorder lay on the table between us, the spools revolving slowly.

Yant formally reminded me that I wasn't obliged to say anything, but that I could do so if I wished. He plainly hoped I couldn't resist. I have to admit I was scared.

It didn't help my situation any that I was three sheets to the wind drunk.

And if that wasn't bad enough, any moment my attorney was going to fall through the door, ostensibly to come to my rescue.

The fact that I had clammed up didn't stop Yant and Wahl taking turns with some intense criss-cross questioning, hoping I'd lose patience and elect to waive my rights and spit out the truth.

They kept asking me about a bracelet.

Thanks to the champagne, everything was still going in one ear and out the other. The uppermost thought buzzing around in my brain was the mind-numbing concept that the District Attorney was actually considering arraigning me for Faith's murder. As far as a bracelet was concerned, I had no idea which bracelet they were referring to, nor its relevance, so I merely tried to concentrate like hell so as to get the adrenalin going in my system to counteract the alcohol.

Ten minutes later the effort seemed to be paying dividends. My mind was clearing. I could tell because I was more scared than ever.

Something had clearly transpired since I'd last seen Yant. Some fresh evidence must have come to light to persuade Goodrich to indict me. Question was, what the hell *was* it? I was innocent – there could *be* no such compelling evidence..

"He's a damned disgrace, that's what he is," I heard Yant remark to Wahl. "The man's drunk as hell."

All I could think of was Nate's imminent arrival.

"You think I'm drunk? Wait till you see my attorney," I mumbled through the onset of a bout of hiccups. I wasn't trying in the least to be funny. It was hardly the time for levity; the words just seemed to slip out. Either way, only Wahl appeared to hear what I'd said, and I didn't give a damn about him. Yant was the primary.

Yant leant across the table and whispered encouragingly. "The bracelet, Mr Benedict. Why not tell us about the bracelet."

Right then the door opened and a detective I'd never seen before ushered Nate into the room.

How he'd done it I shall never know, but the man looked as good as new. The suit was fresh, the shirt was starched, the tie was knotted correctly, adjusted to just the right lengths and tied in a Windsor knot. The pants had a razor sharp crease.

But the most impressive feature were the eyes. Crystal clear, bright and earnest. I made a silent prayer for Mama Poule; she'd worked a major miracle. If I hadn't known Nate better, I'd have sworn the man had taken five lines of the purest cocaine. He was buzzing like a queen bee.

"Nathaniel Berg," he said drawing up a chair and seating himself beside me. "For the record, that is," he added, gesturing towards the tape recorder. "I'd like to speak to my client alone, please."

Yant and Wahl stopped the tape, rose, and left the room. It was my right to a few minutes with my attorney.

As soon as we were alone, the façade of sobriety cracked a bit. Nate was sweating with the effort.

"Don't say a word, Jay. Hear me? Not a word unless I ask you to do so. And I don't see that happening." He looked deadly serious. "Have they hinted about what they've got on you?"

"They've been banging on about a bracelet."

"What bracelet?" It came out sounding like 'braithleth'. Nate stretched his lips several times.

"Don't know," I replied.

Nate thought for a moment. "Well, we'd better find out. That may mean asking them in for a chat. Point is this. I can tell them 'no more interviews' because the arrest's already been made, or I can agree to talk. I think we'll opt for the latter so I can find out what the hell they've got. Otherwise it could take some time.

"They don't have to tell me what they've got on you right now. To tell the truth, if I were Yant I'd give nothing away. He must have persuaded Goodrich to let him go ahead with the arrest. I'd let us sweat if I were him. Unless I was unsure of the strength of the new evidence – whatever it is. The bracelet, I'd say. Then quite possibly I'd want to talk about it."

I agreed with Nate's logic. Whatever he decided was good enough for me.

"Am I going to be here overnight?" I asked. I didn't relish the thought. I was conjuring up a mental picture of my overnight companions.

"We'll apply for bail at the arraignment. Shouldn't be a problem," he said. I could see he was lying to give me confidence. "Whatever bail they set, we'll raise it. Bondsmen can be reached twenty-four hours a day."

Nate then stepped outside and talked to Yant. The two cops re-entered and the interview continued.

There followed a brief description of the nuts and bolts of my arrest – what time, where, the fact I'd been Miranda'd. All formal stuff for Nate's benefit. It was noted that the arraignment was to take place that evening.

Nate stated for the record that there was no question of my innocence. He was dumbfounded that Goodrich should have seen fit to issue an arrest warrant solely on the evidence of the Ruger found in my garden. He was fishing – he wanted them to ask about the bracelet so he could ascertain its relevance.

Almost immediately Yant took the bait.

"Perhaps your client could tell us why he forgot to mention the bracelet at our first interview."

"What bracelet are you referring to, detective?" Nate enquired. "Please explain the significance of your question?"

"Sure will, Mr Berg. Sure will," Yant crooned with more than a hint of a smile. "The Saturday following the fatal shooting of Faith Benedict, I interviewed your client. At that time I questioned him concerning the articles of jewellery taken from the decedent. I showed him a list we'd made. I told him at that time that the list excluded the contents of Mrs Benedict's purse, and her sunglasses. I stated in the clearest possible terms that the list was one of jewellery alone. I asked him to study it closely and tell me whether there were any articles missing – articles Mrs Benedict wore habitually, ones he would expect to have been found on the body. He assured me categorically that nothing was missing."

"So what's your point?" Nate asked.

But I was already way ahead of him. Despite my befuddled state of intoxication the word 'bracelet' had suddenly lit up in four colour neon. The part of the brain that dealt with self-preservation was hitting the panic button hard and often.

How could I have forgotten? Faith's bracelet, for Christ's sake! The one I'd given her on our first anniversary! She never took it off. I'd simply missed it when he'd shown me the damned list. My mind was elsewhere. Dear God, I'd been in a state of abject shock at the time, how the hell could I have been expected to think cogently about details such as how many pieces of jewelery I'd given her, and which pieces she habitually wore!

"My point is this, Mr Berg," Yant continued smoothly, "We made inquiries at the late Mrs Benedict's place of work."

My insides burned red hot. What kind of rabbit was he going to pull from the hat. Judging by the look on his face, Yant clearly thought he'd stitched me up.

"The Design Factory?" Nate asked.

"The same. A Ms Ilse Tilstrom there said she was surprised to find no mention of the bracelet Mr Benedict had given her on their anniversary. Together with her three rings, these were items she wore habitually. Leastways, that's what she told us. She never took the bracelet off. We checked it out with Mrs Benedict's parents."

I was about to speak when Nate motioned me quite vehemently with his hand to remain silent. "So my client forgot to mention the absence of the bracelet. Big deal. His wife lay dead, shot to death in a parking structure off 4th Street. He was in a state of shock. So what? You're not telling me that *that's* the evidence that persuaded Ms Goodrich to lay charges against my client? Come on, detective."

"The bracelet was not recovered at the crime scene."

"Okay. Have you ever considered that maybe it was stolen?"

"It was not stolen, Mr Berg. We know that for a fact."

"Oh yes? How so, detective?"

"Because I have it in my pocket," Yant replied theatrically.

His mother did well never to set him on the stage. He was hamming the thing to hell.

"Do you recognize this item of jewellery, Mr Benedict?" Yant asked, holding up the gold bracelet I'd given Faith. It had been slipped into a transparent plastic sheath.

I glanced at Nate. He nodded his assent.

"Yes, I do," I replied. "I gave it to my wife as an anniversary gift five years ago."

"For the record, Mr Benedict has indicated the bracelet listed on the evidence sheet as number fifteen," Yant drawled.

"Could you please tell us where this line of questioning is leading, detective," Nate asked. "I am anxious to apply for bail on behalf of my client at the earliest opportunity."

"This bracelet," Yant continued, waving it in the air in front of Nate's face, "has been thoroughly examined by forensics. Traces of Mrs Benedict's blood and tissue were found on the inner surface. This indicates that she fell on the bracelet after she was shot. It logically follows that the bracelet was taken from the decedent's wrist subsequent to her death."

"So where did you find it?" Nate asked sharply. "Not in my client's possession. I feel certain of that."

I hoped he was correct. Mama Poule had been watching the police conduct their search of my house. Yet it was entirely possible she'd missed them taking something. After all, they'd been in the house as well as the garden and Mama Poule could hardly have been in both places at the same time. Could the bracelet be another plant?

"No, it was not found in your client's possession, nor at his property. It was found in Harold Corr's bedroom. Mr Benedict put it there to implicate the boy."

My head began to swim.

It was at this moment that I vomited all over the table and the tape machine.

31.

My mother gave me a model boat on my fifth birthday. She'd saved up enough money to take Raymond and me on a short holiday to Brockenhurst in the English New Forest. I took my shiny new boat with me.

The day of its maiden voyage on a lake close to the hotel, it snagged its funnel on the branch of a tree and sank in deep water. Raymond tried to rescue my treasured craft, but failed.

To me that day, I suffered the most crushing loss of my entire life.

It's all relative, isn't it? The loss of a boat when I was five; the day my first love walked out of my life at the end of the holiday at Wraysbury; waiting in the corridor of the West London Hospital; the news of Faith's death – how can anyone judge which is worst?

It can only get better, as Granny was so fond of saying.

Sure.

I looked into the eyes of detective Yant in the interview room and saw written there the certainty of my guilt.

They'd given me a ten minute break to clean myself up in the men's room. An officer had accompanied Nate and me to the door.

He'd waited outside.

At first I thought, *how nice, he trusts me not to try and leg it out the window*. Once inside the washroom I saw the bars, and the size of the window.

"You'd better tell me quickly, before we go back," Nate said as I tried to wash the vomit from the front of my shirt. "It's true? You forgot to mention the bracelet when he showed you the list?"

I nodded.

"Have you any idea how he could seem so certain you placed it in Harold Corr's bedroom?"

"That's complete crap. I did nothing of the kind."

"I have no doubt of that. I just had to ask, that's all. You might have remembered something that happened while you were in the boy's bedroom."

I didn't. But I was thinking really hard.

"It's clear that Yant thinks you're guilty. My bet is he's hoping you'll break down and sign a confession. I'd like to find out what, if any, concrete evidence they have that you stashed the bracelet in Corr's bedroom. That means going back into the interview room. Is that okay with you, my friend?"

"Whatever," I replied, dry-retching.

There was a rap on the door. My stomach was still heaving. I prayed for strength.

"Just remember, I do the talking. Got that?" Nate looked as though he meant business – like he'd punch me if I argued the toss.

I nodded again. I didn't feel safe opening my mouth right then.

Wahl was still cleaning some debris from the tape recorder when we re-entered the room. I presumed it was some small particle of my lunch. He didn't look too happy about it. The room smelled of strong disinfectant.

Wahl finally placed the tape recorder back on the table and snapped it on. The spools began to turn. A look of relief crossed the fat man's face.

"Let's get back to the bracelet, shall we?" Yant began again. "When did you last see it?"

"My client does not at this time wish to answer any more questions. However, I have a couple if you don't mind, detective."

"Be my guest," Yant replied, tilting his chair back on two legs. He was dying to deliver the *coup de grace*.

"What evidence could you possibly have that would lead you to believe Mr Benedict took the bracelet into the Corr boy's bedroom?"

"Pretty compelling evidence, actually."

"Could you share it with us?"

Yant grinned, first at Nate, then at me. Then he nodded to Wahl.

The fat detective left the room, returning a minute later with a television, complete with a VCR on a trolley. He plugged them both in to a power socket, then pushed a tape into the recorder. The television screen lit up.

It was a high angle shot of Harold and myself – a back of the heads shot, so naturally you couldn't see our lips moving, nor the screens on the trestle table.

The picture quality wasn't so good, but it was good enough. It was clear from the head movement that we were talking.

"Is there sound to this, detective?" Nate asked.

"Nah, it's mute. Damned shame."

I might have known it. The kid wasn't stupid. He hadn't run the sound on this one.

Yant addressed his next remark to me. "You'd remember when this was taken, eh, Mr Benedict?"

I said nothing, obedient to the commands of my attorney.

"My client was unaware that he was being taped. It was clearly made without his consent, and is therefore inadmissible."

"We'll see about that. See, the boy contends that he told your client he had live cameras throughout the entire house. It was kind of a hobby of his. No harm there, eh?"

"Seems a pretty strange hobby to me, detective Yant, to want to film your parents without their knowledge," Nate shot back.

"Oh, hell, I'd say it was all pretty innocent. Point is, though, that if he'd made it clear to Mr Benedict that there were cameras all over the place, you'd be pretty dumb not to take it for granted that there would be one in the bedroom as well. So it kind of implies assent to the video, doesn't it? Unless Mr Benedict's going to say the boy never made any mention of the cameras?"

He let the question hang in the air, challenging me to say this was the case.

"The day we searched your client's home, I mentioned the movie the Corr kid had taken of his father and your client. Mr Benedict didn't seem at all surprised to hear I'd seen it. So don't waste my time now suggesting your client didn't know the kid was making movies."

" Come on, detective, you'd have to be insane to plant false evidence if you knew you were being video'd. You can't have it both ways. He either was aware of the camera, and consequently would have been quite mad to plant the bracelet, or he wasn't aware of it, and therefore the tape was made without his consent and is inadmissable."

Nate folded his arms, pleased with the logic.

For a moment detective Yant's expression was blank. I could see his brain ticking over. "It's entirely possible Mr Benedict placed the bracelet behind the table, and only then was told about the cameras."

Nate snapped his fingers theatrically. "Then it's inadmissible. My client didn't know. Simple."

"It's not my job to worry about points of law," he replied quickly, "I leave that side of things to the DA's office. They've viewed the tape, Mr Berg, and are happy to proceed."

Of course the question of whether or not I was aware of a camera in the bedroom would ultimately be a critical one – I knew I'd have to think about it carefully. I had no intention of lying about anything. Once I deviated one inch from the truth, I knew I was lost. Naïvely, I'd imagined that the truth would set me free. I expect a few poor souls had thought the same and lived to regret their gullibility as they were strapped into the electric chair.

Of course if I *did* admit that Harold had mentioned the cameras, then the tape would very probably be ruled admissable through implied assent.

"Okay, let's move on," said Yant, as he gave Wahl a gesture with his index finger to fast forward. Wahl pressed a button.

I watched myself stand and move to the door. All at double speed. It was clear from the angle of my head that I was watching one of the screens rather than Harold. Then Harold grasped a video tape, inserting it into the VCR player. The player was visible, not the television screen.

"Slow it down right there," Yant directed Wahl. The speed immediately slowed to normal.

Harold had his head turned away from me, as though something had caught his attention.

While the boy looked in the opposite direction, I suddenly crouched down and reached in under the trestle table next to the filing cabinet. A couple of seconds later, I stood. It was only then that Harold turned back in my direction.

"Freeze it right there," Yant snapped triumphantly.

I stared at the image. Maddeningly, it was still only the backs of our heads. I would have given a kings ransom for our faces to have been visible; a lip reader could have interpreted the entire conversation. As it was, the whole performance was a grotesque mime; and you didn't have to be Einstein to second guess Yant's next play.

"That," he said, with an air of finality, "was when you placed your wife's bracelet on the floor in Harold Corr's bedroom."

Nate reacted wonderfully. He actually laughed out aloud. If he'd been doing it for effect only, he certainly fooled me. I think he actually thought Yant had taken leave of his senses.

"Why on earth would my client do such a thing?"

"You seem to forget, Mr Berg, that Mr Benedict has been at very great pains to suggest that Harold Corr caused the death of his wife; that it was this young boy who shot her."

Nate started waving a hand. "Hey, hey, hey! Just hold on. Are you seriously suggesting that my client removed the bracelet from his wife's wrist as she lay dead in a parking structure in Santa Monica, with the settled intention, at that exact moment in time, of laying the blame for her death at the feet of an eleven-year-old boy? A child? The son of one of his closest friends? Is that your idea of the thinking of a rational human being?"

Nate shook his head in abject disbelief. It was a thoroughly theatrical gesture to signify that Yant's entire case was quite ludicrous. It impressed me a lot.

Yant stuck to his guns. "Mr Benedict has consistently maintained that the Corr boy attempted to extort money from him for having committed the murder. So I suggest it would be very much in Mr Benedict's interest to implicate the boy by attempting to incriminate him in this way – to wit, by placing a bloodied item of Mrs Benedict's jewellery in the boy's bedroom."

"If my client shot his wife, and she was wearing the bracelet at the time, why did he remove it at the time of her death? The extortion demand came later."

"If there was such a demand, Mr Berg. If!"

Nate again shook his head. "Well, if this is the extent of your evidence, I can't wait for the Grand Jury hearing," he responded with a confident expression.

Yant pulled out a note pad from his jacket pocket and began to read. "*I'd take a search warrant with me, detective, if I were you. And while you're looking for the Ruger, don't forget to check out the computers – the kid's got one in his room. Jack's is downstairs.*" Those are your client's words, Mr Berg. Spoken to me just hours after the video tape we've just watched was made. You see, he was very anxious indeed for us to search the boy's room. That's because he wanted us to find the bracelet that he'd placed there."

It was only then that the thought struck me. I had to speak, even if it meant incurring Nate's wrath.

"Tell me detective Yant. When exactly did the bracelet come to light? Before or after you viewed the tape? And while you're about it, how and when did you become aware of the presence of a camera in the boy's bedroom?"

"Harold Corr's mother turned over the tape to the SMPD of her own volition. It was only then that we asked ourselves what the hell you might have been doing crouching down under the table."

"And that's when the bracelet saw the light of day?" Nate added rhetorically.

"That's correct. Harold Corr had never set eyes on it before."

"Sure," I muttered to myself. Yant clearly believed one hundred per cent in my guilt and the boy's innocence. I'd tried to frame Harold to give weight and substance to an impossibly implausible story.

"Try reversing the logic, detective Yant," I said wearily. "You see, the boy's too damned clever for the both of us. He's got me indicted for murder, and he's got you nailed to the mast. Why can't you see that the kid put the damn bracelet there himself in order to frame me. For Christ's sake, he handed you the videotape on a platter. And what do you do? You say *thanks a bunch, you solved the whole frigging case for me, sonny!*"

"You *knew* the house was under surveillance, Mr Benedict. The boy told you!"

"Answer me this, then. Why didn't the boy give you the video taken in his bedroom the day you went to search the Corr house? He showed you the tape of Jack and myself in the living room, didn't he? Why not the one of Harold and myself in the bedroom after Jack's funeral? Where the hell was *that* tape when you searched?"

Yant's eyes flicked around as he searched for an answer.

"He'd hidden it, detective. Same as he'd hidden all the other things, not the least of which was the gun he used to kill my wife!"

Nate placed a firm restraining hand on my shoulder. "Jay, I implore you to say no more."

"Look, Benedict," Yant said, rising to my anger. "The kid could have told us all about the tape the day we took a look round the house. But he didn't. Want to know the reason? It was because he felt sorry for you, 'cos you'd just buried your wife. That's what his mom told us. He didn't want to get you into any more trouble by handing us a tape of you beating the shit out of him. He said he'd forgiven you. It was his mother who insisted he hand it over, and that was only yesterday when he let slip to her he'd had the camera running in his bedroom for weeks. She thought we ought to have all the tapes."

The scales immediately fell from my eyes. The threat spat out with such venom in the toy store. *You're a dead man, Mr Benedict.* It was only then that he'd decided to go ahead with his scheme. He'd had the bracelet all along in case he'd have to use it to frame me.

I don't quite know how I managed it under the circumstances, but I shut my bazoo.

Not a peep out of me.

32.

I spent the night in a holding cell. I had a cage to myself. Again I was lucky; fortunate not to have been confined with the animal who stared at me throughout the night. He was in the cage opposite. He had the unmistakable look of the serial sodomist.

At 9.20 am the arraignment took place before Judge Mason Earnshaw.

Bail was set at two hundred and fifty thousand dollars.

Where people come up with figures like this defeats me. Go figure. No way did I have that kind of money. What I *did* have was a mountain of debt, a double mortgage and an empty fridge. On the up side I had a deal with Lanyard Bell which I had to presume spelt 'security' to one 'Bull' Longhorn, the friendly neighbourhood bail bondsman with whom Nate had a working relationship.

Longhorn by name, Longhorn by nature – he certainly charged like a wounded one. Twenty-five thousand dollars, plus collateral.

Nate was mightily relieved that I'd made bail. I was damned lucky, he told me later. It never occured to me at the time that I might have been about to spend a prolonged spell in Folsom making new friends that special way only hardened criminals know how – facing the shower wall.

As he walked me to his car Nate confided that he hadn't given me more than a one in a hundred shot of walking free that night. After all, I'd been charged with a capital offense, and it took a pretty brave judge to shoulder the responsibility of letting a man walk free to maybe pick up another gun and do it again. After all, even national sports heroes had been refused bail.

His granting bail only went to demonstrate the weakness of the prosecution in the eyes of Judge Earnshaw.

Nate had argued my case with admirable fervour and conviction. I was a solid citizen – whatever that meant. I had never been charged with, let alone been convicted of, the smallest crime. I had never even been audited by the tax office. I failed to see the import of that one, but let it pass.

The court, Nate stated, should show compassion to a man who's wife had been brutally murdered just two weeks ago, and who now stood wrongly accused of the self same murder on only the flimsiest of circumstantial evidence – a gun that could have been planted by anyone, and a video tape that he would show, if it ever came to a trial, was clearly inadmissable in evidence.

He concluded that he had known me personally for over six years and would vouch for my probity, as would a very long list of character witnesses he could call if the judge so desired. I was in no way a flight risk, and would surrender my passport to the court.

"I personally guarantee my client will be available to stand trial, your Honor," he concluded with an admirable solemnity.

On behalf of the State, Assistant District Attorney Wilson Helmley, standing in for Ms Goodrich, wasn't that bothered about opposing bail which helped matters enormously. Nate told me later he probably recognised the inherent weakness of his case and wasn't about to push it right then.

Apart from the surrender of the passport, there was one more proviso. There was to be a half mile 'Jay Benedict exclusion zone' round the Corr house; I broke it – I was in the slammer for the duration.

I held my hands meekly in front of me, looking downcast – a thoroughly decent pillar of society who had been dreadfully wronged, yet bore no grudge against the authorities.

I hoped the puke stains on my shirt weren't too obvious at fifteen feet - the distance between me and the beady eyes of Judge Mason Earnshaw.

Then I was free. Nate had excelled himself.

"While I think of it, Nate," I said, as I buckled my safety belt, "why the hell would the kid have a camera running in his bedroom anyway? Jack told me no one was allowed access except the cleaner, so what was the purpose of a damned camera? What was it supposed to film? The back of the boy's head?"

"Good point," Nate replied, pulling out a notebook and pen. "Keep that thought and write it down," he said, handing it to me. "Mind you, the kid may say he set up the camera in his room to see if anyone monkied around with his things while he was out; a kind of security measure."

I thought about this. It made sense – to me now, and hopefully to a jury somewhere down the line.

"And while we're talking of the cleaner," I continued. "we've got to find out what day the cleaner came. I'm pretty certain Jack told me it was weekly. If that's the case, then she must have cleaned the house at least once since the day of the funeral. And if she gave the Command Module the once-over *she* would have found it, not the boy."

"Write that down too."

I was hoping for a slightly better reaction to the stroke of genius.

I studied Nate as we fed onto the San Diego Freeway. He didn't look quite as worried as he had earlier; marginally more confident. His eyes were dancing as the after-burners in his brain started to kick in.

"The tape of you and the boy in his bedroom is clearly inadmissable. You didn't know you were being filmed. That's clear as day. I'll fight that one down to the wire. But there's no way we can afford to let that tape be presented in open court. Can you imagine the reaction of a jury to a film show of you beating up on an eleven-year-old?"

A jury? My heart began to fibrillate. He actually saw this going to a jury trial? I'd hoped he was going to say something like '*Relax Jay, we'll have this all straightened out in no time. They'll never let you stand trial on evidence as piss weak as that. Trust me, buddy.*'

Instead my trusty attorney was sweating.

Nate drove me straight to his place. He insisted – said I still looked ill, and he wanted Mama Poule to give me the once over.

Actually, I had the sneaking suspicion he thought I might top myself if left to my own devices, but I didn't want to seem ungracious, so I just went along with his plans. The furthest thing from my mind was any thought of self-destruction – my mum had put me off such a course of action for life.

Nate loaned me a change of clothes the front of my shirt was becoming offensive to the nose.

Mama Poule cooked up a pan of her famous chicken gumbo. It hit the spot very nicely – I'd passed on the gourmet breakfast they'd offered me in the holding tank.

"I'm truly surprised Goodrich agreed to issue an arrest warrant," Nate observed, spooning the chicken soup to his lips. "She's one very bright lady."

"Why don't you try sticking to positive thoughts right now, eh?" Nate had struck a raw nerve. "I want to hear she's made a dumb-ass decision, not that she's smart as a whip."

"What I'm getting at is this. I think she's being pressured. She's not stupid, she's got to know this video tape stuff is flimsy as hell. It just won't hold water. No way."

"And that's all they have, isn't it? How can they move to indict on the basis of that stupid tape. You couldn't even see the damned bracelet!"

"Absolutely," Nate replied, banging the table. "Dead right. For all anyone knows, you could have been tying your shoelaces."

I felt better. For about three seconds. Then I remembered the gun.

"Oh shit. The Ruger. I forgot the Ruger. I suppose that counts."

"No way!" Nate replied emphatically. "Purely circumstantial. Anyone could have put it there. Same as the bracelet. Relax Jay, we'll have this thing straightened out in no time," he concluded, scraping the last few fragments of chicken gumbo from the bottom of his bowl.

At last. He'd said the words. I could have kissed him.

We discussed my position again in the greatest possible detail after we'd finished eating, which in Mama Poule's case took some time. She loved her gumbo.

At 11.30 Mama Poule went through her checklist with both of us. She had some serious investigating to do.

Somehow she'd have to ascertain when the cleaner last visited the Corr house.

Secondly, there was still the bag lady at the Santa Fe Grill to track down. She said she'd chase up her friendly neighbourhood PI, Dan Stir, first thing in the morning.

Then there was the tape. She'd ask the DA's office for a certified copy of the tape to send for independent analysis.

It was fundamentally important to assess whether it had been doctored in any way; and it was vital to prove absolutely that the bracelet was not visible on the tape. Once this was done, it was pure conjecture as to why I was crouching on the tape.

Apart from these two vital tasks, there was a mountain of leg work to do – statements and affidavits to take from the staff of the Santa Fe Grill and Toys Universe on Ventura; establishing whether the red Mustang Phil had been driving at the Galleria had been stolen; timing the trip from the restaurant car park to 4th Street. The list was endless.

At midday Mama Poule asked me if I wanted to catch some shut-eye in the den. I declined her offer. I wasn't tired. Against all the odds I'd managed to catch a couple of hours sleep in the tank overnight. My friend next door had stayed awake – each time I opened my eyes there he'd been, his face pressed to the bars.

I told Nate and Mama Poule I needed some time to myself.

I felt about five years old as she hugged me close. It was incredibly reassuring and comforting. I'd never experienced that kind of physicality from my mother.

For the first night in almost three weeks I didn't feel like weeping.

It was damn fine to be a kid again.

33.

Thirty minutes after leaving Nate's place I was on the road in a rented Jeep. I was off to God only knew where and the idea of an off-road vehicle seemed to make sense. I didn't give a shit where I ended up – I'd reached the nadir of my life where even granny's favourite aphorism held true – things couldn't get worse.

Put it down to a disfunctional childhood, but I've spent the majority of my life braced for a blow. Perhaps I make it sound much worse than it was; I had some wonderful times with mum as well as bad ones. She gave me all the love she had; she wanted only the best for her sons.

Sadly, she often just didn't have the strength to look after Raymond and me. I think she never came to terms emotionally with having been deserted by our father within hours of declaring joyously that she was pregnant with me. It broke her spirit. From that day on she believed she was basically unlovable.

Often Raymond and I had to look after ourselves when it came to keeping body and soul together. No big deal most of the time. If we were short of money, granny would give us a royal feed at her place. The same was true of auntie Eileen. Both she and granny made no secret of their disapproval of mum – she'd demonstrably failed to keep the marriage together.

So all in all things very rarely turned out to be as bad as they might have, and over the years I know I've spoiled many a fine day worrying about phantom problems.

The irony was that now, despite my appalling situation, I felt paradoxically calm. The only woman I'd loved completely and unequivocally was dead, and I was quite sure that Raymond, the single surviving member of the Benedict family, would merely have raised an eyebrow if he'd read my obituary in the London Times.

What could God do to me now? Arrange for me to be found guilty of Faith's murder and be put on Death Row?

Initially I drove in the direction the car was pointed when I picked it up at Hertz. I didn't know where I was headed and it didn't matter. I needed to find space; one with as few people around as possible. Instinct directed me towards the Mojave desert.

I'd called Charlie first thing, asking him to hold the fort at the Cyberkitchen.

He was struck dumb when I told him the police had charged me with Faith's murder. I had to keep asking whether he was still on the line, or whether we'd been cut off.

Eventually he came back to me. At heart Charlie's a simple country boy who lives for his work. Buddies up on 'Murder One' charges didn't figure in his life.

I asked him to tell everyone at the 'Kitchen; I didn't want them to read about it in the papers, or worse still to see it on Eyewitness News.

Go heal yourself, Jay, Charlie told me, *Nancy and I can look after things. Take as long as you like.*

The second call was to Nate. He told me to get the hell out of the city and breathe some fresh air.

I knew if I stayed in town, watching the television for news of fresh slayings I'd go quite mad. Besides, there was every chance the news services would access a photo of me somewhere, and run a story of my arrest.

Harold would just have to do what he had to do. If the cops didn't believe me, too bad. I was not responsible for the safety of the world. Right now it was a question of *sauve qui peut* – I had to look after myself. If I could pull myself together mentally, I'd be in far better shape to see justice ultimately done. That was my priority.

I didn't stop till Devore, a small town on the edge of the San Bernadino National Forest. I reckoned from there I'd travel north through Cajon Junction, up through Pinon Hills to the dry lake at El Mirage.

I wanted to sit in the desert. The emptiness appealed to me, it would mirror my feelings.

Half an hour later I was back on the road. The diner had been friendly and the road food more than adequate.

For a fleeting moment I'd been tempted to sack out for an hour or two in the back of the Jeep. Then the memory of the Santa Fe Grill hit me and I was wide awake.

A couple of hours later I was on a narrow two-lane blacktop heading across the desert. I opened up the roof and wound down all the windows; I wanted the hot desert air to rush in and cleanse my soul.

By the time I passed through the town of El Mirage, a strong wind had appeared out of nowhere, and the temperature had fallen. Not enough to be anywhere near cool, but low enough to dry the sweat on my back.

About five miles the far side of town I pulled off the road and headed across the hard sand towards the dry lake.

At first I thought it was a pile of trash.

It was only when I was about fifty feet away from the mound that I realized it was the seated figure of a woman.

She was sitting on a fair-sized rock hugging her knees to her chest, gently rocking backwards and forwards. She didn't even look in my direction.

I have to say I thought this a mite odd, in view of the fact that mine must have been the only vehicle to have passed that way in many hours, judging by the absence of tyre tracks.

I drove on for a while, watching the rocking figure recede in my rear view mirror. She never looked towards me. Her gaze was set on the sun, which was beginning to drop in the West.

A mile or so on I stopped. It was my insatiable curiosity again.

Why had there been no evidence of any backpack? What could this woman possibly be doing so deep into the desert? Had she walked there? In the heat of the day? Presumably she had, there was no sign of an off-road vehicle. My concern for her grew by the second.

A couple of minutes later I turned the car round and headed back towards her.

I could see her up ahead, sitting in the lotus position, ramrod back, hands folded easily in her lap.

I turned off the ignition and walked out towards her from the Jeep. She now had her back to me.

Rather than scare her, I called out a greeting from a distance of about ten feet.

It was only then that she turned her head. She'd been crying, that much was clear from the dried streaks down her face.

"I don't mean to disturb you. I just wondered if you were alright," I offered.

"That's kind. But yes, I'm just fine," she replied, looking over her shoulder with a friendly face. Her voice had the density of the soft sand around her.

She was slim and fine-boned. I judged her to be around thirty. Her Titian red hair blew free in the increasing wind, the skin of her bare shoulders a patchwork of giant freckles.

"I love this place. I came here with a man many years ago. It's never lost it's romance."

I didn't quite know how to respond. She was speaking so softly it was almost as if she were talking to herself. I had to strain to hear.

"You've visited here before?" she asked, still looking directly at the sunset.

I walked the last few yards and sat in the sand to her right, careful not to invade her personal space. She sat perched on the rock a couple of feet above me.

"This is my first time," I replied.

"You're lucky then. The first time's always magic. I come here every year. Same day, same time. You see, I come here to remember Matt."

I wondered if he'd been the 'man' she'd referred to, but didn't like to ask.

"Your husband?"

"He was my son. I never had a husband. I had a man for a short while."

The strong wind blew some tumbleweed towards her. As it jumped up towards her face, she fended it away with her hand, then turned her head to look at me. "I hope you don't mind my straight-talking. I tell things the way I feel them. Some folks think it's confronting. I don't. It's just the way I'm put together.

"You married?"

"I was. My wife passed away," I replied without thinking.

Passed away? What the hell had I just said? I made it sound as though Faith had died in her sleep of old age, rather than violently at the hand of a psychotic child killer.

I was suddenly angry at my middle-class preciousness. Faith had been *murdered*! This woman told things the way she felt them; I hid behind euphemisms.

"My son was shot to death," she added simply. No theatrics, it was just a fact. Straight-speaking.

At that instant I felt as though I had been struck by lightning. I actually looked up into the sky waiting for the thunder to crash.

"That's terrible," I managed.

"It was very terrible, yes. You must miss your wife as I do my son. He was so very small to be taken, my boy. He was two day's short of his eleventh birthday.

"Do you believe in a God? I have to admit I find it hard. But it's worth the struggle. There must be reasons beyond our comprehension."

This logic had always been a stumbling block between me and my maker. Blind faith. The most terrible things happen to the most wonderful people, and we're asked to accept it as part of God's grand design. And why? Because it's not our's to reason why.

"That's why coming here is so important to me. I can feel him here. He died in Long Beach, but that ain't no fit place for eternity. So I scattered his ashes here." She pointed vaguely into the desert, out towards the horizon.

Faith's ashes. Where had Alice and Hal finally chosen to scatter them? I hadn't even bothered to ask. This woman made me feel I'd deserted Faith's memory.

"It's a very spiritual place, don't you think?" she asked without turning her head in my direction. She didn't seem at all concerned with any replies I might give her, preferring to couch her thoughts in rhetorical questions.

"Spiritus. Means the breath of life," she continued dreamily. *And the Lord God formed man of the dust of the ground, and breathed into his nostrils the breath of life; and man became a living soul.*"

I wondered why she'd been crying earlier, she was so much at peace now.

We sat side by side for the best part of two hours watching the sun creep down the sky. She didn't say another word.

Every now and then I'd look from the blood red sun across and up to her face and I'd see it's twin reflections dancing in her eyes.

The air was very still.

"I have to go now," I whispered, breaking the silence. The sun was long since set and we were now two spooky figures sitting in the semi-darkness of a desert moonscape. The wind had mercifully dropped, yet it was now decidedly chilly.

She didn't reply, nor even look in my direction.

"Can I give you a ride back into town? I'd say it's a long walk."

"I'm not through yet, stranger. But I thank you."

I rose. It wasn't easy – every muscle in my body had seized up.

"You're sure about the ride? It's getting mighty cold you know," I asked again. I was worried for her.

"I'm here with my boy. Safe as can be. No one can touch us."

Only the elements, I thought. Hardly mankind. I knew which I would have preferred. Presumably she thought the same as me.

I pulled the driver's door shut rather than slam it. It was so quiet; just the whistle of the desert wind.

I took a last glance at my companion of the past couple of hours. Once again she was no longer discernible as a person, she was a shadowy pile of trash atop a rock.

I could see the boot marks in the sand where I'd trudged back, and a second fainter set leading foward into the desert. They were both size eleven, my size. Try as I might, I could see no others. I put it down to the wind. The wind and the darkness.

By the time I pulled back onto the blacktop and headed back into town it was raven-black outside. The stars above looked so bright I felt I could reach out of the window and pull a handful back into the car.

It was about fifty miles to Santa Clarita, but I didn't feel tired and I wasn't hungry. So why not drive? Who knew, by the time I arrived there I might well be in the mood for some dinner and a bed for the night.

As I drove through Palmdale I passed a road sign. An arrow told me that off to the left five miles or so was a small town called Harold.

Abruptly my peace was shattered, and nightmare images of fierce blue eyes, chubby cheeks, and short fingers grasping handguns filled my mind.

The steak was rare and tender, the beer cold, and the waitress around seventy.

The El Cordobes Steak House was on the edge of Santa Clarita. The swinging neon sign had appealed to me – it reminded me of the 'Bates Motel', so I'd pulled in.

The joint was pretty empty, which is never the sign of gourmet food. But it was late, so I didn't have too much of a choice.

The elderly waitress sat me down at a table close to the check-out, then hovered over me, pencil at the ready, while I checked out the plastic menu card.

I figured she was anxious to close, so I made it easy. I ordered the twelve ounce grain fed porterhouse.

As I waited for my steak to arrive I became vaguely aware of some white noise behind me.

I turned my head to spot the source of it. It was a television, up on a bracket above the cash register. The sound had been turned down to practically nothing.

Not more than five minutes later, the old girl was scurrying back with my steak, the plate held on the flat of her hand at head height with all the finesse of a professional juggler.

How the chef had managed to cook it in the elapsed time was a mystery. Perhaps they had a combination microwave blowtorch in the kitchen's out here in Santa Clarita.

Whatever the reason, the meat was juicy and full of flavour.

As it turned out I was hungrier than I'd imagined, so it wasn't long before I was standing at the checkout. It was then quite by chance that I looked up at the television.

Ellen Wyborg was reading the news on Channel 5. Even this close I still couldn't make out the words. Right then I wasn't too bothered, I was just filling in the time while the cashier totted up my check.

As I watched, the face of Councilman Michael Gardenas filled a square top right of the screen.

I remember being mildly curious at the time as to what he'd been up to this time. How a man could survive in politics so long with so much dirty money in his back pocket was incredible. Somehow he always did.

I wondered if this time someone had fingered his collar successfully. It would be a brave DA – Gardenas was rumored to have the highest connections, at state and federal levels, as well as in Vegas, Miami and New Jersey.

I laid some bills on the saucer and asked the cashier to recommend a motel. She suggested the Mountain View Motor Lodge a couple of blocks down the main street, and one to the left.

She smiled gratefully as she pocketed the tip.

34.

That night I slept like a baby. My desert friend must have been a spiritually calming influence.

First thing the following morning I walked down to the Golden Cup Coffee House on the main drag for a bite to eat.

Over a lazy breakfast I decided it was time to get back to town; time to contribute to the CyberKitchen. I couldn't leave it to Charlie forever.

Mind you, there was precious little to do right now but count how many times our web site was being hit. The CD's wouldn't be in the stores till the end of the week. That's when the rush would begin.

That's what we hoped, anyway.

It was time I showed my face at the 'Kitchen regardless. I was pretty sure none of the gang would have any doubt about my innocence, but morale might be reaching a fairly low ebb. I'd been freaking out now for close to three weeks. Not the kind of man employees appreciated as their CEO.

Most importantly, it was time I called Nate and checked the state of play.

Time to face the music.

At 9.30 am I was pulling out of the Mountain View Motel. I switched on my cellphone. It began to cheep less than five minutes later.

"Jay? This is Nate. Have you seen the news?"

I told him I hadn't read a paper nor watched TV since Sunday. It was now Tuesday morning.

"Michael Gardenas was found shot dead last night – it broke on the late news last night."

The file photo I'd seen on the television at the El Cordobes flashed through my mind.

"What are you saying, Nate? You think it could be Corr? Come on. Really?"

I was quite naturally stunned. Michael Gardenas? Whacked by eleven-year-old Harold Corr? Was the idea at all credible? After all, Gardenas was a political figure with major underworld connections – everyone knew that, though few would have had the balls to say so publicly. But despite my conviction that the boy had killed Faith, the concept of Harold Corr as a major league professional junior contract killer was still somehow farcical.

"He was shot with the same calibre weapon used to kill Faith. A .22."

"A Ruger?"

"The police aren't releasing too much information right now. I rang a buddy of mine who owes me a favour; he's a sergeant in the Beverly Hills PD. His nephew was up on a drugs charge last Christmas. Possession, not dealing. I defended the kid pro bono."

"What did he say? Was it a Ruger?"

"Says they're not sure right now. Could be. The interesting part is this. It was messy."

"Messy? What do you mean, messy. Messy in what way?"

"Whoever it was had to shoot Gardenas four times to kill him. Three in the chest, and one to the head. My source thinks it was someone trying to make it look like a professional hit, but screwed up badly. He figures it was an amateur."

He paused. I let his words sink in.

"See what I'm getting at, Jay?"

"Did you mention the Corr kid's threats to your source?"

"Naturally."

"What was his reaction? Dismissive? Same as Yant's?"

"No. He was interested. He knew if I was taking the kid seriously, then maybe he should too."

"What's that supposed to mean? That Yant took the attitude he did because I'm a bonehead?"

"You're not that insecure, Jay, so hold it right there."

"You reckon he'll liaise with Yant?"

"He's promised to pass it up the chain of command. His captain would be pretty dumb not to take it seriously and exchange info with Yant. He'll need all the help he can get. The press are crawling all over his office.

"I asked my source to keep me up to speed with developments. Gardenas is undergoing an autopsy as we speak. That should tell us a lot."

"When will they be through?"

"Hold it, Jay. I haven't told you the kicker. Guess when they reckon Gardenas bought the bullets?"

"Oh shit," I murmured. "Don't tell me. Saturday?"

"Saturday."

PART THREE

35.

I pulled off the road and parked. Up till that moment I'd been driving on auto pilot.

"Are you still there, Jay?"

I was holding the phone in my lap as I stared through the windscreen into the desert.

"I'm here, Nate."

"Hey, this is good news, not bad," Nate argued in an upbeat kind of way.

"You call the violent mob-style death of Michael Gardenas 'good news'?"

"Jay, I'm just doing my best for you. You know damn well what I mean. You told Goodrich that Corr planned to kill again sometime Saturday. That's what he boasted to you, didn't he? Well, Saturday came and went, and what do you suppose they were saying? *The man's a complete and utter flake.*"

"Well, now they're going to have to reconsider."

"It all depends on the timing, Nate," I cut in. "I drove over to Tampico's apartment on Montana just after 1pm Saturday. By that time the cops were already in place outside. I don't know how long they'd been there."

"Doesn't matter! One thing I haven't told you yet. The commissionaire at the building was shot dead early Saturday. He was found around 9 am. Apparently the cops didn't check out the building, so they didn't find Gardenas till last night.

"Right now they're not about to say the two homicides are definitely linked. Not until the autopsy tells them that the same weapon was used.

"The Tampico apartment wasn't under surveillance till 10.30 earliest. That means Corr and Tampico could have killed the doorman and Gardenas and got back home before the cops arrived.

"The chances that the killings aren't linked is next to nil in my book. It's a done deal the autopsy will find Gardenas died within minutes of the commisionaire."

Anger and frustration welled up inside me. "Shit, Nate. This is stupid. A big time notoriously corrupt city official is gunned down at his home last

Saturday, and we immediately take it for granted it's the handiwork of eleven-year-old Harold Corr? I mean, hell, what's the world coming to?"

"Jay, listen to me. Saturday morning I went in with you to see Gail Goodrich because you'd convinced me the Corr child meant business; that he was dangerous, had access to weapons, and had every intention of carrying through the threat he made to you. Now, when someone is killed – gunned down with the same calibre hand gun that killed Faith – you turn on me and tell me it's fanciful to believe the boy could have done it. So let's get one thing straight right now. Do you believe Harold Corr shot Faith?"

I had no problem there. "Absolutely," I replied.

"And do you think it's conceivable that, given opportunity and means, Corr could, and would, have shot Gardenas?"

"Anyone in Los Angeles could have killed Gardenas. All I'm really saying is we're drawing one hell of a long bow to jump to conclusions this early in the piece."

"He said to watch the news, Saturday. He knew the guy was famous. Gardenas was killed Saturday, but wasn't found till last night. In my book it's not stretching the imagination to consider Corr a first rate suspect."

"Do you know if he's still under surveillance?"

"He'd better be. I called Goodrich soon as word came through about Gardenas.

"She was naturally very defensive. Said there was not the slightest shred of evidence to suggest that Harold Corr was connected in any way with the shooting in Wilshire. She even surprised me by quoting some scary figures about the average body count in this city. I think what she was getting at in a pretty half-assed way was that just because someone bought it last Saturday, doesn't mean the Corr kid did it."

"But the guy wasn't just *anyone*. He was a major political figure. Harold knew the killing would be on the news because he knew the guy was famous."

"Absolutely right! They carried that poor dumb doorman out of the building feet first, and stuck him in the morgue. Nobody gave a rat's ass about him. Didn't rate a mention on the news. That's the big difference!

"Where are you?" Nate said after a brief pause.

"A few miles outside Santa Clarita."

"You planning to come home today?"

"Right now, Nate."

"Well, why don't you drop by the office on your way?"

It was odd. All day Saturday I'd been breathlessly awaiting the news that heralded the death of a human being. That would have proved me right and Yant wrong. Now that Gardenas' bullet-ridden body had been discovered, I didn't feel too proud of myself.

Nate would no doubt argue that the world was a better place without the likes of Gardenas. But one might as well argue that it would be a fine thing if all criminals were struck down by God's wrath in the form of a terrible disease. Did we only grieve when the nice guys died? Maybe.

As I clicked the 'end' button on my cellphone, I turned on the radio.

As a child I'd always been fascinated that in old Hollywood movies the hero invariably switched on the radio and, wouldn't you know it, the news he'd been waiting for came through right that instant.

Incredibly coincidental, huh?

Well, I'm here to tell you it actually happens. Within seconds of flicking the switch I was listening to a news update on Gardenas.

"The Los Angeles Police Department has just released a further statement concerning the execution-style murder of Los Angeles City Councilman Michael Gardenas in his Wilshire apartment Saturday morning..

The report droned on. I tried to keep a part of my mind focussed on it as a multitude of conflicting thoughts fought for the remaining space.

Wilshire. The report didn't state exactly where.

If Harold had been involved, he would have needed Phil and a car. The red Mustang was most probably stolen since there'd been no evidence of it outside the Montana apartment block. That's why they'd used Tampico's mother's yellow Beetle to go play ball.

It seemed likely that he'd spent the Friday night at Phil's place. The alternative would have meant Phil picking him up at Calabasas in Mrs Tampico's car very early Saturday morning.

If Phil had stolen the Mustang, he could just as easily have stolen another car early on Saturday to get to Wilshire.

...Michael Gardenas has been City Councilman for the 11th district since June 1984, and was Chairman of the Budget and Finance Committee, as well as Vice-

Chairman of the Rules and Elections Committee and a member of the Public Safety Committee, three of the Council's most important legislative committees. During the '92 -'93 Budget deliberations...

Who had wanted Gardenas dead? Whoever it was may have used Jack before, knew Jack's public key, and posted the contract using PGP.

...Michael Gardenas was in the spotlight in February when he was obliged to apologise to the Los Angeles' Vietnamese American community for statements made following a recent official visit to Ho Chi Minh City. Photos of Gardenas in a topless bar in Cholon surfaced recently during a police investigation of a burglary...

An even more fundamental question was this. Suppose for the sake of argument that Nate and I were right, and the contract had been placed with Jack. Who did he or she think they were dealing with now that Jack was dead? They'd surely know that by now. Yant had been right about one thing. No way would anyone knowingly do this kind of business with a child.

...Gardenas was a tireless campaigner to stimulate economic growth in his district. He was sixty-four years old...

I couldn't make out the rest of the news item because of the police siren. I glanced first in the rear view mirror. The Highway Patrol. Then at the speedo. It was registering around ninety.

I'd got myself so wound up I hadn't noticed.

A couple of minutes later I'd racked up another ticket.

36.

I called in at the Cyberkitchen on my way home.

The excitement about the Lanyard Bell contract had worn off slightly, and everyone was hard at work on projects other than Sleuthhound.

Nancy was in the galley making coffee. Her face lit up as she saw me, despite the fact she was staring at a man charged with murdering his wife.

"We're all behind you, Jay," she said.

Lissie, Mort and Scuzz were in the main work area busy developing a new wave of programming tools. They all thanked me for the magnums of champagne I'd arranged to be waiting for them at their workstations when they showed for work on Monday.

No one made any reference to my indictment – I don't think they knew quite what to say.

I appreciated their sensitivity.

Charlie was in his molehole at the other end of the office.

"How are you holding, buddy?" he asked, as I entered.

A length of black material covered the single window. The only source of light were four large computer monitors on the melamine desk in front of him.

"This craziness can only be temporary, Charlie. The police will have to see the light soon. No one can be that stupid."

"Sure," Charlie responded, nodding his head as though to convince himself. "Only a matter of time, eh?"

"Nate's got it in hand. He's cool."

"You're still sure Nate's the man, Jay?" Charlie said tentatively, testing the waters.

"Positive. End of story," I replied firmly. I wasn't about to give Nate the bum's rush at this stage of the proceedings.

An hour down the track I was home. The house was hot and smelly. I immediately opened all the windows to allow what passed for the faintest of breezes funnelling down Sunshine to course through the place.

I knew I'd have to move as soon as was practicable. Every room held memories of Faith.

I checked for messages. There was only one. It was from Alice. Her voice sounded frail and uncertain. Hal had suffered a stroke and was in a coma in a hospital in Mesa.

I called her back at once.

The phone rang interminably the other end. I figured if she was at home, rather than at his bedside, it might take her quite a while to reach the phone, so I didn't hang up.

I was proved right; she was breathless when she answered.

I told her the reason I'd taken so long to call back was because I'd been called out of town on business. I hoped with all my heart that word hadn't reached Tempe that I'd been indicted for her daughter's murder – the news at that particular moment might well have finished her off.

She told me that since she'd last called me, Hal had shown signs of breaking out of his coma. He'd blinked a couple of times. He'd actually squeezed her hand when she'd whispered his name into his ear!

I could tell she was optimistic by her cheery tone. She was a gutsy lady.

I asked if there was any way I could help her. She said it was probably best to keep Hal as calm as possible. No visitors. That's what the doctor had ordered. It was without doubt the shock of Faith's death that had brought on the thrombosis – that was her opinion as well as the specialist's.

My heart turned over as I listened to her. Should I keep the news of the indictment from her, or tell her now so that she could do her best to keep the news from Hal?

I decided to hold fire.

"I have to get back to the hospital, Jay. My place is at Hal's side. I'm going to keep him quiet as a doormouse till he's better. Be a long haul, I don't doubt that, but as long as he's resting, he's getting better."

That settled it. No way was I going to feed her another dish of nightmares. Not right now. If someone else told her, that was too bad; there wasn't much I could do about it.

I told her to call me any time, day or night. I'd be there for her.

She thanked me, blew a kiss down the line, which was quite out of keeping with the conservative woman I'd always known, then rang off.

There were two surprise faxes. The first was a very stiff and formal letter from Great Western Provident Assurance; our insurance company. It was dated the Friday prior to my arrest.

It observed in all the proper sanctimonious legalese that since one of the joint policy holders had been the subject of a homicide *by person or persons unknown,* they felt it was *proper to withhold payment of the insured sum* until the authorities had *conducted a full and proper investigation.* In short they weren't about to cough up the moolah till they felt like it.

I had expected no less.

By and large insurance companies at best take as long as is humanly possible to delay proper response to claims. Quite often they merely write to the insured, stating the equivalent of *tough shit, we ain't payin', schmucky, 'cos we think this one smells to heaven.* Then it's up to the claimant to give them the old squeeze. This invariably involves paying an attorney a small fortune.

I threw the fax in the trash can. The starched white shirted men in the claims department at Great Western Provident Assurance would be breathing a good deal easier now that I'd been indicted. Chances were they were a quarter of a million better off.

The second surprise was far more disconcerting in that while I'd fully expected the kiss-off from Great Western, I'd never in a million years foreseen a fax from my brother Raymond informing me he'd heard of Faith's death and was flying over to give me some moral support.

My heart sank; the thought of having to deal with an emotionally unbalanced brother right now was a horror second only to the thought of the Grand Jury hearing.

What did he want? What was he *really* after? I knew him too well to believe he was acting out of fraternal love. It had to be money. When had it ever been different?

Raymond was the smartest man I'd ever met. I firmly believe he could have done anything he cared to set his mind to. He could have made the world a much better place.

Instead, he chose the path of least resistance, turning to the easy life of the con-man. It was the most terrible waste of a fine and agile mind.

He had the charm and looks of Casanova, combined with the guile of Machiavelli. He could pull the wool over the eyes of most of the people nearly all of the time – at least long enough to separate them from their money.

However, after all these years he no longer fooled me.

But how the hell had word of Faith's death reached the south coast of England? Presumably some journalist had caught a whiff of scandal involving an English national, and sent the news off to the United Kingdom.

I hoped Raymond hadn't scraped every last penny together for the air fare just on the off-chance of hitting me for a cash advance.

The more I thought about it, the more it occured to me that it wasn't beyond the realms of possibility that somehow he'd got wind of my deal with Lanyard Bell, and was coming to collect his share of my 'windfall'.

If that were the case, he was out of luck.

I re-read the final paragraph of the short note. *Arriving Wednesday morning. BA 269, 8.55 am. I'll make my own way if you're busy. R.*

My stomach tied itself into the tightest knot.

Raymond always managed to make me feel as though I were the bad guy. He'd swindle me out of my cash, fob me off with dud cheques, plead with me for large sums of money to pay off criminals who'd threatened to break his legs, then have the affrontery to intimate I was a hard man when I ultimately called a halt to the money drain.

He was so damned devious and manipulative. Twenty minutes with Raymond and he'd make you feel bad about having any money in your wallet at all. You'd feel ashamed to own a home and car, enjoy a happy marriage or good health.

I bitterly regretted ever letting him know my address in America. The only reason I'd done so at all was in case something terrible happened to him. He might just need my help. Call me weak, but I couldn't just desert my own brother, even if he'd always neglected me when it suited him.

Now he was descending on me. And at a time like this.

I can honestly say that at this particular moment I would have traded places with any one of the rats that lived under Santa Monica Pier.

37.

Stella showed the detective into the lounge and offered him a seat, but he replied he'd prefer to stand.

She sat on the sofa, her stomach tightening into a ball of steel. First it had been the Santa Monica Police Department detective, now it was a detective from the Los Angeles Police Department.

Detective Quin, Mrs Corr. LAPD, Robbery Homicide. That's what he'd said, holding up a badge as she'd opened the door.

Quin had the happiest face Stella had ever seen. It looked more suited to delivering the news of a big win on the lottery than the loss of a relative.

"I won't take up too much of your time, Mrs Corr," Quin began. It's a routine visit. I have to follow through on some matters that have come to our attention."

"Does this matter concern my late husband?" Stella felt a touch of annoyance. What questions could they possibly have missed the first time? And why this new guy from the LAPD?

"Not exactly, no," Quin replied without a hint of awkwardness. "It concerns your boy, Mrs Corr. I was hoping you'd be able to clear up something for me."

"Hold it right there, detective Quin. Before we go any further, I'd like to say one thing. Harold is a young boy. He's never been in the slightest piece of trouble. He's a hard working, well-behaved child. To say I'm proud of him would be an understatement. If you are here to ask me more questions concerning the death of Mrs Benedict, you'd better leave right now, because I'm going to get real angry."

Quin nodded sympathetically. "No need to worry. This has nothing to do with Mrs Benedict's death. I'd be grateful nevertheless if you could confirm your son was away from home last Friday night. Staying with friends, maybe? I'm talking about Friday the 16th."

"What the hell do you want to know that for? Jesus Christ, don't start all that again."

"Please, Mrs Corr. This is nothing to get upset about. It's a straightforward routine question."

He knew from the stake-out report young Corr and Tampico were at the Montana address from 10.15 am Saturday. But where had the Corr boy spent the previous night.

Stella's eyes were burning with fury. She took a deep breath as she tried to regain control of her emotions.

"Friday, eh? Yes. As a matter of fact I am able to tell you where my son was last Friday. How about you telling me the reason you're asking?"

Quin merely beamed. "As I say, it's just routine. That's all."

"Well, as *I* say, I'll be happy to tell you if you have the good grace to tell me why you're asking?"

Quin kept the smile well glued as he assessed the situation. It was an impasse. This wasn't going to be easy. He could hardly say he was checking the boy's alibi should a finger be pointed in Harold Corr's direction concerning the Gardenas slaying.

"Look, I'm real sorry, Mrs Corr," Quin continued. "but you have to understand it's a confidential matter. Wish I could be more frank. Rest assured, your kid's not in any trouble. I'd be mighty grateful if you could help me out in this."

Stella ground her teeth. The man was a brick wall.

"Okay. I'll answer this one question. Then that's it. You leave us alone."

Quin nodded.

"He was visiting a friend. Okay?" she replied angrily.

Quin pulled a notepad from his inside pocket and cocked a ballpoint pen. "The address, Mrs Corr? If you would be so kind."

"Apartment 5, 2217 Montana, Santa Monica. *Now* tell me why you're asking."

"He spent the night there?" It was always best to ignore difficult questions.

"That's correct. Now I have a question and I'd appreciate an answer. Has Mr Jay Benedict been spreading any more malicious gossip about my son?"

"Mr Benedict? Not that I'm aware of," Quin lied easily.

"Has detective Yant briefed you on Mr Benedict's claims concerning the death of his wife?"

"It was in his report, yes."

"Well, as far as I am aware, Mr Benedict has recently been indicted for the murder of his wife. I had hoped that now you'd leave my boy alone. He's been distressed enough by that crazy man's allegations."

"You're a psychiatrist, Mrs Corr?" Quin asked. He was just plain curious, and it was she who'd brought up the subject of crazy people.

"I'm a psychologist, detective Quin. There's a big difference."

"Is that a fact?"

"That's a fact. The psychiatrist is concerned with the treatment of mental disorders. I study the human mind and its functions, especially those affecting behaviour in a given context."

"I get it. You don't need to be crazy to come see you."

"That's one way of looking at it, I suppose."

"You reckon Mr Benedict's crazy, Mrs Corr?"

"To suggest my son's a murderer, he'd have to be," she shot back. "You don't know this, detective Quin, but you'd better pass this on to your buddy, detective Yant. Jay Benedict had the gall to call me up on Saturday morning. If you can believe it, the man said he wanted to apologize face to face to my son for what he did to him. Said he'd been out of control the day he attacked Harold at my house. That the violence was the result of taking too many barbiturates. So if I hear one mention that that man's been stirring things up again, I'm going to go buy a gun, go right round to Mr Benedict's house and put a bullet in him. Is that plain enough?"

Quin slipped his notepad back into his inside pocket. "I'll pretend I didn't hear that last remark, Mrs Corr. I'm sure you didn't mean it," Quin said, turning towards the door. He knew if he stayed any longer she'd be badgering him again for the reason he was asking about the boy's whereabouts in the first place. She'd go ballistic if she ever found out. Better to get out, fast as possible.

"Your son. He's at the Montana address right now?" he said at the door.

"Detective Quin. Let me make one thing absolutely clear to you. My son is a minor. If you have any intention of speaking to him in the absence of myself and my attorney, I'd think again. Understood?"

"I hear you talking, Mrs Corr," Quin replied. The smile was gone. He'd had enough aggression from this woman. Next stop was Mrs Tampico's place on Montana.

Betty Tampico was a very different kettle of fish to Stella Corr.

Where the Corr woman was confrontational, Mrs Tampico was submissive. Eager to be of help.

"Yes, Harold spent the weekend with us here, detective Quin. Why do you ask? Is he in some kind of trouble?"

Quin's smile was still very much in evidence. "No ma'am, no trouble. It's a routine question, is all."

"I'm glad to hear that, detective."

"Does Mr Tampico live here with you?" There was no reference to a husband on file.

"Marvin passed away five years ago," she replied, casting her eyes down to the floor.

"I'm sorry to hear that." Quin briefly let go the smile for appearances sake.

"To your knowledge, did your son or Harold Corr leave this apartment before midday Saturday 17th?"

"They were home all morning. I went out around midday for a while. The kids were still home when I got back."

"What time was that?" Quin continued, just to confirm the accuracy of the stake-out team's report.

"Five o'clock, or thereabouts."

Quin folded the cover of his notebook. If Mrs Tampico was to be believed, the kids had been home most of the day. If she was lying, she was doing a pretty fine job. He'd been a cop for twelve years – he thought he was a pretty good judge of liars.

As Quin stood to leave, the door opened and two boys entered.

Quin guessed the taller to be Tampico. He stood around five ten. The file had his age down as sixteen.

The shorter had to be the Corr kid. As yet there were no file mug shots on him.

"Sorry, Mom," Phil said politely, "Didn't know you had company."

"This is my son, Phil. And his friend Harold Corr," Mrs Tampico said. "This is detective Quin from the Los Angeles Police Department."

Quin watched both boys take off their baseball caps, holding them by their sides as they looked him squarely in the eye. A good sign. His experience told him that people with something to hide could seldom bring themselves to hold his stare.

Phil held out a hand. "Hi."

"Hi," Quin responded, as he shook Tampico's hand, at the same time nodding a response to Corr.

"Something wrong, mom?" Phil asked.

"No, nothing. Just some routine questions. The detective is just leaving."

"Yeah, time I was gone," Quin said, making for the door. "Thank you for your cooperation, Mrs Tampico. Nice meeting you boys," he added, again giving the kids the beady eye. Neither looked in the least fazed.

"Likewise, detective," Harold said, just as Quin closed the door behind him.

38.

Phil sat hunched over a copy of Hustler magazine, his legs hanging over the edge of his bed. Harold lay on the bunk bed opposite deep in thought, his hands behind his head, the fingers interlaced.

"Shit, would you check out the hooters on this chick," Phil snorted.

Harold paid him no attention. He was thinking hard.

What was this new guy Quin up to? How did he fit in? He was LAPD, while Yant was a Santa Monica cop. Had the ground rules changed? He hoped not. If Yant was out and Quin was in, then he'd wasted a lot of hard work sucking up to the wrong slimeball.

What concerned him more was what Betty Tampico had told them the cop had been sniffing after. What had they been up to Saturday morning?

"What did you tell them, mom?" Phil had asked.

"Told him the truth, of course," Betty had replied. "That you never set foot outside the apartment till after five."

Harold snorted with laughter. Too fucking good! Dumb old butt-faced wombat. Yeah, they'd been in all morning!

"What's that?" Phil said, glancing across to Harold.

"Read your dumb tits mag, numbnuts. I'm thinking," he replied.

"Harry doesn't like the girlies," Phil jeered in a sing-song voice. "Harry doesn't like the gir-lies!"

Harold stopped breathing for a second. He felt a sudden almost uncontrollable urge to pump a full magazine of hollow-point bullets into the big turd lounging across from him.

Concentrate, Harold told himself harshly. Forget the dirtbag, he doesn't matter! *Just work all the angles and you come out smelling sweet. Miss one, and you're knee deep in it.* It was a one liner from the cop show he'd watched the night before. It had appealed to him.

Saturday. The cop had asked Betty about Saturday.

It had to mean that Benedict had been talking again. He'd blabbed to the cops about their meeting in Toy Universe.

After the show he'd put on with that stringy old geek Yant – he'd been certain he had the dumbass detective in his pocket. What with the tears, hiccups and all. Who would have believed they'd take Benedict seriously? That was real surprising.

He felt a good deal better now they'd found Gardenas. It took the heat off him now that the bosses knew for sure their man had been whacked.

Not so good was the stuff they were saying in the papers. 'Messy'. 'Unprofessional'. He was still learning for Christ's sake! Just thinking about the copy in the LA Times made his blood boil.

It was only my third kill! Give me a break, for Christ's sake!

He took a succession of deep breaths to calm himself down.

So, somehow Benedict had persuaded the cops to check out his movements Saturday morning.

Well, they had their answer, didn't they. He'd been right here listening to some Hip Hop. They could check with the cops who'd stalked them in the car Saturday afternoon.

He looked across at Phil who'd shifted onto his side to face the wall so he could slip a hand down the front of his pants without Harold watching him.

Harold dipped a hand into his satchell and pulled out his favorite Swiss Army knife. He then tip-toed across to Phil.

Harold doesn't like the girlies, eh?

As Phil turned a page, Harold grabbed him round the neck with his right arm and pressed the short blade of his knife to Phil's oesophagus. Phil's body went rigid. "Shit, man. What the fuck –"

"You ever say those things to me again and I'll carve my name in your freaking throat. You read me?"

Phil couldn't breathe. He could already feel the trickle of blood where the blade had nicked the surface of his skin.

He nodded assent, careful not to force his throat down on the blade.

Harold pushed Phil down onto the bed and snapped the knife shut. "You're just a big girl," he said as he lay back again on the bunk bed.

Phil pulled his hand from his pants and dabbed at his throat.

Harold's thoughts returned to Benedict.

Birdturd Benedict. He'd never learn, would he. He'd given the dirtbag a chance to pay him the money he owed. Twice in fact. Now he was paying the price. Indicted for murder.

Yet still he hadn't learned his lesson. Still he was making waves. And people were actually listening to the sonofabitch.

He could hardly believe it, but it was true; the cop Quin was actually checking out where they'd been early Saturday morning, presumably because the pathologist had determined that to be the approximate time Gardenas had croaked.

Maybe it was time to fuck with the birdturd's head.

A thrill of excitement ran through Harold's body like an electric charge.

Yeah! Why not? That'd be cool.

Real co-ol.

39.

Raymond looked so profoundly different as he walked through from the customs area that had it not been for that unmistakable look of devilment in his eyes, I would have missed him entirely.

He'd always been slender, the product of two packs of Capstan Full Strength cigarettes a day, and a general disinterest in any form of sustenance other than booze.

His face was gaunt, his eyes hollow, his cheeks sunken. It had to be illness; thin was thin, but the man that stood before me today was, despite a strangely distended tummy, the meerest reed.

I tried not to appear shocked.

"Little brudder! It's great to see you," he said, clasping me to him. I was suddenly aware of every bone in his body.

In spite of everything, all the resentment I'd built up as a defence mechanism over the years, it was wonderful to hold my brother. He was all the family I had left, and I loved him regardless. Blood is blood, I suppose.

He looked me up and down, a giant grin creasing his face. "You look terrific, Jay. You're such a bastard – you never look a day older."

I was utterly tongue-tied. How was I to respond? He looked as close to death as anyone could and still stand. Yet he was merry as a grig.

"Let's get out of here," I said awkwardly, adding "You're staying with me I hope?" It was purely rhetorical, but it was polite to ask.

"If that's okay with you, little brudder?"

I picked his suitcase from the trolley. It was 1950's, tied up with string. "Of course. The car's in the carpark."

Raymond had a theory. It went like this. If you've ever done anything you feel ashamed of, or are guilty of something others will hold against you, erase it at once from your mind – it never happened. If anyone raises the subject, look puzzled, then deny any involvement.

So, as we drove down the 405, he made no mention of our last farewell.

It was an involved story to say the least. In short, he'd asked me to cash a cheque he knew damned well was a forgery. He swore he knew the signatory and that the cheque was good. When it bounced I was really angry. I eventually tracked him down and held the cheque up close to his eyes.

Shit, what bad luck, was all he said. Not his fault, you see. *How was I to know, little brudder? Really sorry.* No offer of recompense.

I left for America the following day ten grand lighter. It was money I desperately needed.

He didn't even bother to see me off.

That was twelve years ago. He was fatter then.

"Heard about Faith from Freddie. Terribly sorry. Can't begin to tell you. You remember Freddie, don't you? Sends his best. Says he knows you'll come out smelling of roses."

I couldn't make out exactly what he'd heard from Freddie – the news Faith had been shot to death, or that I'd been arrested for her murder.

I didn't much care.

I actually remembered Freddie well. An antique dealer down the Campden Passage in London; a nine bob note if ever there was one. I never liked the man. Smarmy to me because I had more money than he did.

"How did Freddie get to hear?"

"Said he saw it on the Net. Some news page somewhere. Called me right away. He couldn't believe it was true."

"Why didn't you phone rather than fax?"

"I did. No reply."

I can never understand the logic of people who lie in such an obvious manner. Everyone I knew, bar Raymond, had an answering machine or a service, so what was to be gained by saying he'd tried to call?

That was it probably – Raymond didn't have one, so it didn't occur to him everyone else did.

On the way home I gave him a warts and all account of the state of play regarding my arrest. He wore his 'worried' face, and did a lot of tut-tutting and shaking of the head.

I was pretty sure he basically didn't give a shit whether I was found guilty or not, providing in the meantime he had a good holiday and refilled his wallet.

I found it all immensely saddening. All my life I'd wanted to be able to love and respect my elder brother. He just made it impossible.

I asked him what he'd been up to since I'd last seen him in '86.

He was as vague as ever. A bit of this, a bit of that. He'd briefly gone into partnership with Freddie. Then he'd got himself into a spot of bother with some unsavoury people down the East End of London and had been forced to leave the country.

It all sounded like an echo.

He'd gone to Hong Kong and spent several years working for a radio station, hosting a breakfast program. That was Raymond all over – one minute an antique dealer, the next an oriental DJ. He could do anything if he set his mind to it.

"And how's business, little brudder. Hope you're sufficiently cashed up to afford the best defense?"

If there was a way to ascertain the balance of my bank account, yet couch the enquiry in such a way as to appear to show a concern for me, he'd find one.

"My attorney's a close friend. No need to worry, he's one of the best," I replied.

He nodded his head, then continued to pump me for information about my business. I parried most of the questions, but he was relentless.

I eventually confided that things were looking pretty good for the future. Getting in the 'future' bit was important because it intimated I wasn't financially very fluid right now.

I asked him obliquely about the state of his health. He was evasive. This was unlike him. On one occasion he'd stung me for several thousand pounds to pay for what proved to be a phantom heart bi-pass operation. Once I'd parted with the cheque, the matter of his 'dicky ticker' was never mentioned again.

So why was he prevaricating now?

I dropped him off at home to unpack while I drove over to Nate's office. I left a few hundred dollars on his nightstand while he was in the shower. With it was a short note telling him the money was a gift to tide him over till he got to a bank.

I needn't have been so sensitive to his feelings, but I've always been a 'do unto others' person at heart.

A girl I'd never before seen was behind reception when I arrived at Nate's. I told her who I was, and she immediately showed me into the 'inner coop'.

Nate introduced me to a well muscled man of around thirty; Dan Stir, the gumshoe Mama Poule had engaged to do some of the legwork associated with my case. I liked the look of him – he had intelligent eyes.

"There's a vagrant who works an area of about eight city blocks along Ventura, from Laurel to Lankershim," Stir began. "She's quite well known by the local store owners, drives a baby carriage with all her stuff in it. They call her the Road Runner 'cos she moves that carriage real fast if she catches sight of a cop. She's scared to death of the law for some reason. You said she was around fifty, liquored up, with crazy eyes – that about right, Mr Benedict?"

I nodded assent.

"Well I'm not saying it couldn't have been someone else, but I'd say it was her. Problem is she's dropped out of sight. No one's seen her for the best part of three weeks. But if she shows her face, I'll know. You can bet on it."

I really didn't feel like betting at all. I needed the security of knowing something was going to be done.

Maybe the disappointment showed on my face, because Nate stepped in at once with some more positive news. Mama Poule had obtained a certified copy of the tape taken from Harold Corr's bedroom – the one that purported to show me planting the bracelet.

They'd had it examined by experts, and after careful scrutiny had concluded that though there were no signs of editing, neither was there one frame that showed the bracelet. It simply was not there.

The technician was more inclined to think I had been reaching for something, rather than laying anything down on the bedroom floor.

He'd promised Nate that that would be his expert testimony at the trial.

"I had someone check computer records for red Mustangs," Nate continued. "Guess what? A late model Mustang was reported stolen from a parking lot on Ninth Street, Friday 16th. The call was logged at 3.30 pm. Turned up same day, in Ocean Park."

I tried to look excited, but what did it prove? Not a lot. It didn't put the kids in the Mustang. Made my story a tad more plausible if you were that way inclined, that was all.

Mama Poule had taken a whole heap of statements. She beamed at me as she lifted a thick folder from Nate's desk to show me the extent of her labours.

The bar kid from the Santa Fe grill remembered me well. Apparently he was going to refuse me a third jug of Margaritas if I'd ordered it, I was so drunk the Thursday night I'd met Jack. The pisser was, he appeared to have little sense of time. His recollection was I'd arrived around three and left about thirty minutes or so later. He was as vague for Friday. He guessed I'd arrived two-ish and left around three-thirty.

The checkout lady wasn't much more accurate. She thought I'd made it into the place a little before three, and left a quarter to four. Both of them testified to the fact I could hardly stand. This made up for their previous memory lapses, since if you believed them, I could hardly have driven a car at speed to Santa Monica in the short space of time available.

I was feeling quite perky about this positive aspect when Dan astutely pointed out that the prosecution would naturally maintain that I'd been trying to fool them by appearing to be drunk when in fact I'd been as sober as a judge.

"So what did I do with the two jugs of Margaritas, then? Answer me that. Pour them down the front of my pants and hope they'd think I'd pissed myself?" I countered.

Nate immediately made a note of my observation – it was a good point.

I asked Nate if he was any further forward with the Corr cleaning lady. He gestured to Dan.

"That's going to be a very hard one, Mr Benedict. I've had an associate outside the Corr place since Monday."

It looked as though Nate was pulling out all the stops in the manpower department. As far as I was concerned he could enlist an army – I didn't care if I spent my last cent bringing the truth to light.

"Only been one visitor," Dan continued. "apart from the neighbour down the road. That was yesterday, 9 am. My associate figures it's the domestic. Can't be sure, because she wasn't carrying the usual cleaning things you'd expect."

"Uses Mrs Corr's things, Maybe?"

"Could be. Anyway, he made a note of the car's registration and followed through. The woman lives in Canoga Park. Name's Mantilla. Single, small bungalow, not much evidence of a lot of cash. I'd say she's your cleaning lady."

"What did she say?"

"I thought it best to check back with Mr Berg before I went in swinging with questions that might put the woman's back up.

"We've two alternatives here, Mr Benedict. We can be straight-up and subpoena her evidence, hoping she'll be cooperative; or we can be sneaky and offer her a few bucks to talk frankly."

"You not suggesting we try to buy her evidence?" I said, shocked. I'd come this far without any intention of underhandedness, I wasn't about to countenance it now. All I was after was the truth. The last thing I wanted was to manufacture any falsehoods."

"Absolutely not, Mr Benedict. Mr Berg will vouch for the fact I play things pretty straight. I didn't express myself well, that's all. From what I've gathered so far, I'd say the Mantilla woman's the kind of simple soul who gets mighty nervous of the judicial process. She'd be the kind to ask the advice of a friend before she told us anything. That friend would most likely be Mrs Corr. I want the cleaning lady to tell us everything – the way it is. If that means initially waving a few bills in her face, I can't see the harm there. I'm not going to tell her what to say."

"Well, as long as I'm paying the bills, I'd appreciate it if no money changed hands prior to her answering your questions."

"It's your call, Mr Benedict," Dan replied reluctantly. It was clear he considered the rules of the game often justified cutting corners in the interests of justice.

"I agree with Jay," Nate chipped in. "I know sometimes a few bills gets things moving without exactly tainting the evidence, but on this occasion I think it might get us into hot water if the woman tells Yant we've sent someone round with a full wallet."

"How about I go see her," Mama Poule offered. "The woman might be more ready to open up to a woman."

"Done," said Nate. "Tomorrow."

I switched my attention to Mama Poule. "What about the staff at Toy Universe? Any luck there?"

"Naturally I had no way of interviewing the customers in the store that particular day, but I did find one girl who saw the both of you. A store detective. Unfortunately she didn't see Harold fall, just heard the racket when he hit the Leggo display, so she didn't see whether you pushed or punched him, or whether he tripped.

"What's really useful is that she says she heard what he said. I didn't have to lead her one bit. She told me the boy called you 'dad'."

She shuffled through the papers in the folder and pulled out the one she was searching for. "*Sorry, dad. My fault. I'm okay. I must have slipped.* That's her recollection."

I tried to think back. That was pretty close. Close enough anyway. How was the boy going to explain calling me dad?

"And that's not all, I asked her if there was anything unusual about the way he spoke. I didn't want to influence her, so when she asked me what I meant, I told her I meant did the boy have any kind of speech impediment. *No*, she said, *he spoke like any other normal American kid.*"

I was delighted. Now he'd also have to exlain why he was acting all Yankee when he normally affected his British accent. Not a big deal in itself, I grant you, but it would all add up to paint a picture of one strange little boy.

Nate leant back in his chair. "Two great points. But we have a big problem. You see, unless we can pin some substantive wrongdoing on Harold that directly impinges on the indictment, no one's ever going to hear about these things because it's going to be next to impossible to introduce them into evidence. No judge will allow us to subpoena a minor to give evidence against his will unless we have the strongest possible cause to suggest such testimony is fundamental to proving your innocence."

As we all pondered that sobering thought, another one struck me. "One thing, Mama Poule. How did the store detective recognise us? You have photos?"

"Sure do, Jay," she replied, picking a postcard size snap from the folder. It was grainy, but not bad. Head and shoulders; probably taken with a telephoto. She glanced across at Dan.

"Thought a head shot would be useful," he said. "Took it first thing Monday, outside the Corr house."

Dan Stir was going up in my estimation by the minute.

The next point on the agenda was the timing.

Dan checked the notes in his book. "I've made a series of runs from The Santa Fe Grill. All on Thusday, same time of day.

"Naturally the times vary, but not much. Luck plays a part. If you put your foot down and don't care too much about being picked up by the cops, the freeway's fastest by far. The 101 to the 405, then the Santa Monica turn-off at 4th. Best I managed was 22 minutes. Worst was 38. Average was 31. Taking

Coldwater or Beverly Glen wouldn't be an option if time was a factor. Just wouldn't be time to get to parking structure 5 by 4 pm."

"The autopsy report gives the estimated time of Faith's death close to 4 pm," Nate continued. "We could reasonably argue fifteen minutes either side. But so could they. Essentially that means you could have made it to Santa Monica from the restaurant."

I was about to interrupt his flow when Nate held up a hand. "Hold it one second. Right now, I don't see this proceeding to trial. A Grand Jury just won't wear it, because although it's conceivable that you drank two jugs then drove like shit across to Santa Monica, shot Faith and drove home again, it's stretching the bounds of credibility. Even with the discovery of the Ruger, the DA didn't proceed. It was the bracelet that tipped the scales, and I plan to attack each of the three items separately. Inividually they stink."

"Do we know any more about Gardenas?" I asked.

"Yes we do. And that's kind of interesting. The gunman shot and killed the commissionaire of the building on his way up, but there were no signs of forced entry upstairs in the Gardenas apartment. Looks like the councilman opened the door himself. The only other alternative is that the killer had a key, and apparently there was only one – Gardenas had that. The police are working on the assumption that Gardenas knew whoever it was, and felt safe enough about letting him in."

"I thought you told me the cops were calling it a mob-style hit? Why would Gardenas let him in?"

Nate and Dan both smiled. "Easy, Jay. Councilman Michael Gardenas has been on a best pals basis with the top people in organized crime in this city for ten years. He'd be familiar with a lot of their wiseguys. The cops think he maybe thought someone was making a delivery, so he opened the door."

"Their line of thinking is that he wouldn't have opened the door to a stranger?" I asked.

"Right."

"Let's just think this through, Nate. Normally, the commissionaire would buzz Gardenas that there was someone in the foyer. Right?"

"If whoever it was was unfamiliar to the doorman, yes. That's his job, to check people out. Someone he knew, he'd just send them on up."

"Surely that's why the killer is forced to take him out. He doesn't *want* him to buzz Gardenas. He knows that Gardenas won't let him in."

"But he *did* let him in, Jay," Nate insisted.

"Listen to me for a second, Nate. Who else would you open the door of your house to – apart from a friend?"

"You mean a child, don't you?"

"Sure, I mean a child. If Harold hadn't shot the doorman, the man would have buzzed Gardenas, telling him there was a kid downstairs looking for him. Naturally, Gardenas would have told the doorman to get rid of him. But if he could get up to the apartment and knock on the apartment door, quite possibly Gardenas would have opened up just out of curiosity to find out what the boy wanted. You wouldn't give it a second thought, would you? Well dressed angel-faced child?"

"I guess not."

"Have you been able to access the autopsy findings?" I asked. I knew Nate would be thinking along similar lines to me. Would the medical examiner have found anything to suggest the killer was much shorter than Gardenas?

"Only through my source at the BHPD," Nate replied. "What I was interested in was the determination of the angles of entry. Whether the wounds were front to back, above, downward, right to left etc.

"Harold stands around four-eight. If he shot someone in the chest who was significantly taller than him, the bullet would travel on an upward path – unless he held the gun high with both hands and angled the muzzle down. Faith was five six, so he wouldn't have had to reach up that much. But Gardenas was four inches taller."

"What were the findings?"

"Pretty interesting. The doorman was shot in the back of the neck. Here the medical examiner concluded the slug travelled from back to front, upward. Significantly upward."

"What about Gardenas?"

"Gets even better. There were three shots to the chest. All fired at skin touch range. Pressing the gun to the victim makes it easier to control the barrel held up high at head height. However, the entry point of one shot was low, below the heart. This bullet hit a rib and was deflected upward. The entry point of the two other chest wounds were higher. All three missed the heart. It was the shot to the temple that killed him.

"But get this, the report states clearly that there was significant evidence of contusions to the back of Gardenas' head. He took a series of blows; blows administered before death. The conclusion is that there were two people present at the crime scene. Otherwise how could he be shot from in front, yet clubbed from behind?"

"Phil Tampico?"

"Could be. There's evidence that Gardenas thrashed around quite a bit before he took the head shot that killed him. That's why they said it was 'messy.' If the Corr kid had screwed up the first shot – the one that was supposed to bring the man down – then he'd be really vulnerable. That's where having his buddy around would pay dividends."

"Have you had a chance to meet with your source at the BHPD to share your thoughts?"

"He knows my line of thinking, but it's the same old story so far. No one up the chain of command is taking the 'killer kids' theory too seriously yet.

"My guy's not saying it's out of the question, he's just saying his Captain doesn't think much of the theory. Anyway, the word is Parker Center has given the authority for Robbery–Homicide to take over the case because of Gardenas' profile."

"Have they made a determination of the height of the assailant? That'd be a huge step foward."

"Shorter than Gardenas, that's all. It's impossible for them to be more accurate because they can't tell for sure Gardenas was standing straight up when he took the first shot, and they don't know which of the three chest wounds came first."

"What about the time of death?"

"Well, even though they're dead certain whoever killed the doorman went right on up and shot Gardenas, the medical examiner still has to make an estimation of the time of death on Gardenas, and his body wasn't discovered till 9 pm Monday. Even so, the autopsy states the ETD to be around 8 to 9 am Saturday."

"What time was the doorman found?"

"One of the residents found him 9.05 am. The cops were around there five minutes later. Autopsy states he died between 8.30 and 8.45."

"What staggers me is that having found the commissionaire lying in a pool of blood Saturday morning around 9, they wouldn't have checked out every apartment in the building."

"They checked as many as they could – that is, the ones that were occupied at the time. Gardenas' was locked. No signs of forced entry."

I bet the Beverly Hills Police Department had felt pretty embarrassed around 9 pm Monday night.

"Why don't you leave us to it, Jay," Nate observed with a smile. "That's what you're paying us for."

That much was true, and judging by the recent increase in manpower it was plenty. Problem was I'd never been hot on delegation. I found it damned hard to sit back and let other people make decisions on my behalf, especially since right now my life might well depend on these decisions.

For instance, I wanted to make certain someone from the LAPD went right over to the Tampico apartment and asked Phil's mother where the hell her son was around 8.30 am Saturday.

I'm sure Nate understood why I didn't want to go home and twiddle my thumbs. Every morning since Faith's death I had to convince myself there was a reason to get out of bed. Right now there was nothing to do at the 'Kitchen except watch the royalties roll in.

And now there was Raymond.

Jesus Christ! What a life. Even Job would have thought twice about swinging his legs out of bed in the morning.

40.

Harold lay in the darkness of his bedroom, his cheeks wet with tears. He could just make out the voices below on the verandah. It was that man again. Vince Grogan. He was always hanging around the place now, always in his face trying to be pally so he could be with mom. Harold knew Grogan meant nothing special to his mother. As far as she was concerned, he was just a friend. Problem was Grogan most likely thought he could wear her down; the scumbag was so persistent.

The sound of his mother laughing drifted upwards and into his bedroom window, and Harold's blood ran cold.

The way he looked at mom. Like he was taking her clothes off. Couldn't she see it in Grogan's eyes? Didn't it make her want to puke?

Nothing would ever be the same now dad was dead. Dad was the earth and sky. Without him nothing had much meaning any more.

He'd worked his butt off at school for dad. To see that look of pride on his father's face when he saw the grades was the best thing ever. *Straight A's again you little wonder! You've maybe got your mother's brains, but sure as hell you've got my spirit!* That's what he'd said. Then they'd gone to the park for some catching practice.

He grabbed a loose end of the sheet and brushed away the tears. He was suddenly angry. Crying was for kids.

He'd never seen dad cry. Mom cried all the time. Couldn't get through a day now without bawling her head off.

So what was she doing pallying around with that shit Grogan? Jesus, dad was only three weeks in the ground.

There were no tears when Grogan was around. Oh no. Not with cheesy Grogan sucking up to her, pawing her, trying to get close. Why couldn't he piss off and leave them alone? He had no place here.

There'd always been just dad and him. And mom. Now there was mom and Grogan. And him on the outside.

He could feel the tears welling up inside him so he sat up at once and began punching the pillows hard. He'd love to push the Ruger deep into Grogan's mouth and watch the turd's eyes just before he popped him. Man, that'd be the best thing ever!

He knew that was out of the question. The cops weren't complete dummies. Kill a family member or a friend and chances were the cops would get you. Kill a stranger and you never get caught – well hardly ever. He'd read recently on the Net that the clean up rate for random killings was not more than fifteen per cent.

From the verandah beneath he could hear Grogan laugh loudly. A second later Stella joined in.

Screw her! If she'd rather spend time with that dirtbag, then he was better off on his own. He didn't need her. She'd have to get by without his shoulder to bawl on.

He didn't need a living soul. If the older guys at school thought he was a young smartass, that was too bad for them. If they didn't want to be friends, who was missing out? It wasn't him – that was for sure! Shit, who needed friends, for Christ's sake! A slave like Phil was more to the point – some bastard who did what he was told. Maybe some day he'd marry a woman just like that.

He felt a sudden pang of uncertainty. He was totally alone now. He knew that. Dad was gone and mom had her new buddy. But hell, that was not such a bad thing. He'd always been a loner. Just like dad. Well, now he'd make dad real proud. He knew that some place Jack was watching over him, guiding his thoughts, pulling the trigger with him.

The thought of triggers pulled his thoughts sharply back to Jay Benedict. It was Benedict who was responsible for the cops down the road dogging his steps.

Anger swept through him like a forest fire. He hated Benedict with a vengeance. Everything had been just fine, then Benedict had come along. He wanted to hurt him badly. But how? The muscles in his jaw tensed as his mind buzzed with possible options.

A car started up down the road and he abruptly sat bolt upright in bed. Had the cops finally called it a day?

He swung his legs out of the bed and ran to the curtains, pulling back a corner to peek outside.

The road was empty. The Chevy was gone.

Harold punched the air with his fist in triumph.

Victory, man!

He walked across to the trestle table and switched on his computer. A couple of minutes later he was watching the teaser on the Cyberkitchen web site.

Sleuthhound. Available Friday. Heralding a new genre of multipath movies. An experience, not a game. You call the shots. You don't like the way the movie's going? Change it! Sleuthhound. The outcome's different every time.

He watched the trailer. It wasn't the first time he'd viewed the five minute freebie. He'd hit the site every day since it had appeared for the first time Monday morning.

Sleuthhound. Birdturd's new baby.

The graphics looked interesting. Good characters. But the game stank. Who gave a shit that you could change the end? He prefered the old fashioned games. He liked his finger on the trigger, scoring points.

'Course he fingered a very different trigger nowadays.

He chuckled softly to himself.

The teaser finished and a box prompted him – did he want a repeat? He didn't. He shut down.

Back in bed he closed his eyes and considered his options. The cops weren't watching any more. That gave him room to move again.

Perhaps he should play his own game with Birdturd. But how exactly would he go about it?

As if from the spirit world, the answer began to grow and bloom in his mind like bacillus on a petrie dish.

It was as if his dad was feeding his imagination with killer ideas.

His whole body tingled with excitement. It would be the ultimate mind-screw!

The more he thought about the concept, the more he liked it. It was so simple. It was ex-cellente! Soon Birdturd Benedict wouldn't know up from down.

Harold snuggled down under the covers and began to hum softly. It suddenly felt like Christmas.

You'd better watch out, you'd better not cry...

He felt better already. His cheeks were dry as a bone.

41.

As I drove back from Nate's office I did my best to clear my head of thoughts of death. It wasn't easy.

As I approached Veteran I saw two patrol cars either side of a Mercedes. Standing in the centre lane was an EMS ambulance, the doors closed. A uniformed officer was waving us through. The traffic was moving sluggishly because no one could resist the ghoulish temptation to look into the Merc.

I'm ashamed to say I was no different.

The car was empty, yet the driver's seat at head height was awash with blood. I could clearly see three bullet holes in the driver's side window.

The ambulance personnel were standing around, their arms folded, talking to the cops. Whoever had been driving was no doubt in the back of the ambulance, dead as mutton. No one was hurrying. Must have been a drive-by.

As I picked up speed on the 405 heading north, my eyes filled with tears of frustration. What an incredible waste of human life. Ten minutes ago the guy was driving home, most likely to a wife and kids. Now he was a statistic; randomly gunned down in the middle of the day. He was dead, his family scarred for life.

I felt besieged, completely powerless to do anything about it. Life had never seemed this way ten years ago. Quite possibly I was just joining the ranks of the old fools who liked to crow *in my day, son, you could walk the street at night.*

And what kind of a show was I putting up against Harold Corr? I was allowing a small kid to trample my emotions. He'd shot Faith to death and was laughing at the authorities.

In the United Kindom kids got away with murder. Literally. Merely because of their age. The fact that they knew very clearly what they were doing when they stabbed or clubbed their friends, brothers and sisters to death wasn't considered relevant. If Harold had shot Faith in London, social workers would most likely have obliged Harold to undergo a few months psychiatric evaluation, while at the same time giving the poor lad a good deal of 'counselling'. After all, society had to look after it's walking wounded – not get out the big stick. It was no longer the bad old days of 'lock 'em up and throw away the key'. Society knew better, didn't it.

If anything my politics are dead center. Not too conservative, not too radical. I don't believe in the death penalty, I'm pro-choice, and I oppose any form of censorship. Individual freedom is everything – screw the greater good of an ordered society.

Up till a few weeks ago, I'd always seen the police as on my side. I paid for them via my taxes to protect me from the bad guys.

Suddenly I'd crossed an invisible line and the cops were protecting the bad guys from *me*! I wasn't guilty of the smallest wrongdoing, yet if I didn't drop everything at once and put everything I owned into the melting pot to pay for my defense, there was every chance the good guys would put me to death in error.

But that wasn't the worst part. Every minute of every day I was reminded that Harold Corr was out there. He'd murdered Faith and was sniggering at the remembrance of his crime, yet there was absolutely nothing I could do about it simply because he was a child, and no one would believe he was capable of such premeditated barbarity.

Besides, even if Judge Mason Earnshaw hadn't ordered an exclusion zone around the Corr household, what the hell was I going to do? Beat the hell out of the kid? Torture a confession from him? Exact an eye for an eye?

I've never thought that violence solves anything. I've never deliberately started a fight. Finished a few maybe, but never started one.

So, as far as killing another human being is concerned? Forget it. The only circumstance where I could envisage taking a life would be to protect innocent people. If I saw a crazed gunman about to let fly in a shopping mall with an Uzi sub-machine gun, I'd shoot first if I had the opportunity.

But I couldn't kill in cold-blooded revenge, and that's why I don't believe in the electric chair, lethal injection, the guillotine, hanging – you name it.

Nevertheless, I was certain of one thing. No way was that evil child going to walk free. Somehow I'd bring him to book. It was a promise I made myself.

Raymond was doing laps of the pool when I arrived home. He looked like a pregnant grasshopper struggling across a lily pond. It was a very weird sight; his limbs thin as twigs, his stomach one fat Christmas pudding.

He waved cheerily, as he pulled himself out of the water.

"Bloody gorgeous day! Water's hot as horse piss. You guy's have got it made out here in La La Land."

He stank of Scotch. There was no glass in evidence, but I'd have wagered a large sum of money the Johnnie Walker bottle had taken a pasting during the morning while I was at Nate's. Raymond was one of those people who could drink himself to a standstill, yet never stagger around, nor slur his speech.

From his shorts pocket, he pulled out the roll of cash I'd left him earlier. The notes were sodden. "Thanks for leaving the cash, little brudder. Shouldn't have, though. For once I've got plenty." He looked down at the sopping wad and laughed. "Bit bloody wet, I'm afraid. Forgot it was in there. Here," he said, preparing to throw it in my direction.

For the first time in many years I played it smart. All our lives he'd played this silly game of offering money back to me, hoping I'd turn him down. *Oh no, that's far too much.* Please take it. *No, I couldn't.* Go on. *Okay, if you insist.* I do.

"Thanks," I said, "It was really just to tide you over till you got to a bank. Didn't mean to hurt your feelings."

To my surprise, he didn't appear at all bothered that I'd pocketed the money.

"I fixed up the house a bit while you were out," he said as we walked inside out of the heat. "Made us some sandwiches too. Knew you'd have your mind on more important things."

The house was cleaner than I'd ever seen it. Raymond must have slaved his skinny butt off. I felt really bad about my previous dark thoughts concerning the Scotch, not to mention my lack of charity concerning the money. He'd caught me on the emotional hop again. Two minutes down the line and already I felt I owed him one.

I reached for the door handle of the fridge then remembered I'd forgotten to stock it with beers and wine. I swore.

"What's up?" Raymond asked, his face wreathed with concern.

"Oh, it's nothing. Provided you don't mind wine with ice in it."

He grinned. "Forget it. I stocked up for you. Isn't all bad having a brother to stay once in a while, eh?"

He pulled out a tray of beautifully cut sandwiches complete with an artistically prepared Cobb salad. Everything looked mouth-wateringly good.

Game, set and match in the guilt stakes.

That afternoon I took Raymond to Ojai. I wanted to show him somewhere a trifle more lyrical than Silicon Valley.

Raymond made me promise to take the afternoon off from all my worries. Said I had a haunted look. That was fine by me. I agreed.

For some reason I couldn't quite fathom, I felt really close to Raymond that day. Like we were very small children again. All his usual shit and pretence were absent. We laughed as we walked round the town remembering old times.

It was a truly great day. For six hours I didn't feel alone any more. I had my big brother back again and it was fine!

We drove back to town around eight, and I took Raymond to dinner at Orso – movie star hunting.

Spotting a movie celebrity in a restaurant in Hollywood is to the Englishman what clapping eyes on a member of the royal family at an upstairs window at Buckingham Palace is to the American.

He pulled my shirt cuff. "Hey, isn't that George Hamilton? Freddie said he once sold him a pair of candlesticks in the Silver Vaults."

It wasn't, but the likeness was so good I confirmed the sighting; as one would a downed aircraft at the Battle of Britain.

Raymond ate so sparingly during dinner my concern for his health grew by the second. He'd always downed strong liquor as if mum had spent her entire pregnancy with him in the desert. So when he turned down an Armagnac, his favourite after-dinner tipple, I pressed him again.

"Just mending my ways. Got to consider the liver some time in your life. Mind you, still can't resist the odd Scotch now and then," he told me.

I could see he was lying. Whatever the matter was, he didn't want to tell me right now. I respected that.

"Look over there," I whispered, "It's Molly Ringwald." I pointed to a young girl who bore a remarkable resemblance to the real thing.

He scanned the room excitedly, "Is it? Where?" He then swung back to me. "Molly who?"

Back home there was a message from Alice. Hal was much improved. He was actually talking a bit now; very breathy, but she could make out most of the words. It still wasn't time for visitors.

I was making some chocolate in the kitchen around 1 am when Raymond re-emerged from the guest suite.

"Where do you keep the aspirin, little brudder. Sought, but could not find, so I shall ask, for I know it will be given, " he said smiling.

I reached inside one of the cupboards and handed him the bottle.

"Thanks for a truly wondrous day," he said.

"Yes, it was great, wasn't it," I replied.

"But really, we had some fun, didn't we?"

"We sure did. Now get to bed, you look buggered."

"I feel it," he said pocketing the aspirin.

I took my chocolate to bed with me.

Quite often Faith and I drank our nightcaps as we watched the late night talk shows. She always had the clicker. It felt all wrong to have it my side of the bed. Such an insignificant detail, yet one that brought a sudden stab of pain.

42.

For most of my adult life I've been plagued by nightmares.With the exception of that one glorious night in the desert, I can well remember the last night I slept the sleep of the innocent as a child.

It was Christmas night on my fifth birthday. I remember so well the feeling of wonderful exhaustion as my mother lay me down to sleep, and how incredibly refreshed I felt the following morning.

From that day on the dreams came.

When I was little it was tigers running after me through the night. Then in my youth came dreams of loss and rejection.

The day I met Faith the dreams stopped.

Even when she walked out on me, the boogiemen didn't come back to haunt me.

Not till I met Harold Corr.

The night I took Raymond to Orso I was again haunted by images of Harold. He was a stick figure dressed in green, dancing on my grave, his eyes bright torches of white light. *I did!*, he was shouting trimphantly.

My guardian spirits were calling me to action. *Don't let the world happen to you, Jay. Go change it!*

They were right. But what more could I do that Nate and I hadn't already put into action?

Then a thought occured to me. What would I do if I were Harold?

I'd killed three times and I'd got away scot-free. Even though the murdered woman's husband was pointing fingers at me, no one believed him. Better still, thanks to planting the gun and the discovery of the bracelet, the cops now thought *he'd* killed his wife. The slaying of Michael Gardenas had gone reasonably well. So what would I do now?

If the kid was smart, and everyone kept telling me he was in some gifted program, he'd lie low and do nothing. At least for a while.

If he was *really* smart he'd keep the lowest of all profiles until I was indicted by the Grand Jury.

A guilty verdict of my peers, and that would be case closed on Faith Benedict.

I was worried. His lying low would be the worst possible scenario for me. And as yet I had absolutely no evidence to back up what everyone considered were wild allegations. It was imperative I stir up the little brat. I had to make him put his size five foot in his mouth. I certainly didn't want to pressure him to kill again, merely to goad him to boast about his crimes.

But how could I draw him out?

I had to remember I'd be seeing things from the perspective of an eleven-year-old. If I read him right, it was his ego I had to target.

Raymond was keen to see the Cyberkitchen, so I took him to the office with me next morning.

I'm pretty sure the word 'cyber' conjured up some kind of futuristic workshop – something akin to the inside of a space shuttle. I knew he'd be disappointed with the reality, but he insisted on coming.

Raymond and I are about as alike as Jeff Bridges and Woody Allen. When I introduced him around, the expressions of muted surprise were the usual ones.

I could see he'd had a very different vision of the office, but he feigned interest in the gobbledegook on the screens as Lissie enthused in her usual high octane fashion about a new progamming tool.

Charlie told me the initial interest in Sleuthhound had been so intense – over fifteen thousand hits since Monday – that the publishers of the CD were already considering a bigger release.

Tomorrow was D-day, and orders were really strong. Not just in California and the major cities, but America-wide.

All this talk of Sleuthhound whetted Raymond's appetite.

"Can I have a go?" he asked.

"You still don't get it, do you Ray," Charlie said, putting an arm round Raymond's bony shoulders. "You *watch* it, you don't *have a go* at all. It's not a game, you see. You don't win points."

"Whatever. Let me see it, eh?"

I explained in the simplest of terms the basic concept.

The richest man in the Cosmos, Althar Robustus, has invited five of his closest friends to join him on a cruise through space from earth to Trillium, a dark star in the Groton solar system.

To his horror, one of the guests, the beautiful Lastra Garbo, is found dead in her bed. Althar knows only the four remaining guests had access to Lastra's boudoir. Who is the culprit? Could it be Lane Freeway, a cruel underworld figure from the planet Vegas? Trent Truman, Planet Earth's representative on the Cosmic Council? Maybe screen siren Velma Vain, triple winner of the virtual acting award – the Charade. Or could it be Sol Shyster, con-man extraordinaire.

Panicked, Althar calls in the most celebrated gumshoe of the twenty-second century – Sleuthhound; a bloodhound with a steel trap brain, and a nose for the truth.

Pretty silly stuff, I'd be the first to admit, but it was the kind of fun formula that the video consumer found amusing, so who was I to buck the system?

"And how can I change things around?" Raymond asked as we sat him down by a monitor.

"It's a bit like watching a video, except you're part of it," Scuzz said by way of explanation.

Raymond looked puzzled. "I don't follow."

"Well, suppose you're watching the movie of Julius Caesar," Scuzz continued.

"Right."

"Well, just suppose you had your finger on the clicker and *you* could persuade Caesar to beware the ides of March rather more forcibly than Calphurnia. There'd be no death in the capital would there?"

"I suppose not. Wouldn't be much of a play either," Raymond added with a sly grin.

"Scuzz' point," I interrupted, "is that you can change the course of events just by clicking on the mouse every few minutes at the plot points."

"How'll I know when to do it?"

"It'll be obvious. Sleuthhound asks himself questions. Will I do this, or do that? That kind of thing.

"You then influence his decision by clicking on him to go gangbusters and try to coerce a confession from a suspect, or pursue a more circumspect route to uncovering the villain."

Raymond still looked flummoxed. I suggested he go ahead and play the movie. I knew he'd catch on quickly.

Within five minutes he was laughing aloud and clicking away. I couldn't help noticing he was forever urging Sleuthhound to put the boot in.

We all had our work to do, so we left him to enjoy himself.

Just after 11 am Raymond came into my office.

"Great stuff. Loved every minute of it. Trent T was the guilty party first time up. Second play it was Sol Shyster. Ve-ry devious character, that Sol Shyster. Not based on me by any chance?" he asked, giving me the evil eye.

"'Course not," I lied, trying to look as convincing as possible. The fact was I had modelled Shyster mercilessly on Raymond. From his physical attributes – the long limbs and coarse wavy hair – to his terribly English turns of phrase.

Raymond winked at me. "Look, don't worry, little brudder. I take it as a compliment. The man's a con man of extreme distinction and wondrous quality. By the way, the bloodhound's a seriously cute piece of animation. Who's work was that?"

"Mort's," I replied.

This genre of animated game or movie usually stood or fell by the quality of the animation. It was damned good. Mort had really hit the spot.

Raymond joined me for a black coffee, then scooted off in my car, leaving me to get on with my work. He was going to take in Universal City. That's what he said anyway; a couple of hours hard work in the bar would have been more likely.

Around one o'clock I heard Charlie call my name down the corridor. There was a sense of urgency in his tone, so I dropped what I was up to and walked down to his office.

"Too late. It's gone," he said, staring at one of the monitors.

"What's gone?" I asked.

"Same thing as before. Except it was closer this time."

I was confused. "What are you talking about?"

"Someone's been hacking into our system somewhere. About an hour ago here I am working on Cyberstar and up comes a photo. Just for a couple of seconds. Then it's gone. I didn't mention it at the time to anyone. I thought maybe Scuzz or Mort were pulling a fast one on me. Then just now it pops up again. Same picture, only closer."

"A picture of what?"

"The first one, the wide shot, was a pretty ordinary shot of some suburban street somewhere. People walking around. Leafy shot. Nothing special. This last one was the same picture, just closer. As if the photographer was zeroing in on someone. Looked like a pretty girl."

"How old?"

"Hell, I don't know. Twenty, twenty-five? It was only there for a second or two. Full length shot. Took me by surprise. That's when I called you."

"Have you run a check on the system?" I asked. I was suddenly nervous that someone was considering scrambling our network.

"Yes, I ran Vigilante right away. Everything's cool," he replied. 'Vigilante' was his own invention. Any extra-network tampering with files was highlighted in orange automatically as a matter of course.

"Do you think it might be accidental? Is that possible?"

"I'd say it's highly unlikely. Someone's jerking us around. Having a bit of fun at our expense. Probably something to do with Sleuthhound. Like it'll all end up being some stupid note of congratulations."

At that moment Mort arrived at the door. Close behind were Lissie and Scuzz. "What was that all about?" Mort said.

"The photo?"

"That's right."

They'd all seen it. Only Lissie could give a more accurate description. The girl reminded her of Lastra, the corpse in Sleuthhound.

The moment she mentioned it they all agreed with her; with the exception of Mort – Lastra's creator. He begged to differ. Lastra was drop dead gorgeous, he said, while the girl in the photograph was merely pretty; though she did have the same jet black hair and reasonably similar features.

"Think we should introduce added security into the system?" Charlie asked.

"If whoever's doing this is as good as we think, changing a password's not going to phase him much. Besides, if we make it impossible for him to re-enter our system we shut out the possibility of tracking him down in the future, if we need to. If he's done any damage, we'd be sensible to try to ID whoever it is. Maybe it's better to restrict his access to sensitive stuff without him knowing, yet allow him to use the machine."

Mort, Lissie and Scuzz drifted back to their workstations.

I was two steps down the corridor to my office when the shout went up from all the offices. It was the photo. It was back on all the screens.

I raced through to Charlie's office. I caught a subliminal glance – then almost instantly it was gone.

A head shot.
Mort was dead wrong. She *was* beautiful.

43.

I often wonder whether in the real world witnesses are as accurate as they are in the movies.

On the tube I can watch detective Andy Sipowitz grill some waitress about a customer she had in her place three weeks ago last Friday, and the dizzy girl instantly recalls the guy down to the tattoo on his wrist.

By contrast I couldn't tell you the name of the management executive Charlie and I dealt with at Lanyard Bell, let alone tell you what she'd looked like.

Mind you, if she'd had the charm and charisma of Katherine Hepburn it might have been a very different matter. Ditto if she'd been a colorful eccentric and had behaved really badly when we'd met. It's all the in-between people who are so instantly forgettable.

The following morning I speed-read the guts of the LA Times over breakfast, and consequently missed the photo connection entirely.

Of course you have to bear in mind I'd only caught a subliminal flash of the photograph in Charlie's office before it disappeared from the screen. The others had seen it for a good five seconds.

I was halfway down Sunshine when my cellphone rang. I thought it might be Raymond.

He'd been up most of the night in the living room, hitting the Jose Cuervo and watching an all-night Russ Meyer moviefest.

Before leaving for the office I snuck into the guest room to see what he had planned for the day, only to find his bed hadn't been slept in. I didn't worry overly; Raymond had often been prone to taking off at a moment's notice. He was well able to look after himself. He was, after all, my big brother.

Instead the call was from Charlie.

"Jay? Have you seen the LA Times?"

He sounded really agitated.

"Yes I have. Whatever it is, I missed it. Something in the computer section?"

"It's nothing to do with the company. It's the photograph we saw – the one on the screen yesterday. You remember?"

"Of course I remember. What's the panic?"

"She was found dead last night. On Ocean Avenue down by Inspiration Point."

I pulled over to the side of the street and took a few big breaths. Death was becoming a staple of my day to day life. I was becoming a veritable Jonah.

"Hold it a second, Charlie. You're sure it's the same girl? Absolutely sure?"

"Hundred per cent. And it's not just me, Jay. It's all of us. We're all sure. Mort, Lissie, Scuzz. We're all here in my office right now. There's no mistake."

"Give me a second," I said, as I reached across to grab the copy of the Times that lay on the seat beside me.

Charlie read my thoughts. "It's on page fifteen. See for yourself," he said.

The photograph looked like a college yearbook snap. Frankly I was hard pressed to put the snap on page thirteen together with the flash on the screen I'd seen the day before. I told Charlie exactly that.

"Well, it doesn't really matter, Jay. You only saw it for a second. We're all certain. Anyway, I called the police and told the duty officer. They're sending some detectives to see us this morning to check it out."

My heart sank. The SMPD. I wondered what the chances were that Yant would miss the opportunity to flash his badge once again in my face. Would he associate the company address with me? I really hoped not.

There was always the chance they'd send someone else. Surely there were plenty of guys to choose from in the squad room.

I was clutching at straws.

"Hope I haven't screwed things up for you. I know the last thing you need right now is a visit from the Santa Monica detectives. We couldn't just let it ride, though, could we? A young girl's dead."

"Of course not," I replied. "If it's the same girl, then the photo was placed there for a reason. We gotta do what we gotta do. Simple as that."

I told him I'd be with him in around fifteen minutes.

On the way over to the office a thought that had been buzzing round my brain for the past few days continued to nag me. It concerned the gun used to kill Gardenas.

If Phil Tampico had driven Harold over to Wilshire that Saturday morning, and the pair had then immediately raced back home to the sanctuary of the Montana apartment, then they'd have had to take it home with them or dump the murder weapon somewhere on the way, in which case it was most probably in some homeboy's pocket right now.

Exactly how many weapons had Jack possessed when he'd died?

Harold had already planted one of them in my garden. If Harold saw himself running short of weapons, he'd think very seriously about getting rid of one of the most convenient guns. After all, the Ruger Mark II was light and thereby suited his physical needs admirably.

If he'd decided to keep the murder weapon, the best way to conceal the gun would be to disassemble it, then hide the components separately somewhere in the Tampico apartment.

Once he'd seen the cops staking out the apartment building, he'd know there was no way he could take the Ruger home with him to Calabasas, just in case the police gave him the once over on the way or on his arrival home. They'd searched once, he couldn't be sure they wouldn't again.

If I was right and Harold had determined to hang on to the Ruger he'd used to kill Gardenas, then it was logical to assume the gun was still hidden somewhere in the Tampico apartment. He'd never risk carrying it outside until the police called off their surveillance.

I immediately called Nate.

"Not much further down the road, Jay. We're dancing as fast as we can," he began defensively as soon as he heard my voice.

Before he could continue, I leapt in. "Easy, Nate. One thing I need to know. Are the cops still keeping tabs on Harold Corr?"

"No they're not, I'm afraid. Dan told me yesterday. They called it quits Wednesday night, late. Why do you ask?"

I told him my theory concerning the Ruger. Of course now that nobody was keeping tabs on the pair, the gun could be anywhere.

"Even if Harold was still under surveillance, we'd have no chance of persuading them to ask for a warrant to search the apartment. In their mind, there's no probable cause. No judge would issue one."

Nate was right. It was true. It was the same old eight-ball. No one believed the kid had done anything. He was the innocent moppet.

"Didn't have much luck with the cleaning lady, I'm afraid," Nate continued. "Mama Poule said she'd worn her most charming hat, but the lady wasn't talking. Señora Mantilla said she'd have to call Stella Corr before she could breathe a word to anyone. You'd think she was Stella's confessor!

"That's when Mama showed her the big stick – told her we could subpoena her testimony if the need arose. Didn't make the smallest difference. The woman immediately called up Stella Corr, and that was that. Told Mama Poule to go to hell. Pity, eh?"

It sure was.

As I stared at the burgundy Chevy two-door parked outside the building, I felt as though Atlas had temporarily rested the world on my shoulders while he'd ducked out in search of doughnuts.

In the conference room, Yant was chatting with Charlie. As usual, detective Wahl was stabbing at his teeth.

Scuzz, Lizzie and Mort were seated in a semi-circle around them.

They all looked around as I entered.

Yant's eyes flicked up to meet mine. "Good morning, Mr Benedict."

"Detective Yant."

Wahl didn't even bother to glance in my direction, his attention rivetted to the bloody tip of his wooden toothpick.

Yant returned his attention to Charlie. "What time did the third photograph appear, Mr Krale?"

"Must have been just before 1.30 pm," Charlie replied. "I didn't look at my watch, but that'd be about right, wouldn't you say, Jay?"

"I wouldn't argue with that," I agreed.

"And you've no doubt it was the same photo on all three occasions; 'cept the second and third were in greater detail?"

"That's right," Charlie answered. "As if whoever was sending them was drawing attention to the figure of the girl."

Wahl pushed himself off the wall and walked towards Charlie, easing his fat butt onto the edge of the computer desk. His short legs dangled in mid air, his feet several inches above the floor. "I guess I don't know too much about computers and stuff, so maybe you can tell me something. This photo. It's not a photo like *I* know a photo. Am I right?"

"If you mean was it film or digital, I'd say the chances are it was digital."

"Oh yeah? How so?"

"I suppose I think I can tell the difference. Most people couldn't. I think I can, is all."

Wahl nodded his head slowly as he progressed from thought to thought.

"Correct me if I'm wrong, but with a digital camera because there's no film you snap away and you got pictures. No need for a drugstore. No processing, no muss, no fuss – you can see it right away?"

"That's right. Connect it to your computer and scroll through around ninety-six snaps then and there."

"So that's how he, or she, sent them to you?" This time it was Yant speaking. He shot me a quick look on the 'or she' bit. He was clearly making a point; quite what, I wasn't exactly sure.

"I'd say so," Charlie replied.

"How can someone make a snapshot appear from nowhere on someone else's computer screen?" Yant asked. "I mean, if someone sends me E-mail, it doesn't just spread itself across my screen in the middle of what I'm doing. I have to call it up and read it. I do that when I feel like it."

"I tell you something," Charlie replied. "Whoever did this knows what he's doing. I'd have to think twice about it myself. The actual hacking into our network here at the Cyberkitchen wouldn't be too hard. All you'd need to know is our user number and password.

"A lot of hackers enjoy the guesswork. If time's an issue they resort to other means, some very high-tech, involving personalized software systems that instigate structured searches.

"Most hacking isn't very clever at all – insider informants sell the passwords. And quite often a search of the dumpsters will reveal a password scribbled on a scrap of paper prior to being committed to memory."

"Which would it be in this case? A mole on the inside?" Wahl suggested evilly.

No one spoke. Clearly no one felt like dignifying Wahl's question with a response.

Yant ran a hand through his thinning grey-flecked hair. "So once he or she knows your user name and password he or she'd be in, right?"

Yant had been deliberately ignoring my presence, so I chose to chip in and answer his question. "He'd have to know the modem number of our central machine. Everyone at the Cyberkitchen is connected with this machine. We share all its resources. Plus we have access to each others work."

"How would he know the central machine's modem number?" Yant was clearly interested in all the technicalities," I replied. "There's an apparatus called an 'automatic dialler' which will repeatedly dial possible modem numbers.

"You see, if I know the target company's central computer's modem number starts with the prefix 228 – and I'd know that because all the telephone lines to that company would have the same prefix – I tell the automatic dialer to dial all the numbers beginning with 228. I then let it run all night. In the morning I check the log file. My auto dialler will then write a log entry for every modem it finds, because it can determine the difference between a handset telephone, a fax and a modem. I check all the numbers in the range I've searched which are modems, then check all of them one by one till I get my target machine. Pretty damn simple."

"And once he's inside, he can do what he likes to the network? Put up photos of nude gals? Screw up your work?" Yant asked.

"Well, once he's logged on to our network, he can use the native messaging system. Messaging systems are presently text based, but if I put my mind to it I'm sure it'd be possible to create a program to make them graphical as well. And while he was at it, he could also type in commands to find out who else is on the network. The central machine will give the user name and number of every individual machine. He could talk to that person using the messaging sytem."

"Couldn't we trace him?"

"Only when he's on-line. If he thought you were instigating a trace, he'd quickly log out and disconnect. Once he logs out you'd never be able to."

"What if we bugged all lines in and out of here?" Wahl cut in. I saw Charlie's jaw drop. "With your permission, naturally, Mr Krale," Wahl added with a sugary smile.

I was presumably chopped liver.

"Look, all the guy has to do is find the user number and password of a legitimate user and send the message via them," Charlie explained. "The police can only trace a call while it's connected. After that they can't track where that phone call was initiated, only the user name used.

Yant looked thoughtful. "Let's get back to the photograph," he said. "What was the young lady wearing?"

"A simple white dress," Lizzie offered. "Ann Taylor'ish."

Yant and Wahl exchanged a meaningful glance. I concluded this was what she'd been found dead in.

"Oh, and tan pumps," Lissie added as an afterthought.

"You remembered the *shoes*?" Yant was incredulous. "Jesus."

"I'm a girl. What can I tell you."

"What time was the body discovered," I asked Yant.

"Yesterday at 3.40 pm."

"She was wearing the white dress?" I continued.

Yant ignored me. Suddenly I was invisible. One answer was all I was going to get. "None of you has ever seen this girl before?" he asked, addressing the room at large. "You're all quite certain of that?"

Everyone either nodded or agreed verbally.

"So, let's get this absolutely clear, Mr Krale. When you saw the photograph in the paper this morning, you said to yourself *that's the girl in the photograph.* Right?"

"Right. Well it looked mighty like her. The similarity was pretty amazing."

"So you checked with your colleagues? Asked them what they thought, eh?"

"Sure. We all agreed."

"Well, I've a Polaroid here," Yant said, reaching into his jacket pocket. "It's a shot of the dead girl. Would you be so good as to take a look at it, Mr Krale. You're not obliged to."

Yant offered it to Charlie, who gingerly took it. I understood how he felt.

He studied the shot then passed it to Scuzz.

"That's the girl. There's no question. That's exactly how she looked."

"The photograph printed in the paper was over a year old. The hair style was a bit different, yet you still recognized her. You'd make a fine witness."

The Polaroid did the rounds then was passed back to Yant, who slipped it back into his inside pocket.

He leaned back in his chair, lacing his fingers behind his head. "Can you think of any reason whatsoever why the photographs would have been electronically mailed to you here at the Cyberkitchen?"

"Whoever it is, he's clearly taunting us," I said. "Or maybe he's taunting the police department via this office."

Yant turned his stare on me. "That would seem to be the case, yes. Pretty self-evident, Mr Benedict. Question is, is it you or us?"

"Maybe both?"

Wahl eased off the desk and stuck his hands in his pockets. "Why should anyone wish to taunt you in particular, Mr Benedict?" he asked, eyeballing me. "Got someone in mind?"

"Maybe," I replied.

"Goin' to share that *maybe* with the Police Department?" Wahl took a couple of paces towards me. "See, that's what we're here for. We ain't here to play video games." Wahl was, as usual, beginning to turn nasty.

"I think you know who I might have in mind, detective. Whether or not he has anything to do with the death of this girl is debatable. However, I would say the coincidence is remarkable."

Yant gave me a studied long-suffering look. "You figure the person you have in mind stuck an ice-pick into this girl's chest just to get up your nose? That about right? Not much of a motive for killing someone, is it?"

Wahl chuckled. The others cut glances between Yant and me – they could sense this was becoming personal.

"Make what you like of it, detective," I said. "You asked me what I thought. I told you. Next time I'll remember to keep my thoughts to myself."

Yant smiled. "Oh come, Mr Benedict, let's not get snitty, eh? I get a real buzz listening to your whacky theories. Never helped me much, but they're certainly always very colourful."

Before I had a chance to respond, Yant stood.

"Thanks for calling us, Mr Krale," he said, holding out a hand to Charlie. "If anything else comes to mind, give detective Wahl or myself a call, will you?" He tossed a card on to the table.

Charlie nodded.

"Naturally, if any more photos pop up on your equipment, you call us right away."

Charlie showed the two detectives out. Neither looked in my direction.

I returned to my office to think things over.

Perhaps Yant was right on the button. Perhaps I now saw the hand of Harold Corr at work everywhere. Was it an hysterical reaction? Or was it conceivable that the kid had sunk to the horrific abyss of thrill-killing?

Logically anyone could have been responsible for the death of the girl. Anyone could have sent the photos; for countless weird reasons.

Though Yant and Wahl had chosen to share next to none of their findings with us, I figured that the girl had to have been photographed by the killer sometime yesterday morning. The killer then took time out to send the digital photographs to the Cyberkitchen, somehow hacking his way into our network. He then retraced his steps, sought out the girl again and killed her.

I kept returning to two fundamental questions. First of all, if Harold Corr wasn't responsible, why had the killer chosen the Cyberkitchen's computers to air the trailer to his murder? Why had he not sent it to the police department, or to someone who knew the girl? Was it harder to hack into the police department computer system? Was that the only reason?

Secondly, was the similarity to Lastra purely fortuitous? Or did the movie play some part in all this? Perhaps the killer was some crazed serial killer who'd always had a fascination for our products.

I don't believe in coincidences of any kind. Never have.

Lastra had short jet black hair, a thin face, big brown eyes. So did the dead girl. The hairstyle was practically identical. Lastra was a corpse. So was the girl.

It only struck me then that no one had mentioned to the detectives the similarity of the dead girl to our animated body in Sleuthhound.

I made a note to call Yant.

Just then the door to my office opened and Charlie joined me.

"You saw the photo for longer than I did, Charlie. How close would you say the girl's resemblance was to Lastra? A vague one, a good one, or one that hit you between the eyes?"

"Pretty striking. 'Course you have to remember Lastra's animation." He looked at me, trying to second-guess my thoughts. "You think it's got something to do with Sleuthhound?"

"Too early to say. You'd have to stretch the imagination pretty far to believe it yet. What would be the point anyway?"

"Someone's out there killing people and leaving us messages. *Hey look! I'm going to kill. Watch me!* That's what he's saying. He doesn't necessarily need a reason."

I sincerely hoped Charlie was right – that the killer was unknown to us.

Though it was appalling enough to consider the possibility that a psychopath was killing people and sending us the press releases in advance, the thought that the killer could be Harold Corr, that he was murdering innocent people merely to piss me off, was absolutely horrifying.

I was about to go make both of us a coffee when Nancy poked her head round the door. Her face showed concern.

"Jay. It's your brother. He's in a cab outside. He's unconscious."

44.

The Hispanic driver was doing a lot of arm-waving. I couldn't make out if he was speaking American or straight Spanish, his speech was so incoherent.

Raymond was lying across the rear seat, face up. I'm no doctor but he looked to be at death's door. I handed the cabbie a fifty and told him to drive as fast as he could to the nearest hospital.

The big bill was a major attitude changer. The cabbie's anger was replaced in a flash by the most unconvincing look of concern I'd ever witnessed.

As we sped towards Valley Presbyterian, the closest hospital to the office, I sat in the back of the cab with Raymond, holding him in my arms.

His breathing was practically non existent, his shirt was soaked with sweat, his skin sheet white, and his eyelids three-quarters closed. I gently raised one of them with the tip of my finger. The pupil looked small as a pin-prick.

I was scared to death for him.

I carried Raymond into Emergency where I told the triage nurse he was my brother, and that he'd collapsed. I made it crystal clear money was no problem, I'd be paying by credit card.

They immediately put him on a cart and wheeled him away. I didn't want to get in the way, so I hovered in the corridor just close enough to be able to see what was going on.

Someone gave him a couple of injections. I watched as they undressed him, checked his airways, gave him oxygen and checked his vital signs.

Within minutes I saw Raymond's feet move; they were sticking out from under the hospital sheet. He was coming round. I almost cried with relief.

As I walked forward to Raymond's bedside, one of the staff waved me away.

I retreated to the waiting area where I was immediately collared by the triage nurse. She wanted a whole heap of details – Raymond's name, my name and address, my social security number, and most importantly my visa card number.

Fifteen minutes later the young doctor who'd been attending to Raymond walked over to me.

"That's your brother over there, isn't it, Mr Benedict?" he asked.

"That's right, doctor," I replied. "Is he going to be all right?"

"Sure. He slipped into an hypoglycaemic coma, that's all. We've stabilized him."

I thanked him.

"You know you shouldn't allow him to drink to excess, Mr Benedict," he continued sternly, "The amount of alcohol in his system right now could easily have killed him."

Quite how the doctor thought I could prevent a grown man of over fifty from drinking while my back was turned was a mystery to me.

Besides, if Raymond was a diabetic, it was news to me. And now that I'd been assured Raymond had postponed his breakfast meeting with the grim reaper, I was angry with him. The bubble had burst. He was back to the old Raymond – the one who tested my patience, stole my money and gave me heart attacks.

The doctor told me they'd given him what he referred to as a 'bolus' of dextrose as first line management, then some Narcon, just in case he'd OD'd.

"He's awake now. You can go see him if you like. He won't be making much sense for a while – he's pretty confused."

"When can I take him home?"

"Couple of hours. That should do it. Then a couple of days bed rest. No less."

"Should he see a specialist? Is there a serious problem?"

"I'm afraid I'm unable to discuss your brother's condition with you. Sorry, but it's a matter of ethics. I can tell you this, though; I think he should have his abdomen scanned at the earliest opportunity. Can't say any more, I'm afraid."

I was annoyed. It was okay for him to inform me Raymond was a diabetic, but not that he had a possible heart condition? What about renal failure? Or AIDS? It made no sense at all.

I didn't bother to argue the toss. I merely thanked him again for what he'd done already, and walked back to Raymond's cubicle.

Raymond had been crying. His hair was standing on end like a rag doll, and his face was a waxy death mask.

"I've been a bad lad, haven't I, little brudder? Got pissed as a fart. Should have known better, eh? Silly bugger."

"*Very* silly bugger," I agreed, running a hand across his forehead, wiping away the cold sweat.

I noticed he was shaking, so I collared a passing nurse and asked her for a blanket, which I immediately draped over his body.

"What the hell were you up to, you old reprobate?" I chided gently.

He held out a bony hand and grasped mine tightly. "Just having some fun while I still can. Found some cracking good night spots. Met a few lovelies. Had a ball, I can tell you."

He grinned, though I could plainly see there was an all-encompassing fear in his eyes.

He stared at me for a good ten seconds. The ER was strangely quiet. Then a child began crying behind a curtain somewhere close-by.

"I'm dying, Jay. Sorry," he said simply, like a child who'd been caught smoking behind the lavatories, and hoped dad wouldn't be too angry.

I suppose subconsciously I'd seen something like this coming since I first saw him at the airport. I just hadn't allowed myself to believe death could be an option.

"Who told you you're dying, Raymond?" I asked.

"Doctor back home. Nice chap. Pancreas is all fucked up, you see. Hence the pseudo-diabetes. I asked him how bad it was, and he said, *Raymond, old fellow, is there anywhere you've always wanted to go for a holiday?* "

He laughed shortly, then winced. It must have hurt somewhere. "You see, I wanted to see you, little brudder. Say sorry for all the nasties in the past."

He squeezed my hand. "Can we go home now?"

"Right away," I replied.

45.

Raymond was asleep within minutes of my getting him to the car.

The doctor at the hospital had said to give him a couple of hours rest before moving him, but Raymond kept begging me to take him home. In the end I gave in.

Rather than leave him alone, I asked the daughter of one of our neighbors, who I knew did a bit of baby sitting, to sit in the house while I returned to the office. I didn't want Raymond to wake up disorientated, wondering what the hell was going on.

The young girl, Gretel, was glad of the money. I told her to let him sleep as long as possible, then make him something to eat.

I left Raymond a note.

Back at the 'Kitchen a technician from the LAPD had installed a video camera in front of a monitor Charlie had hooked up in his office.

If another picture appeared on our network, Yant wanted a permanent record of it.

By five o'clock it was up and running. The police technician asked me if I could have a secretary switch it off at the end of business each day. His logic was that if the idea was to advertise a murder, no one was going to transmit a photo knowing the machines were switched off.

Just before 6 pm Nate rang. He had great news. Dan had finally tracked down the bag lady of Lankershim.

"The good news is that against all the odds she remembers you."

"You sure that's not the sound of Dan peeling a few notes from his bill fold?

"Absolutely not."

"You mean she remembers a man sleeping in his car in a parking lot the best part of a month ago? How come?"

"She's been in a half-way house for the last three and a half weeks. She was involved in an accident the day Faith died. Broke her hip. Had nowhere to go, so she persuaded Welfare to shift themselves.

"How come she remembers me so clearly?"

"You were the last thing that happened to her before she was hit by the bus on Ventura. She blames you; says you're some kind of a ju-ju man. Her words."

"So where does that put me? In the clear?"

"I've had a call through to Goodrich since three this afternoon. She hasn't got back to me yet. The only negative aspect of all this is that the old lady's as mad as a hatter. Maybe Goodrich will buy her testimony, maybe not. Maybe she'll think we suggested the times to the old fool. We'll have to wait and see.

"My bet is Goodrich will have to think very long and hard about continuing with the prosecution now that someone has put you in a parking lot on Ventura the same time as Faith was shot in Santa Monica. The old lady may be a crazy fool, but no way is she going to change her mind about seeing you. Dan says she's scared to death of you; thinks you're some kind of witch doctor who put out a curse on her and made her walk in front of that bus."

"So your guess is Goodrich will drop the charges?"

"She'd be ill-advised not to. There'll be pressure on her from the DA."

It was the best news I'd had for an awfully long while. I don't think I realized till then the affect it was having on me – being charged with Faith's murder. I'd never consciously come to terms with it.

I was also still terrified of the effect the Grand Jury proceedings would have on Hal and Alice. How would they react to the news of my commital? Would they be able to dismiss the idea out of hand as all my friends had?

I was deeply concerned for them both, particularly Hal. So the news that Nate thought the charges would shortly be dropped was the most wonderful relief.

"Tell me something, Nate," I said, as my thoughts changed track. "Would Dan be prepared to do a surveillance job on Harold Corr for me this weekend?"

"I'd have to ask him, Jay. Why? He's been working eighteen hour days for me for ten days now."

It was only then that I realized I hadn't told Nate of the appearance of the photo at the office. I'd been so concerned with Raymond's welfare, I hadn't gotten round to calling him.

I proceeded to give Nate a detailed version of the events of the past few hours.

He naturally upbraided me about failing once again to call him – a major judgment error to his mind.

"I know you've been through the ringer lately, Jay, but our job is hard enough as it is. You have to let us know what's happening. This office can't function without all the facts."

"I'm truly sorry, Nate. I'm really grateful for all the terrific work you, Mama Poule, and Dan are doing. I'd have called you right away, it was Raymond –"

Nate cut in. "You don't have to apologize to me. I understand. Just remember to try to keep me informed in future."

"Of course I will," I assured him. "In the meantime, do you think Dan could do the job this weekend?"

"What's on your mind, Jay? Why this weekend in particular? Even if you're right and it is Corr and his friend who stabbed the girl to death –"

"You don't think so? You think this is all coincidental? Come on, Nate! Now it's you doing backflips! Harold Corr murders Faith, then shoots Michael Gardenas. You really think that quite by chance some other psychopath now targets the Cyberkitchen as a PR vehicle for his bloodshed?"

"Easy, Jay. I'm with you, remember?"

Immediately I was chock full of remorse. "I'm sorry, Nate," I said. "Really."

"Don't worry about it," Nate replied. "It's just in my nature to consider all possibilities, then discount the improbable. The point I was going to make was that if the Corr boy can't send you an electronic message on the computer till start of business Monday, why would you think he'd be up to anything over the weekend?

"Surely the whole point of what he's doing is to taunt you with a photo of his next victim, *then* kill them. Right now he can't reach you till Monday."

"All that's true, but only if we're correct in assuming he plans to use electronic messaging. Suppose next time he calls me from a payphone?"

Nate didn't reply for a few seconds.

"I'll call Dan. See what he's got planned for the weekend. It'll cost you, Jay. Dan's time doesn't come cheap. Could be over fifteen hundred for the weekend. Double that if he takes a partner. Can't watch and observe all day and all night without a relief partner."

The money wasn't an issue. Right then there was one focus to my life. Harold Corr. If there was any way at all I could fix the responsibility for Faith's death on that evil child, I'd take it.

"If he says he can do it, tell him to go right ahead. I want to know every step the boy takes."

"Until when?"

"Until further notice. I'll sell the house if I have to."

There was silence the other end of the line.

"Come on, Nate, I know you understand. Faith's dead, I'm still accused of her murder, and this bastard of a child is running round sticking ice-picks into innocent people while the cops look in every direction but his. If it were up to me I'd go round there personally, but you made me swear on my mother's grave not to. And if that weren't enough, Judge Mason Earnshaw said he'd lock me up and throw away the key if I was found inside a mile of the Corr place. I tell you frankly, Nate, it's driving me completely nuts. I HAVE to do something!"

My mind went temporarily blank as though I'd run into a brick wall. It was only then I became aware that my chest was heaving, the blood was racing through my veins and, without thinking, I'd been shouting like a man possessed.

For a moment I wondered if Nate was still on the line. If it had been me, I'd have called in the men in the white suits. I knew I was dangerously close to losing mental control.

"Nate?"

"I'm still here, Jay."

"Jesus, I'm sorry, Nate. I don't know what's happening to me right now."

"Just stop saying you're sorry. Do me a favor buddy and take a deep breath. Mama Poule is deeply concerned about you. Matter of fact, so am I. I tell you what; here's the deal. You come over to our place right now and I'll get Mama Poule to fix up a genuine West African cook out. Meantime, I'll call Dan and organize the stake-out on the Corr place. I'll tell him that if he can't do it personally, to get a couple of guys he trusts to do it for him. Deal?"

"Sounds great to me, especially the cook-out. But I've got one very sick brother staying with me."

"No problem. Bring him with you. We'll make it a beach party. Get a bit of fresh air into the Englishman."

I laughed. Nate had always thought of me as an American despite my hybrid Anglo-American drawl.

"Thanks a million, Nate. I'll see how Raymond feels when I get home and call you back."

"Sure," Nate replied. "You do that."

The traffic was as bad as I'd ever known it on the way home.

A pile-up just before Laurel was the cause. Judging by the rescue vehicles and ambulances the casualties were pretty major. Wherever I went, death seemed to be dogging my steps.

To my surprise, on my return home Raymond was up already and lounging by the pool, a glass in his hand, a cigarette in the other. Gretel was lying beside him on another banana chair, obviously lapping up my big brother's sharp wit and good humour.

She caught sight of me and waved. I smiled back then took a long look at the blood red glass in Raymond's hand.

"Would I do that to you, little brudder?" Raymond said, offering it up to me. "It's a Virgin Mary. Don't believe me? Try for yourself."

By eight-thirty that night Raymond, Nate, Mama Poule and I were standing on the low garden wall of Nate's Venice beach house looking out across the sand towards the Pacific. The extraordinarily wonderful smell of Mama Poule's Blackened Fish did considerably more than scent the evening breeze.

Nate had knocked up a low alcohol punch. I'd had a word in his ear when we arrived. Not that we'd have fooled Raymond for a second – he could judge how generous the measure of Stoli was within a couple of mils.

We laughed a good deal and ate a good deal. Raymond had clearly dismissed all dark thoughts of death from his mind, determined to enjoy what remained of his life.

Mama Poule and Raymond took to each other immediately; they shared a similar wicked sense of humor and sparked off each other the entire evening.

Just before we left, Nate took me aside and told me Dan had agreed to stake out the Corr house till Monday morning. He'd charge twelve hundred, plus expenses, for each twenty-four hour shift.

He'd be working with an assistant, whom he vouched for as very reliable.

We drove home to Studio City around midnight. Raymond had the window wound down, his elbow hanging out listening to golden oldies on KCSFM. He seemed happy enough despite the significant lack of hard liquor all evening. I think he considered himself reasonably fortunate to have survived the day.

Though I didn't press him , I desperately wanted to know exactly how ill his doctor thought he was.

When he said he was dying, was he talking in terms of years? Or was it months, or even weeks. I determined to ask him later, I'd wait a couple of days.

46.

It was 2.50 pm.

Harold stood at the door of apartment eight at 1031 Lindbrook Drive, Westwood Village and rang the bell. Next to the button was a cut-down business card. It read 'T. Thorne'.

Harold had picked the name out of the phone book before breakfast. Any name that had double T initials.

He'd felt like the grim reaper, scything his way down the T page with his penknife.

The tip of his blade had halted randomly at T.Thorne.

Tough shit for Mr Thorne, he'd thought with a chuckle. Now he was about to see the face of his next victim. Some kind of good fun, wasn't it!

He and Phil had watched a short man with thick dark wavy hair enter the apartment ten minutes earlier.

Of course it was entirely possible that their target was already inside, and this was a visitor – hence the letter in Harold's hand, one which he'd extracted from letter box number eight half an hour earlier.

Harold heard the chain being swept aside, then a couple of keys were turned. Finally the door opened to reveal the short wavy-haired man.

It was a foolproof way of gaining entry. Everyone's fortress mentality crumbled at the sight of a fresh-faced kid through the spy hole.

The thought made Harold's smile come easily.

"Excuse me, are you Mr T Thorne?" Harold asked, all sweetness.

"Yes, that's me. What can I do for you, kid," the man said without any warmth.

Kid. Harold felt a sudden tightening in his stomach. *Don't give me that 'kid' shit. Right now, it's up to me whether you live or die, asshole.*

"Come on kid, out with it. What d'ya want? Ain't got all day." The man was wearing a brilliant white towelling dressing gown. Maybe he'd been about to shower.

Harold held out the letter. "I found this lying out in the street. It's got your name on it; saw it written outside this building. Thought I'd drop it in, sir."

"Oh yeah? Well give it here."

Harold held it out and it was snatched away.

For fun, Harold had made sure it was a bill. The wavy-haired man looked at it, made a face, then walked inside and closed the door without a word of thanks.

Harold stood for a moment at the door.

You're a dead man, Mr Thorne. You just pulled the trigger yourself. Called me kid.

Thirty seconds later he was back in the stolen Toyota van across the street, scrolling through the seven high resolution photos he'd taken of Thorne on his Kodak DS Zoom digital camera earlier.

"It's him," Harold said matter-of-factly.

Phil grinned as his fingers tapped on the dash in rhythm to the Hip Hop music he'd stuck in the tape deck.

"Hey please, man. Do I get to off him?" Phil pleaded. Harold shot him a quick glance. Phil was begging with his eyes, like a faithful hound eager to please its master; he'd swim the fastest river, jump the highest fence.

"Sure," Harold replied lightly, returning his attention to the camera, "Hell, why not? You've earned yourself a piece of the action."

Phil smacked his fist into the palm of his hand. "Un-fuckin'-real!"

Harold knew that it had to be that way. This time it had to be Phil. He'd need to be far away when Thorne took the bullet to the head.

Of course Phil didn't have to know that. As far as he was concerned, Harold was doing his buddy a real big favor.

Some time he'd have had to give Phil a shot anyway; his friend was getting crazier each time they whacked someone. Harold would have to hit the release valve. Phil was like a savage dog you had to let loose every now and then on a cat or a rabbit, just to keep it sweet. So why not now? It suited his plan so nicely.

"You need the gun? Or do you reckon you can handle the pick?" Harold said, trying to goad Phil into choosing the pick by appealing to the macho side of his personality. He didn't like setting Phil free with the Ruger, it was too precious. Without it he'd be down to the Sig Sauer Pistole and the Lahti L35. Both were pretty small and easy to handle, neither too bulky. But both were 9 mm, and he only possessed a handful of slugs for them. It wouldn't be easy to replenish stocks.

He preferred the Ruger anyway – it had been his father's signature piece in the past; it would be his in the future. He didn't want to lose it.

"So which is it to be, killer?" Harold joshed, putting the camera aside and ruffling Phil's hair with both hands.

Phil laughed. Harold could see his buddy was thrilled at the prospect of a kill. *He* was going to be the killer dude now. Finally it was going to be *his* turn. Harold could see Phil was busting to do it.

"I want the gun, man. The gun. Got to be the gun."

Harold felt a surge of annoyance.

There were the leaders, Harold thought idly, and those that blindly followed – the lemmings that would follow even to their own destruction.

If it hadn't suited his plans, he'd never let Phil loose on Thorne alone. But this time everything had to be different. So Phil had to come into the equation.

"Okay," he replied grudgingly. "you get to use the Ruger. Just remember, you screw up and I'll make sure you end up dead as that girl you thought was so cute. You better believe me."

"Sure, I believe you, man. That's cool," Phil replied. Right now he didn't care. He'd been given a license to kill. It was his turn to be Doctor Death. It was the most extreme buzz imaginable. It was awesome.

Harold scrolled through the seven shots on the viewfinder at the back of the camera. The last was the best without question. It was a full length shot of Thorne, but that didn't matter. The highest resolution setting on the camera gave excellent results, retaining most of the quality, even when enlarged to double the size. Cropping a good head shot would be a piece of cake.

"You go in the second I leave. Okay?"

"Check."

"Remember, he's got to think he's got a chance. The moment he thinks you're going to top him, he'll scream like a baby."

"Right," Phil replied. His fingers were tapping ever faster on the dash. He was so excited he felt he'd burst a blood vessel. He would have jumped through a hoop if Harold had had one in his hand.

"Why can't I whack him straight off? Why wait till five, man?"

"I've got to have time to get home, haven't I, shitbrain? I've got to post the freaking picture! Jesus, you're one dumb asshole at times, Phil."

"Okay, man. Take it easy. I can buy that. But why not wait out here till five, and then go in and kill the dude?"

Harold's jaw set in anger. "Just do it the way I tell you, man. What if Thorne decides he wants to go out before five? What do you do then? Gun him down in the frigging street?"

Phil thought for a moment or two. "Yeah, that's right. I see where you're coming from."

"You hold the gun on him till five. You need a place to hide out. That's what you tell him – you're hiding out from the cops, okay. He'll buy that. Watch some TV to pass the time. Make him think it's all going to work out. Then come five o'clock you whack the guy."

Phil snorted with laughter. It was kind of funny. He couldn't wait.

Harold reached over and grabbed the sports bag from behind his seat, pulling out a twelve inch Teddy Bear.

"Once you've shot him dead, you wipe the gun clean, then strip it," Harold said, pulling at a thin strip of velcro at the side of the bear to reveal the metal parts of the gun, wrapped in tissue paper. "Check for blood and tissue traces anywhere on the grip, trigger guard and barrel. There shouldn't be any, but you never know. Could get unlucky with splatter, so make absolutely certain, okay?"

Phil nodded, his eyes rivetted to the gun.

"Then you put all the pieces back in here," Harold continued holding up the Teddy Bear.

As soon as he finished assembling the Ruger, Harold loaded the clip, then screwed on the noise suppressor.

"Here, take it."

Phil grinned wide as he felt the cool metal in his hand. He'd waited all his life for this moment.

"Now take it apart," Harold commanded.

Phil immediately did as he was told. Slowly and carefully.

"Now put it together again."

Again he did as he was told.

"After, you take the bear to Miriam's place. You got that?"

"Sure, Harold. Sure." Phil couldn't take his eyes off the gun. It was so damned beautiful.

"Okay, tell me one more time. What do you do?"

"I go in the moment you leave. Tell him I need to hide out from the cops. That he'll be fine. Then at five I whack him. Right, man?"

Harold nodded. In the sports bag, next to the big brown bear, was the FedEx package he'd sent himself two days ago. Phil would go in with the parcel. No one knocked back deliveries of goodies.

"Soon as he takes the parcel and looks down at it, you push him backwards, close the door, and stick the gun in his face. Tell him, if he shouts he's a dead man. It's vital you keep the guy from screaming, so get the message across real quick."

An expression of irritation clouded Phil's face. It wasn't lost of Harold.

"Something bothering you, shitbrain?" Harold spat out the words. It was important to spell out who was in charge here.

"Man, we've been through all of this so many freakin' times," Phil whined.

"So we go through it again. What happens five o'clock? Tell me!"

"I walk over to the dude, real casual. Then I give him one in the chest, up round here," Phil said pushing a finger into Harold's ribs.

"Not just *somewhere*, man – right in *there*!" Harold grabbed sharply at the gun, shoving the barrel into Phil's chest exactly in the killing zone.

Phil winced as the metal stabbed against his chest.

"Okay, man. Chill out, for shit's sake. I know the place!"

"What then, numbnuts?"

"Then I push him down backwards, stand on his neck and give him the head shot." He pointed his index finger at his temple.

Harold studied Phil for a few seconds. His friend was looking a bit dejected. He obviously hadn't enjoyed being made to look like an amateur by the boss.

Harold put an arm round his friend in a gesture of camaraderie as he looked up and down the quiet suburban street. Maybe Phil needed a little man to man bonding.

"I'll do it good, man. Trust me," Phil said.

Harold reached for his schoolbag containing his laptop computer, then pulled the door open. "I know you will, Phil. I know you will."

The Tampico grin was immediately back. "He's a dead man, dude. You got my word on it," he said as Harold stepped onto the sidewalk.

As Harold reached the corner of the street, he looked back briefly. Phil was walking up the steps to Thorne's apartment, the FedEx parcel in one hand, his other hand inside his jacket.

Harold couldn't think of anything he'd left to chance. Even Phil could manage this one.

His only concern was that a cruising cop car might make a note of the license plate of the stolen van between now and five. If they collared Phil he'd be hard-pressed to distance himself from his buddy.

Harold picked up a cab outside the Central Pacific hotel, handing the cabbie a fifty he'd stolen from his mother's purse.

Within seconds the laptop was out of the schoolbag, the digital camera was cabled in and Harold's chosen photo of Mr T Thorne was downloaded and accurately cropped to a neat headshot. Then it was added to the short computer program Harold had written the night before, one that was set to run at the instigation of a short sequence of commands.

Harold snapped the lid of the laptop shut and leant back, looking to his left as the blue Pacific flashed by.

He was dog tired. The program had taken him all night. It was his best work to date.

Scanning the Cyberkitchen's data banks had been a daunting prospect, but Frisk, the search tool Harold had devised himself, had been well up to the task, scanning at speeds even he had thought impossible up till then. It had only taken just over five hours to locate the file that mattered.

He closed his eyes tight shut. *Dad would be so proud of me*, he thought as he ran a chubby hand lightly over the seat beside him.

It was as if Jack was sitting beside him in the cab. Everything was set to run. He merely needed a phone line.

At the corner of Sunset and PCH he asked the driver to pull in by a payphone. He said he'd be a couple of minutes as he stepped from the cab, his laptop under his arm.

Two minutes later, he was back in the cab on the way home.

He'd made his call. It was 3.50pm. The fix was in.

47.

Raymond was up early Saturday morning. This was unlike him. Maybe it was a new experience for him to have gone to bed reasonably sober.

During coffee he suggested we spend the day on the beach at Venice. He'd clearly fallen in love with the place the previous evening.

It seemed like a pretty good idea to me. I packed a couple of towels and something to read and we took off around nine-thirty.

On the way, I called Dan on the cellular number Nate had given me the previous night.

"Dan Stir. Who's this?" he answered.

"It's Jay Benedict. I wanted to thank you for taking on this job for me. I know it was pretty short notice."

"That's fine, Jay. It's what I do. That's how I pay the school fees."

He'd never mentioned he had kids. I'd had a vision of him as a tough loner.

"Where are you now?" I asked.

"Outside the Corr place. The boy's at home; I saw him this morning at a window."

"Did he see you?"

"I'd hope not. We're not sitting in a car across the way, you know," Dan replied, his voice rich with humor. "I'm more expensive than most because I reckon I'm that much better. So the answer is no, he wouldn't know we're around."

"Can I call you later, Dan?"

"Sure can. If I'm switched off, wait a while and try again."

We spent the morning on the beach.

Raymond read a copy of the London Times he'd bought on the way. He then drifted off to sleep.

I stared up at the sky and concentrated like mad on absolutely nothing, hoping I might miraculously slip into a yoga trance that would free my mind of thoughts of murderous children.

Thirty minutes later I gave up. Eleven-year-old demons were running amok in my consciousness.

I picked up Sogyal Rinpoche's *The Tibetan Book of Living and Dying*, ironically a book I'd started reading the week before Faith's death. I began at the chapter called *Bringing the Mind Home*. I was soon both absorbed and spiritually comforted. Mum had been on the right track after all.

Raymond didn't wake till close to midday, when I took him up to a restaurant along the main drag for something to eat.

As we sat down, a waiter brought a couple of great looking Margaritas to the next table. I watched Raymond's eyes roll. I'd seen a similar expression of thirst only once before – on Humphrey Bogart's face in the movie *Sahara*.

I checked with Raymond that he'd taken his shot of insulin, then ordered us a pitcher.

The afternoon was spent again on the beach. Raymond had bought a wind-up frog on the boardwalk, one that paddled along in the water. He thought it was the best thing he ever seen. He looked happier than the three year old beside him who was playing with a bucket and spade. I was reminded of holidays Raymond and I had spent when we were very little.

At four o'clock I called Dan again.

"Dan Stir. Who's this?" he said in a low voice.

"Jay Benedict, Dan, I wanted –"

"Call you right back. You on your cellphone?"

"Yes," I replied, then pressed the end button.

Fifteen minutes later Dan was back on the line.

"You caught me at a bad time. The kid's just got back home."

"Where's he been?" I couldn't help myself, I had to know right then and there. After all, that's why I was paying the man a basin of money.

"The kid was home all last night. Picked up 10.55 this morning by his buddy Tampico. The older kid was driving a yellow VW. The vehicle is registered to a Mrs Elizabeth Tampico. That's the boy's mother.

"The two kids drove over to Tampico's apartment on Montana. Exited the building at 1.20 pm.

"They walked to the corner of Montana and 3rd Street Promenade. Then they split up.

"Ethan was on a break so I had to make a choice. I knew the Corr kid was the priority, so I stayed with him.

"He walked along to Wilshire then up to 5th and down to the Post Office."

For a second I thought the line had dropped out, I wasn't expecting Dan to simply dry up.

"Dan?" I said, just to check he was still there.

"Look, I feel real bad about this, but that's when I lost the kid. Until I picked him up again just before 4 pm."

It was the last thing I'd expected, and I was furious. Dan was supposed to be good. That's what Nate had told me. I was paying the guy and his assistant Ethan a whole heap of money to follow an eleven-year-old boy. Harold wasn't some international criminal or a member of the KGB for Christ's sake – he was a young boy!

And I'd thought the guy had intelligent eyes. Well, as granny used to say, appearances can be deceptive.

I stayed silent. I knew if I said one word, I'd regret it.

"I wasn't expecting the kid to pull one of those moves. He was standing by the bus stop outside the library. I was across the street. Then he walked to the corner as if he was going to cross the street towards me. Some traffic passed between us. When the lights changed and the crowd started crossing he wasn't there any more. He'd just vanished."

"How could that be, Dan?" I asked with what I thought was admirable restraint.

"He must have been picked up on the run by one of the vehicles passing by. That'd be my guess."

"Do you remember any vehicle that might have fitted the bill?" I asked with an edge of sarcasm I hadn't really intended.

"I've thought about it, Jay, and I'd say it had to be a van. See if it was a car, whoever was driving would have had to stop to open the door. But if it had been a van, then the door could have been open all the time. The kid could simply have ducked in while the van slowed down at the crossing."

"Was there a van?" I pressed.

"There was. A white van. Toyota as I remember. I can't be more specific because I was looking for the kid, not making notes of the vehicles."

"So what did you do then?"

"I called in Ethan and we made a grid search of the area. There was no sign of the kid, so after twenty minutes we drove over to the Tampico house and stayed there till 3 pm.

"Then I left Ethan at Montana and I drove back to the Corr house in Calabasas. Harold Corr arrived home in a cab a couple of minutes before 4 pm. He's still inside."

"So between 1.30 pm and 4 pm you've no idea where he was. Is that right?"

"Correct. I'm truly sorry. It'll be reflected in the invoice."

I took a deep breath. As if the fact I was going to get a rebate for his having lost sight of the kid was some kind of a comfort! Hell, Harold Corr could have attended a massacre during the missing hours. The whole fucking point was to follow the kid from go to whoa!

"What about Tampico?"

"I checked back with Ethan five minutes ago. Still no sign of him."

"Look Dan. It's a shame things turned out the way they did. Don't worry about it. Just make sure you stick to Harold Corr like superglue from now on."

"I'll make sure of that, Jay."

I rang off.

Raymond didn't want to go home, so we bought a six pack of beers, walked along the shore for a couple of miles, then sat at the water's edge.

"Can I stay at your place for a while, Jay?" he said, as I popped a can and handed it to him.

"Sure you can. Haven't seen nearly enough of you in the last forty or so years." It was true. We'd been strangers most of our lives. It was good that we'd found each other at last, even if it looked as though my brother was soon to be taken from me.

"I've never felt like croaking in Blighty."

"Stay as long as you like, big brudder," I replied. I never thought I'd hear myself saying it. But times had changed very radically. I was determined to look after the old fool if it killed me. He wasn't going to die alone. If I had my way, he'd die at home with a cigarette in one hand and a Scotch in the other.

There'd been moments all day when I'd been tempted to leave Raymond to his own devices and drive over to the Cyberkitchen.

It was my damned curiosity again.

If I powered up the computer what would I find? A message from Harold? Another photograph?

The reason I didn't go to the office had nothing whatsoever to do with my willpower conquering my curiosity.

My reasoning was simple. If Harold had sent the photograph, and I was convinced this was the case, then it was quite possible he intended at some time in the future to send another one. His game was to send a photograph of his victim, and only subsequently to kill. Well, those had been the rules so far.

It followed then that if the central computer at the Cyberkitchen was turned off for the weekend, Harold would know that there was no way he could put a photograph on our office screens. Besides, no one would be there to see it.

So, short of sending an E Mail, which we might not download till Monday morning, he could not play his game until the start of business Monday morning.

I'd just finished lulling myself into some semblance of security when my cellphone beeped in the sand beside me.

"Jay? It's Nancy. There's a problem."

My first thought was that someone had broken into the Cyberkitchen and had turned the place over. I had no particular reason to assume this since our security contract at the 'Kitchen was costing us a fortune. Alarms everywhere, not to mention a twenty-four hour armed response.

"Tell me," I answered.

"It's our web site. It's been interfered with. A friend of mine called me a few minutes ago. She noticed it. I'm looking at it now."

"Interfered with? What do you mean? How interfered with?"

I asked the questions, yet I had a gut feeling I knew the answers. It was Harold. He'd caught us all napping. He'd outsmarted us again.

"It's the teaser. Trent Truman's head's been altered. There's a photo where the animation should be. It moves around with the character. Looks very strange."

"What do you mean 'moves'?" I couldn't believe the photograph could have been anything but a still shot. Charlie's work on his new program Cyberstar was ground-breaking, and even he would have been hard-pressed to engineer a re-configured 3-D headshot of a human being.

"The photo is the same size as Truman's head. It's not animated, it just moves around when Truman does, like it's mounted on his neck. So if he turns right, the head's still facing left. Weird."

"The head – do you recognize the guy?"

243

"Not at all."

"Does he look at all like Truman?"

"Not a bit. Thick black hair, slicked down."

Truman had been bald.

"Who else knows about this?" I asked. Apart from probably about a thousand people around the country who were right then studying our web site, confused by the change in animation.

"I called you the moment I logged in."

"How long has the photo been on the site?"

"I don't know. I'll do some asking around and get back to you."

I glanced at my watch. It was a few minutes before 5 pm.

"That'd be really useful," I said. "Are you home this evening?"

"I am now. Just in case you need me for anything."

I thanked her, then immediately called Dan.

"Dan Stir, who's this?"

"Jay Benedict, Dan. Are you still sitting on Harold Corr?"

"Sure am. He's in a car with his mother, about five spaces ahead of me."

"Where are you?"

"Highway 101, just short of Thousand Oaks. They left home 4.35 pm."

"Stick to him. Another photo's just shown up. Don't let him out of your sight."

"I never make two mistakes in the same day, Jay. Believe me."

"Call Ethan. I want to know if the Tampico boy has surfaced."

"Will do."

Next call was to Charlie.

It was all news to him. He mumbled a few blasphemous expletives, then asked me to wait while he booted up his home machine and dialled into the Net.

"Jesus," I heard him say, sotto voce, after a few seconds silence.

"What's it look like to you?"

"You haven't seen it yet?"

I'd forgotten to tell him I was still a few feet from the water's edge at Venice Beach.

"Well, Jay. All I can say is that a lot of people watching this site right now may be thinking it's a bit primitive, but I'm here to tell you the kid's one clever little dude."

I was busting a gut to be able to see the image Charlie was looking at on his screen. "How do you mean? What's he done?"

"Well, we know he has our user number and password, 'cos he hacked in before with the photo."

"That's right," I agreed.

"So we know he can get into the central machine, upload whatever info he wants, then place it where it's accessible to our website."

That bit I knew – that Harold could have hacked in and modified a file. The question was how had he managed to modify the digital image of Trent Truman's face?

"He's got to have accessed *all* the files. That scares the shit out of me, Jay. Christ alone knows how long it took him to figure out which was which," Charlie continued.

There were approximately three thousand files that controlled the movie. These were over and above the backgrounds that were stored on the CD. Of these three thousand, possibly twenty controlled the graphics of each actor. If Harold had wanted to 'glue' his digital photograph to the head of Trent Truman, thereby obscuring his animated features, he'd have to have viewed each file until he'd come up with the Truman's face file.

"He's got to have reverse engineered our file format, Jay. He's maybe even changed the linkages. Shit, this is major bad news."

One thing was for sure, Harold was living up to his image of the gifted child.

"Run Vigilante," I said, attempting to calm him down. "I'll call the SMPD"

"I'd like to lock up the central machine, Jay. Put a twenty figure ASCII password on it."

"Can you hold off till I speak to the cops?"

"I can, but I think you're crazy if you don't agree to do it right now. This kid's worse than a virus. He could kill Sleuthhound right this minute if he wanted to."

"Don't exaggerate. We've got back-ups. Fact is, he doesn't want to kill Sleuthhound. Believe me, Charlie." I was begging now. "He's out there killing people. The site's our only potential link to him. We've *got* to keep it open."

"I think you're wrong on this one, Jay. Very wrong. You're simply playing along because it suits you – because you want to beat him at his own game.

Well, somewhere along the line, you may be taking the 'Kitchen down the tubes with you. I'm sorry to be so blunt, but it has to be said."

"I hear you loud and clear. Just give me an hour or so to clear my thoughts and call the cops."

"Take as long as you like, Jay. You call the shots, always have, you know that. So long as you think things over long and hard, I'll go along."

"Oh Charlie, can you download the photo on Truman's face right away? It's the first thing the cops will ask for."

"Sure. Meet you at the 'Kitchen."

I rang off, briefly dropping the arm that held the phone to the sand. It suddenly felt as though it weighed fifty pounds.

Twenty feet in front of me, Raymond was up to his knees in the surf, a beer bottle held to his lips, his trousers rolled up to his knees in true English style.

I pulled Yant's card from my wallet and dialled.

48.

Everyone beat me to the office because I had to drop Raymond off home on my way.

I decided not to tell him of the new crisis – the last thing he needed right then was something fresh to worry about.

I told him I had to pick up a few things, and that we'd grab a bite at Carney's when I got back.

Charlie introduced me to a detective from downtown; Quin from Robbery-Homicide. He didn't refer to Yant. The antipathy had been so evident the last time we'd met, I think he didn't quite know what to say.

Yant's mood was darker than ever. It didn't take too much guesswork to conclude that Quin had been assigned Yant's case, and that Yant's presence was merely for the introductions.

I couldn't have been happier; after all, it was entirely possible that Quin was a bona fide human being, with blood rather than venom running through his veins.

Charlie's monitor was running the web site. Both detectives were holding blown-up black and white photos that Charlie had downloaded.

"So no one has the first idea who this might be?" Quin asked as I sat.

Charlie shook his head. I said nothing. Quin looked at me and took my silence as a 'no'.

"Well, we'd better find out double quick who the hell he is, 'cos the outlook's pretty bleak for this guy," Quin added, waving the paper in his hand.

He looked surprisingly jolly for a homicide detective who was anticipating any minute being called to a crime scene to view a warm cadaver.

"Mr Krale says this man bears little or no facial similarity to any of the characters in your movie. Would you agree with that, Mr Benedict?"

"Yes, I'd agree with that."

"So why this guy? Any ideas?"

I presumed Quin was brain-storming rather than simply asking me to do his job for him. "On the last occasion," I began, "as detective Yant will tell you _"

Quin cut me short. "He already has, Mr Benedict. The dead girl looked the spitting image of the dead body in your movie."

Yant must have received my message concerning Lastra.

Quin's attitude wasn't in the least aggressive, it was clear he wanted to move along as quickly as possible. Time was not on his side.

"So we have to assume there's another link. Question is, what? Could it be the name? What are your characters called? The male ones, that is."

"Althar Robustus, Lane Freeway, Trent Truman, and Sol Shyster," I replied. I felt pretty damned stupid coming up with a list like that, given the very serious circumstances of the moment.

Without thinking, my eyes flicked defensively to Yant. Our eyes met. His expression was one of utter disdain. Stupid me – my fault, I'd looked.

"Possibly this person's been chosen because he shares the same profession as one of the characters?" Quin offered.

"Politician, con-man, criminal, and rich sybarite," I replied.

"No difference between the first three," Quin quipped. "What's the last one? Sounds like a sugar substitute."

"A self-indulgent person devoted to sensuous luxury."

"Well wouldn't you know it, yet another word for a politician."

Charlie laughed.

Right then my cellphone rang. It was Nancy. She'd done some asking around on the web. The first sighting of the altered web site that she'd come up with was 4.45pm. It could have been up there earlier, but no one had seen it.

I relayed the information to Quin.

"Why don't you get the TV stations to broadcast the picture," I suggested. "You don't necessarily have to say there's a serial killer on the loose. If the guy's still alive, I'm sure he'd appreciate it."

Again, without thinking, I was coming across like a smart-ass.

"I faxed it through to Parker Center ten minutes ago, Mr Benedict," Quin replied, fixing me with a semi-hostile expression. "I'd say it'll be included in the 6 o'clock news. We probably missed the 5.30 edition."

Suddenly the atmosphere wasn't quite as jovial as before. Quin had clearly taken offense. In a few short minutes I'd again managed to put a man who'd up till now shown me nothing but politeness, completely off-side. I swore inwardly. Getting along with members of the police department clearly wasn't my strong point.

I was determined to win back Quin's respect as soon as possible.

"I'm sure you know exactly what you're doing," I said. "However, if I were in your situation, rather than sitting around here, I'd be sitting on Harold Corr and his friend Phil Tampico. I'm convinced it's the Corr boy who posted the photos on our computers yesterday and today. He stabbed that girl to death yesterday – that's a fact."

"A fact is it? Do you have evidence to back this up, Mr Benedict?" Quin asked languidly. Judging by his enthusiasm, I might have been suggesting the moon was made of mozzarella.

"Harold Corr shot and killed my wife, detective. He planted the murder weapon in my garden, then manufactured a story that I'd accidentally dropped a bracelet belonging to my wife on the floor of his bedroom following the funeral of his father. Frankly I'm staggered that detective Yant here has failed to appraise you of all the facts. The reason I believe –"

"Hold it, Mr Benedict," Quin cut in strongly, holding up his hand. "You're quite wrong there. Detective Yant has told me every detail of your case. However, it's you the District Attorney's decided to charge with Mrs Benedict's murder, not Harold Corr.

"The case against you is, I'm told, a strong one; while there isn't the smallest shred of evidence to link the Corr child with your wife's death. If Robbery-Homicide thought for one second that Harold Corr was responsible for the slaying of that girl yesterday, we'd be on the Corr kid's doorstep right now with a warrant to search the premises."

"Well, you'd have missed him," I snapped back. I was sick and tired of being lectured to by hard-nosed Los Angeles detectives. Quin's attitude seemed as intransigent and set in stone as Yant's.

Yant raised his eyebrows. "Oh yeah? How so, Mr Benedict? You know something we don't?"

I knew at once I should have kept my big yap shut.

"He's on Highway 101 with his mother, heading west," I replied lamely.

"How come you know that, Mr Benedict?" Yant continued, as Quin watched the exchange with interest. "You got someone watching the boy? Would that be right? I'm not sure how pleased Judge Earnshaw would be to hear that. Last time I heard, you were under orders to leave the kid alone. That right?"

There was no point in denying it. "I was told to keep away from the Corr boy personally. Didn't say I couldn't have him watched by a private detective."

Yant smiled. He would have done a Cheshire cat proud. "Well, I guess we've got nothing to worry ourselves about, have we?" he said, looking at Quin. "Mr Benedict's private eye's got the kid nailed down. I don't see him and his mother going on a murder spree – not with a PI on their asses."

"Harold Corr may already have killed that man," I stumbled on, pointing at the black and white photo, unsure of my reasoning. Yant suddenly had me firmly on the back foot.

"I thought you told us that last time the picture came first and the killing followed?" Yant continued, like a dog with a bone.

I nodded vaguely. It was true.

"Well, tell me this. How long has your personal gumshoe being trailing the kid."

He had me in a corner. I didn't feel at all like making his day.

"Don't be shy, Mr Benedict. You'll have to share this information with the LAPD soon enough."

"Since last night, detective Yant."

"And is this person still on the kid's case? Right now?"

"He is, yes," I had to admit.

"Well, unless the kid's killed someone while your private eye was sleeping, I'd say we don't really have to worry about Harold Corr." He fixed me with a triumphant stare. "Do we, Mr Benedict?" he prodded.

I said nothing. Charlie ran a hand over his face. I knew he felt for me.

Yant chuckled. "Cat got your tongue, eh?"

His self-saitsfied remark did the trick. I leaned forward. "Detective Yant, I'm concerned that Harold Corr's buddy, Phil Tampico, is at this moment out there on the streets about to kill the man who's picture you are presently holding. I know damed well Harold Corr isn't in a position right now to kill anyone. But his buddy is unconstrained. Is that too difficult to comprehend?"

"So now you think it's the *other* kid that's the killer," Yant persisted. "Would that be about right?"

This time I locked eyes with him. Push was fast becoming shove.

"That's entirely right. At approximately 1.30 this afternoon, Harold Corr and Phil Tampico left an apartment on Montana and split up. My man followed Corr, but he gave him the slip –"

"You're not paying him enough, Mr Benedict," Yant cut in, shooting Quin a look.

I stood and walked over to Yant. He rose to face me. "Detective Yant, my investigator picked up Harold Corr again at 4 pm when he returned to his home in Calabasas. We're still trying to locate Tampico. I suggest to you that it is entirely possible Harold Corr sent the photograph from his home before he left with his mother, while Tampico is about to kill right this minute. He may already have done so."

"Now you listen up, Mr Benedict," he replied in what was only just above a whisper. "I'd say your private dick puts you in contempt of court. While I don't give a damn personally, I'd say Mrs Corr would make it her business to see your bail revoked if she ever got wind of what you were up to. What do you make of them apples?"

At that precise moment no one in the room was smiling. Not even Quin.

Charlie broke the silence. "Couldn't you make a list of all calls made from the Corr house between 3 and 5 pm?"

I could have kissed my old buddy. He'd managed to come between Yant and me, diffusing the tension. I wasn't at all sure that Yant didn't have it in mind to punch me then and there, and to hell with his pension.

"Can't make a list without a call analysis machine locked on to the house lines," Quin replied, "and we'd need a judge to agree that. Otherwise, there'd only be records of long distance calls. If you're dialling into the Net it's a local call, right?"

"Right," Charlie replied.

"I'm not a computer man myself, Mr Krale," Quin continued. "But it must be possible to track which computer was dialling in?"

"If he's screwing directly with the site via the Net, he's got to have an Internet connection somewhere. Of course he could always have hacked his way into an Internet service provider's data base, creating himself a false account, in which case he'd be the mystery man – you wouldn't know who he was unless you caught him while he was actually on-line.

"But if I wanted to smokescreen you guys, I could dial out to one machine, connect via the Internet to several other machines, then dial out from one of those. The cops could never chase me back. Are you with me so far?"

I looked at the faces facing Charlie. They were twin mirrors of confusion.

"Why don't you give me a for instance, Mr Krale," said Quin,

"Sure. I can connect to a machine in the Ukraine and make that machine dial a modem. Then I can hop and skip from one machine and modem to another machine and modem, and continue to do so until I've lost you. Like using several cars for a getaway."

I noticed a glimmer of understanding register on Quin's face at the mention of car switches.

"There was a famous case recently. Kids in West Germany were dialling out of Frankfurt using a fake account. They used a satellite connection to the United Kingdom, then another satellite connection to the States, covered their tracks by scooting in and out of about twelve university networks around the country, finally hacking their way into the military networks. Only the combined efforts of FBI, CIA and three countries' computer cops busted them."

My eyes flicked quickly from Quin to Yant. I'm sure I had a similar expression on my face when I'd looked down at my first Latin examination paper at school when I was thirteen.

Quin stood. "Well, we've got to get back. I'd like to take a copy of your movie back with me, if you have one available, Mr Benedict."

I gave Quin a Sleuthhound gift box of CDs on his way out.

The detectives were clearly in a hurry. Any minute now the photograph of the mystery guy would be flashed across the television screens of the city, and with any luck the phones would be ringing off the hook. They had to hope to reach the poor bastard before the killer did. My guess was that rather than knocking on the guy's door to warn him, they'd soon be at a crime scene, looking at his body.

"You think my theories concerning Corr and Tampico are nonsense, don't you," I said, handing Quin the box of CDs. I took particular care not to sound aggrieved.

"Mr Benedict, I listen to everything," Quin replied in a reasonably friendly fashion. "I'd be pretty dumb not to. Right now, I don't happen to share your opinion we're dealing with a couple of murderous kids. I think there's every possibility we've got one sick serial killer out there, and it scares me to death. Not to mention the DA and the Mayor."

"Look, I've absolutely no place to ask you this favor," I said, crawling right up Quin's butt. "But couldn't you please do one thing for all of us?"

"We got to get moving," Yant called out from the door.

Quin held up a hand. "What's that, Mr Benedict?"

"Check the whereabouts of Harold Corr and Phil Tampico between 1.30 and 5 o'clock today. Then you can tell me I'm an asshole. Who knows, I very well may be. I think it's worth a shot, that's all."

Quin debated my request for a couple of seconds. "I'll do what I can, Mr Benedict. Maybe I should wait till a crime's been committed."

"There's a dead body out there right now, detective. Believe me."

Everyone, including Charlie stared at me. I was close to shouting again without realizing.

"Let's hope you're wrong," Quin said as he walked through the door.

I called after him. "Detective Quin! One more thing. When you find the body, ask around at the crime scene. I'll lay odds someone tells you there was a white Toyota van standing nearby sometime during the afternoon."

Quin was reaching for the the door handle of the Chevy. He turned and walked back towards me. Yant followed.

"You'd better tell me right now what you mean by that last remark, Mr Benedict," Quin said.

"The investigator who was following Harold Corr this afternoon thinks the boy slipped him by jumping into a white van in Santa Monica at an intersection. I'd lay odds the van was stolen earlier by Tampico. Why don't you run a check for any white vans stolen around midday in Santa Monica. Worth a shot, isn't it?"

"Tell you what, Dale," Yant replied with a smirk, "Let me handle that one. Be a pleasure to oblige you, Mr Benedict."

I turned to face him. The tone of his voice left me in no doubt that he was sending me up.

"You're a real mensch, detective Yant," I replied with an easy smile.

As he turned towards the car I added, "Oh, one more thing, detective Yant. Don't take it too hard Parker Center's jerked your case from under your feet. It'll leave you freer to make my life a misery, won't it?"

If looks could have killed.

49.

It concerned me greatly that I didn't seem to be too much in control. I was making instinctive decisions, saying things without considering their consequences. One minute I'd be calm, the next I'd be ready to punch whoever disagreed with me.

I knew I had to chill out and take stock. Problem was, however carefully I attempted to tread, every five minutes the lights went out and someone threw a dozen banana peels in my path.

Charlie and I had a pretty intense discussion concerning my theory that it was Harold who was sending the photos.

To my mind there was absolutely no doubt whatsoever that the boy was pursuing a personal vendetta against me. The reason? Purely and simply because I'd crossed him the day his father was buried.

"You really think he's killing these people just because you pissed him off? Come on, Jay."

"Hold it right there, Charlie," I said, grabbing his arm. "I was right there when the sonofabitch looked me in the eye and told me he'd put a gun to Faith's head and blown her brains out."

"Slow down, Jay. This is a discussion. Okay?" He was staring accusingly at my hand which was fastened to his elbow. I let go at once.

"You see, I'm not talking about Faith, Jay. I'm talking about the girl who died yesterday, and now the guy who showed up on the website."

"I know that, Charlie. I know that. But I also know damned well that Harold killed these two people. It's his vengeance. I'm certain he killed them as a pay-back because I wouldn't pay him money for killing Faith. He genuinely thought he was doing me a favor when he killed her."

"But he's got nothing to gain by pursuing you!"

"For Christ's sake, Charlie, you're attributing normal reasoning to the kid. He's *not* normal. He may be a genius when it comes to electronics, but at bottom he's an eleven-year-old who thinks it's cool to kill people for money!"

"Jay, there's not one shred of evidence that it's Harold who killed that girl yesterday. Sure, your hunch is that it's the kid. It'd be mine too. Put me in your shoes, I'd be paranoid about the little sonofabitch. But I have to tell you, I can see it from Quin's POV too. I'm with you all the way about Faith's death. But the rest's conjecture."

"Charlie, at the toystore he told me he was going to kill someone Saturday! Gardenas died Saturday, shot in the head execution style with a Ruger! The same gun as killed Faith!

"When I told him to go to hell; that I'd make it my life's work to see him in Juvenile Hall, he told me I was a dead man! So, how the hell can you stand there and tell me it's sheer conjecture to believe Corr's the killer?"

Charlie didn't answer for a few seconds. "You gotta take it easy, Jay," he said finally. "You're driving yourself to madness. I'm really worried for my best buddy, and that's a fact."

Before I left the 'Kitchen, Charlie and I agreed to keep the computers switched off. I managed to persuade him to leave the central computer password unaltered. At least for the present.

I argued, I thought quite reasonably, that whoever was doing the hacking was without doubt smart enough to get in, whether or not we changed the password.

Logic dictated that Corr was merely using our web site to post the photographs. If he'd meant to damage our data bases and tools, he'd have done so already.

Besides, Charlie had backed up every shred of information that existed in our data banks, so what real harm could he do now?

Before I left for home I called Nate, detailing the events of the past couple of hours.

He was shocked to the core. He told me he and Mama Poule had just seen the photograph on the news. Of course, at the time he'd had no idea of its relevance.

Dan had called him earlier telling him that he and Ethan had cocked up their surveillance. Nate apologized to me on their behalf.

"Nothing to do with you, Nate. One of those things, is all. Tell me, is there anyone downtown who could run a check on a stolen vehicle for you?"

"What exactly do you mean? Like you have the plates and want to know if the car's stolen?"

"No. I want to know if anyone reported a white Toyota van stolen in the Santa Monica area any time today."

"Well, I've got a contact, yes. Whether he can do me a favor like that, I don't know. I'll ask him anyway. Who do you reckon stole it? The Corr kid?"

'You got it, Nate. More exactly, Phil Tampico. It doesn't look too good for the guy in the photograph, does it?"

"You're convinced it's Corr and Tampico that are behind all this, aren't you?"

"Nate, let's get this straight," I said. My nerves were now really jangling. "Are you with me on this one, or not?"

"Sure I am, Jay."

At that precise moment, I wasn't exactly sure that he was. Sounded as though he was trying to convince himself.

"Any word from the DA's office?" I asked. I'd been fully expecting Nate to call to tell me they'd decided to drop the murder charge. That they'd not yet done so was a major disappointment.

"Nothing yet, Jay. Remember, it's Saturday night. Difficult to get anything done."

I was suddenly really angry again. "Oh yeah? Well I wouldn't want to put Goodrich to any trouble, would I? I'm sure she's got better things to do Saturday night than tell me the DA's office no longer thinks I'm a murderer."

"Call me if you need me," Nate said, ignoring my childish outburst. "Call me anyway. You know where your second home is by now."

And to think that only a few weeks ago I'd been in two minds whether to bend to Charlie's pressure and dump the man as my lawyer. He was a tower of strength.

I was only two blocks from home when my cellphone started ringing. I reached out and pressed the 'send' button.

"Jay? It's Raymond. I don't know where you are right now, but if you're on your way home I'd turn right round and make for the hills."

My immediate response was to take my foot off the gas and pull over. What the hell was he talking about?

"There are four TV crews outside the gates. I'm next door at the Agrams' place. Couldn't ring out from home – they've jammed the lines. They don't know I'm your brother yet – I told them I was the pool man."

Raymond chuckled. It was all a big game.

They had to have found the body. There was no other reason I could think of for the media frenzy.

The moment the photo had been shown on the news, every TV station in greater Los Angeles would have smelled one major deal story.

It was quite possible the newshounds had beaten the police to the crime scene. People are more inclined to offer information to a TV station and stash a few dollars in their hip pocket, than call the cops and give it away for free.

Why were they on my front door step? The answer wasn't too hard to fathom. The World Wide Web is a very powerful tool, accessed every second of the day and night by a fair cross section of the world at large. I'd have laid odds that someone watching the 6.30 news, while chuggalugging a cold beer, said to himself, *Hey, isn't that the dude that popped up on the Cyberkitchen web site?*

So he calls the networks pronto. *I got some mighty interesting news for you.* he says.

Five minutes later someone in the newsroom pulls the Cyberkitchen's company records. Up comes my name.

Shit, the journalist says to the news director, *Jay Benedict's the guy who mudered his wife a few weeks ago?*

The news director rubs his hands together. It's all beginning to look like strawberries and cream for the late night news. Now the media are pressing the LAPD really hard for details of the death.

And what would be their dream scenario? Well, a serial killing would be numero uno, of course! Could they possibly link the death of this guy to the death of the gorgeous babe the day before? Holy shit, that would really be something!

I sat in the car, the engine idling, debating what I should do. Turn around and make for the hills, or front up and face the music?

Ten seconds thought told me taking off wasn't an option. They'd find me soon enough, and how would that make me look?

It was vital I showed them I had absolutely nothing to hide.

It was also entirely possible that I could turn the situation to my advantage, put the media on my side, show them a travesty of justice was in the air, and that I fully expected a complete about-face by the DA's office on account of my newfound unshakable alibi. I didn't have to spell out to them that it hinged on the testimony of an elderly mentally challenged alcoholic, did I?

Besides I couldn't throw Raymond to the wolves. They'd soon figure he wasn't the pool man, and they'd be hounding him till I returned to take the heat off him. He was too ill to take that kind of a beating.

There was, of course, another reason. I was damned curious. What the hell had happened? Who knew, with a bit of luck the guy I'd presumed to be dead might well have turned the tables on his assailant.

So who was dead?

I pulled out into Ventura and drove the final couple of blocks.

The news vehicles were parked both sides of the street. I pulled up fifty feet down the road. The moment they caught sight of me they started running towards me, so I drove on up to the gate where they surrounded the car.

I've seen better order at a UN food drop in Mogadishu.

Surrounded, I leant out of the window and told the ravening reporters I'd be happy to give them an impromptu press conference poolside in ten minutes if they let me pass.

I'm sure they realized it was that or nothing, so the Red Sea of news hacks parted, and I drove on through.

Through the den window I could see them chatting amongst themselves on the lawn as I dialled Nate's number. A tall man in a double-breasted Italian suit was talking earnestly to camera. It must have been the lead up blurb to his forthcoming interview – one with a murder suspect in his Studio City home.

Well, this man had a surprise or two coming.

"Hello? Nate Berg speaking."

"Nate, it's Jay."

"I've been calling your home number for twenty minutes. Called your cellphone too."

"I was calling Raymond. It's a three-ringed circus here. Media everywhere. You've got to tell me what's happened. I missed the news. I know nothing."

"They found a body at 6.30, or close to it. Westwood Village. Execution-style shooting. No struggle. Guy in the upstairs apartment called in the DOA's address almost as soon as it was aired. LAPD were round there within minutes. His name was Thorne. Supposedly an accountant."

"Hold it, what do you mean by that? Supposedly?"

"Just about to tell you. My source at the BHPD says they know Thorne quite well. Get this, he's a numbers man for the local mafia."

This really threw me for a loop. "What the fuck–?"

"Yeah, me too. And here's another weird one. Dan Stir's assistant called me ten minutes ago. Phil Tampico just walked *out* of his Montana apartment. You follow me? Not *in*, but *out*. And guess where Harold Corr is right now?"

No guesswork there. "Santa Barbara?"

"Close. Montecito. Dan called and told me. He's outside a private home now. The Corr kid and his mother are both inside."

Nate's line of thinking was clear as day. He was having second thoughts about Corr and Tampico's involvement. The hackles on my back were rising. O ye of little faith.

"So what are you saying, Nate. tell me."

"Not saying anything else other than Harold Corr was nowhere near Westwood Village; and Ethan could have made a mistake about Phil Tampico. He could have been home."

I decided to let the remark ride. No point in getting angry just because Nate was leaning against my theory. Nate had every right to voice his opinion, and he was always going to take a cautious approach anyway. I couldn't blame him for that. Fact was, Ethan couldn't have watched the back and front of the Montana apartment at the same time, could he? Tampico had obviously sneaked in the rear entrance.

The reporter in the suit was now tap-tapping at the den window to gain my attention.

He smiled inanely as our eyes met.

"I'll call you right back, Nate. Got to go, I've got some idiot at the window, and five news crews in the garden. They want to talk."

"One thing!" he shouted into the telephone. "Jay – don't talk about the case. Your case. Whatever else you do, don't do *that*! Please!"

"Trust me, Nate. If they ask about Faith, I'm going to tell them I'm an innocent man. That's it. Don't ask me not to. I want to tell the world. I need to!"

"Okay. If you must. But please don't antagonize the DA's office! Life's hard enough. Don't make mine any more impossible."

"I promise," I said.

"Jesus, Jay. Can't you wait till I get down there? Why the hell do you have to go off half-cocked right now?"

"Because they're there. Like Everest," I said, trying to lighten Nate's mood.

"Nice try, Jay, but I'm not in the mood to be soft-soaped. Promise me one other thing."

"Anything. You're my lawyer, after all."

"Don't name names. If you do, I won't be your lawyer a second longer. And that's *my* promise."

I agreed, then hung up, promising to give him a precise account when I'd talked to the newshounds.

I chose a woman who reminded me very forcibly of Lois Lane; she'd be my focus during the barrage of questions. It served the suited guy right for the discourtesy of knocking on my den window when he could see I was on the phone.

"Gina Davies, Channel 9. Mr Benedict, we believe a photograph of the dead man, Travis Thorne, appeared on your company's web site this afternoon. Is there any connnection between the dead man and your company?"

"I didn't know the man," I replied. "I had no idea he was dead till two minutes ago."

"Can you think why anyone would want to place a photograph of Mr Thorne on your company web site?"

I bit my tongue. How I'd have loved to come out with it all in front of the city's media; tell them everything from beginning to end, and let them make of it what they liked.

But Nate was absolutely right. What purpose would it have served? These guys would lap it up, but who was I talking to? Bernstein and Woodward? Absolutely not. These guys were looking for a story; the whackier and more outrageous the better.

And who's side would the news director take? A clean cut eleven-year-old middle class kid, or a forty-two year old raving lunatic accused of murdering his wife?

I also had to bear in mind that as far as the Thorne killing was concerned, Harold now had a rock solid alibi.

No, naming names wasn't an option. The second I even hinted that I believed Harold Corr killed Faith, Stella Corr and a team of lawyers would own me lock stock and barrel.

Then a better alternative came to mind. Maybe I could say just enough to put the skids under the LAPD.

"Mr Benedict, can you confirm that this is the second time a photo has been sent to you electronically at your company offices." It was the suited guy.

"That's correct," I replied.

"And on both occasions the subject was found murdered?"

"Correct again."

"And you can think of no common link?"

"I have a theory, yes. One I've shared with the Los Angeles Police Department. I'd rather leave it to them to make the decision whether or not to release this information to the media. I'll certainly not be interfering with the course of justice."

A short sweating man in shirtsleeves pressed his way to the front. "Mr Benedict, do you think there's any link between the deaths of these two people and the death of your wife?"

I liked this guy enormously right away. I could have fed him the question word for word.

"I do."

The newspeople pressed forward ever more eagerly, cameras thrust in my face. They were all shouting for my attention.

How are they linked, Mr Benedict?

Does the LAPD have a person or persons in mind?

Over here, Mr Benedict!

I held up a hand. "I am innocent of the charges that have been laid against me. New evidence has recently come to light that completely exonerates me –"

"What evidence is that, Mr Benedict?" the short sweaty guy asked.

That's when I called a halt to the interview. I fully hoped they'd now go ask Quin about the evidence. Besides, I'd already overstepped the mark as far as Nate was concerned, and I knew it.

"That's it. I have nothing more to say for now," I said, walking back to the house, the newspeople in hot pursuit.

I had to send Raymond out to talk to them ten minutes later. They didn't appear to have any intention of leaving. Raymond reminded them they were on private property and formally asked them to get lost. He'd had personal dealings with the media when he'd been arrested for passing dud cheques. He'd always had a more than healthy dislike of them, and welcomed the opportunity to be less than polite.

A few minutes later the hounds and their camera crews grudgingly did as instructed.

Before I had a chance to call Nate, the phone rang. I picked up the receiver. "Nate?"

It wasn't Nate. It was Alice. My stomach turned over with apprehension.

"Jay, it's Alice. Hal and I want you to know we are behind you all the way. We love you, and feel so sorry for what's happening to you right now. It's a terrible, terrible mistake and they'll all come to see that soon."

Her words were such a surprise, and so moving, I was instantly choked with emotion. I couldn't speak. My eyes filled with tears that rolled down my cheeks. And after all, we were talking about the death of her daughter.

"Jay? Are you still there?"

"I tried to keep it from you both. I was worried for Hal. I didn't know how he'd take it."

"I knew that must have been it, Jay."

"How is Hal?"

"Taking him home tomorrow. He's fit as a flea. The doctors had to chain him to the bed."

She sounded happy and relaxed.

"You take care, Jay. The world will come to its senses soon and you'll be able to put all of this behind you. Meantime, come and see us soon."

"I'll do that first chance I have," I replied.

As I put down the receiver, the phone rang. It was Nate. I was a good lad and told him everything – rather than just the bits that wouldn't make him angry.

"So you did everything but name names. Thank you so much, Jay. You're a real help to me in this time of crisis."

"My crisis, Nate."

"And getting worse by the second when you're left to steer the ship. Pressuring Quin's just going to antagonize him. Same with the DA's office. They're not going to drop the charges right now, even if they were going to do so, because it'll look as though they're caving in to media pressure. So, all in all, you've done a pretty thorough job."

"I've never been one to take the easy option. If something's got to be said, then I'll say it. To do otherwise, merely because it'll make life run a bit smoother, is plain gutless."

"Sure, thing, Caped Crusader," Nate quipped wryly. "Are we going to see you this evening?"

"I'm taking Raymond to Carney's. We'll drop by tomorrow if that's okay with you two – Raymond wants to go shopping beachside."

The chili dogs at Carney's tasted better than they'd ever done.

Raymond's experience with hot dogs was based on the fast food guys at Wembley Football Stadium in London, with their steaming aluminium carts of smelly sausages and boiled onions. He was instantly transported to chili dog heaven.

On our return he clicked on the tube, surfing the channels for a news report.

A few minutes later he struck pay dirt. There I was, a small photo in a box to the right of the newsreader's head.

Raymond sat goggle-eyed. Somewhat ghoulishly, I thought, everything considered.

Were the deaths of Raylene Kelly, the girl who'd looked so much like Lastra, and Travis Thorne, the body found earlier in the evening, the work of a serial killer, the anchorman asked?

"Jay Benedict, a co-director of a San Fernando Valley computer games company, The Cyberkitchen, agreed to be interviewed this afternoon at his Studio City home."

Suddenly Raymond and I were watching my press release on the lawn. They included my every word.

"What evidence is that, Mr Benedict?" the short sweaty man asked finally, referring to the new evidence that was to exonerate me of Faith's murder. As I turned away from camera we cut back to the anchorman.

"Mr Benedict preferred not to answer that question. Nor were the LAPD willing to add to their 6.30 statement."

The newsreader cleared his throat briefly then added, "Mr Benedict is currently on bail, charged with the murder of his wife earlier this month."

I turned off the television.

As usual Nate had been right. I'd come across as a complete asshole. A dangerous one at that – one that most probably had killed his wife earlier this month.

I bade goodnight to Raymond, took a couple of Nembutal and went to bed.

I'd fucked up enough for one day.

50.

I still felt drugged when Raymond woke me the following morning. I regretted having taken the Nembutal, and cursed myself for such weakness of spirit. I'd have to face up to things sometime really soon, I couldn't just hide behind chemicals.

At 10.30 am Raymond was anxious to get down to the beach.

"Funny thing isn't it. The moment mum tells you you can only swim for another ten minutes, you know you've just *got* to do it all day. What I'm saying is, now I know my days are numbered, life tastes so damn sweet."

I chewed slowly on Raymond's French toast. A chef he'd never be, but right now he was high on my list of heroes.

"I think everyone should be lied to by their doctors when they hit forty," he continued. *"You've only got six months to live, Mr Jones, make the most of it.* Everyone would be so damned grateful they were still around seven months down the track, they wouldn't give a shit about the tax man, the traffic, the weather, the lack of parking spots, bad service in restaurants. You name it!"

Before I left home I put in a call to Dan.

He was still in Montecito. Harold and his mother hadn't moved since they'd arrived.

Ethan had called Dan at 10 am to report that Tampico was still at his home.

There wasn't much else I could do at home, so Raymond and I set off for the beach.

Venice was wonderfully hot, crowded and sweaty when we arrived.

It took us half an hour to park then an hour and a half to be carried from one end of the boardwalk to the other amongst a seething wave of humanity.

Somewhere along the way, Raymond managed to buy a pair of sunglasses, twenty pairs of white socks, and a Jimi Hendrix beach towel that he'd instantly fallen in love with.

We stopped by our Margarita watering hole for a jug and some salsa. Then it was back to Raymond's favorite sun-bathing spot on the sand near Muscle Beach.

Five minutes later he was asleep and I was deep in thought, trying to make some sense of what was happening to me.

What would be Harold's next step? Up till now I'd never even got close to second-guessing him. It was time for a serious re-think.

Harold couldn't possibly have shot Thorne himself. It had to have been Tampico. But Robbery-Homicide weren't going to have much time for my theories now that Harold had a cast iron alibi.

The link with Sleuthhound was pretty straightforward as far as the victims went. Raylene Kelly was practically a double for Lastra. And Travis Thorne? It had to be the initials; the same as Trent Truman. Double T's.

Was there more? If I analyzed the game in more depth what more, if anything, would I come up with? Would I be able to pre-determine his next move? Because the horrifying possibility was that Kelly and Thone weren't the end of the matter. It was a fair asumption that Harold planned more deaths. Would they too be based on characters from Sleuthhound?

Althar Robustus? Lane Freeway? Sol Shyster? Who'd be next?

I tried to think laterally. Why had Harold chosen the Lastra figure first, and Trent Truman second? Had it been random, or was there a sequence?

The movie was structured so that each time the viewer played the movie, the branching options allowed him or her to alter the outcome. Depending on the advice the viewer gave Sleuthhound, the canine gumshoe, the killer could turn out to be any of the major protagonists. That's what made the game interesting.

This thought led me back to square one – any one of the characters could be next up if Harold was bent on continuing his killing spree. Again I'd hit a brick wall.

The fact that I was powerless to do anything to stop the boy, short of putting Dan Stir on his tail day and night, was driving me crazy. I was heading inexorably for a nervous breakdown. Either that or I'd simply lose the balance of my mind entirely and take a gun round to the Corr house to take the law into my own hands.

The long and short of it was that I was getting absolutely no further forward in bringing Harold to justice, and the police seemed content to wait around till another photo appeared on the web site.

A frisbee crashed to the sand two feet from my head, bringing me sharply back to reality. A girl ran up, apologising to me as she snatched it back.

The sun suddenly felt as though it was flaying the skin from my body, and my blood was racing round so fast I thought my brains were frying.

I sat up abruptly and took some deep breaths as I looked out towards the deep blue Pacific.

At 2 pm Raymond woke, and I put aside the *Tibetan Book of Living and Dying*. I'd just reached the chapter entitled *The Process of Dying*. I snapped the book and suggested we have a bite to eat. Raymond agreed readily. I knew which bar he had in mind.

The boardwalk was only slightly less busy at 2 pm than it had been at 10 am. It was as though every eccentric from San Francisco to Arizona had chosen this day to spend a few hours in Venice. Old men with beards on monocycles weaved in and out of the crowd; fat girls in bikinis scythed past on in-line skates; dogs dressed in Harley jackets and dark glasses panted their way down the sidewalk under the watchful gaze of their adoring owners; sixty-year-old refugees from Haight-Ashbury sat in the sand, incense and tarot cards close to hand.

Halfway down to our margarita joint I caught a flash of a girl roller-blading at speed down the sidewalk past us; tight denim shorts, blonde hair tied in bunches, long long legs, and a yellow singlet that covered only about five per cent of her upper body.

Where had I seen her before? Perhaps earlier in the day somewhere.

I didn't bother too much with the thought.

Raymond and I sat at a bartop that faced out onto the boardwalk, so that we could eat, drink, and watch the world stroll by.

We ordered a double plate of nachos and a pitcher of Margies, and stared vaguely at the weirdos as they paraded by.

Maybe it was the Nembutal the night before, possibly it was all the concentrated thinking I'd done while Raymond was asleep. Either way, two drinks and a lot of tortilla chips later, my mind was in a relaxed state of grace that any self-respecting Yogi would have killed for. My brain was barely ticking over. My eyes were open yet seeing nothing but walking blurs. I was a laptop in 'sleep' mode.

It was Raymond's raucous laughter that brought me out of it. I tried hard to focus my eyes. Raymond was calling out to a young girl who was standing on the boardwalk right in front of us. The world around me was a mass of vague shapes.

I shook my head to clear my befuddled brain.

That's when I saw her.

It was the same girl. Long long legs, tight shorts, yellow top, blond hair tied in bunches. She was there in front of us, a camera held to her eye, snapping away at me.

The adrenalin kicked in at once and I was suddenly wide awake. It was only then I knew where I'd seen her before. It was the Jodie Foster look-alike.

By the time my brain had booted up sufficiently to be able to give a panic message to my legs to get on after her, 'Jodie' had taken off like a rabbit, scything her way in and out of the tourists with all the skill of ice-skating gold medalist Eric Heiden.

I vaguely heard Raymond call after me as I barrelled my way through the crowds.

I had to catch her. She was Harold's girl, and she'd been sent to get a photograph.

It was a losing battle from the first second. She had a head start on me. She was on skates, I was on foot.

But I wasn't thinking logically at the time. I was so emotionally charged I suddenly had the strength of five men.

Every ten yards or so I'd catch sight of her ahead of me as the crowds parted. I was shouting at the top of my voice. *She's taken my wallet! Stop the girl on skates! Someone stop her!*

I was about fifty yards down the boardwalk when the first cop flung his arms round me and wrestled me to the ground. He was aged about twenty, one of the detail of bicycle cops that patrolled the beach front.

"Stay down!" he shouted at me as he pulled my right arm round my back. I went limp; there was no point in fighting him or trying to explain, the girl would be long gone by now.

Within seconds another cop in shirt-sleeves and shorts was squatting next to me.

A crowd had gathered around us.

"What's the problem, mister?" the cop shouted in my ear.

"Someone stole my wallet," I replied, my face still pressed into the roadway. "A girl. I was trying to catch her. Would have 'cept you chose to help me out. Thanks a bunch. Mind if I get up now, officer? This is really painful. I'm the victim here, for Christ's sake!"

The young officer let go and helped me to my feet, giving me a very wary look. "Have I seen you before someplace?" His expression suddenly lightened. "Hey, you're not famous are you?"

"I'm not an actor, if that's what you mean," I replied. Over the cop's shoulder I could see Raymond jogging his way down the boardwalk.

"Can I see some form of ID please?"

Now that he'd established I wasn't famous, indentification was clearly a must.

"She stole it, didn't she," I replied. What else logically could I say?

The two cops exchanged a glance. Did they buy my story?

"You want to file a report, or you going to let it ride, Mr –?" the young cop said pulling out his pocketbook.

"Benedict. Look, I haven't time right now. Thanks all the same." I replied.

As the cops climbed back on their mountain bikes, Raymond arrived at my side, completely out of breath.

"What the shit was all that about?" he whispered in my ear in between gasps.

He then turned aggressively on the semi circle of rubber-neckers who were still staring at me, open-mouthed.

"You'd better stand back, guys. FBI," he said authoritatively. "This man here has the Ebola virus."

You've never seen a crowd melt so fast.

On our way back to the beach I explained my fit of madness.

Raymond was suddenly no longer so flip. He was worried.

I reassured him as best I could. I didn't feel threatened personally. No way would Harold Corr try to harm me – too many people were watching his every move.

I wished to God the LAPD were.

I left Raymond to while away what was left of the afternoon on the beach. I was hot and hyped-up in a very major way. To tell the truth, for the first time in a month I was optimistic of a positive outcome to all this horror.

At last. Harold Corr was coming after me.

51.

I'd been home for less than an hour when I heard someone buzz me from the gates. Curious, I looked through the window. I recognized the car at once. It was Stella's.

I felt a jolt of angst, the last thing I wanted right now was to have to face Stella.

Had I met her twenty years ago I could easily have fallen in love with her, but right now she was the mother of the child who had shot and killed Faith.

My quarrel was not with her. I felt deeply sorry for the woman; the day Jack had died her life had inexorably turned into a living nightmare.

I buzzed her through, then walked outside to meet her. I stood there wondering what could possibly be sufficiently important to have persuaded her to come to see me personally.

Had it all been too much for her – was she about to step from the car, pull a gun from her purse and shoot me dead?

I opened the driver's door as the car drew to a halt. She stepped out.

"May I come inside Jay. We need to talk," she said, her voice cold as the grave.

"Of course, Stella," I replied, indicating the open front door.

In the living room , she walked over to the mantelpiece, then turned to face me.

"This won't take more than a minute or so, Jay. I felt it best to discuss the matter face to face so that there'd be absolutely no possibility of our misunderstanding each other."

"Won't you sit down?" I asked, in what I hoped sounded a conciliatory tone.

"No."

"Can I get you anything, then?"

"Nothing," she replied curtly. "Let's get right to it, shall we? Are you currently paying someone to watch my son?"

The remark took me absolutely by surprise. I stood facing her, speechless.

"It's a pretty simple question, Jay. I'm referring to the person who's been following us all damned weekend. Is he paid by you? That's what I'm asking you. Because if that's the case, you'd better call him off this very minute or I'll have your bail revoked so fast your head'll spin all the way to Folsom."

She hadn't raised her voice much above a normal conversational level, yet I was very much aware she was struggling for emotional control. She was fighting mad.

"What makes you think I would do such a thing?" I asked, trying to look as surprised as possible. I had to think very clearly before I admitted anything. If I apologized, thereby admitting I had indeed hired Dan, there'd be little Nate could do to keep me out of prison while I awaited trial.

"Harold pointed the man out to me before we left for Montecito. He followed us all the way up there, then sat in a car in the street outside the house the entire weekend. Right now he's sitting in a car a hundred feet from my home, spying on Harold through binoculars."

"Maybe he's a policeman?"

"Don't play stupid games with me, Jay." Her tone hardened perceptibly. "I'm an intelligent woman. I've called the authorities, and he's no detective. They asked me if I wanted them to come up and check the guy out, but I declined their offer."

I stared at her in silence, still completely stymied as to how to reply.

"Don't you want to know *why* I declined their offer?" she asked.

"Okay. Why?" I mumbled feebly. Her unblinking stare was unnerving. Same as Harold's at Jack's funeral.

"Because I want to give you one last chance. God only knows why, but I feel one small grain of compassion for you. You see, I don't think you're a bad man, Jay. Jack loved you dearly. I have to remember that. You're ill. You must know that. Jack wouldn't want me to hit you while you were down and on your knees."

I didn't quite know how to take all this. If the FBI weren't a million miles off-base, my ex-buddy Jack Corr had made it his profession to do exactly that – to hit people when they were down. To be more precise, to execute them. But much as I wanted to point this out to the fiercely sanctimonious woman who stood before me, I said nothing.

"So you call your man right this second and that'll be the end of it. I will not have Harry upset any further. He's been terrified you might hurt him or me ever since the day Jack was buried. He actually believes you've sent this man to kill us! Can you believe that?"

"I've no intention of harming you or your son, Stella. I only want to see those guilty of Faith's murder brought to justice."

Stella glared at me. It was clear as day what I meant. "If you *ever* again suggest that my boy had anything whatsoever to do with your wife's death I'll make it my business to sue you from here to Moscow!" she exploded. "Now call your investigator right this minute, or I'll call the police and let them do it. Then they can take you downtown for contempt of court! I'll give you one minute."

What the hell was I going to do? It was a classic Catch 22. Call Dan and I admitted he was my man. Stand my ground and she'd call the cops and I was dead in the water.

I picked up the phone and dialled.

"Dan Stir. Who's this?"

"Jay Benedict," I replied as Stella stood across from me in solitary fury.

"I'd like you to please call off the surveillance of Mrs Corr's property. She's with me right now and she's pretty damned angry. She says you've been scaring her boy."

"Jesus," I heard Dan breathe at the other end of the line. "Can she hear me?"

"No. Just leave the area," I replied.

"I'm really sorry, Jay. I should have called you."

"I'm sure you didn't mean to scare anyone. We'll talk about it later."

I rang off, then looked at Stella. "Okay?"

"Okay."

She walked to the door and out to the car.

"I'm serious, Jay. You or anyone come near Harry from now till your trial and I'll see you in prison. You need solid psychiatric help, you know that, don't you. If you're not getting it already, do so."

She climbed into the car then wound the window down and looked up at me. The primrose hair drifted lazily in the breeze. "Whatever you might think, I'm not a vindictive person, Jay. At times my heart goes out to you. You were very sweet to me when Jack died, and I'll always remember that. You see, I don't for a second think you killed Faith. But I have to remember I'm a mother first and foremost, and for that reason I have to see Harry protected from your madness. And believe me, I'll do exactly that."

I looked deep into those piercing blue eyes of hers. I wanted so much to be able to communicate with her; to tell her how deeply I felt for her, how much I wished our friendship hadn't been shaped, controlled, and ultimately destroyed by her evil son. She had no idea of the tragic path she was on.

She opened her mouth to speak then hesitated.

For that fraction of a second I sensed the ice melt. She was the same frightened lonely girl I'd seen sleeping like a doormouse in her basket chair on the verandah the night I'd visited her in Calabasas.

For just that second she was my friend again.

Then the engine roared into life. "Goodbye, Jay. May God protect you."

52.

Imagine this. Suppose the starter of a Formula One Grand Prix race chose to hold the cars at the red light stage for days on end?

It's quite inconceivable, isn't it?

The drivers brains would most probably fry, and their hearts would burst during the first hour of slipping the clutch and standing on the brakes.

Well, that's exactly how I felt the entire week that followed: strung out, brains scrambled by expectancy, as I waited for the second shoe to fall.

I was running the Sleuthhound teaser on a loop at home twenty-four hours a day.

At work, monitoring the site was Nancy's responsibility. Her brief was to keep her eyes riveted to it every minute of her working day and dial 911 if anything came up.

I'd called Quin Sunday evening, doing my very best to convince him that I was a rational human whose thoughts were worth serious consideration.

I informed him of my brush with Harold's girlfriend at Venice. Unfortunately, he wasn't too impressed. Quite reasonably he asked me if I knew the girl's name or address so that he could make an identification and ultimately interview her. I had to say I didn't know the girl from Eve. When pressed, I was forced to admit I'd never even exchanged a single word with her.

Quin then inquired whether I was absolutely certain the girl who'd taken my photograph was the same girl I'd seen before at the Galleria. I assured him that on this point there was absolutely no doubt in my mind.

"What makes you think she was on a mission for young Corr, Mr Benedict?"

"She was in the stolen red Mustang with Tampico at the Sherman Oaks Galleria on the 17th," I explained.

"That only puts her in Tampico's car on that particular day. Doesn't mean she knows Corr, does it?"

"The car they were in was a stolen car. That must count for something."

"You know for a fact the Mustang was stolen? You made a note of the plates?"

"No. At the time I had no reason to think it might be a stolen vehicle. However, a red Mustang was reported stolen that morning in Santa Monica. That *is* a fact. You can check it in records."

I heard Quin sigh at the other end of the line.

"One hell of a lot of cars get stolen every hour of the day, Mr Benedict."

"It's another coincidence, detective Quin."

"True, but it still doesn't make her Corr's buddy."

"She was with them both the following day at softball practice," I argued.

"Same again. Doesn't make her Corr's friend. She could well be Tampico's girl."

"Either way, why the hell would she want a photo of me?"

There wasn't a quick answer to that one. Quin changed tack immediately.

"Was it a digital camera she was holding?"

"Yes."

"How do you know?"

"The Kodak DS looks more like a video camera. Take it from me, it's distinctive."

"And you're sure it was the same girl?"

"Positive," I replied.

Quin didn't sound too convinced.

"Why didn't you say something to her while she was standing there taking snaps?"

"It was hot, and my brother and I had had a few drinks. I was drowsy. I suppose I didn't notice her at first."

"Hold on one second. A minute ago you were prepared to swear on oath it was the same girl, now you're telling me you were the worse for liquor at the time, not paying too much attention to her?"

"It was the same girl."

"Look, Benedict, I'll give it to you straight as I can. First you tell us eleven-year-old Harold Corr shot your wife, executed Councilman Michael Gardenas, stabbed the Kelly girl, and shot Travis Thorne. Then, when it's proved Corr was fifty miles away from the crime scene when Thorne was killed, you change your story."

"I never said Corr shot Thorne," I protested.

"Whatever. Now it's Corr's buddy Tampico who's the killer."

"It's the most logical answer."

"Just hold your breath one minute will you Mr Benedict. I'm doing the best I can."

"And I appreciate it, detective Quin. I really do." A good time for a spot of belly-crawling.

"Don't mention it," Quin replied, then cleared his throat. It sounded as though he'd lost his train of thought. "So, today you're calling me up to tell me that Tampico's girlfriend is in on the act too. That about right?"

"Right."

"Now this young lady would only be around fifteen years old. Thereabouts, anyways. Right?"

"Maybe less. Not older."

"See, my problem's this, Mr Benedict. If you're to be believed, then there's a whole gang of yuppie kids out there, bent on murder and mayhem, and, well, frankly I don't buy it. Really sorry, but there it is. Plain and simple."

There was little point in pursuing the conversation further. He was beginning to think like Yant; that I was a card-carrying kook.

I gave appeasement one last shot.

"Look I understand your position, detective. Your job's not easy, I appreciate that. What I'm suggesting may sound very implausible to you. But put yourself in my shoes for a second. Looked at from my point of view it's pretty clear that I'm next up. Wouldn't you be looking over your shoulder?"

"We'll take care of you, Mr Benedict. So you can rest easy on that score, take it from me," he said as though coaxing a sharp instrument from a toddler.

"Any sign of the white truck outside Thorne's place?" I threw it in – it was worth a shot.

"Not just yet. It's on my list. We'll be asking the question. You leave it to LA's finest, eh?"

I thanked him through clenched teeth, then hung up.

Who exactly did he think was going to take care of me? I didn't see any cops hanging outside my house, or patrolling the streets by the office.

The plain fact was Quin had no intention of 'taking care of me'. He just hoped I'd fade away so he could get down to the serious business of tracking down the serial killer responsible for the two recent deaths. As far as he was concerned, the Cyberkitchen central computer and Sleuthhound the video movie were just conduits for a seriously deranged killer.

I was so jumpy that Monday morning there was no way I could even contemplate spending the day at the 'Kitchen waiting to see myself grafted to one of our characters on the Sleuthhound web site.

Fear didn't come into it. I wasn't in the least bit scared of Harold Corr, though logically I should have been – five dead people were testament to that. I was hyped up fit to bust, and I relished the prospect of coming face to face with the evil kid.

Raymond was adamant that I should get hold of a handgun.

"What if he breaks in here one night? What are you going to do, fend off the bullets with your bare hands like Superman?" he joked over breakfast.

It was a good point. Maybe it wouldn't be such a dumb move to arm myself. I'd feel pretty dumb if I found myself looking down the barrel of Harold's Ruger exactly as Faith had done only a month ago.

The whole focus of my life now was to avenge her death and bring Harold Corr to justice. I couldn't conceive of becoming his next victim.

However, as far as equiping myself with a brand new handgun, I knew I'd have to fill in forms swearing I wasn't insane, a convicted felon, or presently charged with a crime. Then there was the fifteen day cooling-off period during which various police checks would be made. How was it going to look if it came to the attention of the cops that Jay Benedict, a man recently released on bail, charged with the shooting murder of his wife, had just gone shopping for a revolver?

No, I decided to pass on a gun. I'd never fired a handgun in my life, let alone owned one. I most probably wouldn't have been able to hit a barn at fifty paces.

After once again suffering Raymond's vile French toast, I drove him round to a rent-a-car company in the Valley; one that he'd found in the yellow pages. He wanted to have a little independence – to be able to shoot off down to Venice as and when it suited him, rather than have me drive him.

This arrangement suited me down to the ground. If I was to be a moving target, I didn't want Raymond caught in the crossfire. Better he should be lazing at the beach, enjoying what was left of his life.

I have to say the charges at Plain Jane Rentals were almost unbelievably low. A hundred bucks a week, insurance and unlimited mileage thrown in!

I revised my opinion when I saw the car. The oil-stained hood was positively steaming as it sun-baked by the front door of the weatherboard office on Woodman and Sherman Way. A two-tone '68 two door Buick.

Had it been mine, I would have paid someone fifty bucks to cram it in a dumpster. But Raymond thought it was just dandy, and it fitted his limited budget, so who was I to give a damn?

Two minutes after filling in the rental agreement, Raymond disappeared in a cloud of thick exhaust gases in the general direction of the beach.

I saw him wave cheerily at me in the rearview mirror.

It was time to drive home. I wanted to be somewhere Harold could get to me.

It's an eerie experience to spend every minute looking over your shoulder.

In every shadow lurked a child with a gun. Every sound was the footfall of young Corr.

If Harold planned to come get me, how would he plan his moves?

So far, everyone had been killed during the day. Presumably the rationale was that his mother would notice his absence if he left the house at night.

Any time up till say 10 pm would be fine – he could always say he was out with Tampico. Any later would arouse suspicion, and that he wouldn't want. Especially if he was coming after me – the one person who knew his secret.

It was a relief to think that if my thinking was on the button, no more innocent people would be placed in the firing line. One way or another it would be over soon. It'd be him or me. I'd be dead, or he'd be in Juvenile Hall.

At midday I had an in-house power lunch downtown at Nate's office.

Present were Nate, Mama Poule, Dan and myself.

Dan looked very embarrassed. With good reason.

Nate told me he'd at last spoken to Goodrich. She'd been quite obdurate when it came to his suggestion she drop all charges. She'd be making her own inquiries with the Department of Welfare regarding our witness, and knew we were stacking our hopes on an unstable witness to say the least.

Nate looked me dead in the eye as he made a point of emphasizing the fact that up till my press conference on my lawn, his relationship with Councillor

Goodrich had always been smooth. Now she was anything but accommodating.

Another black mark for me.

"There's no question of Dan and Ethan continuing their stake out now that Stella Corr knows they're there," Nate stated simply.

This really worried me. "But they're running free. The police aren't watching them. If we don't, no one will. We have to know what they're up to."

"I agree," Nate replied. "It's a problem. But Mrs Corr's right. She complains to the LAPD about our harrassing her little boy, and you can kiss your freedom bye-bye."

Mama Poule began serving the lunch on the boardroom table. Today it was a vegetarian dish of beans and okra. It smelled wonderful.

"What you need is a bodyguard, Jay," Mama Poule suggested as she ladled the steaming food into bowls.

She was wrong there. The last thing I wanted was to be hog-tied by having a strong-arm man at my elbow day and night. I was more than happy to be the Judas Goat. The last thing I wanted was to put obstacles in Harold's path. If he came at me, I'd be available.

I obviously had a huge physical advantage over the boy; that wasn't the point. There was the Ruger to consider. And Tampico. The key was to outsmart the kid; somehow outmanoeuvre him so that I'd be ready for him when he came – with or without his buddy, Phil Tampico.

My major obstacle was the fact Corr could always plead the 'Help me! This big man's going to hurt me,' angle.

I was painfully aware I wasn't thinking too clearly; my head was full of too many movie scenarios – spaghetti-western heroes and villains facing each other over ticking fob watches in the desert.

"I don't think a bodyguard's the way," I answered Mama Poule, "and that's no reflection on your abilities, Dan," I added, so as not to embarrass him in front of Nate. It was a bald-faced lie. Given Dan's recent track record, I felt better off alone.

After lunch we discussed more legal aspects of my case, not in too much depth.

Nate seemed pretty confident that it wouldn't even get as far as the Grand Jury hearing, despite Goodrich's present intransigence.

Even given the worst possible scenario, that the DA's office would insist on proceeding with the prosecution, Nate was certain he had sufficient ammo to have the case thrown out of court.

I spent the afternoon sitting by the pool, wracking my brains for a plan of action. There had to be some way I could deal the cards myself, rather than wait around for Harold Corr to do so.

Ever since the day he'd killed Faith, he'd had all the aces and I hadn't even had a pair. He'd always been in a position to call the shots.

If he decided to call a temporary halt to the bloodshed for a few months till things cooled down, what was I to do? Go to the trial and take my chances with the murder charges because I hadn't been smart enough to force Harold's hand. That was unthinkable.

Then again, it was entirely possible Harold had no intention of killing me at all. What if sending the girl to take my picture had been a cruel joke merely to put the fear of God into me? What if his sick game was to observe my anguish at having to stand by while innocent people died on my account?

If I was right about this, then there was no question whatsoever that Harold Corr was mentally ill. Although I'd always disputed that criminality was entirely the product of social conditioning – the fashionable opinion of the day – it was hardly credible that a clinically sane, albeit extremely cruel, boy could randomly kill innocent people merely for the fun of watching another human being squirm. To take a life in such a detached manner was fundamentally horrific.

If this was the case, then I could no more blame Harold Corr for his actions than a baby for vomiting its formula on a thousand dollar suit. Corr's place was in a mental home, to be treated by experts.

Raymond didn't return home till after 8 pm.

The moment I heard his old banger drive through the gates I switched on the house security system – I'd made some adjustments during the afternoon.

Fundamentally it operated in exactly the same way as before. The major difference was that, as the circuit was broken, lights as opposed to bells alerted me that someone had broken into the house.

When Raymond opened the front door, I was upstairs in my bedroom. Nevertheless, a flashing blue light told me that someone had entered the house, thereby breaking the circuit.

The whole point of the lights was that I actually *wanted* Harold inside the house. That necessitated making it easy for him to get inside – I didn't want him scared off by any alarm bells.

If I could catch him inside, and hold on to him until the police arrived, he'd have a hard time explaining what he was doing there. If he'd come to kill me, he'd have an even tougher time explaining away the Ruger or the ice-pick. I'd be vindicated, and Harold would be put in a padded cell. End of story. If it ever came to a struggle, it wouldn't be easy making sure only his prints were left on the automatic - I'd just have to busk that one.

I looked at the blinking light with satisfaction. The sytem worked. If Harold decided to break into the house I'd know immediately that he was inside.

The one drawback was that I had to sleep sometime, I couldn't watch the lights day and night. So I had to switch the system back to the bells between 3 am and 6 am, times when I felt Harold would have difficulty in explaining his absence from home to his mother.

I'd also installed a wide screen computer screen in my bedroom close to the alarm console light. The screen displayed the web site day and night. This meant I could monitor both at the same time.

Quin's precinct number was now a one-touch number on the home telephone system. If I needed to call help quickly, one stab of the finger and I'd be through.

Raymond was impressed with my electrical handywork. He also liked my line of thinking.

"I hope the little bugger tries something while I'm at home. I'll twist his ear till it comes off in my fingers," he said. He still had a vision of Harold as a naughty boy, rather than someone who had killed several times.

Raymond was in great form all evening. He knew time was running out, so he was making the most of things. Every moment was golden. If you could ignore his distended abdomen, he looked surprisingly healthy. His face was tanned, and a newfound inner peace shone through his eyes.

I took him to the Lincoln for dinner, and he ate like a Trojan.

That took care of Monday.

Tuesday crawled by. Raymond was on his way to the beach by 9 am. I spent all day inside the house, alternating my attention between the monitor and the blue light, waiting for Harold Corr.

He never came.

Nor was my photo posted on the Sleuthhound teaser.

Nor did the telephone ring once.

The entire day was torture by apprehension.

Every so often I'd think I'd hear something, and my eyes would flick to the blue warning lights by the console as the hairs rose on the back of my hand. My pulse would begin to race. Seconds later I'd realise it was a stray animal outside, or the neighbour's children playing ball. But the damage to my nervous system was done.

This was my life from the moment Raymond left for the beach at 9 am to the moment he returned at around 8 pm.

All day, disjointed thoughts flashed through my brain.

What was the significance, if any, of the fact that Thorne had been a mobbed-up accountant? Was Thorne's murder a contract killing? Did this mean that his name wasn't picked at random after all? Was the double T an incredible coincidence? Would Quin be true to his word and ask around about the white Toyota van? And, if so, would anyone have seen it standing outside Thorne's apartment?

Twenty-four hours a day there were a thousand thoughts fighting for space in my brain.

Wednesday, Thursday, Friday were no different.

I couldn't concentrate on anything other than the computer monitor and the alarm lights for more than a few minutes. I'd watch them all day and night.

Then at 3 am I'd take half a valium and switch on the bells, setting an alarm clock to wake me up at 6 am.

It went without saying that when the alarm clock went off at 6 am I'd jump out of my skin every time, convinced it was the security system alerting me to an intruder.

By Saturday morning my brain was close to meltdown. If it hadn't been for Raymond's calming influence every evening that week I think I would have gone stark raving mad.

"Why don't you take a break; spend a few hours at the beach," Raymond suggested as he juggled two fried eggs from the pan on to a slice of toast. Mercifully he'd tired of French toast.

I declined his offer of a break at the beach. I knew I'd arrived at the end of the line as far as my sanity was concerned. Now wasn't the time to relax. I had to take the initiative. The alternative was no kind of life at all.

On an impulse I picked up the phone and dialled directory information.

53.

I pushed my Gelson's trolley down towards the fish counter. It was already chock full of things I didn't need.

I'd called the Tampico apartment at 9.50 am. No judge had told me to stay clear of him.

His mother answered. She seemed very friendly. I asked to speak to Phil, as though I was a friend.

A few seconds later he was on the line.

"This is Jay Benedict, Phil," I began. "Shut up and listen hard. You tell Harold right now we have to meet. Gelson's on Wilshire. 11 am today. The kid doesn't show up, you'll *both* be very sorry. If he's scared, you just make him do it."

I didn't wait for any response. I hung up.

I checked the time. 11.20 am. I'd been in the supermart for thirty minutes now. It was vital I looked as though I was shopping, so every minute or so I had to stick some random grocery item into the damned cart for the sake of appearances.

My concentration was set so sharp I could have sworn I could hear the ice melting amongst the tuna, swordfish and mahi-mahi.

I tried to put myself in Harold Corr's shoes.

A trap? Maybe. But he could always pretend it was pure chance that he'd come to the supermarket.

See, I was banking on the kid's curiosity. It had always been insatiable. Like mine, come to think of it. I hoped my message would infuriate him. *What was Benedict up to?* he'd think.

Also I wagered he'd consider the message a personal challenge. *Scared? Never!*

I threw in the word 'kid' for good measure because I had experience of how he reacted to being patronized. It was his personal red rag.

I pulled another jar of decaf from a shelf as I neared the fish counter. The gentle musak tinkled in my ears. It did nothing to soothe my nerves.

As I pushed off once again, this time towards the bakery section, I heard my voice being called. It was a girl's voice. I swung round.

It was 'Jodie'.

She'd appeared like a wraith out of nowhere. We were separated by nothing more than two giant wire carts.

Her eyes cut quickly left and right as she scanned the supermarket. Her lips then relaxed into a smile. "Hey, aren't you that weirdo who spied on Phil and me at catching practice?" she said. "Fancy meeting you here. You following me or something?" She'd never make it as an actress. The soaps maybe.

I realized immediately what her game was. She was concerned I might be carrying a police wire. She wasn't going to compromise herself. If there was a tape running, then her words would indicate *I'd* been following *her*, rather than the other way round.

"Where's Harold?"

"Who?" She winked at me as she opened a sheet of paper that had been folded four ways. It was about six inches square. On it was printed. *McDonalds. Century City. Midday. Come alone.*

The girl gave me a few seconds to read the note, then she scrunched it up in her hand and put it down the front of her bra.

She winked again, then casually walked towards the exit.

I didn't follow.

It was 11.40. I'd have to hurry if I was to make the midday meet.

On my way over to Century City I considered my options.

If he wanted to, Harold could scream blue murder the moment he saw me enter the restaurant. I'd be apprehended and taken downtown to have my bail revoked. He'd be in a crowded fast food outlet, so he didn't have to fear any physical danger from me.

But it was worth the risk. I'd made first base; he'd risen to the bait.

I had to quickly consider whether he actually did have it in mind to see my bail revoked, and laugh as I rotted in prison awaiting trial while he carried on his murdering spree, or whether I was right and he just had to know what I could possibly have to say.

I didn't even think twice about it. I made for the car.

I parked on level two at Century City and made my way up to the shops.

The adrenalin was pumping like crazy.

I'd told no one where I was heading. No one could help me now. Not Nate, not Charlie. No one. It was him or me. What scared me most was that I had absolutely no plan at all. The idea was to confront him head on and see what happened. Anything was better than the mindless waiting.

However, I knew I was functioning on automatic pilot with no coordinates punched in. One way or another I'd crash sooner or later.

It was two minutes after midday as I walked into the restaurant. My head was pounding; my blood molten lava.

I stood just inside the door, my fists balled at my side. If Harold's plan was to scream for the cops, he was on to a good thing. I looked like a crazed escapee from an asylum.

I took several deep breaths as my eyes scanned the seething room of fast food junkies. I still couldn't see him!

I walked slowly forward, weaving my way through the tables towards the rear.

It was then I felt his presence. It was the strangest thing. As if someone at a nuclear power plant had lowered the protective screen and I was suddenly being cooked by radioactive fuel rods. My bones were turning to jelly.

"Why don't you join me, Mr Benedict? I've plenty enough fries for two," I heard a voice from a table two across to the left.

He was sitting alone. Even though the restaurant was crowded, no one sat with him. It was as if he was surrounded by some evil aura of which everyone was subconsciously aware.

I sat opposite him, then patted my clothes to show him I wasn't wearing a wire. A brief look of contempt flashed across his face.

"You wouldn't dare, Benedict. Besides, too much peripheral noise."

"I'm alone," I said.

"I know you are. I'm not a complete klutz," he said with a smirk. "Finally come to pay me the money you owe me, eh? Give up?"

Before I could open my mouth he grasped his Big Mac with both pudgy fingers and was lifting it to his mouth, obscuring ninety percent of his face.

When he lowered the bun, my eyes became fixed with morbid fascination to a small spot just below his left eye, where some mingled ketchup and mayo had squirted onto his cheek.

He was quite unaware of it.

"Haven't got all day, Birdturd. What's all this about?"

He was confident as hell. He knew I didn't have the slightest chance of being able to jump him.

His left hand stabbed at the fries in front of him.

"Help yourself. Got to get 'em while they're hot and crispy."

I leant foward across the table so only he could hear my words. "You killed the girl."

Harold smacked his lips then tore another couple of inches from the bun. His cheeks were twin tennis balls. The ketchup and mayo bobbed up and down.

"Sure I did. Got real lucky, eh. What a killer match," he replied.

"That was it? Just luck?"

"That she was the dead spit of Lastra? Yeah. Some good things, eh? But look, it just saved me time. I'd have found someone cute and dark. Whoever – you'd have clocked the similarity. That was the buzz."

His eyes twinkled with amusement.

"And Thorne?"

In a flash, he'd put down the bun and raised his hands. His eyes shone with mock horror. "Hey, officer. You can't pin the wrap on me!" he said, then shrieked with laughter.

"It was Phil, wasn't it?" I asked, purely thetorically.

He merely winked as he chomped on the two all beef patties, special sauce, bacon, cheese and tomato.

"Did you know Thorne was mob-connected?"

"Nah! That was some weird thing, eh?"

Munch, munch, munch.

"Doesn't matter though," he continued. "They'll never know who did it."

Abruptly, he leant forward, his eyes wide with feigned fear. "Unless *you* tell them, Birdturd. Ooooooo, shit, I hadn't thought of that! I just *know* they'd believe you." Again, he peeled with laughter.

I studied him closely. I couldn't believe I was so much in control. The panic that had gripped me when I'd stepped through the doors of the restaurant had vanished, replaced with a deep and abiding fascination for the boy's each and every response.

"Why?" I asked.

"Why what? The killing? You just don't get it, numbnuts. Doesn't have to be a why! 'Cos I'm all mixed up? 'Cos I found out dad was a real bad man? 'Cos I'm a lonely little boy? 'Cos I'm so damned clever and I can't relate to kids my own age? Yeah, yeah, yeah..."

He chuckled.

"You know something, Birdturd? I think about these things every now and then. Like when I can't get to sleep. And you want to know something? If ever anything went really wrong, and the cops had me nailed – that's when I'm going to come out with all those old favourites. That's when I'll cry my way to a few months counselling, 'cos I'm SOOO mixed up."

He poured a sachet of salt over the fries. "In the meantime, shit-face, I do what I want to do, twenty-four hours a day. Anyone else can go screw themselves."

He paused to dip some fries in the ketchup, cramming them into his mouth. "Let me tell you something interesting, Birdturd. One of the first things I remember was sitting in my pram. I couldn't have been more than three. There was this bug. Flew right in, started walking on the plastic right by my face. It bugged me. So I squished it." His eyes lit up, and he snickered. "The bug bugged me, what do you think of that, eh? Pretty funny."

He put down the bun and fixed me with a steady look. He was deadly serious now. "See my point? The bug was alive. Then it was dead. Who gave a damn? It never knew, did it. The world was the same, 'cept there was no bug around. It's the same with people. Life means nothing." He lifted a lazy fat hand, "Well, that's not exactly true. *My* life does, but then I'm me on the inside looking out, aren't I?"

"You killed that girl and Thorne for no reason at all?" I was incredulous. My pulse was rising despite the iron fist I thought I had on my self-control.

"Not exactly. I did them for you. See, first you insulted me. Wouldn't pay me the money you owed. Then you did your feeble best to make life difficult for me. It was kind of a fun pay-back."

He reached for yet another bunch of fries, stuffing them into his mouth.

Pay-back? This boy had stuck an ice pick into a beautiful young girl just to get up my nose? My beathing was beginning to come in fits and starts.

I stared mesmerised by the self-satisfied face across the table as Harold picked up a paper serviette and casually wiped his mouth , missing the ketchup and mayo under his eye. He looked like the sad clown.

"Your father would be ashamed of you. You know that, don't you.
Immediately his eyes narrowed. I'd hit the spot.

"Don't you ever talk to me again about my father –" he stammered.
I'd made better contact than I'd thought. My heart leapt with hope.

"I knew Jack better than you ever did. I knew him as a man. To Jack, you were just his little kid."

"Oh yeah? You knew my dad? Sure you did. Ten years and it never crossed your stupid mind what he did for a living. Yeah, that's knowing him." He snorted with derision.

"What about Stella? You love your mother don't you, Harold?"

"What the fuck's that got to do with the price of apples?" He balled his fists on the table top.

"No one's all bad. Not Jack. Not you."

"Sanctimonious dickhead," he mumbled. But he was listening.

"Mighty long word, kid."

He fixed me with one of his 'you wait' looks. I could feel the malice flood across the table.

"I knew your father once," I continued. I was getting to him, I could tell. "A long time ago. Of course I knew a very different man. Jack had a heart then.

"You see, once we were very close. He was a very good friend to me. Whatever happened later, happened. I can't explain it – it's beyond the realms of my understanding. But I do know this much, he was damn proud of you. You became his life. If he could see what's happened to you he'd be screaming his way round hell in an eternal loop. You see, you're determined to turn yourself into a nothing. A worthless evil bag of nothing."

"Says you, Birdtird! What the hell have you ever done? Friggin' games for dumbass kids!" His expression was one of abject scorn. "Some achievement!"

"It's good enough for me. I bring happiness into the world. You bring death."

"Death's fine. I hand it out like candy. Good enough for dad, good enough for me. Damn fine living."

"And what about Stella? Does she know she has a punk killer as a son?"

I was stunned by the reaction to this one. His face went completely white. He moistened his lower lip with his tongue. For the first time he was tongue-tied. His eyes didn't seem to be focussing on anything in particular.

This was the button! I'd found it. He was reeling emotionally. I went in for the kill.

"When she finds out, it'll kill her."

Just then a middle-aged couple appeared at the table, smiling politely at me for the unstated permission to join us.

"Mind if we join you? There ain't much room else."

"Scram!" Harold hissed at them.

The couple stood transfixed, staring in disbelief at the horror face of evil looking up at them, one pink cheek bespattered with mayo and ketchup.

A couple of seconds later they just backed off. Never said a word. Harold Corr had that power.

But the brief moment of vulnerability was gone. Harold cut his glance to me. His eyes were pure poison. "My mother will *never* know."

"You'll go down, Corr. That's my promise to you. She's going to have to know."

"Oh yeah?" He licked his lips and leant forward. "Well listen up smartypants. I told you once you're a dead man." All pretense of the Little Lord Fauntleroy accent was cast to the wind. "You better listen *real* close now, 'cos I'm going to give you one last clue. And clues are what makes all of this one *real* gas eh?"

"Clue?"

"Yeah. Clue. We're playing a game, aren't we? So you gotta go figure." He braced his hands on the table and leant even further forward, so his cherubic face was just inches from mine. "You're a dead man, Mr Benedict!"

"That's it?" I asked, my voice the merest whisper.

"That's it. I'm out of here."

He stood, then weaved his way towards the exit without a backward glance.

As he reached the door, I'm pretty sure I caught sight of Phil Tampico outside on the sidewalk. He must have been keeping watch for cops.

I felt like a butterfly trapped in a beehive, the noise around me was so maddening. I tried to unscamble my thoughts to think clearly.

You're a dead man, Mr Benedict?

Some clue.

54.

I sat at home all afternoon trying to assess whether I'd made any ground whatsoever.

The boy had appeared quite unfazed by my request for a meeting. He'd handled his side of the logistics beautifully, a true professional. Like father like son.

It had been his choice of venue, there'd been no chance of my carrying a wire, and he'd always had the option of screaming blue murder the second things looked to be turning bad, while acting the innocent kid.

The only chink in the boy's armour had been Stella.

Like any kid, deep down he loved his mom. And he knew she wouldn't understand. If she ever found out about him, it was all over – he stood to lose the love of the one person who fundamentally mattered.

Secure as he was, this was always in the back of his devious little mind. He knew I was the only one on God's earth who considered for an instant that he was anything less than mom's little darling.

Stella hadn't believed my ravings up till now, why should she in the future? Nevertheless it was Harold's continuing private nightmare.

You're a dead man, Mr Benedict.

He'd said it before and I'd believed him. The threat reiterated made it all the more chilling.

I stared fixedly at the Sleuthhound teaser, waiting for my image to appear. The moment it did, it'd be one on one. He'd be down in Juvenile Hall or I'd be dead.

I didn't think for a second he'd ask Tampico for help. He'd want to kill me himself. His ego would feed on that personal satisfaction.

Well, I was ready for him. Most would have considered it a complete mismatch; an eleven-year-old kid against a grown man.

I decided to tell no one of the meet at MacDonalds. What could possibly be gained? Nate would kill me. Mama Poule would heave one of her gigantic sighs of disappointment. Charlie would think I was a fool.

My meeting with Harold? It never happened. Simple as that.

Raymond returned from the beach at 7 pm, lively as a Mexican jumping bean. I'm no doctor but it was as if he were in remission. Either that, or he was squeezing the last drop of sunshine out of his life.

Nate called in the evening. Not much news. I didn't care. Mama Poule told me a very dirty Senegalese joke that against all the odds made me laugh a lot. Charlie popped round for ten minutes to check on me.

There was nothing in the fridge so I decided to take Raymond back celebrity-watching to Orso for dinner.

The food was as good as ever, but the atmosphere that night was weird as hell.

None of the diners were interacting. Everyone in the place was staring vacantly around all the time. Then it suddenly struck me – we were all nobody's waiting for a 'somebody' - anybody. It was quite insane.

Raymond swore he spotted someone across the room. The guy was table-hopping. Raymond said his name was Shoe. Could have been Show. Shaw? Whatever.

I tried to look impressed, I had no idea who the hell the guy was.

Raymond wanted to finish the evening taking in the table dancers on Doheny, but much as I wanted to show him a good time, I couldn't bring myself to go through that tawdry ritual right then, so we drove home.

I didn't even sleep the wolf-shift between 3 and 6 am, I was so pumped. If ever in my life I needed my wits about me it was now. No way would Corr defeat me. I owed it to Faith and all the people who had died as a result of this boy tormenting me.

More importantly, I owed it to any future victims should I fail.

Sunday took a week to pass. I was aware of every microsecond as they ticked in syncopation to my racing pulse.

Raymond scooted off to the beach as usual while I waited for my nemesis.

He never came.

That was the beauty of the torture seen from Harold's perspective. He would choose the moment. Meantime I sweated.

There's no real English equivalent to the phrase 'cabin fever', but I'll tell you by the time Raymond got back 7 pm that night I was three cents short of the dollar.

I knew I couldn't wait out Harold for ever, cooped in the house twenty-four hours a day. There had to be some relief.

So Monday morning I bowed to Raymond's constant pressure and agreed to join him at the beach.

I had to drop by the Cyberkitchen first to attend to some stuff which couldn't wait – papers to be signed, that kind of thing.

"You got to feel part of the wonderful living world," Raymond said as he prised open the creaking door of the Buick. He was the doctor.

"I'll be with you at the seaside, Jay. We'll fight the little runt together if need be."

Raymond was being so wonderfully supportive – how could I refuse?

So at 11.15 I was stuffing my personal computer, a few floppy discs and some paperwork in the trunk of the Pontiac, while I racked my brain as to where I could buy an English paper on the way to Venice Beach. I knew Raymond lived for the London Times.

Don't for a second think my mind wasn't absolutely focussed on my situation. I was watching my back and front at all times. I even scanned upper windows.

But deep down I knew the kid would have to kill me the way he'd killed the others. It would be a pride thing. Somehow or other he'd have to get close enough to be able to put the killer bullet through my brain, or the pick in my heart.

I parked outside the Rose café just before midday. It was as close as I could get to the beach.

I ducked in to see if they had an English paper.

They didn't.

A few minutes later I was on the beach.

Raymond was in his usual favoured spot. Asleep. The LA Times was draped over his body from just under the chin down to his belly button. Beside him was his cooler of white wine spritzer, mixed at home in the kitchen at breakfast.

This was Raymond to a T; reformed con-man turned Venice eccentric.

I loved him.

I sat in the sand beside him for a good ten minutes, watching the newspaper rise and fall as he slept. There weren't too many people around on the sand; a few kids playing touch football thirty feet closer to the water, a vagrant searching through a dumpster behind us near the cycle path.

"Well, how-de-doody, little brudder," Raymond murmured as he opened his eyes, becoming aware of my presence. "Ain't this the best thing? All my life I've been swindling old ladies in the cold and rain back home, always one step ahead of the law. And just think of it, I could have been a bum here all my life." He grinned across at me devilishly. "Don't you ever come here, Jay? It's so good."

"It's the old story, I suppose," I replied. "You never appreciate what's on your own doorstep."

He poured me a spritzer of wine and soda, and we chatted for an hour or so.

The temperature was nice. The sun wasn't too harsh.

At 2 pm I decided to get back home. There was still a voice deep within me that told me Corr would come for me only when I was alone. So I had to make myself available, didn't I?

I walked slowly down the promenade towards Rose.

I'd just turned the corner when I felt my cellphone throb in my jeans pocket.

"Jay! He's posted the photo," I heard Charlie say. "Less than a minute ago."

A thrill of extreme excitement rushed through me.

"Are you there, Jay?" Charlie continued. There was something very wrong about the tone of his voice. I could sense it. There was something he wasn't telling me. Suddenly my blood ran cold.

"Tell me, Charlie."

"Oh Jesus, Jay. It's Raymond. The photo is of Raymond!"

There are no words to describe the feeling I experienced that second. I threw my head up towards heaven and screamed for pity.

Dear God, don't let him die! I screamed at the top of my voice.

I was vaguely aware of a black American woman beside me who instantly chimed in a resounding 'Amen!'

Then a tidal wave of anger kicked in, and I was running wildly back down the boardwalk.

I'd been so incredibly dumb.

You're a dead man, Mr Benedict. That had been the clue.

It had never been me, it had always been Raymond. He'd been my model for Sol Shyster, for God's sake! They were physically identical! When 'Jodie' had taken the snapshot, she'd been concentrating on Raymond, not me.

My body did me proud as I pounded the asphalt back towards Raymond. No bursting lungs, no legs that threatened to give out on me. Just a free-flowing sprint as I ducked and weaved through the tourists.

And with each footfall I kept calling my brother's name.

Raymond! Raymond! Raymond!

It can't have been more than three minutes from the time I'd spoken to Charlie that I leapt across the cycle track and pounded across the soft sand towards Raymond.

I could see him lying there ahead of me, same as I'd left him, LA Times from chin to belly button, his head resting to one side.

Relief flooded me.

I screamed out to him but he didn't hear me. I screamed again, and a volley-baller thirty feet to my right waved; he must have thought I was calling out to him.

As I crouched down beside Raymond my heart burst. I knew even before I lifted the newspaper that my big brother was dead.

I pulled the sports page to one side. The pick was stuck in his chest. Up to the hilt. There wasn't much blood.

I turned his head towards me and saw the entry wound. Skin-touch range. There were massive powder burns on his temple.

I was still screaming Raymond's name when the black and white arrived, lights flashing, siren wailing.

The cops held me back as they covered him with a sheet.

Big brudder was dead.

55.

I rode in the back of the ambulance to the morgue. The cops and paramedics tried to dissuade me, but I was really wired and they must have known it. So they left me alone.

The anger I felt at that particular moment was so intense I could taste bitter gall on the roof of my mouth.

When we arrived downtown, the paramedics politely asked me to step aside, pulled the sheet back over his head and took him away on a metal cart.

I gave the detectives a statement, then took a seat in an empty corridor and stared into space, collecting the thoughts that were crowding my mind.

Something had happened to me during the trip in the back of the EMS ambulance to the morgue.

I was Kafka's beetle – but instead of my body, it was my brain that had undergone the radical metamorphosis. I was profoundly changed in every conceivable aspect – everything I stood for had been turned on its head, everything I'd always believed in.

I was absolutely focussed on one thing, and one thing alone. Harold Corr was to die. I was going to kill him. There was no question of that. I just hadn't quite determined the manner of his death. Nothing else mattered.

I was unbelievably calm and composed. My heart rate couldn't have been higher than forty beats a minute. Grief was on the back-burner. My focus was the cold logistics of premeditated murder. I was thinking more clearly than I'd ever done in my life

The fact that the intended victim was so young never even entered my thinking.

A door down the corridor slammed shut, interrupting my concentration. It made me aware my cellphone was chirping in my pocket; how long it had done so, I had no idea.

I reached down and switched it off. I didn't have time for other people. I had too many things to do.

Whichever way I handled it, every detail would have to be carefully planned. I'd need to be very careful. No way was the demon child going to bring me down.

I left the building and headed in a vaguely westerly direction.

I must have walked for the best part of two hours. A glance at my watch told me it was 4.10 pm. I was on Wilshire, coming up to La Brea. I'd been speedwalking on auto pilot, I'd covered an awful lot of ground without realising it.

A sudden realisation hit me that I was getting close to Nate's building, so I quickly turned down Sycamore. The last thing I wanted was to bump into my friend – I needed total mental freedom to think things through clearly. There was no way I was about to be diverted from my purpose.

I was fifty or so yards down the street when I saw the 'Open House' sign on a lawn across the way, and an idea began to form in my mind.

The house looked expensive; a three, maybe four bedroomed family home. Well kept garden. Shady trees.

Possibly the realtor had forgotten to remove the sign. I opened the gate and walked up the drive.

The front door was open. A woman in tan slacks and floral blouse looked up from a folder she had open in front of her on the hall table.

"Hello. My name's Susan Field. Of Field & Tate. How can I help you?" she said, holding out a hand.

"Brad Hersham," I replied. "I'm looking for a place to move into right away. I'm a writer. I'll need the place for around six months or so."

"Is it just yourself, Brad?" Field asked.

"That's right. My wife's back in London."

"Well, I'd say this place is just perfect. Short term lease would suit my clients just fine. They're in London themselves as it happens. Till next June. He's a producer."

My eyes roved round the living room.

"Everything's here that you'd ever need," she continued. "All the utilities are connected. Even the phone. Just need to change the account names, that's all."

"Mind if I take a look around?" I asked.

"Sure, go right ahead, Brad. I think you'll like what you see. Works out to just over three thousand a month."

I walked through into the huge open plan kitchen.

Of course there was no way I could have used the house I was now in. The realtor had seen me. But this was one of hundreds of open houses. Any one of them would probably suit my needs. I'd just have to make damned sure the phone and electricity were both connected – without them both, the plan I had in mind would fail.

Ten minutes later I was on my way out. "I'll be in touch," I told Susan Field. She made a note of my name, and gave me a business card.

I walked on down Sycamore to San Vicente, analysing every foreseeable problem – all conceivable stumbling blocks.

At the corner of San Vicente I called a cab to take me back to my car in Venice. While I waited, I made some more calls.

In all, I called seven realtors. Affecting a quasi-Italian accent, I enquired about houses for lease in the area that suited my needs. The area I'd mentally mapped out was bounded by Melrose Avenue to the north and Beverly Boulevard to the south, Larchmont to the east, La Cienega to the West. It was a portion of the Hollywood flats; a reasonably quiet well-heeled area with little to no through traffic.

I told the realtors I had a medical research document to write, and was in a hurry to find the right accommodation – somewhere quiet. Money was not the issue.

I only made notes of the properties the agents informed me were immediately ready for occupation. I explained I'd drive by the houses, and then get back to them if any of them looked suitable.

Of the seventeen houses suggested, eight were geographically suitable, six were furnished, but only two had all utilities connected including the telephone.

I was about to call yet another agency when the cab arrived.

It was close to five-thirty when I cruised past the house on Sierra Bonita in my Pontiac.

Initially the house looked promising. The curtains were drawn and there was no evidence of a realtor's sign in the front garden.

I parked down the street and walked back on the opposite side to the house.

This time I saw problems. The front and sides of the house were pretty exposed. No trees in the garden, and the shrubs were scarcely two feet high. If I were to break in at the side or the rear of the property I'd have little or no cover.

Nevertheless, it was a possible.

Three minutes later I was back in the car on my way to the house on Orange Grove.

On the initial drive-by it looked ideal. The house stood opposite a school. It was still the school holidays, so there'd be no prying eyes there.

Another plus was the garden. A hedge ran round the front and side perimeter. A massive oak stood three feet from the front door, casting shadows everywhere.

Once again I parked and walked back.

The street was peaceful. Just the sound of a sprinker, and the chirping of the birds.

I crossed over as I neared the house so as to get a closer look down the side to the yard at the rear, but a high rhododendron bush blocked my view of a side entrance.

This was ideal. This had to be the perfect house for my needs. I hoped the various locks wouldn't present too much of a problem.

I was back home just after 6.30 pm.

I checked my messages. Both Nate and Charlie had called. Would I call them. They were concerned for me.

I returned their calls right away.

Charlie told me to call him if I needed anything. He'd be there for me.

Nate wanted me to spend the night at his place. I declined. I told him calmly that I needed to be alone. Nate seemed reassured as to my mental state.

Then I sat down at my desk and began to think things through in sequence.

My plan was to use the Finnish site Harold had shown me so proudly the day of Jack's funeral. Penet remailer. I knew Jack's public key, Harold had told me. 666jACK666.

Providing he hadn't changed the key number as threatened, I could post the boy a message and he'd receive it in micro seconds. But what would his reaction be? Would he read it as genuine? Or would he smell a rat – would instinct save him?

I cast my mind back to that night in Harold's bedroom.

This is how my father did business, Mr Benedict. How he took his orders, so to speak.

That's what Harold had told me.

It was always quite simple. A name, an address, sometimes a sense of urgency, sometimes not.

The words were stamped on my memory like a brand.

Only a very few knew the keys, and as far as Jack was concerned it didn't much matter which one of them was sending the message.

It seemed logical that Jack's employers didn't always make it clear who they were. This simplified matters a little - I wouldn't have to sign off. This was just as well, since I hadn't the first idea how I'd accomplish that.

Dad's reply was action or lack thereof.

So sometimes Jack passed on a contract. Interesting. It made sense. There were bound to be times things didn't feel right. That was his prerogative as a pro. However, Harold had only received one contract to date – he'd be champing at the bit to take another and complete it successfully. Certainly after the debacle with Gardenas.

Payment was arranged through a numbered account in the Turks and Caicos Islands

Maybe I could throw in a reference to the Turks and Caicos somewhere so as to add a convincing touch of authenticity.

I mentally juggled the guts of my message.

I was banking on the fact that Harold wouldn't recall giving me such detail all those weeks ago. If he did, then all my plans were worthless.

The next most pressing question was how often did Harold check the remailer for messages? If he was serious about his future in the killing business, it'd be prudent to do so at least twice a day. Morning and night.

In order to have two bites of the cherry, it'd be wise to send the message tonight.

Secondly, he'd have to believe implicitly that the message was genuine. This wouldn't be easy – Harold had a steel trap mind. The chances were it was part of his routine to check out the name and address with the phone book before he even moved from home. There he'd find no entry. But my guess was that this wouldn't necessarily arouse his suspicion. After all, the message didn't purport to inform him where the victim *lived* – merely where he could be *found*.

Thirdly, he'd have to be physically able to do as he'd been asked – namely to complete the job in the timeframe stated. If he delayed, I was out of luck. I'd have to think again.

I planned to break into the house on Orange Grove around 5 pm the following day. He had to show sometime during that evening. I couldn't remain there any longer – the chances were the realtor would stop by the house to check on it every so often.

I posted the message on Penet remailer at 9 pm.

I gave a name, the address of the house on Orange Grove, adding *Most urgent. Tomorrow. 3rd Sept. Arrangements as usual via Turks and Caicos.* I was flying by the seat of my pants, but there was little else I could do.

I was still wide awake at 3 am, despite the Nembutal – still mentally covering all the bases over and over again.

I knew that despite all my best efforts there were a thousand things that could go wrong. That was too bad. I'd have to take my chances. After all I doubted that any murder was foolproof.

I closed my eyes but sleep wouldn't come. I knew what Tuesday held for me, and I couldn't wait for the morning.

Finally vengeance would be mine.

56.

"Go to bed, Jay. Sleep on it. It'll all seem like nothing in the morning."

That's what granny told me so many times as a child. She was always right. How many times I'd gone to bed seething with anger at something Raymond had said or done to me, and each time I'd woken mystified that I'd allowed my temper to affect me so greatly.

Tuesday morning was different. When my eyes snapped open at 7.25, my attitude was quite unchanged.

Raymond's death had somehow tipped the scales. I wasn't a reasoning human any more. I was obsessed. Faith wouldn't have known me.

Yesterday as I'd sat in that souless corridor at the morgue I'd proclaimed myself judge and jury. The verdict had never been in doubt. Guilty of five counts of murder in the first degree.

Today I was the executioner – I was now the servant of the court, my duty to see sentence carried out. Six innocent people had died at the hands of this monster – I was determined no one else would.

There was no need for a weapon. Harold Corr would provide the instrument of his death himself. This was an essential ingredient to my plans. There would be nothing to link me to the killing.

At 7.30 am, I changed into a pair of dark blue cotton Dockers and a navy short-sleeved shirt, and left the house. I didn't want anyone showing up unexpectedly, asking me questions about what my plans were for the rest of the day. I didn't want to have to turn down any dinner invitations. Questions might be asked somewhere down the line.

I drove into the hills. Sometime during the day I'd have to buy some thin rubber gloves in a supermarket. Then it would merely be a question of waiting till evening.

57.

I turned left off the street, walking down the side of the house as though I owned it. It was dead on 5 pm, and Orange Grove was silent. If anyone was watching me, it had to be from behind curtains. Hopefully they'd take me for a tradesman come to repair a tap in the kitchen, or check something in the yard.

I pulled on the thin latex gloves. The yard door was a breeze; the simple slip lock gave on the second hard push of my shoulder. A second later I was in the kitchen.

Inside the house the air smelled stale. Most likely it hadn't been opened for a while. A fly buzzed inside a lampshade somewhere.

I immediately hit the light switch. No hitch there. A globe lit up above my head. I decided to leave it on; a light that remained on would draw less attention than one that was snapped on in the darkness later, and I figured the boy might well be intimidated by a house completely shrouded in darkness, so I'd need a light. He had to believe there was someone inside.

I walked quickly into the living room, searching for a phone.

I found it was on a small table next to the sofa. Relief flooded through me as I picked up the receiver and heard the dial tone.

Okay this far.

The next twin priorities were to check the lock on the front door, and settle on a vantage point inside the house where I could look up and down the street.

The door was no problem. The deadbolt operated from the inside. I unlocked it, and drew the security chain aside.

The curtains on all the windows had been drawn shut. I inched back the corner of the one that was dead centre and looked out.

Not so good. I could see right up the street to the right, but my view to the left was obstructed by a tallish shrub.

I moved further down, away from the front door, and again pulled back an edge of curtain.

Much better. I could see at least a hundred feet up the road in each direction. I'd see anyone coming. The added advantage was I could reach out to the phone from where I was.

I turned on a table lamp beside the sofa. It shone quite brightly, so I substituted it with a forty watt bulb I found in the bathroom. I needed light to attract my 'moth', but not too much – shadows suited my purposes better.

I pulled up a chair, and sat looking through the smallest of openings up and down the street. There was nothing to do now but wait.

I felt my first tinge of uncertainty at around 7.55 pm. Maybe he wasn't coming. Ridiculous as it may seem , I was reminded of similar feelings I'd experienced as a kid, waiting for girls to show up on dates. I'd be convinced they'd never turn up, but they always did.

If I'd been a betting man, I would have placed even money on Harold falling for the fake message. If he did, my next bet would have been that he'd show up around six-thirty.

If a kid knocked on my door around that time, I'd open the front door without a second thought. But if a strange albeit straight-looking kid showed up on my doorstep at ten at night I'd wonder what was going on. So, to catch the average guy on the hop, the earlier the kid arrived the better. Certainly that had been Corr's MO to date.

It was now past 8 pm.

I'd been sitting motionless by the window for over three hours. Every so often a car would glide down the street and park close by. Each time my hand would reach out for the phone. But each time the door of the vehicle would open and some innocent stranger would climb out.

The minutes passed very slowly.

I didn't look at the time again till five to nine.

For over half an hour I'd been getting a weird feeling in the pit of my stomach. The real Jay Bendict was fighting to gain control. I did my best to ignore him. There was no room for second thoughts. The dye had been cast.

My eyes returned to the gap in the window and immediately my pulse leapt to around a hundred and fifty beats a minute.

A dark blue Buick was cruising down the street in my direction. It was travelling slowly – around twenty miles an hour, as though scanning for street numbers. No headlights, just sidelights.

As yet it was too far down the street to be able to make out how many or who was in the vehicle.

Immediately I crossed to the front door and opened it only a matter of two inches.

Three seconds later I was back at the window.

The Buick came to halt maybe thirty feet down the street under an oak tree, the furthest point from the closest street lamp.

The sidelights were immediately doused. No one stepped out.

Without realizing, I was holding my breath.

It had to be Corr and Tampico. Who else would just sit there in the darkness?

The minutes passed. Five, six, seven. No one stepped from the Buick.

Eight, nine, ten. Still no movement.

Then the passenger door opened, and a figure stepped out onto the sidewalk. He turned to face the house.

It was Harold Corr.

I willed him to keep on coming.

As the boy began to cross to my side of the street, I watched the Buick. Would Tampico remain in the car? I'd banked on his doing so for at least the first few minutes.

Keeping my eyes rivetted to the driver's door, I picked up the phone and made the 911 call.

There's a guy outside! He's got some kind of heavy duty automatic weapon, I whispered fearfully. *He's sitting in a dark blue Buick. Please hurry.*

Judging exactly where the Buick was parked, I gave an estimated street number, then rang off without identifying myself.

The question now was, would fortune smile on me? I needed Harold inside before the cops arrived, and I needed the cops to arrive before Tampico even thought of backing up his friend.

I'd been afraid he mightn't stay in the car, but would rather hang around the back of the house in case there was any trouble.

If he had, I would never have made the emergency call. I'd have switched to plan B, and that meant taking out both of them. Harder, but not impossible.

The way I saw it, Harold had had help when he'd shot Gardenas, the forensic evidence was proof to that. There were heavy duty contusions to the back of the the deceased's neck, as though he'd been clubbed to the ground. My guess, bearing in mind the three shots he took to the chest, was that

Harold had failed to kill the man with the first shot, and had consequently needed the help of his buddy before he could fire the killing shot to Gardenas' head.

All of this suggested Tampico would be watching for any signs of trouble. One shout and he'd be in here, backing up his friend.

I could hear the blood in my veins, it was so quiet. Outside, I could see Harold ambling down the sidewalk on my side of the street; he was now about two houses down. Every so often he'd glance around. One hand was inside his jacket – fingering the grip of the gun more than likely.

Tampico was still in the Buick – I could just make out someone behind the wheel.

I was suddenly aware that I was sweating. It was going to be a close run thing.

I let the curtain drop and moved my head back from the window; the gap between the curtain and the window frame was now the meerest sliver. But through it I saw Harold Corr stop at the gate, pause for a second, look back down the street, nod towards the Buick, then walk up the pathway to the front door.

There was still no sign of a patrol car.

I padded silently into the kitchen.

There was a light rap on the front door.

"Mr Bonoventure?"

I didn't reply. I had to play for time. The cops were taking forever!

"Mr Bonoventure? Are you there?"

I was standing near the yard door, straining for sounds of a patrol car.

"Mr Bonoventure? It's Tim Grady from down the street. Can I talk to you for a moment, sir?"

The voice sounded closer this time; I guessed he'd pushed the front door open and had walked in.

This was perfect.

Just then I heard a car somewhere outside in the street.

"In here, kid," I called from the kitchen in a lazy drawl, trying to mask the sound of the approaching vehicle. "Come right on in. Door's open."

I could hear footsteps on the hard wood floor in the next room.

"Close the door, will ya, kid?" I added. I needed to close any avenue of escape.

"Sure thing, Mr Bonoventure," Harold called out cheerily. It wasn't a voice one might fear – that was the horror of it.

I heard the dead bolt on the front door click shut.

"I'm here in the kitchen," I called out.

Next thing I knew, I was somehow aware of him coming through the kitchen door from the living room even though I had my back to the boy.

I was leaning over the kitchen table. It was a chance I had to take. The moment he saw my face, he'd either shoot me, run, or just scream for help. I had no idea how he was going to play it, but I needed to have the jump on him. It was absolutely imperative he came close enough for me to be able to grab him before he could use the gun.

I figured he'd stick to routine – wait for me to turn, then stick the gun in my chest, same as all the others. None of them had been shot in the back.

When I guessed he was less than a couple of feet away, I pivotted sharply and threw myself at him, wrapping my arms round his upper body and crashing him to the hard wood floor.

As we fell through the kitchen doorway into the living room, I distinctly heard shouting from down the street. At least two men, possibly three.

I slammed down on the boy with the force of a lead blanket, crushing the air out of his lungs.

Before he could draw breath, I clamped one hand over his mouth.

He hadn't had time to draw the gun. I could feel the outline of the boy's arm and the gun pressed sideways, flat against my stomach. I guessed he still had his finger on or near the trigger.

We stared at each other for several seconds. Harold's eyes were straight from Hades.

Then his face began to turn a bluish tinge, and it was immediately obvious he couldn't breathe. Instinct made me pull my hand from his mouth. Just a fraction of an inch.

Harold began to gasp for air– he'd been severely winded by the weight of my body as we'd fallen. His body was rigid.

"Looks like you screwed up, kid," I whispered. "Jack'd be tutt-tutting in hell."

Unexpectedly, the kid's body suddenly relaxed, and he smiled. It made my flesh crawl.

"No Mr Bonoventure?"

"No Mr Bonoventure," I replied.

"Birdturd Benedict. Starting to use your brain at last, eh?"

He was breathing hard, but he still managed a giggle. There didn't appear to be a shred of fear in his small body.

"So where do we go from here, Birdturd? It's your call. You going to turn me in?"

I was too busy thinking about how to make a move for the gun to reply.

" 'Cos if you've got that in mind, you'd better think again," he continued, as he caught his breath.

I began to feel the slightest movement between us at stomach level – the level of the gun. I'd have to do it now. He was trying to free his hand to turn the gun towards me.

I tried to move but couldn't. The mesmeric eyes were paralysing. I was completely frozen.

A voice deep within me was shouting, but I wasn't listening. *You came here to kill, so kill the bastard! Do it NOW!*

The boy looked away, twisting his head round towards the front door.

Harold was looking for the cavalry.

"He's not coming," I said, a sudden renewed sense of purpose flooding back. "There's no one to save your sorry ass this time."

The head snapped back.

"It's payback time," I said quietly. "I pity your unfortunate mother. Stella's going to suffer so damned hard."

"Look, asshole," he spat out with incredible venom. "You think you've got me fixed? Forget it! I'll think of something; you'd better believe it. No one can link me with this gun. Dad's guns are clean as snow. So what have you got? Sweet nothing, asshole. What was I doing here? I was out for a drive with Phil, that's all. He stole a car – big fucking deal!"

He again craned his head towards the door. He couldn't believe Phil wasn't coming.

I knew I'd have to make a move for the gun right now. Better I make the move than Harold.

He was a micro-second ahead of me.

The explosion between our bodies punched mine upwards.

A sudden rush of air burst from the boy's mouth. I felt his knees jolt against my thighs as he tried to snap them up violently towards his chest. His gun arm clutched at his stomach. He was staring up at me, his face a mask of abject terror, making low gutteral noises.

Saliva was bubbling from his mouth. Tears were flooding down his cheeks.

Horrorstruck, I instinctively rolled off the boy to the left – my heart banging violently in my chest.

His performance was so utterly convincing that I never saw the blow coming. It was a move of sheer brilliance.

Pain exploded upwards into my brain and I felt a violent blast of light in my eyes as he stabbed them hard with straight fingers. The agony was indescribable.

My hands shot up spontaneously to my face as a second blow slammed hard into my throat.

I couldn't breathe. I began retching and gasping for air as I felt fingers bury themselves in the hair at the nape of my neck. Then my head was jerked violently backwards.

He was kneeling – his face now inches from mine. The breath smelled of lemon candy.

I felt the wide barrel of a gun jabbed viciously in under my chin.

"You are one *pathetic* excuse for a man, Birdturd," he hissed at me. "You know that don't you. Big grown man, at the mercy of little ol' me. Makes me want to laugh, Birdturd."

I struggled to open my eyes, but vision was still a blur. A live current of pain shot from my eyes to the back of my head and back again.

"Now tell me something," the boy cooed, teasingly. "You ready to die?"

He snickered briefly as he punched the gun again hard into my throat, making me gag.

" 'Cos I was. Just now. I took my chance. Had to. And guess what? I lucked out." He raised his eyebrows and grinned inanely. "That's me all over. Just one lucky hound.

" Course I knew the odds. Must have a feel for a gun. Just like dad, wouldn't you say? Anyway, most I would have felt would have been a flesh wound. Then again, *you* might have taken the bullet rather than me – hard to say exactly – but who'd have given a shit about that? Not me, Birdturd."

My eyes darted down to his stomach area. A small tear in his shirt was the only evidence that a bullet had passed through. There was no blood.

I was suddenly aware that my arms were free. He must have seen the realization in my eyes, because he giggled, pushing the gun still harder up under my chin into the flesh. I could now see why the barrel felt so wide – a short suppressor had been screwed to the tip.

"Touch the gun and I'll kill you right here and now," he snapped.

My head was still swimming. There wasn't anything I could do now but keep the boy talking.

"You're not going to kill me – that wouldn't be any fun at all," I managed.

He wiped his running nose with his free hand. It was a thought that hadn't occured to him.

"You know something, Benedict, you may be right."

His eyes narrowed.

"Guess I just can't make up my mind."

He laughed, then began rocking his head from side to side like a clockwork toy. "Eeny, meeny, miney, mo..."

He was having a really good time now.

"Is that the gun you used to kill my brother?" I said. I had to keep conversation going. "Guess you're a pretty big guy when you're holding a Ruger."

"It's a Lahti, stupid! Don't you know anything, pissbrain?" He spat the words out with absolute derision. "I felt like a change – they say it's as good as a holiday."

He snickered and angled the gun outwards so I could just see his hand on the butt of the gun.

"Hey, tough guy, watch my finger. I'm squeezing."

I held my breath. I knew if I budged at all, it might give him the mental impetus to pull the trigger. Right now he was toying with me like a cat with a bird – I don't think he'd made up his mind whether to kill me or not.

A couple of seconds passed in silence.

"You know the difference between us, Birdturd?"

"Tell me," I replied, really careful not to move my head.

"I could pull the trigger and watch your brains fly out the back of your head. Wouldn't bother me at all. But you, you're such a damned coward – you're weak as piss."

"Easy to say – you've got your finger on the trigger," I replied.

A big smile spread across his face, as he opened his eyes wide.

"Oh yeah? You think *you* could do it?"

I stared into his eyes. There was madness there – no question.

He pushed his face forward so his nose touched mine. The barrel was rammed so hard into my throat I was again beginning to choke.

"Think you could pull the trigger, yellow-belly?" It was a whisper. "Do you? Do you? Do you? I don't think so."

At that precise moment I really thought that he'd do it. Cold sweat was running freely down my back. I was going to die. I closed my eyes and began to mouth a prayer.

The seconds ticked by.

... *As we forgive them that trespass against us...*

Abruptly the pressure on my throat was gone.

Silence.

I opened my eyes.

To my amazement the boy was holding the Lahti to his temple. There was a taunting look in his eyes.

Don't ask me why, but though my arms were completely unfettered, I simply couldn't move a muscle. I was still trapped in a macabre surreal dreamstate.

"So you think you can do it?" he snapped at me. "Think you've got the guts to kill me?"

He grabbed my right hand and raised it to the gun, pushing my forefinger onto the trigger.

"Come on, then! Pull it! Here's your chance, pissbrain!"

His left hand shot out again, grabbing my head, pulling it to his till our foreheads were touching.

"You think this doesn't take guts, man?"

His eyes were ablaze. He was loving it. Every second. It was some kind of exquisite extreme game. He didn't give a shit whether he lived or died at that particular moment; to him it was the ultimate rush to look death in the face second by second.

"PULL IT! " he screamed.

His mouth was closed, his nostrils flaring as he took in short bursts of air.

I stared into the acid blue eyes. The pupils were widely dilated. The boy was absolutely wired.

My finger took up the first pressure.

I searched for some change in his expression. Nothing. He knew he was a microsecond from eternity. His breathing quickened marginally – that was all.

"That's it, big guy," he coaxed in a chillingly soothing tone. "You got the idea. Go ahead. Do it. Do it. Do it."

Then he began to sing the words. "Doooo it, doooo it, doooo it."

The blood was pounding in my temples.

Right then my nerve broke. I slackened my grip on the trigger. There was no way I could do it. Even if this meant my own death, I couldn't do it. He was a *child* for Christ's sake!

I pulled the gun away from the boy's head. He didn't resist.

"Piss weak bastard. Just like I said," he said, snorting at me in disgust. Though I'd never read fear in his eyes, he was breathing hard.

My hand was still closed over his on the butt of the Lahti.

"Well, right now I'm going home asshole, and there's not a damned thing you can do to stop me," he whispered. "You had your chance and you blew it."

I pulled the gun from his grasp.

I fully expected him to resist. Once again I was proved wrong.

"Keep it, Birdturd. 'Cos it ain't mine. I'd say it's *your* gun now. You lay one finger on me – you even think of getting in my way and I'm going to scream so loud every man woman and child in the neighborhood's going to hear me. And you know what they'll find? A man with a gun scaring the shit out of a poor helpless child."

Then he leaned forward till our bodies were touching.

"We were never here. You understand me? You play it any other way you'll be very sorry 'cos they're always going to believe me."

"No way, Harold. You're going down."

"In your fucking dreams, you spineless shit. You're the one they'll put away. You point the finger at me, and I'll find a way out of it. You'd better believe it! That's the way it's been till now, and that's the way it'll be. Know why? 'Cos I'm so damned smart! And guess what? I'm going to do it all again, and send you messages. Just like before. Maybe I'll start with that fat black bitch!"

He chuckled at the thought.

"And where are you going to be in all this? Locked up in Folsom, that's where! Dead wife. Dead bro. Dead brain. Just watching me whack your buddies. So, go screw yourself, asshole!"

There was a white bubbling froth forming at the side of his mouth, such was the intensity of his invective. His blue eyes were practically popping out of his head.

The evil was so powerful, his face was so utterly grotesque, that it held me absolutely powerless, as if I were in the grip of some irresistible spell.

Then the devil before me began laughing again, and his eyes were dancing. He was clearly relishing my horror.

"Give me that," he cooed softly, prising the Lahti from my fingers.

"Why don't you do the right thing and 'off' yourself. Can't kill me – may as well kill yourself, eh? Life's not going to be worth a damn from here on in – I can tell you *that* right now!"

A ghoulish smile spread across his perfect face, as he straightened up.

"This is the way, Birdbrain!" he said, slowly pushing the barrel of the gun into his mouth. He began to shake his head left and right, rolling his eyes, making the same gurgling sound as before.

Harold Corr was having the time of his life. This was the ultimate game. Life and death practically fused together.

That's when I managed to kick start my brain.

I made a lunge at the Lahti. There was no way in the world I could let him walk out of there, ready to kill again. If I didn't have enough of the 'right stuff' to kill him, I'd do whatever I could to drag him with me to the cops. They wouldn't believe me – they'd probably locked me up for life, but that was just too bad. Anything was better than doing nothing.

As my hand slashed forward and slapped onto the boy's wrist to pull the Lahti from his mouth, Harold's smug expression suddenly bled to one of panic. It was the only time I saw genuine fear register on his face. It was as if he knew in that microsecond that the terror of oblivion had become a reality.

We were nose to nose when I felt the jolt go through me. I never heard a thing, though looking back I know there must have been some kind of muffled sound from the gun.

Either way, his head kicked violently back away from mine. Then he slipped to the floor. His body shuddered briefly, then was still.

58.

I stood over the body of Harold Corr for several seconds in a state of cataleptic shock, watching the blood pool next to the boy's head.

My brain was turning over faster than a Pentium processor, yet every other physical motor function had shut down. Nausea swept through me in mountainous waves.

I couldn't take my eyes off the the figure of the boy at my feet. Splashed blood and tissue spattered the back of his head and neck.

My hot blood was rushing through my veins, while Harold Corr's spewed forth from the opening in his head and onto the floor. The silence around me was so intense I was certain I could hear the blood pumping from the boy's body.

I couldn't move. A irresistable rigor gripped my mind and body like a vice.

Then the sound of laughter drifted through the night air and into my consciousness. I could actually hear someone laughing.

It came from the street. A girl's carefree laughter.

Then others joined in. There were several people laughing now. Happy people on their way home somewhere.

Mercifully that's when my instinct of self-preservation fired up and I broke free of my trance.

If I didn't think clearly now I was a dead man – same as Corr. There was no way back now.

Do what you've planned, the voice in my head shouted! *Don't let him take you down with him. Don't be a sacrifice!*

I immediately closed my eyes, straining for any further sound or movement in the street.

More gentle laughter. Then car doors opening and closing. Finally the sound of a vehicle driving away down the street.

Fifteen seconds later silence returned. It was overwhelming.

I laid the gun down on the floor next to Harold Corr's head. Not a trace of an assassin's print, just Harold's. It would be another riddle for Yant and Quin.

Despite my best intentions, my eyes kept returning to the body on the floor, and the ever-growing pool of blood on the hardwood floor. The boy's eyes were following me, as though he were mocking me.

Get the hell out, Jay! You know what you have to do, my guiding spirits screamed at me. *Get moving, for Christ's sake!*

I looked down at my clothes. There was no blood. On my right hand glove, yes. But not my clothes.

I washed both my gloved hands in the sink by the yard door.

I encountered no one on my way back to the Pontiac on the corner of Edinburg and 3rd.

Next stop was the payphone I'd scouted out earlier on La Cienega.

I parked and popped the trunk, taking out my PC, a floppy disk and a small roll of plastic tape. I walked to the pay phone.

Less than a minute later it was done, and I was back in the car, driving home.

59.

A photograph of Harold Corr appeared on the Sleuthhound web site twenty-five minutes before I got home to Studio City.

Messages from Charlie, Nancy and Mort were on the answering machine.

I called Charlie back at once. I was suitably shocked by the news of the photo. I told him I'd taken some pills at lunchtime – I'd only just come round. I was still drugged to the eyeballs.

They didn't find the boy's body till 5 pm the following day. That's when the realtor chose to check on the house.

Goodrich dropped the charges against me on Monday. She gave Nate no reason.

I heard via Nate's source that Tampico had been arrested and charged with Grand Theft Auto late Friday night. Apparently the kid said he'd stolen the Buick as a dare, then he and Corr had had a spat, and Harold had walked off into the night. It was then that the cops had arrived on Orange Grove and arrested him. That was it, end of story.

Well, what else was he going to say? That they'd come to kill someone?

The word was that the police thought Tampico was somehow involved in Harold's death. It was the computer tie-in that was the stumbling block. Whoever had sent the pictures of the first three victims had presumably transmitted the photo of young Corr.

That line of thinking suited me fine.

The cops didn't even bother to interview me. They respected the fact that I had to bury my brother – another victim of the serial killer.

Stella Corr never learned her son's secret. That much was spared her.

The LAPD did their best to track back the electronic messages, to identify the origin of both Raymond's and Harold's photos. They used their best tech boys. They were unsuccessful. The serial killer was clearly a computer whizz.

To this day, to the best of my knowledge, the files on Faith Benedict, Michael Gardenas, the commissionaire of his building, Raylene Kelly, Travis Thorne, Raymond Benedict and Harold Corr are still open.

Phil Tampico's still out there somewhere. On probation.

Question is, how many other Harolds walk the streets?

Scary.

OTHER BOOKS BY SHANE BRIANT

THE WEBBER AGENDA

Set in Europe as the Berlin Wall is pulled down, this page turning novel examines what may have happened to the billions of dollars that were in banks across the world to fund the East German secret service - the Stasi. This is perhaps my favourite novel. Don't miss this one.

THE CHASEN CATALYST

The sequel to The Webber Agenda, yet with a different plot - how much money and corrupt goods are being transferred across the globe via the 'diplomatic bag. Guy and Marysia are back - with Marysia's daughter! This thriller will keep you guessing to the final page.

BITE OF THE LOTUS

My one 'saga' novel. Set in Washington, Sydney, New York, Hanoi, Hong Kong and Vietnam, 'Bite of the Lotus' was WAY ahead of its time. Before suicide bombers, before planes being used as missiles. The plot concerns international money laundering at a time when a new American president is about to be elected. The finale is breathtaking.

GRAPHIC

Set in Sydney, the plot centers on a graphic novelist who morphs into his central character, Sainte-Claire. Two rival crime gangs are vie for the number one spot in Sydney - the Parramatta Asians and the caucasian Sydney mob. Who will win out?

WORST NIGHTMARES

Published by The Vanguard Press, this is my darkest thriller to date. An Internet imposter professes to cure people of their worst nightmares, only to track them down and visit their worst fears on them. NOT TO BE MISSED.

THE DREAMHEALER

The sequel to Worst Nightmares. Read WN first. Then carry on and be even more terrified.

ALWAYS THE BAD GUY

This is my autobiography. It has all my private stories concerning my 40 years in the film industry, starting withHammer Films. I've worked with Huston, Newman, Joffe, Mason, Irons, Hurt, Harmon, Rush, the list goes on! My most recent film is Roland Joffe's film 'Singularity' to hit the international film festival circuit early 2012.

ACKNOWLEDGEMENTS

My thanks to Michael Morton-Evans for creating the cover.
All my wonderful friends in Los Angeles, some who fed me, some who
gave me board and lodging. Jeffrey, Carole, Nicky and Sheelagh.

And...
Wendy, my wife, for her excellent editing.

www.ingramcontent.com/pod-product-compliance
Lightning Source LLC
Chambersburg PA
CBHW070219260626
47160CB00002B/606